Cathead
Crazy

Rhett DeVane
2012

Cathead Crazy

RHETT DEVANE

Wild Women Writers
An Independent Publishing Company

Cathead Crazy

This book is a work of fiction. Names, characters, places and incidents are either the product of the author's imagination or are used fictitiously. Any resemblance to actual persons, living or dead, or to actual events or locales is entirely coincidental.

ISBN: 978-0-9829015-6-4

Published by Wild Women Writers, Tallahassee, FL
March 2012
www.wildwomenwriters.com

Cover photograph by Rhett DeVane
Cover design by Donna Meredith

Logo design by E'Layne Koenigsberg of 3 Hip Chics, Tallahassee, FL
www.3HipChics.com

Printed in the United States of America

Dedication

For my mother, Theresa DeVane.
I was proud to be your caboose, then your engine.

For my sister, Melody DeVane-Kight.
You left way too soon, hon.

Acknowledgements

- To my family: both the blood-lines and the love-lines, may God bless you all.
- To the three Fletcher sisters: thanks for always being there for me. Special thanks to Denise Fletcher for her camera expertise. And to Wayne for just being Wayne.
- To my friends: whether I have known you for years, or less—you have made my life rich. Thank you for listening, coming to my aid, and reading my books. Where would I be without you?
- To Donna Meredith of Wild Woman Writers Publishing: thank you for your support and hours of hard work.
- To Paula Kiger: appreciate your green pen, hon.
- To the Wild Woman Writers critique group: I have learned so much from you ladies! Love each one of you.
- To Mary Menard, RN; Dr. Roberta Burton; and Peggy Kassees. Thank you for your help.
- To the staff of Woodmont Assisted Living: you are the true angels. Thank you for your patience, kindness, and compassion. You were there with us every step and stumble.
- To my fellow humans on the caretaker path: be gentle with yourself. This book is as much for you as it was for me.

Chapter One

"Yuck. What's that, road kill?" Hannah Olsen steered around a brown lump and squeezed into a parking space in front of Chattahoochee Drugs.

The lump: a pair of pantyhose resting in an oily mud puddle. Hannah's thoughts went first to sex. Some woman in such a big hurry she had ripped off her clothes? Had she and her lover/husband/partner let it fly in the back of the family minivan, right there in front of God and everybody?

At least someone's caught up in passion, Hannah thought. She imagined a different scenario for the discarded pantyhose: some harried working woman like herself—wedged between insolent teenagers and an aging parent—stressed out and fed up.

Bless her heart; the stockings must have pinched the poor woman's torso like a sausage casing, squeezing the middle-aged belly fat into a double roll beneath her breasts. Perhaps the lady had flung the hose off in a fit of aggravation similar to the one Hannah felt looming over her shoulder. The scene popped into Hannah's daydream: a woman after a long day cursing her computer, pulling into a tight parking slot, and then proceeding to have a total meltdown.

The cold, pissy early-February drizzle increased to a steady thrum on the SUVs roof and snapped Hannah to reality. She glanced toward the rear seat. "Great. No umbrella."

When she stepped up to the pharmacy counter, water droplets dangled from the tip of her nose and eyelashes. Hannah turned over her mother's soggy prescription, plopped down onto a hard orange plastic molded chair, and used a crumpled lipstick-smudged tissue to dab her face and neck. "That's plain-out common," her mother would say. "Women of quality should always use a cloth hankie, preferably one with embroidery." At last count, Mae Mathers had over thirty handkerchiefs, some printed with violets and cabbage roses, others plain white linen with crocheted edges. None had been left behind in her move to assisted living. Heaven forbid.

The elastic band in Hannah's bra cut into her skin and she felt so bone-weary, breathing was a chore. How pathetic that she would welcome the brief respite in a cramped aisle of Chattahoochee Drugs.

Hannah wondered if her sixteen-year-old daughter would be speaking to her this evening after the morning's heated fashion altercation. The outfits these young girls wore! Well, no daughter of hers would so much as step foot from the house with two miles of bare belly and that much cleavage showing. No sir-ee!

Her thoughts slipped to her elderly mother. Another kidney infection, this one compounded by a chest cold. The day had consisted of phone-tag calls to Mae's doctor's office and an order for another round of strong antibiotics. All of this, crammed into a business schedule already full of enough hassles. And she still had to go home and scrounge up something for dinner.

Hannah felt her damp pantyhose tighten like a famished boa constrictor. An old man with a bubbly, hacking cough lowered himself into the vacant chair beside hers.

"Afternoon, Ma'am." He squeezed his bulk into the chair and coughed into his cupped hand.

Country music blared from behind the counter—some screechy-voiced female whining about losing her man to a floozy, or to a whiskey bottle, or both. The rumble of the man's phlegm added a steady annoying rhythm. Hannah prayed her immune system was up to the challenge. Everywhere she went people shared germs faster than Santa Claus scattered toys to good girls and boys in one globe-circling night.

Sometimes Hannah felt like the star of some cosmic *Candid Camera* episode, or perhaps a cock-eyed version of *Survivor*. Put a woman through trial by fire, piss and vinegar, and see if she ends up in a padded room. Good thing there was a mental hospital within easy access, two blocks down on West Washington Street.

Wouldn't that be nice? Hannah's mind changed channels to her favorite fantasized version of a voluntary admission lock-up: A quiet white-walled room. A single cot. No sharp utensils. Plenty of mind-numbing medications. A psychiatrist to dutifully listen to her litany of woes. Maybe a pot-holder arts and crafts class.

All she wanted in this life was a small slice of peace. Maybe add in some attention from her husband. Respect from her kids. A clean house. But she'd settle for peace.

Peace would be nice.

She picked up a worn copy of a typical women's magazine, one with the latest diet craze announcement posted next to a glossy picture of the cake of the month. Give me a break.

Mr. Phlegm Man leaned over and motioned to the full-page photo of an eight-layer coconut confection. "My mama used to make cakes looked just like that 'un."

"That's nice," Hannah said.

What was it, her girl-next-door face? No matter where she went, people wanted to talk to her. The few times she had flown, Hannah had felt like the official in-flight counselor. Even if she wore earphones with her head buried in a novel, some stranger would sit down beside her and relate intimate details about a contentious divorce or botched hemorrhoid surgery. That or she would pull babysitting duty for the biggest freak on the plane, the one who white-knuckled long before they closed the hatch.

Mid-way through ads touting every kind of beauty emollient known to modern chemistry, she spotted a self-help article on women as caretakers. The term "sandwich generation" caught her attention. The expression pegged her perfectly, one of the many women smashed between parenting children and caring for elderly relatives. If the analogy held, Hannah served as the mayonnaise gluing the pieces together.

Images of skinny models popped from the magazine's glossy advertisements. Slick red baboon-butt lips. Jowls that didn't meet their bird necks. Eyes clear of red veins. No cottage-cheese thighs. Hannah felt the warning flare of a hot flash, her own personal summer. She dug in her purse for an unpaid bill envelope and used it to fan her face.

How long had it been since she felt remotely hot, the kind of woman men licked with their eyes? Hannah didn't feel sexy. At all. The one black lace negligee she owned strained to corral the extra bottom fat. She longed to be touched, but maybe from across the room, certainly not close enough to communicate additional body heat. God forbid. She surveyed the males in the room: Mr. Phlegm Man. The pharmacist. One juvenile near her son's tender age.

"Paul Johnson?" the pharmacist called.

Hannah watched the jowly man cross in front of her to retrieve his medicine. He hacked so hard, she was sure he'd hawk something up on the tile.

Ugh. Definitely not him. Guilt set in immediately at the unkind thought. Guilt: Hannah was good at that, if nothing else.

Twenty minutes later, the paper pharmacy bag clutched in hand, Hannah dashed to the second-hand Chevy SUV in the now-sheeting downpour. By the time she flopped into the driver's seat, no part of her remained dry. The pantyhose bore the slimy consistency of a garden slug.

Hannah kicked off her ruined leather pumps, then peeled the hose from her skin, lowered the window, and flung them to the pavement. A second nylon lump stood in the muddy pool. She laughed—a giggle, then a full-fledged falling-out fit complete with tears and staccato air snorts. When she finally decompressed, mascara rivulets stained her cheeks.

"Oh for Pete's sake," she muttered.

Hannah jumped from the car long enough to retrieve the discarded hosiery—hers and the other pair. No use to be a litter-bug, even if it had felt briefly empowering. She tossed them into the back seat floorboard, sending an arc of muddy water through the air, then used a wad of fast-food napkins to dry the bottoms of her feet. She smeared a generous dollop of alcohol-based germicide onto her hands and waved them back and forth to dry. A month back, she would have been hysterically sobbing and grinding her molars to a gravelly mush.

"Hannah, forget getting sedatives for your mama," her cherished sister-in-law Suzanne had advised. "You need drugs for yourself. Call your doctor and get on something, honey!"

Hannah hated the idea. She barely took an aspirin for a headache. But she had to admit—in less than a week, when the antidepressant finally reached a proper blood level—she felt almost human again. Able to think in a straight line. Able to smile. Able to rip her pantyhose off in a parking lot and cackle like a budding nutcase.

Able to do most anything.

Hannah steered from the drugstore lot, stepped on the gas, and covered the three miles from Chattahoochee, Florida, to Interstate 10 West. She tore up the on-ramp like a NASCAR driver leaving pit row. Worry rolled off her as the mile-markers passed. By Marianna, she wouldn't be a mother. By Pensacola, she wouldn't be a wife. By New Orleans, she would cease to be Mae's daughter. Maybe by the time she crossed the California border, she would be someone else entirely. Even the Angel of Lost Things—the heavenly entity her mother called upon to locate most anything misplaced—wouldn't be able to find one shed hair, one tire tread, one fingerprint.

Right, she thought. Get real, Hannah. Like you could really do something like that. Who do you think you're kidding?

She turned around at the next exit and headed east, back into town.

Hannah squeezed the SUV close to the curb in the cramped parking lot of Rosemont Assisted Living. A mishmash of emotions vied for first place; a weary sadness won out.

What kind of mood would her mother be in? Anyone's guess. On a good day, Mae Mathers and Hannah might hover over a jigsaw puzzle, reminiscing about family history and local affairs between lapses spent searching for a missing piece. Hannah assembled the edges and corners, leaving the sky to her mother. Mae found little challenge in the straight-edged sections and her "baby daughter" loathed the eye-crossing sameness of the heavens.

Bad days came as regularly as Monday mornings, though less predictable. The set of Mae's jaw held the initial clue to her mood: often clenched, held tightly together as if by doing so, death couldn't steal her life's breath.

The anger and small hissy-fits were easier to overcome than the tears. Mae cried for pent-up hurts, real or imagined—a collection spanning eighty-five years.

Hannah nodded to a couple of residents and signed in at the front desk before heading down a long carpeted hallway to her mother's section: the Camellia wing. She triple-tapped then used her key to enter room 104. The spacious efficiency apartment held a queen-sized bed, bureau, writing desk, a recliner, and a small upholstered rocker. A walk-in closet and bathroom took up a fourth of the room. Bright light filtered into the bedroom from three tall windows. The walls displayed clusters of family pictures and two framed monarch butterfly photographs, a gift from Hannah's sister Helen, from Helen's photography phase.

"Ma-Mae?"

"In here," a faint voice answered from the bathroom.

"Don't know why I eat greens," her mother said as she pushed into the room, "gives me the Hershey-squirts every time."

A wave of putrid, lily-of-the-valley air wafted in Mae's wake. Hannah wasn't sure which was worse, the fecal odor or the cloying floral spray. She dropped the pharmacy package on the bed and hugged her mother. "At least you're not constipated, Ma-Mae. Here's your kidney medicine."

Mae coughed. "When do I take it?"

"Once a day."

"God knows I have enough to keep up with, without having to take it more often."

"I'll put it in your pill organizer. That way, you won't have to worry about missing a dose."

Mae shuffled to the faded blue recliner and flopped down. "Sometimes, I don't know why I'm still on this earth. I can't seem to shake this cough. I'm scared to death I've got that new virus that's been going around."

Hannah cleared a spot on the bed and sat. "Long as you wash your hands and be careful, you should be okay. You're not exposed to many folks outside of Rosemont. Lately, you won't even go to Wal-Mart with me."

Mae poked a stray strand of white hair into the bun atop her head. "Still, it's going around. Sweeping the country, from what they say on TV."

"What virus is that, Ma-Mae?" Hannah dropped pills into slots in a clear plastic organizer: Monday through Sunday, a.m. and p.m.

"That computer virus. Everyone's getting it!" Mae jabbed a finger in the air. "Causing business to all but shut down."

Hannah fought the smile threatening the corners of her lips. Forget Candid Camera; life had become one big freaking sit-com and the writers had seriously outdone themselves on this episode. No use trying to explain technology to her mother. The ensuing stress would overwhelm even Zoloft's capacity.

"Ma-Mae, you don't have to worry. Only people with computers get computer viruses." *Not exactly a lie.*

Her mother's blue-gray eyes studied her. When Hannah was a child, the same look had withered her into honesty. "All the more reason I shouldn't ever get one, at my age. But you'd best watch out. You got them all around you."

"My office has virus protection." Hannah held her breath for a second.

Mae coughed several times. When she was able to catch her breath she said, "That's a weight lifted off my mind."

Hannah slowly exhaled. Conversations with her mother felt like tip-toeing through a smoldering peat bog wearing flip-flops. She snapped the lids closed on the pill organizer and returned it to a spot on the bathroom vanity.

Mae picked up a crocheted afghan and spread it across her legs. She frowned. "Women your age shouldn't go bare-legged, dear. You still have a nice shape to your legs, but nylons help to hide those little spidery veins. Besides, it's still too cold to be fanning around without anything covering your skin."

For a second, Hannah flashed back to adolescence, a time when nothing she did met with her mother's approval. The adult supervisor in her psyche snatched back the controls and she stuffed the urge to roll her eyes and snipe a reply.

"I had a run in one leg. Took them off in the car." Hannah's gaze roamed across the row of family pictures. One caught her attention: the three Mathers children—Hal, Helen, and Hannah—dressed in starch-stiff Easter finery, wicker baskets top-heavy with colored eggs. One egg had fallen to the ground and the eight-year-old Hannah stretched to return it to the fold, a pinched expression on her face. Her brother Hal looked as if the tie choked the life from him. Helen looked her usual self—available to emote at will.

Mae's voice snapped her back to the room. "Long as you don't stop anywhere else on the way home. I taught you better, than to be doing such in public. When you bringing my grandbabies to see me?"

When I can tie one down long enough to get him or her to the car, Hannah thought. "They're not babies anymore, Ma-Mae. Justine is sixteen and Jonas will be thirteen in a few months."

Her mother's eyes narrowed. "How can that be?"

"Time passes, Ma-Mae. Time passes." Hannah flopped back down on the bed.

Mae hacked phlegm into a handkerchief—purple printed on white cotton, with "New Jersey" scripted across an outline of the state. When had Mae been to New Jersey? Her mother tucked the hankie into the edge of her robe sleeve then shifted her weight to the opposite hip with an audible grunt. "You know who gave me this cold?"

"It's that time of year. Could be most anyone."

Mae pointed in the general direction of the rest of Rosemont. "That new lady from California brought it in."

Hannah leaned back on her elbows. For the first few months after the family helped move Mae into assisted living, and Hannah morphed from daughter to caretaker, she had felt a bit off-kilter—like stepping into a play in the midst of the second act without the benefit of a program.

"How you figure that, Ma-Mae?"

"The mudslides triggered it."

"Mudslides."

"Yep." Mae nodded once. "All that soggy earth out there slipping and sliding around has stirred up evil bugs. That new woman brought those mudslide cold germs to Florida."

Amazing, how events across the country could have such a debilitating effect. "I see."

Forgetting the one tucked in her sleeve, Mae dug in her pocket for a clean cloth hankie—white linen with dainty pink crocheted edges—and blew her nose. The noise reminded Hannah of the gaggle of Canada geese that had honked its way across Lake Seminole a couple of days prior. The dirty clothes hamper no doubt held a mound of sticky handkerchiefs.

Mae gestured with a wave of the cloth. "Bless her heart. That lawyer son of hers flew her in and stayed put long enough to check her in here. He tore out the next morning on the first plane! Good thing she has another son over in Tallahassee."

"Sounds like you've made friends with her."

Mae coughed several times before answering. "Passable. She was a teacher. English."

A retired teacher like her mother. Another potential new best friend. Part of the great cosmic order of instructors.

Hannah jumped up and removed a bottle of water from the small refrigerator in one corner. "Here, drink this. Good for your kidneys and it will help your dry throat."

Mae took two small sips and set the bottle aside. So much for hydration.

Hannah said, "You have something in common. That's good."

"She ain't got good sense anymore. Can barely pour piss from a boot. Even the Angel of Lost Things couldn't find that woman's mind. Poor thing. I had to help her to her room twice yesterday. There she is—a Ph.D. doctor, mind you—and she can't even so much as find the way down the hall. She's just plain cathead crazy."

Cathead crazy: the Mathis family's phrase for having less than a brain. Coined from her brother Hal's childhood reaction to the home-made Southern biscuits Mae cooked every Sunday for breakfast—made with lard, big as a cat's head. Hal would spin and giggle and act like he'd lost his last marble until they came from the oven, piping hot and ready for butter and honey.

Mae leaned forward and whispered in a conspiratorial tone. "Age is the great equalizer, you know."

"Those new?" Hannah pointed to her sister-in-law's red bejew-eled flats.

Suzanne grinned. "Not T-totally. I got them at Shoe World over in Tallahassee, end of the season last year. Just haven't worn them much."

Hannah refilled her favorite pottery mug and joined her sister-in-law at the kitchen table. Her cup's rim had chips in two places and the inside held ghosts from coffee and tea past, but she would throttle the fool who tried to shuffle it to the garbage. Milk-rings from the morn-ing's cereal bowls created abstract tabletop artwork. Hannah sighed and grabbed a wet dishcloth. Good thing coffee existed, or she'd have to kill one of her kids. "How many pairs are you up to now, fifty?"

Suzanne's giggle typified the expression *infectious laughter*. No matter how tired and stressed Hannah felt, her brother's second wife could always lift her spirits. Why couldn't she share the same closeness with Helen? If her sister lived in town, maybe things would be different. Maybe not.

"Sixty or so, unless you add the boots. Then it's closer to seventy. But who's counting? Your brother has three pair: black, brown, and those God-awful, rat-hole-infested, worn-slap-out sneakers."

The kitchen timer trilled and Hannah rose to remove a baking sheet of cinnamon rolls from the oven. She squeezed a packet of glaze over the crowns and spread it with a knife.

"Look at you, Miss Dolly Homemaker. I'm impressed."

Hannah licked a stray glob of icing from one of her fingers. "Don't be. I popped these from a can. Who has time to make anything from scratch?"

"I get mine from Joe Fletcher's little bakery uptown. He makes them better than I ever could." Suzanne dug in her purse, then studied her reflection in a compact mirror. "Lord have mercy! I've got to get by the Triple C Salon and have Melody to wax my brows. I'm beginning to look like a Cro-Mag-Nonnie." She snapped the lid shut. "How's your mama? I need to get by to see her this week."

Hannah placed a stack of napkins and a heaping platter of frosted cinnamon rolls on the table. She bit into one and groaned. Comfort food had to be the best balm for a sore, worn-out spirit. "Depends on which day you ask. She still has that cold, and now we're treating a kidney infection. Her cough's pretty bad and that's worrisome. Last spring, she ended up with bronchitis. Everything seems to go straight to her lungs."

The scent of warm sugar and cinnamon drifted through the small kitchen. Hannah flashed back to childhood when her mother stirred up confections from scratch and let her lick the raw batter from the beaters afterwards. Never a thought of salmonella.

"If it ain't one thing, it's twenty-five. My mama's the same way." Suzanne studied Hannah for a moment as she chewed. "You look a little pale."

"I'm fine." Hannah tapped the end of her nose three times, a gesture she and Suzanne shared as a private joke. *Touch it to see if it grows because I am lying, lying, lying.*

Justine bounded into the kitchen, snatched an apple from the wooden bowl on the island counter, and darted toward the door, a blur of long yellow hair and pink chenille. Regardless of her mother's admonition over showing skin, a sliver of Justine's midsection flashed above tight blue jeans. "Bye Mom, Auntie Suzanne!"

"Wait, wait, wait!" Hannah called after her daughter. "Where're you off to in such a hurry?"

Justine paused in mid-dash. "Brittany's. Huge bio quiz Monday."

"And dinner?"

Justine idled in place, an impatient teenager with more important places to be. "Probably grab a burger uptown at Mr. Bill's."

"Be home before ten," Hannah said. "And keep your cell phone turned on."

"Yeah, what—ever." Justine threw the parting comment over her shoulder like a discarded fast food bag and slammed the door on her way out.

Suzanne dabbed frosting from her lips. "See she got the belly ring."

"Have to choose my battles, Sis. If not, we'd scratch each other's eyes out. Some days I swear, if I hear *whatever* one more time, I'll yank my hair out by the roots."

Suzanne waved one hand dismissively. "Makes me glad I had boys. Then again, there's no such animal as an easy teenager. That any of us make it through without our parents choking the life from us is a miracle."

"It was either that navel piercing or a tattoo. I have Ma-Mae to thank for helping me out on that front."

"Really?" Suzanne's perfectly arched brows shot upward.

Her sister-in-law's petite features were almost too perky—naturally curly blonde hair framing pale blue eyes, a button nose, impish smile. If Hannah didn't adore her, she would've been terminally jealous.

Hannah bit into a still-warm roll. Glazed sugar icing formed a ring around her lips. "Ma-Mae told her, at least a little hole in her navel could grow over if she got to the point she didn't like it anymore. Then Ma-Mae described in detail some of the tattoos she'd seen on her elderly cronies, amidst age spots and rolls of muscle gone to fat. Justine came away from that little grandmotherly-love talk with a profound distaste for permanent body art."

Suzanne laughed. "My mother-in-law surely knows how to put a spin on things."

"When she takes a mind to, yes."

Chapter Two

The call came as Hannah eased into a chest-deep, hot bubble bath. The kids were at friends' houses for the evening and Norman was playing poker with his work cronies. An unread novel—one she had looked forward to starting for over two months—rested on a padded vanity stool beside the cordless phone.

"Hannah Olsen?" a female voice asked when she answered on the second ring.

"Yes?"

"This is Lora Strong at Rosemont."

"Don't you usually work weekdays?"

"I do. We have three people out with the cold that's going around." The nurse cleared her throat. "About your mother—"

"Yes?" Hannah stepped from the tub, trailing water onto the ceramic tile and fuzzy blue bath mat. The beat of her heart thumped in her ears.

"Miz Mae called me down to her room a few minutes ago," the nurse continued. "She's having great difficulty breathing and her temperature's hovering around a hundred degrees. I advise sending her to the hospital."

Hannah felt an immediate rush of adrenaline, plus the requisite sting of stomach acid. Several thoughts collected at the gate like frightened cattle awaiting slaughter: *God, what now? Is this it, the start of the last lap? Ma-Mae, I love you, you know I do.*

She grabbed the first towel handy, frowned at its rank odor, then threw it into the dirty clothes hamper. Honest to Pete, Norman and the kids would leave a damp towel or washcloth hanging in a wad every time, no matter how often she explained the concept of spreading them out to dry. She yanked a fresh white towel from the cabinet over the toilet and mopped moisture from her skin, balancing the phone between her ear and shoulder. "She's had a cough and cold for a few days."

"We have six residents quarantined with the same thing. I've already sent two to the hospital this week. It's very easy at your mother's age for this to develop into pneumonia."

Hannah's mind raced. "I'm on the way."

"I'll call the ambulance and get the paperwork ready. Do you have a preference as to the hospital?"

"Tallahassee General. Her doctor's there."

Hannah hastily dressed then threw a few toiletries, a change of clothes, and a back-up copy of her mother's emergency papers into a small bag. On the way to Rosemont, she called Norman's cell. The serenade of some female country music star twanged, then cycled to the automated voicemail announcement.

"Norman, I can't believe you don't have your phone on! I'm heading to Rosemont, then to Tallahassee. Ma-Mae's on her way to the hospital. Again. Call me as soon as you get this." She snapped the phone shut, thought a moment, then opened it and jabbed the speed-dial number for her sister-in-law. Forget Hal. He never turned on his stupid phone either.

A two-minute conversation with her sister-in-law sounded the Ma-Mae Alert. Suzanne would take care of calling Jonas and Justine, gather Hannah's brother, and meet the ambulance at the hospital.

When she screeched to a halt in front of Rosemont, Hannah noted no emergency vehicles. Wow. She had the timing down after so many close calls. Even the first responders couldn't beat her. Good thing she hadn't passed any police cruisers.

She dashed through the lobby with a quick nod to the young girl sitting behind the front desk, and jogged down the hallway. When Hannah entered room 104, the pungent scents of mentholated rub and urine slammed her nose. The charge nurse glanced up from the clipboard she held and nodded a greeting.

"Thanks so much for calling me." Hannah cast her purse onto the chair, sat down on the bed and held her mother's feverish hand. "Hear you're not feeling so great, Ma-Mae."

Her mother opened her eyes briefly. "You got to get me some help," she said in a weak voice. "I'm slipping fast."

"I'm right here, Ma-Mae. We'll be taking you to Tallahassee General as soon as the paramedics arrive." A rush of intense love washed over her, as fierce as the protective emotion she felt when one of her children took ill.

Lora motioned toward the small bathroom and Hannah stood and joined her. "Your mother self-medicates, correct?" the nurse asked in a low voice.

Hannah nodded. "She and I have been working together on that. I put her drugs in one of those daily divider boxes."

Lora pointed to the jumbled countertop beside the sink. "In this?"

Hannah picked up the plastic container. "Jeez. This was full when I left her this morning. That means . . . oh, Lord help. She's taken two days' worth of pills in one afternoon!"

"Looked that way to me, too." The nurse hesitated. "But it's often hard to tell. If memory issues are part of the equation, she might've thrown them out or put them somewhere else. I've seen it all."

"I'm sure you have." Hannah took a deep breath and exhaled slowly to calm her nerves.

"Could be part of why she's feeling so bad. What prescription meds is she on?"

Hannah scrolled through the lengthy list. Two blood pressure medications, anti-anxiety, anti-inflammatory, diuretic, sleep-aid and an assortment of over-the-counter pain relievers, sinus relief and vitamin supplements: a chemical soup.

The nurse pursed her lips. "Be sure to let them know at the ER. Doubling up on the blood pressure and anti-anxiety meds is probably adding to her weakness."

"Guess it's time to turn this over to you guys. Her memory the way it's been lately . . . " Hannah smacked her forehead with her palm. "I should have seen this coming. What's wrong with me?"

Lora rested a hand on Hannah's shoulder. "Don't be so hard on yourself."

"It won't happen again. I assure you."

Every task provided by the trained staff came with a price tag. *I was trying to save your money, Ma-Mae. And protect your precious independence.*

"All we need is authorization from her doctor, and we can take this worry off you." Lora motioned to Mae's bed. "We'll address this when she's better."

The silver and black wall clock showed 12:30 a.m., but Hannah could've sworn they had been lingering in the emergency room much longer than three and a half hours. No more than two visitors could stay with the patient at one time, so Suzanne and Hannah shared a shift, leaving their husbands in the waiting room. Though the minutes sailed along at a usual breakneck speed outside, inside the hospital, time slowed to a barely detectable creep.

"Sure wish that doctor would come back," Suzanne said around a yawn.

On the gurney, Mae erupted with a series of wet, rumbling coughs, then grunted with the effort to breathe. Hannah studied her mother. Once a substantial woman—solid and strong with plenty of muscle— now Mae looked depleted. A husk with most of the life sucked out. Shrinking and curling up. How was it happening so fast? It seemed like just a few months ago when she was able and sure of herself; in reality, a long time had passed since Mae had stood as the stalwart, formidable head of the family.

Hannah ran her fingers through her damp, shoulder-length brown hair. "The doctor poked his head in here about an hour ago, right before you came back, long enough to look at the chart, then he took off like a shot dog. This place is a total zoo tonight."

Suzanne glanced around the small room. "It surely is an improvement over the old ER. Remember it? Most times, it was standing room only, and they had to line people up in the hallways 'cause they didn't have enough space. This one's decorated nice, for a hospital."

"If I hadn't been following the ambulance, I might have missed the entrance. The doctor she had before practiced out of the other hospital."

In the hall, a gurney rattled past. Hannah caught a glimpse of white sheets and a chrome IV pole through the door's narrow window. Muffled conversation sounded in the adjoining room, punctuated by the pounding footsteps of someone dashing down one of the long hallways. Hannah imagined different life or death scenes playing out around her. The sounds melded into the background like elevator music. Predictable and familiar. Way too familiar, in the past couple of years.

"I could find my way around this place in a blackout." Suzanne stood and stretched her arms overhead. "My mama's been here twice in the past five months."

Hannah frowned. "You should call me. Only fair that I come wait with you too."

"Hal and my boys are good about helping out, honey. You got enough to worry over. Besides, I'm getting to the point I'm an old pro at this medical nonsense. It may be like the blind leading the blind sometimes, but I can help you muddle through all of the Medicare and insurance stuff, if you need. And your brother wants to help, even if he doesn't always know how to show it." Her sister-in-law plopped back into the chair.

"You don't know how much I appreciate that, Sis." Hannah squeezed Suzanne's hand. "Suppose our husbands are going cathead crazy in the waiting room?"

"They were talking power tools when I left 'em. Ain't hurting them to wait. Hal said he'd come in and take a shift, if it's too much longer."

"Good thing Hal's here to help Norman pass the time. My husband's like a little fidgety boy."

"They're all little boys, hon."

Suzanne's soothing voice continued as Hannah's gaze took in the orderly room. No clutter on the countertops. Clean, shiny tile floors. Nothing extraneous. So unlike her house. Norman could make a sandwich and leave deposits on every surface. No matter how much she nagged, the kids left a slipstream of books, discarded clothing, and dirty dishes in their wake. And stinky towels.

Mae shifted and coughed. She opened her eyes and squinted at the overhead fluorescent fixture. "Can't someone shut that off ? It's too bright."

"Be right back." Suzanne jumped up and left, returning shortly with a soft white hand towel. She folded it twice and placed it over her mother-in-law's closed eyes. "There you go, sugar." Then to Hannah, "they keep the clean-linens cart parked in the hall past the nurses' station."

"And there's a room with a little kitchen on each wing in this hospital, from what I recall." Hannah rubbed her burning eyes. "We could give tours." Her mind raced to its normal point: at least one step ahead. "Once we ever get her up to a room, if they admit her, I want you and Hal to go on home. No use in all of us being here all night. Norm and I can stay until she's settled in. Of course, I'll make him go home to be with the kids. I brought a bag so I can stay." *And Ma-Mae's updated meds list and the medical power of attorney directive and Living Will and signed Do Not Resuscitate order . . .* If she ever left the house without the paperwork she called "The Tool Kit," Hannah would feel naked.

Mae moaned and moved her legs beneath the stiff white sheet. Mae appeared to be half-conscious, but Hannah knew her mother was tuned into the conversation, regardless of how bad she felt.

"Did you call your sister?" Suzanne asked.

"I reached her on the way over. Told her I'd phone her first thing tomorrow morning. She'll drive over if I need her."

Suzanne shifted her gaze to Mae and purposely lowered her tone. "You better start letting Helen lend a hand."

"I hate to bother her."

"You'd rather have a nervous fit than ask for help. You beat all I've ever seen." Suzanne shook her finger. "What you're not stopping to consider is that Helen might want to be involved." Suzanne's voice slipped to a barely-audible whisper. "On down the line, when all is said and done, Helen might feel kind of slighted if you don't at least give her the chance to help out your mama. I have it all on my shoulders, me being an only child, but you—you have two siblings who will share the load if you let them."

A burst of laughter sounded in the direction of the nurses' station. Mirth seemed out of sync in this place, like knock-knock jokes at a funeral. The ER was about waking in the wee hours in a panic, or with something bleeding and hanging off at an odd angle. About bruises and body fluids and foul-scented emissions. Life disrupted. The Reaper cheated, or not.

A rattle on the opposite side of the door announced the arrival of Dr. Timmons, a thin, twitchy, balding man in his late fifties. He shot into the room, flipping through the clipboard chart. Behind him, the heavy door swung slowly open as if another patient's disoriented newly-minted ghost had trailed the physician.

Hannah jumped up. "Here, let me close that. We've gotten the hang of making it stay shut."

The doctor threw up his hand. "No."

For a couple of minutes, Hannah and Suzanne watched as the emergency room doctor studied the door and its faulty latch. He mumbled to himself, visually measuring the gaps above and below, opening and closing the door several times. Meanwhile, Mae coughed, writhed, and moaned on the gurney. The automatic blood pressure cuff inflated and deflated, sending updated data to the overhead monitor.

Dr. Timmons stepped over to a wall phone, jabbed a series of numbers, then consulted with Joe in Maintenance.

The doctor turned to face the bewildered stares of Hannah and Suzanne. He flashed a sheepish smile, as if the reason for his second appearance in room six had suddenly come to mind. "Got to handle these things as they come up."

Suzanne glanced at Hannah, then back to the doctor. "As long as you keep a mind to detail that much with my mother-in-law, we'll get along just fine."

The doctor nodded once then said, "The chest x-ray shows signs of congestion. Possibly the start of pneumonia. You said earlier that she seemed confused?"

"Her memory's been a bit fuzzy lately," Hannah said. "But some of it, at least right now, might be because of her medications. We're pretty sure she took a double dose of her Xanax and Avapro."

"Her blood pressure's low, but not dangerously so." He nodded toward the gurney. "I'll order a CAT scan of her brain."

Mae's eyelids flew open. "My brain? Nothing's the matter with my brain!"

Hannah leaned over and grasped her mother's hand. "I think what the doctor is worried about, Ma-Mae, is ruling out anything terribly wrong."

Mae tried to sit up, but collapsed with the effort. "I don't want no scan! Ain't a gosh-darn thing wrong with my brain!" A series of coughs left her breathless for a moment. "I got the consumption! I need some help! You don't do something and my next stop will be the bone yard."

Dr. Timmons snapped the chart closed. "She clearly doesn't want a scan. I'll consult with Dr. Rawlings. I'd like to admit her, start her on breathing treatments and IVs." Before either of them could reply, the doctor left, a flurry of green scrubs and white lab coat.

Suzanne propped her hands on her hips. "That was surely short and sweet."

Hannah eased her mother's arms beneath the sheet and smoothed the edges. Melancholia washed over her. How many times had her mother tucked her into bed in the same fashion, promising to keep the night-light on, telling her to "sleep tight and don't let the bedbugs bite?" No matter how much she butted heads with Mae, Hannah had always felt protected. Now she felt powerless to reciprocate. "I'm sure he's busy. They've always been good here, so I have to trust."

Hannah sank down into one of the vinyl chairs. She caught a whiff of stale sweat and urine and wondered if it came from Ma-Mae—her mother worried constantly about smelling like an old person—or if the odor free-floated in the ER air like cologne.

Suzanne huffed. "They don't want to mess with this family. I may look like a little bitty thing, but I can come out snorting if you ruffle my feathers enough."

Hannah patted the chair beside hers. "Might as well smooth those fanny feathers and sit down. Looks like it's gonna be a long night."

Suzanne glanced at the wall clock. "Done been night. Morning, now."

Hannah knew the routine. At least seventy-two hours in the hospital—the minimum for insurance purposes before Ma-Mae would be transferred to some kind of rehab facility. Then, several weeks of therapy to restore mobility and health before moving her back to Rosemont. For Hannah, extra hours spent burning the forty miles between home and the hospital. Collecting and washing soiled clothing. Consulting with teams of doctors, therapists, and case management staff. And work. And family.

Hannah felt exhaustion drape across her shoulders like a shroud. On the gurney, Mae had settled into a fitful sleep. Her chest rose and fell rhythmically. At least one of them was getting some rest. The inevitable wash of guilt circled her heart.

Dang, Hannah. How could you think of yourself when your mother is lying on a hospital bed? she thought. What a pitiful excuse for a daughter you have, Ma-Mae.

Ma-Mae's Buttermilk Cathead Biscuits

2 cups flour
4 teaspoons baking powder
1/4 teaspoon baking soda
3/4 teaspoon salt
2 tablespoons butter
2 tablespoons shortening
1 cup buttermilk, chilled

Preheat oven to 450°

In a large mixing bowl, combine flour, baking powder, baking soda and salt. Using your fingertips, rub butter and shortening into dry ingredients until mixture looks like crumbs (do this quickly so the fats don't melt). Make a well in the center and pour in the chilled buttermilk. Stir just until the dough comes together. The dough will be very sticky.

Turn dough onto floured surface, dust top with flour and gently fold dough over on itself 5 or 6 times. This isn't like working bread dough. The less you handle it, the fluffier your biscuits will turn out.

Press into a 1-inch thick round. Cut out biscuits with a 2-inch cutter, being sure to push straight down through the dough. You can also pinch off dough (about a palm's full) with floured hands and pat into rounds. True catheads are larger 'round.

Place biscuits on baking sheet so that they just touch. Reform scrap dough, working it as little as possible and continue cutting. (Biscuits from the second pass will not be quite as light as those from the first.) Bake until biscuits are tall and light gold on top, 15 to 20 minutes. Slather with butter. Good with Tupelo honey, cream cheese, or your favorite jam or preserves.

Go walk a block or two. You'll need to.

Chapter Three

One of life's true little pleasures: the chocolaty-rich aroma of ground Colombian beans. Hannah closed her eyes as she breathed the puff of exhaled air from the vacuum-packed coffee bag.

"Gah, Mom." Justine stood at the kitchen threshold, hands propped on her slender hips. "You are so freakin' bizarre. No wonder I'm such a head case."

Hannah ignored the invitation to spar. Too early. Too much other crap raining down over her head. She measured several heaping table-spoons into the paper-lined filter cup, added cold water, and flipped the power switch on the expensive brewer. She might wear rags, but by golly her coffee maker had to be the top of the line. "If they made cologne that smelled like this, I wouldn't have to sniff. There're a few turkey bacon strips on the stove. Want me to fry you an egg?"

"Not even. I'll grab something later."

The urge to give her daughter the importance-of-breakfast spiel nudged. Not today. No energy for motherly well-intended needling. "Suit yourself."

Justine's brows knit together. Hannah could almost read her daughter's thoughts: Like, what's up with this? No lecture?

"You going over to be with Grand-Mae this morning?"

"Later on. Your Aunt Helen is with her."

"Oh."

Hannah grabbed the insulated coffee carafe and poured a quick cup. Coffee brew-us interrupt-us, she thought, love that feature! She sipped, savoring the flavor. Rich, sugar-less, jet black. Nothing to wa-ter down the heart-jarring punch.

"You 'kay, Mom?"

"Sure, why wouldn't I be?"

One of Justine's shoulders lifted slightly, then fell. "I'da know. You're acting a little strange—more than usual."

"Don't you have somewhere to be, honey?"

Justine slipped a hot-pink backpack over one shoulder. "At Brittany's if you need me."

This was new: her teenage daughter revealing her plans sans the interrogation. Hannah watched Justine sweep from the room with her cell phone clutched in her hands, her thumbs tapping a staccato rhythm. The child probably texted in her sleep.

The blare of the television in the den announced the awakening of her son. Jonas teetered at a pivotal age: old enough for the stirrings of hormones and young enough to still love Saturday morning cartoons and sugary cereal.

Jonas acknowledged her on the way to the cupboard. Hannah watched as he carefully measured out cereal to within an inch of the bowl's rim, then added a heap of precisely sliced bananas and milk. His thick, shiny brown hair hung in uncombed hanks across his forehead. Blue eyes with lashes any woman would die for. And dimples surrounding a slightly lopsided smile. One day, he would be a real lady killer. God forbid.

"Napkin?" She offered as he passed by on his way back to the cave-like den.

Jonas stuck the napkin in the edge of his T-shirt collar. "Thanks."

When had her kids become separate nations unto themselves? She had blinked and missed it.

Earthy male cologne announced her husband's arrival. "Mornin', hon." Norman's lips barely brushed her cheek as he reached past her for coffee.

"You want anything to eat?"

"I'm playing a round with Rich Burns this morning. We'll grab a sausage biscuit."

"All righty then."

What about your cholesterol? And your promise to take the car in for an oil change? And the fact that your mother-in-law is sick as a dog, lying in the hospital in Tallahassee? Hmm? Hate to interrupt your golf game.

Norman stopped long enough to study his wife's expression. "You all right, hon?"

"Just peachy."

Norman snapped the lid on a commuter mug. "I'll have the cell on." He delivered a drive-by kiss before grabbing a worn set of clubs and disappearing out the carport door.

"Ma-ummm!" Jonas's sing-song voice echoed from the bowels of the den. "Slug yakked again!"

"Jeez." Hannah grabbed a handful of paper towels, an old dish-rag, and the beacon-red, economy-sized bottle of carpet spot remover.

Slug walked in deliberate circles around a gelatinous mound of purged hair, then raked the surrounding carpet with one clawless paw. True to his name, each movement the aging feline made expended as little energy as possible.

"Thank you for at least trying to cover it up," Hannah said to the family fat-cat.

Slug sat back on his haunches and studied her with big yellow eyes.

Hannah used a paper towel to remove the hairball, then sprayed the foaming cleaner and dabbed with the damp rag. "You know, you wouldn't have this ongoing little issue if you'd stick to cat food."

The former stray ate hair—human or otherwise—as if driven by addiction. Even frequent vacuuming and hiding the family hairbrushes couldn't squelch his quest for the favored dietary supplement. Slug stretched in one long, luxurious motion, then padded over and twirled in slow circles around her, purring loudly. Hannah picked him up and cuddled him in her arms. Slug reciprocated with an affectionate head-butt, followed by rubbing the sides of his mouth along her chin line.

"You don't have to mark me. You had me wrapped around your little paw from the first day you appeared at the back door."

Hannah buried her face in his silky black fur and mused about the difference between cat love and dog love. Dog love was the all-slobbering, total devotion, clingy sort of love. Hannah had to earn cat love; it wasn't doled out to humans as a matter of fact. Slug was the only creature in Hannah's life who didn't make demands on her time. He didn't need her. The most delicious moments—rare, lately—were when she and the old Tomcat simply sat together, doing absolutely as little as possible while still breathing.

Hannah walked over and parted the curtains. Sunlight streamed into the room. "It's a beautiful day outside, Jonas. A little cool maybe, but still nice. Please don't sit in here glued to the boob tube all day, son."

Jonas eased into channel-surfing mode before settling on a station with an old Star Trek rerun. "'kay, Mom."

After she refreshed her coffee, Hannah threw on one of Norman's old cardigan sweaters and carried Slug outside to the deck. When she and Norman had purchased the small, ranch-style brick house on Morgan Avenue, the backyard living space had consisted of a cracked and stained ten-by-ten foot concrete slab circled by overgrown boxwood shrubs. Deeply eroded ruts in the surrounding three-quarter acre lot attested to neglect and improper drainage.

Two years after Jonas's birth, Hannah had initiated a gardening make-over. Hal and Norman created a series of stepped terraces to tame the sloping land. With the help of several neighbors, they designed and built a bi-level deck with ample room for Norman's grill, a wooden porch swing, and three wide bench seats. As money allowed, they had added trees, shrubs, and flower beds.

Hannah normally would have been happily rooting in the deck planter boxes, preparing the soil for a variety of flowering annuals. This year, the cracked dirt lay fallow with wisps of dead stems and leaves sticking out haphazardly like Norman's morning hair.

She deposited Slug onto a bench cushion and plucked the remnants of the past year's plantings from the pots. Between work, family, and attending to Mae's increased need for nurturing, no time existed for hobbies. Hannah was lucky to bathe and don clean underwear. Snooker bounded onto the deck and sniffed the cat, then tail-wagged over to his owner. The beagle lifted his head for a pat and hand-lick before darting after the bold squirrel foolish enough to trespass in his yard.

A set of wind chimes rippled music in the breeze, reminding Hannah of her father. She wondered where all the homemade chimes he had fashioned from pieces of discarded pipe had ended up after her mother's move to Rosemont. Probably stored on the back porch of the old house on Satsuma Road.

"Hey, Pop. Nice day, huh?" She looked to the heavens. "I feel kind of sorry for those poor folks up north. Here we are, feeling the first little bit of warmth, and they're still digging out from under snow and ice."

Hannah remembered tilling and planting with her father. His vegetable gardens had been legend. In the small space behind the house on Satsuma Road, he had grown enough for their family to eat and can, plus gifting paper grocery bags of fresh produce to the next-door neighbors.

"I could use some help with Ma-Mae, Pop, if you could look down for a bit. She's really sick. I think she wants to give up." A gust of wind twirled the suspended discs in the chimes' centers and they rang out, a signal that her father was surely listening.

Tears gathered in her eyes. "If it's her *time*, that's okay. She's told me over and over how she's ready to see you. But . . . " She sank into the porch swing. "I don't want to put her through a ton of awful tests or anything like that. Then again, I don't want to be negligent. The doctors throw out all these options. She has so many issues, it's like patching a leaky dam."

Sometimes Hannah wished nursing had been her profession rather than computers. The answers might come easy, or at least she would know the right questions to ask.

"God, what to do?" She closed her eyes and leaned her head back, pushing her feet to make the swing move. "What to do . . ."

"Mom?" Jonas stood in front of her, out of range enough to avoid being hit by the swing.

Hannah snapped to attention so quickly, she felt the bones clack in her neck. "You scared me half to death, Jonas! How do you do that, slip up on a person so silently?"

The expression on his face held a mixture of confusion and concern.

Hannah patted the cushion beside her. "Come sit."

As the swing pitched gently back and forth, the creak of the aluminum support chains accompanied the morning songs of the birds battling for space at the feeders. Snooker took up position at Jonas's feet and waited for a head-pat at each downward pass.

Jonas studied her from beneath his thick bangs. "Who were you talking to?"

"To your Grandpop, and myself."

"Oh." He sat, silent for a moment. "Does that mean you're losin' it? Talking to your own self and someone who's . . . dead?"

She tousled his hair. "Some days honey, talking to myself is the best conversation I have all day."

"Okay. I guess."

"Other than talking to you, of course." She paused. "I often talk to your Grandpop. Makes me feel better and I do believe, somehow, he hears."

Jonas tilted his head. "Phone's ringing."

"I can't believe I didn't bring it out here. Would you run and get it, sweetie?"

He returned shortly and handed her the cordless headset. "It's Aunt Hell. She's all fired up about the doctor or something."

So much for rest and sanity. Hannah grabbed the phone and clutched it to her chest to muffle the mouthpiece. "Don't call your Aunt Helen such an awful name, Jonas. If she ever heard such, she'd fall to pieces. She's very sensitive."

"If you say, Mom. I didn't come up with it anyway. Jus did. She calls y'all the three H's—Han, Hal, and Hell."

The hospital cafeteria teemed with its usual blend of haggard family members and scrub-suited personnel. Hannah and her older sister sat at one of a long line of wooden-laminate café tables.

"Try to eat a little of your salad, Helen. You're going to end up getting sick too, if you don't."

Her sister pushed a hunk of iceberg lettuce aside and speared a cherry tomato. "I know I need to." She rested the loaded fork on the side of the plate. "My appetite's shot, what with our mama curled up in that bed upstairs. Three days already. You'd think she'd be turning around by now. That cough still sounds so bad."

Helen used a thin paper napkin to dab tears from her red-rimmed eyes. "She didn't even want to watch 'The Young and the Restless!' She'll miss out on 'The Bold and the Beautiful,' but she watches Y & R like it was a religion. She's had a thing for that Victor Newman character for years. Every single time I talk to her on the phone, she rants like those actors are real people. She keeps up with who's had an affair with whom and which one's had this or that one's baby."

Hannah reached across the table and rested one hand over her sister's. "We have to keep the faith, Sissy. Ma-Mae's strong-willed. At least, she's in here where they can give her IV antibiotics and breathing treatments, and someone's looking out for her twenty-four hours a day."

"She was listing folks for me to call this morning . . . like she's expecting to die." Helen blew her nose with the crumpled paper napkin.

"She periodically does that. I suppose when you get to be her age, you wonder if every day might be your last, especially when you feel as rotten as she does right now." Hannah studied her elder sister's face—so much like her own, but softer and more rounded. The compassionate features of someone you would like to sit by your sickbed and hold your hand for hours.

Both sisters had inherited Mae's good skin and hair. Other than a few faint smile lines at the corners of their eyes, aging had taken little toll. Helen's dark brown waves showed a few gray wisps at the temples, though Hannah's remained unchanged. The older sibling wore a little extra cushion around the mid-section that her height helped to conceal, and Hannah was within eighteen pounds of her weight at high school graduation twenty years back—though the extra padding had positioned on her hips instead of her stomach. Helen had inherited Mae's blue eyes; Hannah's were hazel like her father's. Both women spoke in a gentle Southern drawl with well-modulated speech. Similar gestures punctuated their conversation.

One of Hannah's back teeth sent a shockwave of pain through her lower jaw and she jumped.

"What's wrong?"

"I have a tooth that's trying to act up. Started last night."

"Better get yourself to the dentist. We have those hard teeth like Daddy's, but they crack up sometimes. I've had two crowns in the last three years for that very reason."

"I don't have the time to deal with this right now."

Helen pushed her plate aside. "Life has a way of raining down over you, like Mama always says. We've had a monsoon, here lately. I came out yesterday to a flat tire. Nail in it. Charlie had to put on the spare so I could come over here. Then, my washer started to smell funny like it was burning up. Sears is delivering a new one sometime end of the week. Old one was shot. Had it for going on twenty years. The dryer's on its last legs. Takes two times to get towels dry. Guess it'll be next."

Come try my life for a while. I'd give anything if flat tires and crappy appliances were my only issues. Hannah scolded herself for the mean thoughts as soon as they breezed from her brain. "You could move that set of Ma-Mae's to your house. "

Helen's expression darkened. "I couldn't do that, Sister. That'd be like I was already picking over her stuff."

Hannah flicked specks of Styrofoam from her cup. "She would

tell you to take them, but suit yourself."

"Won't hurt us to buy new machines."

"Did you ever find out why the doctor ordered the EKG?" Hannah asked after a few minutes.

"He rattled off some long something-or-other. I didn't understand the half of it." Helen paused. "He did the strangest thing, though. He was on his way out the door when he turned back to me and asked in a quiet voice, 'you do realize your mother has signed a Do Not Resuscitate Order?'" Helen's eyebrows furrowed slightly. "Sounded so ominous. Like he was trying to tell me she was going to die."

"You know how Ma-Mae feels, Helen. She's had a Living Will for years. He probably wanted us to know they wouldn't be doing any heroics if she started downward."

"Maybe that's all it was." Helen raked a curl from her eyes. "I hated to call you. You've spent more than your fair share of time up here. I just got so scared."

"Michael Jack's signed on to help tomorrow," Helen said as she pushed the door open to Room 606. "His boss told him to go and do whatever he needed to, for his grandmama."

Helen's eldest was Mae's favorite grandchild, no secret about that. As the firstborn, he had been showered with grandmotherly affection from the start. The two not only shared a bond, but a birthday as well.

"That's good," Hannah said. "I can be here by one o'clock to relieve him. I think she does better when some of us are here off and on during the day."

Helen stopped short when she spied the vacant bed. "Now, where've they taken her off to? She couldn't be up and about by herself, especially with that rolling IV pole tagging along."

Hannah motioned toward the bathroom. "Shh! Listen."

Mae's muffled voice sounded through the slightly ajar door. "Have you washed *possible* yet?"

"Ma'am?" a voice with a thick Jamaican accent replied.

"You wash up as far as possible and you wash down as far as possible—" Mae's voice paused dramatically before delivering the final line, "—and then you wash *possible*."

They heard the nursing assistant chuckle.

Helen dabbed the corners of her eyes with a tissue. "Isn't that the sweetest thing? I had forgotten all about that saying."

"I used to tell Justine and Jonas the same little ditty when they were children."

"All three of my boys grew up hearing it too."

Helen walked around the room, straightening and tidying as she talked. This side of the building had a view of the street instead of rows of AC units. "Isn't it funny? I used to think she and I were so different. There was no way I could ever be like Mae." Her expression softened. "Now, more and more, I find I'm just like her."

Hannah forced down the ache of emotion and thumbed through a stack of opened get-well cards. "She's not such a bad old gal. I can't think of anyone I'd rather mimic. Most days."

Chapter Four

"Hold this so you can see your mouth." Dr. Emery passed Hannah a hand mirror. In the intense glow of the overhead dental lamp, the pores around her nose looked like forty miles of pock-holed back road and the single hair on her neck stuck out a good inch.

Oh, for heaven's sake, she thought. I came out in public like this!

Wolf hair: the term she and Suzanne had coined for the erroneous, whisker-like hairs that sprouted seemingly overnight from the oddest places. Not only had she started to cultivate a healthy patch of chin stubble, three wolf hairs had recently picked her cleavage for a new home.

"See this little crack?" He motioned with the tip of a dental instrument. "The x-ray shows no evidence of an abscess yet, but I'd lay even odds that your pain is coming from that first molar. Sad, it doesn't even have a restoration. A virgin tooth."

She mumbled around his fingers and instruments, "Didn't realize I had anything *virgin* left."

"Well, this tooth is. You only have two pinpoint fillings in your entire mouth. What are you doing breaking a tooth?"

"Grinding in my sleep or something?" *Great. Add that to the list of bad habits I've acquired.* She winced as a jab of white-hot pain shot through her jaw. "Man! Now I know for sure I'd never have a career as a spy. If they captured me and messed with one of my teeth so it hurt like that, I'd give up the President's underwear size."

Dr. Emery laughed then rolled his operatory chair over to a long counter and scribbled into her chart. "Good thing you came in. You're overdue for your cleaning and check-up too."

One side of Hannah's lips lifted. "I'm overdue for everything. Between work, teenaged kids and my mother, I barely have time to brush."

"Life can be somewhat entertaining at times." He closed the chart. "I'll refer you to Dr. Koch's office for a root canal After that, you'll need to come back so I can put a crown over that molar. We can make you a bite guard to wear at night, unless you want to help me buy a new car or maybe a set of tires."

Hannah rested her throbbing jaw in one hand and groaned. "Root canal."

"When you aren't terribly infected and swollen, it's generally routine and painless. Less drilling than a filling."

"It's not that. My life has been so . . . challenging here lately with Mom so sick and all." She offered a weak smile. "Maybe it will be nice having my head numbed up."

A line of pigeons and sparrows balanced on the telephone wire spanning North Monroe Street. Each day as Hannah traveled between her state job and Tallahassee General Hospital, she noticed the birds. How did they choose the designated perch of the day? Who decided? Was there an alpha male or female, as in a wolf pack?

As she pulled to a halt at one of Tallahassee's busy intersections, a cluster of young people jogged by, each wearing black shorts and a gray T-shirt with ARMY printed across the front. How many would have their budding lives snipped short by yet another "peace initiative" or "police action"—the popular political synonyms for "war?" Given a few years, her son or daughter might run with such a well-intentioned group of patriotic men and women. Maybe peace and goodwill would prevail before that point.

Hannah huffed. "And maybe drunk pink donkeys will fly loops around Uranus too."

The epiphany struck her suddenly: she had no control over political edicts or war, no more than she had over birds on a wire.

No control.

Not over which of the jogging youths would die. Nor over when her mother would, as Mae so often quipped, "leave for her reward in the sky." A higher power dictated the storyline and all she could do was play her role. Stress and struggle would make no difference to the outcome—good or bad.

The ever-present knot nestled deep within her stomach eased slightly. For the first time since her mother's most recent illness, she inhaled a deep, unrestricted breath. "Nada. Zip. Not one teensy-tinesy little hair of control."

What would this morning bring? An increase in her mother's congestion and fever? Mae's endless inventory of last wishes? When Hannah entered room 606, Mae was propped up in bed picking at the dregs of dry scrambled eggs and congealed grits.

"Hey, baby-doll. I didn't expect you till later on."

Hannah deposited her purse on the vinyl padded chair next to the bed. "I'm going in a little late this morning. Thought I'd stop by and see how your night went."

"I had a pretty good sleep." Mae pushed the rolling table to one side. "Them breathing treatments make my mouth taste like the south end of a north-bound mule, but I surely have been able to harvest some phlegm. My chest doesn't feel near as heavy."

"That's great!"

"You got to do one thing for me, darlin'."

"What's that, Ma-Mae?"

"Run to a Hardee's and get me a sausage biscuit and a big cup of strong coffee. And soon as I can, I need to have my head washed. I look like who shot Sam! I scared myself when I looked in the mirror."

For the first time in over a week, Mae cared how she looked. The smallest miracles were the sweetest.

Chapter Five

When she pulled into the circular drive at Enable Healthcare facility the next day, Hannah spied her sister-in-law's ruby red minivan pulling from a parking slot. She tooted the horn and Suzanne waved before easing back into the space.

"Hey!" Suzanne's smiling face appeared at the driver's side window. "I was just slipping out to grab lunch. I'm starved slap to death. Want me to help you carry anything inside before I go?"

"I'm hungry too. Hop in and we'll ride up to that little Chinese place on the corner."

Suzanne bounded around to the passenger's side and crawled in. "Sounds like a 'wiener' to me." She grinned. "It'll give us a chance to catch up."

Hannah gunned into the swift current of noon Mahan Drive traffic. "Where's Hal? I thought he was staying with Ma-Mae this morning."

"The new sheriff called a meeting first thing. Hal wants to get a feel for how he's gonna run things. My mama's doing okay, so I told your brother I'd pinch-hit for him."

Hannah vulture-circled the strip mall parking lot until she noticed a truck vacating a spot near the Chinese eatery. "I had forgotten how noon is over here. I usually pack a lunch when things are . . . normal."

"You still car-pool?"

"Generally, yes." Hannah grabbed her purse from the back seat. "I'll need to rob a dang bank to cover my gas bill this month. With me trekking to the hospital and the rehab facility, I've had to provide my own transportation."

"Know what you mean. Three of Mama's doctors are over here. I burn up the pavement most every week for one thing or the other."

After they placed the orders, they sat at one of six small tables.

"I've never been here," Suzanne said.

"One of my co-workers says it's the best in town, and he's Chinese, so I think that's a pretty good recommendation."

"Thought you said you were hungry. But you surely didn't order a whole lot."

Hannah rolled her head to ease the cramped muscles in her neck. "My stomach's been a little off. The hot and sour soup is the only thing that sounded good."

A petite Asian woman delivered two brown paper bags to the table and skittered back toward the small kitchen.

Suzanne slipped back the lid on the Styrofoam container. Tantalizing scented steam rose in a puff. "This is a pile of food. Maybe I'll split this up and take some back to your mama."

"Good idea. She's not too keen on the food at the rehab facility."

Suzanne popped a forkful of cashew chicken into her mouth. "Gah! This is G-double-O- D, Good!"

"Would I lead you astray?"

"Honey, I wouldn't have the time or the energy even if you had the notion to lead me there. I get to going so hard sometimes, I feel like I'm wearing the soles clean off my shoes."

"At least you have plenty of backups," Hannah said.

Her sister-in-law's expression grew thoughtful. "Something dawned on me today, about Miz Mae."

"Hmm?"

"She's been pretty down since they moved her to rehab."

Hannah crumbled crispy-fried noodles into the rich, steaming soup. "She sits and stares into space a good deal of the time. And she doesn't really talk unless you ask her a direct question. I'm starting to wonder if she might've had a minor stroke. Maybe that ER doctor was on target, and she should've had a brain scan."

"I had a different thought. She believes we've put her in a nursing home."

"No." Hannah paused. "You think?"

"I've noticed her crying when she thinks no one's looking."

"It's a beautiful day for late February." Hannah wheeled Mae onto a small porch at the facility's main entrance.

The sky was the blue of Paul Newman's eyes, so intense it almost looked contrived. A few songbirds fooled by the deceptive early warmth sang courtship hymns. Hannah backed her mother's wheelchair into a wind-protected nook, a spot drenched in sunlight.

"That feels good to my back," Mae said.

Hannah tucked a lightweight white cotton blanket around Mae's legs. "I thought we'd sit outside a little today. If the breeze proves to be too cool, we'll go back in. I don't want you to get sick again."

A young man wheeled through the glass entrance doors and rolled to the opposite side of the narrow porch. An FSU baseball cap shaded his face. He slumped in the wheelchair. At first, Hannah thought his snuffles might be the sign of allergies. The first hint of North Florida spring brought a fine dusting of pollen to every horizontal surface, sometimes as early as the end of February. The young man's body quivered, then shook with muffled sobs. Tears splashed onto his collegiate sweatshirt.

Mae's vacant stare altered to one of sympathetic interest as she directed her attention to the young man. "It'll get better, honey. You'll see. It will get better." Her mother's voice held the soothing tone of maternal concern. Tears gathered in Hannah's eyes. The man's weeping continued for a few moments, then ceased abruptly. Mae slipped a hand into her robe pocket, flipped through her collection of clean hankies, selected a plain white cloth, and handed it over.

He dabbed his eyes, blew his nose, and lifted his gaze to Mae. Something invisible passed between the two. His lips quivered into a brief, shy smile. He fumbled in a bag and donned an MP3 player's earpieces, closed his eyes, and separated himself from their company.

Mae resumed her vacant stare.

"Ma-Mae? How do you feel today?"

"Tired."

"How did therapy go?"

"All right."

Hannah patted one side of her mother's sprayed coiffure. "I see the lady did your hair."

"Yes."

"She did a good job."

"Yes."

Hannah rummaged for a subject. "Looks like spring may come early this year."

Her mother grunted in response.

"The therapist said you might be getting out of here end of next week if you work hard enough." Hannah waited. Her mother blinked.

After a few minutes, Mae said, "This is the place I've been sent to die."

"Only if you choose to do so, Ma-Mae." Hannah positioned her chair so that she could look directly into her mother's eyes. "Do you honestly think that I, that any of us, would put you somewhere to die? Do you *really?*"

Mae narrowed her gaze. "Well . . ."

"No Ma-Mae. We wouldn't. Not even in a full-time nursing home, unless you were so ill that you absolutely needed around-the-clock care. I would never do that to you, nor would Hal or Helen." Hannah cupped her mother's chin gently in the palm of one hand. "Part of this facility is a nursing home, but you're in the acute care wing. They're doing everything in their power to help you get strong enough to go back home to Rosemont and all of your friends. But you are going to have to pull yourself together and work with them."

Hannah sat back and crossed her hands over her chest. "You want to die? You go right ahead. It's your choice."

Immediately, guilt at being harsh with her mother clawed a hole in her conscience. Was this the "tough love" all the therapists were so fond of touting? It didn't feel so good.

Mae lifted one white eyebrow. "You might want to take you a little ladies' pink pill, baby. You get a bit peevish when you need a good cleaning out."

Oh yes. Laxatives: Ma-Mae's cure-all for everything that ails ya. Hannah chuckled. The piss and vinegar still simmered inside of her mother.

Chapter Six

"Mm-mmm!" Hal Mathers stomped the dirt from his shoes before entering the kitchen's back door. "Something surely smells good, Pookie."

Hannah smiled as she did practically every time she heard her brother's nickname for her: Pookie, after a shaggy brown stuffed bear, her constant childhood companion.

Her brother filled a tablespoon with steaming red sauce and took a tentative taste. "Dang, woman. You make a mean spaghetti sauce for a non-Eye-talian."

"Thanks. My sister-in-law's not feeding you well?"

Hal rubbed a hand across his spare tire. "Do I look like a man who goes without?"

"Thought you bragged you wore the same pants size you wore in high school."

"Sure I do. Just—they fit a few inches lower down now."

Hal tore off a hunk of Italian bread and dunked it into the sauce pot. "I'm starving and Suzanne's over at her son and daughter-in-law's. Their baby's teething and ill as a sprayed hornet." He chewed. "Speaking of ill, I don't know what you said to Ma-Mae, but it surely worked a charm. I stopped by to see her when I rode over to Lowes to get some lumber. Ma-Mae met some lady she knew from Greensboro, across the hallway, and she was in that old woman's room talking up a storm when I got there."

"I think we've dodged the bullet, this time." She offered him a napkin.

"Know what Ma-Mae told me? Don't know if she shared it with you or not."

"Hmm?"

"She wants us to put her house on the market." Hal dabbed tomato sauce from the corners of his lips.

Hannah's eyebrows shot upward. "Really? What brought that on?"

"Dunno. Said she doesn't like the notion of the house sitting there vacant. Said she's not ever going back there to live, and she knows it. Wants us to sell it and use the money for her expenses."

"She doesn't usually talk to me about big important money things. She saves that heavy stuff for you 'cause—," Hannah gave him a playful arm slug, "—you're the boy." *And I'm the lowly daughter who pays all the bills and keeps up with her accounts.*

Hal screwed up his mouth the way he always did when he was being her big goofy older brother. "Slap me on a bun and pass the mustard. I must be something really special."

"You're special all right." Hannah smiled in spite of herself. "I take it, since you're over here sponging off your sister, you're batching it tonight."

He nodded. "Suzanne's gonna be baby-sitting for the entire evening."

Hannah ran her tongue over her back teeth. *Maybe if I grow some new teeth and get all cranky, someone will come and baby-sit me. What a whiny pain in the butt I'm becoming!* She ripped off a wedge of bread, dunked it in the sauce, and joined her brother. Red sauce glistened on their lips.

"You know the good thing about us doing this?" he asked around a mouthful. "Suzanne assures me it doesn't have any calories if you eat it standing up."

Hannah licked a trickle of sauce from her lips. "I love that woman."

"So do I." His expression softened. "These past two years have been the best of my life."

"Suzanne already feels like a sister to me. Your former wife, not so much." *Not that I'd ever admit this to you, but I secretly called Charlene "Attila the Hun with Boobs."*

Hal hesitated before he spoke. "I hear Charlene's getting married."

Hannah searched her brother's rugged features. "You okay with that?"

"As a matter of fact, I am. There were hurt feelings for a while. Anyone tells you divorce is easy is a fool and a liar. And I'm married again, so why should I begrudge her?"

Hannah thought about the time Charlene had dumped her brother's belongings in trash bags on Mae's front lawn in broad daylight. How the whole town had gossiped about the break-up. How their mama had suffered the fall-out. Maybe Hal had forgiven her, but Hannah wasn't so inclined. "You heard from Natalie?"

"Nope." Hal's gaze dropped. "Maybe one day."

"I ought to give her a call."

He shot a warning glance. "You'll do no such thing. She's a grown woman."

"She's your daughter, Hal. It doesn't seem right."

Hal raked a large work-hardened hand through his graying hair. "She blames me for leaving her mama, Pookie. Heck, there're still folks in this town who won't so much as give me the time of day. And I've known 'em all of my life."

You're not the only one who has to swallow the bile. People cutting their eyes at me like I'm the sister of the ultimate sinner. I want to scream at them. What of Christian compassion, that whole "judge not lest you be judged" thing? Guess that only applies in theory.

Hal walked over to the island counter, poured two tall glasses of iced tea, and handed one to his sister. "Takes two to make a marriage, and by God, it takes two to screw it up. I was the one who finally pulled the plug. So . . ." he spread his arms wide. "I'm the bad guy. What folks don't understand is that it's as hard to be the one who's leaving as the one who's left behind. The one left behind gets all the sympathy."

Hannah hugged her brother. "I know what kind of man you are, Hal. The others—"

"—will just get glad in the same pants they got mad in," he finished with one of Mae's favorite sayings.

"And some of those biddies have some pretty big britches too," Hannah added.

"Looks like two pigs fighting in a croaker sack when they're walking away from you."

Hannah pointed upward. "Good Lord's going to strike us dead one day for being so mean-spirited."

"Nope." Hal shook his head. "He likes a joke as good as the rest of us. Otherwise, He would never have created our family."

"Want to stay for dinner? Both of my kids might actually—miracle of miracles—be here."

"Thanks for the invite, Pookie. That half a loaf of bread and sauce will hold me. I'll root around and find something at the house later. I want to get on home and work on our back deck. I hope to get to the railing before this next weekend, if the weather holds out."

"Always tearing up or building something." Hannah kidded.

When Hal smiled, his entire face got involved, a feat Hannah found truly amazing. His forehead and ears shifted back slightly, his blue eyes twinkled, and the skin around his eyes and mouth crinkled with deep, twin cheek dimples for punctuation. "I'm thinking about constructing a big dog house next."

"You don't have a dog."

"For me."

"What did you do?"

Hal made prayer hands. "Nothing. I'm a perfect angel as always. But if my wife brings home one more pair of shoes, I'll have a place to stay."

When Hannah parked at the rehab facility, sadness washed over her and she allowed herself to cry. Eight years back, she had lost her father. Now her mother's eventual death loomed. The circular dance between healthcare facilities and assisted living confirmed the fact.

Mae roamed the halls and sitting rooms of Enable in search of interesting conversation. Since discovering the afternoon Bingo game, she had coaxed the physical therapy staff into scheduling her sessions in the morning. Mrs. Eva, the hair stylist who curled and stiff-sprayed Mae's white hair once a week, claimed relatives from Chattahoochee. The two women had become fast friends, dissecting the lives, loves, and daily minutiae of small town life. It didn't hurt that Eva was as passionate as Mae about "The Young and the Restless."

Hannah took a shuddering breath and dabbed the mascara from beneath her eyes. Maybe she should wise up and quit wearing any.

"What the heck are you crying for, you big dope?" she asked her reflection in the vanity mirror. "Ma-Mae's better and she'll be back at Rosemont soon. Stop blubbering, blow your nose, and get moving," Hannah preached to her mirror image. "Hannah, you are like your mama. She's always giving herself little pep talks."

Hannah finally located Ma-Mae in the sun room. "There you are.

I was beginning to think you'd taken off." She sat on the cabbage rose-print love seat beside her mother.

"Can't move fast enough to break out. But give me a couple more days." Mae motioned toward the woman sitting in a wheelchair beside the sofa. "Hannah, this is June McConnick. She took a tumble and ended up here. Broke both her ankles, one in three places."

June smiled and extended a hand. "You must be the 'baby daughter' Mae has spoken of so often."

"Pleased to meet you," Hannah said.

"June's getting out of here 'round the same time as me," Mae added. "She's been here going on three months. She's started to use a walker a little each day, haven't you honey?"

The younger woman nodded. "Your mother and I have become good friends in the past few days. I feel like I've known your family for years, what with Mae's stories."

The television blared. Down one long hallway, someone moaned.

"She tells me you're quite the computer expert," June continued. "That's a talent, especially these days. I know enough to send a few emails, maybe type a letter."

"Don't believe all of her bragging," Hannah patted her mother's hand. *Amazing, since she saves a list of things I've done wrong.*

"Hannah, if your mother isn't one of your biggest fans, then you do have a problem." June chuckled. "I believe my kids hang the moon."

Mae swung her cane in cadence with her slow, deliberate stride. They walked the long highly-polished hall leading to her mother's room. The omnipresent cloud of green apple deodorizer—a smell Hannah had initially liked, but now loathed—did little to cloak the mixture of urine and stale sweat. Hannah willed her stomach to stop rolling and forced a light-hearted tone into her voice. "Gosh, Ma-Mae. You're making good progress. No more walker!"

"I parked that baby yesterday and told David—he's my main therapist—that I was ready for my hikin' stick. This one here is a loaner. I'll have one measured to fit before I leave for Rosemont."

A petite, elderly female lifted a shaky hand as they neared her wheelchair. Mae said in a loud voice, "Afternoon, Miz Pansy. Glad to see you up and about." The woman nodded and mumbled a reply, completely understood by Mae but unintelligible to Hannah. "Yeah, sugar. It's turning early spring. Sure is. You get one of those aides to wheel you outside for a spell. Fresh air'd do you a world of good." Her mother touched the old woman's bony shoulder. "I'll be down later to visit."

A thin line of spittle dibbled down one side of Pansy's paralyzed face.

"Poor old thing. She's a throw'd-away," Mae said when they were a few feet down the hall.

Hannah glanced back. "Shh, Ma-Mae. She'll hear you."

"She's deaf as a stump. Couldn't hear a fart in a jug." Her mother pointed her index finger for emphasis. "But sweet as the day is long. Though for the life of me, I can't figure why anyone in their right mind would name a poor gal-child Pansy. Daisy, Rose, Lilly—I can see them—but, Pansy?" Mae stopped mid-hall. "You know what I wish?"

"What's that?"

"I wish I could have a real, soaking-style bath, or a shower: a good washing down. They're regular with the sponge baths, but I swannee, I just don't feel all-total clean."

"Do they even have showers here?"

Mae motioned with a tilt of her head. "There's a big one, end of this hall."

Hannah said, "Wait here."

"I'll go sit in my chair if it's all the same." Mae shuffled toward her room, two doors down.

Hannah returned shortly carrying a tall stack of clean white towels and a bottle of liquid soap. "The nurses gave me permission to help you, Ma-Mae, if you're up for a shower."

"Grab my little carry-all. It's got my body powder and deodorant and such." Mae rocked twice before she was able to stand. She pushed past Hannah, narrowly missing her daughter's foot with the rubber tip of the cane. "Lord a-mighty! You'd think I just won a ticket to see the Reverend Billy Graham. That's how excited I am."

The twenty-by-twenty-foot shower room was divided into four areas containing bench seats and hanging privacy curtains. Hannah sat the stack of towels on a slatted bench and glanced around the small room. *Do they get some kind of discount on this mint green tile? They must buy it by the boat-load. It's in every facility I've ever visited.*

A nursing assistant stuck her head through the entrance door. "Y'all have everything you need?"

"Think so!" Hannah called. She helped Mae remove her cotton house robe.

"I forgot to mention," the attendant said, "turn the nozzle all the way to the right. It'll take a couple of spins. It's a little finicky. When you get hot water, ease it back to the left slightly until the temperature's where you want it. Hit one of the call buttons if you need help."

Mae waved. "Go on about your business, honey. We can manage." Then to Hannah, "get the water started. I can shuck my clothes. I ain't that feeble yet."

As soon as Hannah twirled the single-handle control, cold water coursed from a hand-held nozzle, soaking one of her shoes.

"Dad-gum!" No matter how she tried to position the hose, it managed to whip around and wet some part of her lower body. "This thing is possessed!"

Mae hugged her arms to her naked chest. "Leave it hanging there and help me to the stool. My goose bumps are growing goose bumps."

"All right, Ma-Mae." The second she turned the nozzle loose, it whipped around and sprayed her other foot. "Sh—!"

"Watch that potty mouth, youngun, or I'll wash it out with some of this squeeze soap."

Though she had tried to curtail cursing since becoming a mother (and therefore role model), Hannah often failed. When she stubbed her little toe on Jonas's leaden equipment duffel, conveniently left in the middle of the living room, the only word she wanted to use wouldn't have met Mae's approval. She tried substituting "sugar" or "shoot fire," but most of the time the intended word blurted out. Norman took a different tack: he mumbled barely audible profanity under his breath.

After she pulled the privacy curtain shut, Hannah tested the temperature, then held the nozzle so that a stream of warm water coursed down her mother's back.

"Lordy be!" Mae closed her eyes and smiled. "That feels so-o-o good."

Taking a body part at a time, Hannah gently soaped and scrubbed, rinsing between. Each time she released her hold on the hose, the nozzle swung in wide arcs, spraying the walls, curtains, and the few dry threads of her clothing.

Hannah laughed. "I'm getting more wet than you."

"Here, give it to me." Mae held out a hand. "I'll wrestle with it while you finish me up."

After washing Mae's feet and legs, Hannah helped her mother stand, took the spray wand, and handed Mae the wash rag. "You get to clean possible, Ma-Mae. That's where I draw the line."

Mae giggled. "What's the matter? I washed your bare bottom many a time."

"A fact I am well aware of and greatly appreciate you for. I'll rinse." Hannah aimed the warm spray in the general direction of her mother's privates.

"You're missing the target all together!"

"I could use a little direction. I am flying blind." Hannah adjusted the spray slightly. "Better?"

"Passable." Mae flipped blasts of rinse water into the air with each swing of her wash cloth. By the time she finished, Hannah's pants and the lower half of her shirt glommed to her body.

Their peals of manic laughter alerted the nurses at the nearby station. A concerned voice called from the opposite side of the curtain, "Y'all doing okay in there?"

"As well as can be expected." Hannah said. She turned the control lever and the hose abruptly ceased its spinning samba. "Good thing I brought extra linens."

Hannah guided Mae to a bench. After she helped her mother dry, powder, and dress, she used a fresh towel to blot as much moisture as possible from her own clothes and shoes.

Mae grabbed her daughter's hand and gave it a weak squeeze. "Thank you, sugar pot. I know that was a trial. Never thought I'd live to see the day when one of my own would have to bathe me. This old age trip I'm on is full of surprises."

As much for me as you, Hannah thought. "We'll get through it together, Ma-Mae."

Mae slipped her arthritic feet into a pair of fuzzy slippers. "When you were a baby, I called you my caboose, on account of you were my last child. Now it seems you've turned into my engine."

Hannah's throat constricted. Had her mother paid her a compliment?

Later when Hannah recounted the scene to Suzanne, she said, "I've done some things in my life—thought I'd had some pretty amazing experiences. But until I took a shower with my eighty-five-year-old mother, I had not truly lived."

Chapter Seven

Hannah scrolled though the family-locator roster. Helen was taking a turn at Enable Healthcare, a list of questions in hand for the attending doctor. Hal and Suzanne had taken Jonas to a movie in Marianna. Norman had volunteered, finally, to take her car in for a tune-up and oil change, and Justine was hanging out with Brittany. Lately her daughter spent more time at her best friend's house than her own.

Why should she feel bad about taking a few minutes of down time? It had been a heck of a week. Three people were out sick at the office, and the extra workload shifted to the remaining personnel. Each day at lunch, then again after work, she trekked to Enable for the daily visit and update on her mother. Then she drove the forty-five mile commute home to Chattahoochee. To make dinner. To wash clothes. To be the mother, wife, and loving companion. All the places she *needed* to be.

The gift of time had been air-dropped at her road-weary feet, tied up with a plump, pink bow and a card that read: *Good for a few minutes of solitude. Use it wisely.*

She settled into her favorite worn easy chair and rested a tall mug of lukewarm coffee and a plate on the end table. Heaven forbid if anyone stopped by for an unannounced visit. Her sweatshirt was gray with age, the jeans faded and ripped at the knees, and her unwashed hair was clipped haphazardly on top of her head. No makeup. Bliss. Slap 'em if they didn't like it.

After a bite from a warm banana-nut muffin and a swig of coffee, she opened the chiller-thriller novel she had checked out—for the third time in three months—from the public library. A Delta Airlines electronic ticket fell onto her lap.

"Emily Tucker," she read. "Flight 1274. Seat 28-C. Origin - Tallahassee. Destination - Atlanta. One checked bag. Departs 7:10 a.m., Gate B 01. January 31."

Hannah sipped the tepid coffee, careful to funnel it to the side opposite her errant tooth, and stared absently at the e-ticket.

"Where were you going, Emily Tucker?" Since Atlanta provided the hub for this part of the U.S., it could've been most anywhere. She studied the pristine paper. No multiple fold-lines, like one might have after clearing the ticket-counter, then cramming it into a pocket or handbag.

"Wait a minute! Maybe you didn't go? You poor dear."

The scenario unfurled in her imagination: Emily Tucker at the Tallahassee Regional Airport. Excited, a little flushed. She hates to fly, but wants to be anywhere else besides here. One bag is delivered to the handlers, the other trails behind her like a tethered dog. She visits the Starbucks counter. Orders and pays. Sips the sweet latte, licks the foam from her upper lip. She strolls at a leisurely pace around the lobby watercolor exhibit. Time to kill. No need to rush.

It's a beautiful morning outside. Perfect flying weather. The front from the previous two days has pushed through, and now the skies promise to remain a clear crystalline blue—a perfect end-of-January day in the Panhandle of Florida.

Emily passes through security. One small handbag and the novel in the plastic bin. The carryon bag flat on its side. A security officer motions her to one side where she pirouettes as the sensor wand passes over her. She fights the urge to strike a silly ballet pose.

After a few minutes of rereading the same passage of the novel Hannah now holds, Emily Tucker's cell phone trills with the stupid ditty-song her son programmed from the Internet. She hates the little communication device. Loathes the intrusion into her privacy. She senses before answering that she'll never leave the ground this morning. She talks—nodding, frowning—retracing her steps down the concourse to sweet-talk the counter staff into locating her luggage. So close. So doggone close.

Poor, poor Emily Tucker. She really could've used the vacation.

Hannah returned the boarding pass to the back of the book where it would wait to serve as a handy bookmark. She read the novel's first page three times before glancing up to enjoy the view from the sun porch. A number of trees, tricked by a hint of early warmth, had sent out tentative shoots of lime green. Her gaze wandered to one of three hanging bird feeders—a cylindrical piece of hand-worked pottery fashioned on two sides to resemble long, comical faces, with tongues sticking out for perches. The early spring rains had prompted some of the seeds to sprout, making the feeder appear more of a planter than a haven for chickadees and wrens.

Amazing, she thought. You turn your focus away for a few weeks and everything goes to hell in a hand basket.

She closed the novel, not bothering to mark her place, and left the house for the yard. The small pre-fabricated greenhouse that doubled as a tool shed was packed with tender potted plants.

"You guys can't come out to play just yet," she said aloud as she rooted beneath layers of greenery for the rake, garden gloves, and a bin of birdseed.

Hannah surveyed the yard. Should she remove the dead limbs from the butterfly bush? Was it too early to fertilize?

The first weeks of March in the Florida Panhandle could be deceptively cruel. One day, the temperatures might creep into the low eighties. A collective jolt of greenery would ripple through the countryside. Then the winds would shift, coming from the north with a howling growl to nip the innocent early buds. Gardeners followed the siren song in droves to purchase plats of annuals and perennials, only to grudgingly replant in three to four weeks when spring regained its grasp.

Hannah used a stick to rake the moist goop and sprouted seeds from the bottom of the feeders, then refilled all three. Safflower seeds had proven the least delectable to the marauding squirrels. No matter which brand of tamper-proof feeder she had wasted money on in the past, the fuzzy little yard rats managed to dine with ease. The previous year, Norman had proudly presented Hannah a battery-powered squirrel-proof feeder for her birthday. Woo-pee. Some inexpensive jewelry would've been nice.

According to the manufacturer's claims, the offending raider would be swished around in circles, thwarting plans for free seed. Hannah's squirrels quickly organized a strategy conference and arrived at a solution. Taking turns on the spinning feeder, they rode it like rednecks on a one-price-for-all fair tilt-a-whirl until the two C-batteries expired. The entire punch-drunk extended family feasted until every morsel of the expensive wild-bird mixture disappeared. As frustrated as they made her, Hannah had to admire any creature with such tenacity and total lack of shame.

Snooker dropped a filthy tennis ball at her feet and wagged his tail. "Gross! You expect me to touch that thing?"

Snooker barked twice.

"Oh all right."

She picked up the foul toy with two fingers and lobbed it through the air. As she raked around the daylily bed, the game of slime-ball continued. Slug ambled across the yard, narrowly dodging the charging dog. The Persian padded over to where Hannah stood and twirled in lazy circles at her feet.

Slime-ball and all, Hannah had to admit how peaceful she felt. Breathing the warm, scented air—so different from hospital atmosphere—eased her tangled spirit. The sudden slam of the sunroom screened door caused her to jump. Justine spied her mother across the tiered backyard and charged in her direction. So much for tranquility.

"Hi Mom!" Justine flipped her long blonde hair and stood with her slender hips cocked to one side.

Hannah studied her long-legged, willowy daughter—the kind of coquettish teenaged girl men of every age lusted for, pawed over, and lured with promises. God help her and Norman to get this one to eighteen without bloodshed. Or an unplanned pregnancy. Too bad chastity belts had gone out of fashion before the turn of the last century.

Justine turned on her orthodontist's-vacation-home smile. "What cha doin'?"

"Playing a rousing game of pitch and filling the feeders. Keeping the country safe for generations to come, winning the war against drugs. Important stuff like that."

Justine rolled her blue eyes and dragged out the word Mom until it had at least four syllables.

"And you, what's happening in your young and increasingly dramatic world?"

"Stopped by to pick up some money. Brit and I are gonna ride over to Wal-Mart in Marianna with her mom if that's okay."

"You came to the National Parents' Bank and Trust for a quick withdrawal?" Hannah smiled. "There're a couple of twenties in my purse. Enough?"

"Guess so."

"If you see anything you simply must have, tell Missy I'll pay her back. Bring me the receipt."

Justine dug at the dried grass with the toe of one Nike.

"Something else on your mind?"

"You know, Mom. Spring break's coming up."

"Honey, your father and I have already discussed it. I don't think we can take off to the beach this year. Not until your grandmother's well enough to go back to Rosemont. I know how much you and Jonas look forward to St. George Island, but—"

"That's not it."

"Oh?"

"Brit's cousin has a place on the Ochlocknee River. She asked if I could go with her this year."

"Brit's mother going?" Hannah's trouble-radar zoomed in.

"No Ma'am. Just her cousin and husband. And a couple of other girls from class. Like . . . no big deal."

"I'll talk it over with your father, sweetie. As long as you aren't by yourselves and there are adults supervising, I don't see a reason why you can't go."

Justine flung her arms around her mother and blessed her with the brush of a kiss. "You're the best." She pushed away and dashed toward the house.

"Hey!" Hannah called. "Leave me a little cash, will you?"

Inside, piles of soiled laundry waited like an unwelcome boarder. Jonas's socks alone could be used to win the war against terror. Hannah took one last sweeping look around the neglected yard, then returned her worn yard gloves, rake, and birdseed dispenser to the shed. Maybe tomorrow she'd start the novel. Again.

Chapter Eight

The floral-upholstered wingback chairs in Rosemont's front lobby were filled with the residents Hannah referred to as "the regulars"— Miz Maxine, Miz Nancy, and Mr. Barney—along with two elders she recognized, but didn't know by name.

"Hey!" Beth, the front desk manager, called when she saw Hannah. "I heard your mother was back with us. I must've been at lunch when she came in."

"It's been a long, hard road."

"We still have two over at Enable. One with a bad fall and one had the same bug as your mother," Beth said. "We've had some of the staff out too. Maybe if the weather holds and stops flipping from cold to warm, we can finally get everyone well."

"Amen to that." Hannah signed the visitors' log.

"Hey, Sugar." Barney Thompson held out his shaky arms.

Hannah stepped over to his chair, bent down, and hugged the small elderly man. He kissed her lightly on the cheek. Barney reminded her of an overgrown leprechaun. His shamrock green eyes danced with mischief and the corners of his thin mouth turned upward in a permanent smile. The ravages of age had stolen a few inches of his height, but none of his impish spirit.

"How's your mother? Heard she's back."

"I'm on my way down to see her right now. I'm sure she'll be up and about soon."

Barney nodded. "Good. I miss her at Bingo. It isn't as much fun without my darlin' Mae." He patted Hannah's arm and winked. "Be sure to give her a hug and a pinch for me."

"You bet, Mr. Barney."

Maxine called out, "Tell your mother I'll be down to visit later. All of us have missed her, not just him!"

Maxine fired a glare in Barney's direction. The two seniors kept the fires stoked of an on-going, lively feud. No one could explain their differences. They bristled in each other's company, but were seldom very far from each other. Barney sneered back and jabbed a finger in the air with an eyebrow-raised nod.

"All right you two." Beth shook her head.

Hannah chuckled as she walked down the hall to her mother's room. She knocked softly, then used her key. Mae rested in bed amidst a pile of clothing and toiletries.

"Lord help! Can't a person get a dab of privacy?" The furrow deepened between Mae's eyebrows. "Oh, it's just you."

"Sorry, Ma-Mae. I was trying to be quiet. I thought you might be sleeping."

"Who could sleep? It's like someone ran a freeway through my room. First the nurse dropped by, then it was that young gal who runs this place, then folks who've caught scent of me being back. I'm purely worn out."

Hannah picked up a stack of folded underwear. "Everyone's glad to have you home."

"Leave those be. I know where I want them put." Mae's tone sounded sharp. "I'll be glad to be back to normal. Everyone's kicking up such a fuss."

Hannah settled into the rocking chair. "You're certainly in a mood. Thought you'd be happy."

"I am happy, and I'm not in a mood." Mae shoved a king-sized pillow behind her back and slugged it several times before nestling into place.

"I saw Mr. Barney on my way in. He missed you. Every time I stopped by to check your mail while you were gone, he asked about you."

Mae fanned the air with one hand. "I'm not studying him."

"But he's so sweet, Ma-Mae. And he seems to genuinely like you."

Mae narrowed her eyes. "I didn't move in here to find a boyfriend, daughter of mine. I was married for fifty-two years to your father— a perfectly wonderful man—and I certainly don't need anybody to care for, at my age."

Hannah couldn't stop herself from goading her mother for a reaction. "They take care of them for you here, Ma-Mae. You could always pick out one to play with, if you wanted."

Mae sniffed. "Men are after one of two things when you get to be my age. They're either looking for a purse or a nurse."

Hannah bit her lower lip to avoid laughing, given her mother's testy disposition.

Mae frowned. "And that Barney? He's a player!"

"Really?"

"He's broken his share of Rosemont hearts, and he's not gonna get a'holt of mine."

Hannah rocked gently back and forth before deciding to drop the subject of romance. "I can help you unpack."

"You most certainly will not. I can do it myself."

Mae Mathers's spunk had returned with a ticker-tape parade and fanfare.

"Is there anything you need, or want? I can run to the store and—"

"What I need is to be left alone. I'll get up a list later. I got to rest up. The therapist from e-Bay's starting in on me tomorrow."

Had she missed something? Had someone started a physical therapy department on the popular Internet site? "e-Bay?"

"e-Bay. You know, that place I just come from. Lord, your memory is as long as my pecker."

"*Enable,* Ma-Mae. It's *Enable* Healthcare."

"Yeah," Mae nodded emphatically. "What I said. e-Bay."

Once her mother fixated on a thing, it was futile to fight; e-Bay it would be from this point forward.

"One of those therapists is coming three days a week to work on my walking. I can do the exercises on my own—I told them that—but they're coming all the same. I told them it best be in the mornings, 'cause Bingo's in the afternoons."

"Wouldn't want you to miss that."

"Get yourself on home, now. Hal and Suzanne fed me a good lunch at the buffet place in Tallahassee before carrying me here. I'll be going down to supper in a few minutes, if I can muster the gumption."

Hannah rose to leave. "Okay, Ma-Mae. If that's what you want, I'll go on."

"One thing, though. You kids need to get on the stick about my house. I want it sold to a good family, one who'll love it like we did. Hurts my heart thinking of it sitting empty."

Hannah sensed the emotional minefield looming. "You really ready for us to do this?"

Mae surveyed her cozy apartment. "It's mighty hard to live in one room when I've been used to a whole house. I wish I could go home."

"Ma-Mae," Hannah said softly, "it was your decision to move to Rosemont. Aren't you happy here?"

"Happy as can be expected, I suppose." Mae's eyes watered. "I guess I miss the idea of home—the way it used to be." She smiled wistfully. "When it comes right down to it, what I really wish is that I wasn't so darned old."

"Think of dealing with your mama like you were riding a roller coaster," Suzanne said. "One day, all will be fun and games and she'll be like a little kid with an all-day lollipop. The next day, her lip will be hanging half-way down to her navel and she'll be crying and carrying on like no one in the world gives a hoot."

Hannah propped her feet on a hassock and settled in for a long phone counseling session. "The things she says sometimes—I feel like I can't ever do enough."

"You can't. You can't make her young and healthy. You can't bring your father back. And you can't take her days and make them exciting and full."

"When I try to do too much, she crawls all over me. Like today—she couldn't run me out of her room fast enough."

"She's tired of you being up her butt-hole."

Hannah laughed. "You *do* have a way with words."

"So I've been told."

"Okay, my beloved counselor, what am I supposed to do?"

"Leave her alone for a few days," Suzanne said. "I'll get Hal to call and check on her. Helen will be phoning—you can bet money on that. Mae knows where you are if she needs you."

A sharp stab of pain reminded Hannah of her impending dental appointment. "Crap!"

"I don't think it exactly calls for that much emotion, hon. You off your pills?"

Hannah massaged her jaw. "No, my tooth's doing a tango again."

"You need me to ride over to Tallahassee with you tomorrow?"

"Nah. I'll be okay. Just numb afterwards. And believe me, it will be a relief to get this taken care of."

"Hope you took the day off. I'd hate to think of you banging away at your computer with your tooth like it is."

Hannah sighed. "I've been so spacey the past month, I think my boss looks forward to a day without me. I'm amazed I still have a job."

"You don't stop being down on yourself, I'm going to ride over there and slap you silly. Then you'll have more than a toothache!"

Hannah laughed. "I'll be the first woman in history who takes off to one of those women's refuge houses to get away from her sister-in-law."

Chapter Nine

Squinting in spite of dark sunglasses, Hannah negotiated a tangle of traffic with the right side of her face and jaw numb and her pupils fully dilated. Perhaps scheduling a root canal and a yearly eye exam in the same day had not been such a great idea. Her cell phone chimed.

"Mom?"

"Yeth baby?"

Justine hesitated. "You sound funny."

"Jus num-bah." At the next stop light, she dug in the console for a tissue and dabbed a line of saliva from the corner of her mouth.

"Oh, yeah. Right. Grand-Mae just called and wanted you to call her back A-SAP."

"Did she say what she wanted?"

"Nope, just for you to call."

"She sound upset?"

Hannah heard Justine's labored sigh. Though she couldn't see her daughter, she knew Justine was rolling her eyes and standing with her hip jutted out to one side.

"I don't know, Mom."

"I'll call her. You going to be home this evening?"

"Maybe. Maybe not."

Did other parents have as much trouble getting a simple, sensible answer from their teenagers? Hannah clamped her teeth together, then jerked them apart. Stop, you idiot! Do you want to pay for another root canal and crown? "When your father gets home, either you or he needs to call out for supper. Pizza, chicken, I don't much care. I don't feel like cooking."

" 'kay, Mom."

"Where's your brother?"

"On the 'puter playing stupid video games. Where else?"

"I'll be home in about forty-five minutes or so. I'm just now getting onto the Interstate."

"Drive carefully, Mom."

Hannah pressed the Bluetooth earpiece to end the call and returned full attention to the merging traffic. "Must be the spring break thing. She's being awfully accommodating and suck-up sweet." She used the voice command to dial her mother's number.

Mae answered on the second ring. "Lordy! I'm surely glad you called. I plain-out forgot to ask you about the party."

Hannah turned the volume down on the classical piano CD. A semi roared past in the other lane, rocking the SUV with its slipstream. "Party?"

"The St. Patrick's Day party! It's too late now, to get Helen to come over here. I know Hal won't even get home until after six. It's a family thing. They've got the dining hall all gussied up and a band's coming to play Irish jig music."

Hannah released a slow exhalation. If someone from the family didn't show, Mae would be depressed for days, counting herself with the "poor throw'd-aways."

"What time, Ma-Mae?"

"Five thirty."

She glanced at the digital dash clock. Three forty-six. Exactly time to drive home, change clothes, and schlep back out to Rosemont. "Sure. I'll be there."

"Good. Oh, and honey? Wear green so Barney doesn't feel he has to pinch you. He always aims straight for the butt."

"Festive." Hannah glanced around the Rosemont entrance parlor then signed the visitor's register.

Shiny green curled ribbon and four-leaf clover cut-outs glommed to every vertical and horizontal surface, and clumps of emerald and white balloons bobbed in the corners. A massive arrangement of white carnations, ferns and green-tinged flowers stood on one end of the reception desk. In the hallway, two residents shuffled by, pushing tinsel-clover, garland-trimmed walkers.

"Wait till you see the dining room," Beth said.

Catharen O'Kelly, the new social director, swept by, trailing a line of streamers.

Beth smiled. "I'll be surprised if there's any room left for the residents and family members. Catharen has really outdone herself."

"I assume she's Irish?"

Beth nodded. "Very. Wouldn't be a bit surprised if she's wearing green underwear too."

"She seems to be working out well."

"I worried, after April left, that we'd have a heck of a time finding someone good to fill her position. We've really found a gem in Catharen. She loves the residents to death, and they love her."

Mae walked around the corner, clad in shades of green. Even her walking cane bore an emerald ribbon. "Glad you got here. Maxine's saving a couple of seats."

Beth finger-waved. "Y'all have a good time."

"Want us to bring you some supper, Beth?" Mae asked.

"I'll be on down later. Thanks."

Mae turned her attention to her daughter. "You look mighty nice."

"This sweater was all I could find, and I stole it from Justine's closet. It's not that I don't like green, I just don't wear it often." A nerve in Hannah's tongue sparked. Some of the numbness had faded from her lips and lower jaw. At least she could drink and eat something soft without dribbling.

"It's becoming. You should." Mae smoothed the front of her shirt. "Found this shoved in the rear of my closet. Made it years ago. Your mama can sew, you know. Or I used to, before this old 'author-itis' crooked up my fingers. I can barely thread a needle anymore."

Both she and Helen had bounced through childhood wearing Mae's whimsical creations: dresses with rows of smocking and pinafores trimmed with intricate hand-embroidery. Hannah had learned the basics in a home economics class in high school, but who had the time to sew, or to even shop for clothes? If not for Internet stores, she'd be naked.

"They've been cooking up a storm. Irish food. Green cake. Even green beer!" Mae's face glowed with excitement.

"I'm so glad you're feeling better, Ma-Mae."

"My energy isn't back up to par just yet," Mae said as they joined the line leading to the spacious dining hall. "I can't keep up the pace I did before I went to e-Bay. My get-up-and-go has got up and went."

Midway through the Irish-themed party, as the last plates filled with cabbage, corned beef, and beef stew were delivered to the long tables, a four-member Celtic ensemble began to play.

Hannah spotted Barney standing at the end of their table, his eyes trained on Maxine.

"Uh-oh," Mae leaned over and mumbled behind her hand, "trouble's brewing."

Though he could have taken a more direct route to his seated family members, Barney chose the pathway immediately behind his arch nemesis. Flame and pitchforks shot from Maxine's eyes. She slid her chair back to block Barney's passage. Everyone clapped furiously as the band played a fast-paced jig.

Barney stood beside Maxine's human barricade and scowled. "Move it, old woman! Let me by!"

Maxine crossed her arms across her ample chest. The muscles of her jaw pulsed as she clenched her teeth. Barney leaned over and hoisted Maxine, chair and all, a few inches off the carpeted floor, then dropped her with a loud grunt.

The hand-held drum beat a demented pace to accompany the fiddle.

"Oh for heaven's sake, Barney!" Mae called out in a loud voice. "Find another way to go!"

Before the little man could hunker down for another pass at upending Maxine, the social director appeared with an aide. "Come on now, Mr. Thompson. Come with us, please," Catharen coaxed.

Barney shook his head and pointed down to Maxine. "Make her move!"

"Now Mr. Barney. I don't want either of you upset. Your family's wondering where you are." Catharen tugged gently on his arm.

"C'mon Mr. Thompson." The aide towered a good two feet over Barney and outweighed him by at least sixty pounds. "Let's not ruin the party, eh?"

Barney shot one final squinty glare down at Maxine, huffed, and allowed the social director and aide to usher him to the far end of the room.

Maxine hopped her chair back into place and sipped her green beer. The Irish reel came to an end, everyone clapped and cheered, and the servers appeared with rolling carts of green-colored cake with cream cheese icing.

After the party, Hannah and her mother walked down the hall toward room 104.

"I didn't know we'd get drama along with dinner." Hannah chuckled. "He picked her up! Who would've thought he had that kind of strength?"

Mae shook her head. "Those two just beat all."

"Why do they dislike each other so fiercely?"

Mae slowed her pace. "Like I told you before, he's a player. This started before I moved in, but I've heard talk. Seems Barney had intentions, or so he acted, toward Cynthia. She's the one sits opposite of me at the dining table. Good woman. Sweet woman. Barney broke her heart. Maxine's one of Cynthia's best friends from way back, so there you go. More wars have been fought over misunderstood affections than over all the gold in China."

Chapter Ten

Elvina Houston, head of the Chattahoochee little-old-lady hotline and front office manager for the Triple C Day Spa and Salon, glanced up and smiled when Hannah entered. "Morning, Miz Hannah." Elvina grabbed a red felt-tip pen and placed a checkmark on the appointment book. "Right on time."

"I'm not really sure why I'm here. Norm dropped me off."

Elvina stepped from behind the antique mahogany desk and led Hannah to a cushioned high back chair in the lavish parlor. A small fountain trickled water music. "You're here, dear, because your husband and children ordered our Day in Paradise package for your birthday." The old woman moved to a teak side table and picked up a porcelain tea pot. "You take sugar, artificial sweetener, or Tupelo honey?"

"A little honey, please."

"This is chamomile tea. Good for the relaxation process." She handed Hannah the rose-patterned china cup and matching saucer. "I have decaf coffee brewed in the kitchen if you'd prefer." Elvina's black-painted brows lifted.

"This is fine. Don't go to any trouble."

"It's not a bother at all, Hannah. That's what we're here for."

When Elvina moved her head, the pastel silk butterflies clinging to her bun vibrated slightly. Not only had the seventy-plus-year-old assumed the administrative duties of her bosom buddy Piddie Longman, she had morphed into a facsimile of her deceased friend. Elvina's bun could never reach the height of Piddie's beehive-on-steroids, but her swirling gray hair mimicked the artful presentation. Elvina wore an ELF-Wear designer spring dress by Evelyn Fletcher, Piddie's daughter. Samples of Evelyn's signature line hung on long suspended poles behind the front desk.

"How's your mama?" Elvina asked. "Heard she was back at Rosemont."

"Better. It's been slow."

"Takes awhile for us senior citizens to bounce back." Elvina patted Hannah on the shoulder. "I won't run my mouth, much as I'd love to. You're supposed to be relaxing. Sit back and savor your tea and Stephanie will be out to get you in—" she glanced at her diamond watch "—about ten minutes."

Hannah absorbed the serenity of the massage therapy room: pale blue walls and ceiling painted with billowy, white clouds; blue-gray slate tile floor; a thick, tufted wheat-hued rug. Soft light filtered through linen-draped windows.

"This your first massage?" Stephanie glanced up from Hannah's health history form.

"I had one in college from a muscle-bound woman with forearms like a marine sergeant. Felt like I'd been slugged and spit out."

"I'm no brute, so I hope you'll feel more relaxed this time." She motioned to one corner. "You can undress behind the folding screen. Most folks remove everything, but go to your level of comfort. Though I would suggest no bra. Too confining. I'll have you fully draped at all times."

Stephanie moved to the massage table. "Tuck yourself between the sheets, face up. I'll let you get settled and I'll knock before I come back in."

Under the therapist's expert coaxing, Hannah's taut muscles released the collected tension of the past few weeks. By the time Stephanie finished an hour later, Hannah felt like a simmered noodle.

"Take your time getting up," Stephanie said in a soft voice. "A robe and slippers are waiting for you. I'll be back to escort you to the next part."

Hannah had died and gone straight to heaven. Had she fallen asleep and drooled on the rug through the horseshoe-shaped head rest? Probably. She had managed to snore during a root canal. She sat up and gathered her clothing. Wrapped in a terry robe, Hannah shuffled behind Stephanie to the wet treatment room for an hour of exfoliation, then to the hair salon.

Stylist Mandy Andrews patted the cushioned seat of her chair. "Sit yourself down, hon." She flipped a plastic shoulder drape into place and ran her fingers through Hannah's damp hair. "Your ends are a little damaged." Mandy studied her client's reflection in the work station mirror. "What do you think about updating your style?"

"You mean move into this century?" Hannah smiled. "At this point, after a massage and that decadent scrub-down, you could talk me into shaving my head."

Mandy laughed. "I knew there was a good reason why we let Steph get a'hold of you first." She rested her hands lightly on Hannah's shoulders. "I think you'd look smashing in a shorter style. Maybe a little up-flip on the ends, some layers to add a little more bounce."

"You're the boss."

"I love it when someone tells me that."

Melody, the manicure specialist, walked by carrying a basket of nail enamels. "I get you next. And I just received my shipment of spring colors."

"There's more?" Hannah asked.

Mandy snapped her gum. "Oh yeah, hon. You still have a mani-pedi to go, after I glam you up."

Wanda Orenstein Green, the second master stylist, strolled in carrying an enameled tray of sliced carrots and cucumbers, finger sandwiches, and chocolate-dipped strawberries. "How 'bout a little snack?" She held the dish in front of Hannah. "I'll get you a drink. Water, soda, coffee, tea?"

Hannah nibbled on a strawberry. "Water will be fine, thank you. Do y'all treat everyone this way?"

Mandy led her to a shampoo station. "The 'Day in Paradise' is all about total sensory overload." She worked Hannah's wet hair to a soapy froth. "How's Miz Mae?"

"Much improved. Still a bit more tired than usual. I need to get her in to you for a fresh perm. She was fussing yesterday. Since she had her hair cut short, it's easier for her, but she needs some curls."

Mandy clucked. "Your mama's a card. She'll let Adrian at Rosemont do her wash and roll-ups, but swears I'm the only one who can handle the chemicals." The stylist's experienced fingers massaged Hannah's scalp as she talked. "Let Elvina set up an appointment for Miz Mae before you leave."

Later, when Mandy twirled her around to view the new style from all sides, Hannah marveled at the woman reflected in the mirror. The short bouncy cut drew attention to her hazel eyes. "I look so much better!"

"You have excellent bone structure. All you needed was a hairdo to complement your face shape," Mandy said. "And no offense, hon, but it looked like you'd been trimming your bangs with a butcher knife."

Melody stood behind them. "I think you should go all-out and choose a bright color for your polish. If you're going to look years younger, might as well let it extend to your fingers and toes."

An hour later, Norman whistled softly when he spotted Hannah in the Triple C parlor. "If you weren't already my wife, I'd have to court you."

They heard Elvina chuckle in the reception room. "You better watch out for her, Norman Olsen. She's one hot number now!"

Norman offered his arm. "You ready to go home, birthday girl?"

"If I don't leave soon, I might as well move in. This must've cost a bundle."

"Not really," Norman said, "considering how much stress you've been under lately. The kids have a surprise for you at the house."

"What, did they clean their rooms?"

"Won't wedge a word from me. I don't want to spoil it. They've been working all afternoon."

When they walked into the house, the aroma of garlic and oregano greeted her.

"Wait!" Jonas called out. "Don't look yet, Mom."

Norman stepped up behind her and slipped his hands over her eyes. Hannah heard the sound of scurrying and the clink of glassware.

Justine yelled, "Okay, Dad. Lead her in."

Norman steered Hannah into the formal dining room, an area used for holidays and special occasions. When he removed his hands, Hannah beheld a festively decorated table set with tall tapered candles and the fine china.

"Wow. You guys did all this?"

Norman gestured to the kids. "Don't give me any of the credit. I was in charge of the spa appointment."

Justine held the back of one hand to her forehead. "I slaved for, like, hours."

Jonas grinned. "I made the salad and garlic toast."

"Don't *even* think I baked the pie. I got it from the bakery uptown." Justine pointed to the sideboard.

Norman pulled out a chair and helped his wife to be seated.

"I don't know how to act." Hannah unfolded the linen napkin.

"Sit right there and we'll bring on the chow." Jonas dashed to the kitchen, followed closely by his older sister.

That night when Hannah lay in bed beside her husband, she marveled over the entire experience. Her daughter, Princess of Self-Absorption, had cooked a superb lasagna dinner and managed to stay off the phone. Her son's room appeared spotless, without the usual flotsam of soiled clothes and rank shoes. The entire house had been vacuumed and dusted, and no dirty laundry lurked in the garage. When Hannah felt Norman's hand caress the triangle of skin at the small of her back—the signal for lovemaking—she wondered if she had beamed into another woman's life by mistake.

Helen and Hal had called. Her nephews and friends left chirpy Facebook messages. Co-workers signed a card. Suzanne and Becky Weston, an old high-school chum, sang off-key tributes on the cell phone's voicemail.

She hadn't heard one growly peep from Ma-Mae. Hannah felt sad, in spite of her family's lavish attention. Mae had forgotten her baby daughter's birthday.

HELEN'S HOT CORN

1 stick butter or margarine
8 oz. pkg. cream cheese
2, 12 oz. cans shoe peg corn, drained
1, 4 oz. can chopped green chilies
Jalapeno peppers to taste (1 Tbsp. chopped)
Salt and pepper to taste

Preheat oven to 350°

Melt butter or margarine in saucepan over low heat. Add cream cheese and stir until melted. Remove from heat. Combine cheese mixture with remaining ingredients. Bake in a 2 quart casserole dish, uncovered, for 30 to 40 minutes.

Chapter Eleven

Hannah pulled Norman's truck onto the grass in front of the modest frame house on Satsuma Road. Good, she was the first one to arrive. Time to gather her wits before dealing with Helen's inevitable torrent of tears.

She shut off the engine and sat for a moment. Thinking about the previous night, Hannah felt a blush of warmth creep up her midsection—for once, not a hot flash. What the heck had gotten into Norman? Mr. Lights-off, Four-second-foreplay, Under-the-covers Man? They hadn't made love like that since their twenties. Had she raked Norman with her freshly-painted nails? She surveyed her hands; the polish was intact. Hannah made a mental note to check Norman's back for scratches. No need to court infection. Poor man. It had just felt so good, better than sniffing a fresh coffee bag. She still felt all glow-y and sore, in a good way.

Hannah forced her mind from the marital bed and studied her family's old home. In spite of Hal's maintenance, the house and yard had assumed a deserted, hang-dog appearance. Prickly Smilax vines laced the overgrown azaleas. The flower beds sprouted as many dandelions as perennials, and tentative shoots of centipede grass crowded the brick walkway leading to the front steps. The official greeting goose—fondly named Lucy Goosey, a two-foot-tall cement yard ornament—had developed a thick layer of dark green mold. Hannah frowned. The stupid goose had more little hand-sewn outfits than she could count, and had always been decorated with an ensemble reflective of the season. Now it stood neglected and naked, not good for a goose with a taste for fashion.

It all added up to this: if a building could convey emotions, the house looked lonely, abandoned and forlorn. Hannah grabbed a stack of cardboard boxes from the bed of the truck and dug in her purse to locate the key ring.

Inside, the house smelled of accumulated dust, stale air, and the faint aroma of cinnamon and spices. Hannah smiled slightly as she dumped the boxes on the living room floor. When her mother had lived here, the air always carried a blend of bleach, lemon-fresh Pine-Sol, and the homey scent of her latest baked creation. Mae would pitch a fit and fall in it if she knew her house smelled musty.

Hannah walked through the living room and dining room, flinging open windows along the way, until she reached the kitchen. Over the years, more succulent Southern meals had emanated from the cramped space than from most of the cavernous designer kitchens she had seen. Mae bounced from the stove to the work table, to the diminutive cupboard, and to the sink and back like a quicksilver pinball caught between springing flippers, her cotton ruffled apron polka-dotted with cake flour, oil, and traces of whatever sauce she was concocting.

Hannah left the kitchen to visit the three small bedrooms. Hal's was located at the end of a narrow hallway, across from a somewhat larger master bedroom. The middle room had been shared by the two girls until Helen married, allowing Hannah to sprawl luxuriously in her own space. Mae had converted the girls' room into a sewing and art project nook several years after her final fledgling married and moved out.

For years, the house contained only one bathroom. When it became clear that three women sharing vanity time and space was a recipe for misery, Hannah's father had overseen construction of a small add-on restroom immediately off the master bedroom.

Helen routinely took "forty-forevers" in the bathroom. Hannah recalled the times she and Hal spent pleading and banging on the hollow wooden door, doing the I-gotta-go dance. If a drop of hot water remained after one of Helen's marathon showers, it was truly a miracle. Hannah learned early on to douse quickly, turn the water off, lather, then turn the water on for a quick final rinse. Hal had learned to cope with cold water washes.

Hannah and her sister united for one common cause: teaching their brother to lower the toilet seat. Even though his first marriage had failed, it wasn't on account of leaving the lid up for his unsuspecting wife. Helen's stern warning echoed in Hannah's memory: "Rules is rules, bubba-boy. Next time I nearly-'bout fall into this toilet because of you, I'm going to stick your head in it and give you the worst swirly-flush any human being's ever gotten!"

As far as she could recall, the lid stayed down from that point forward. Helen was never one for empty threats.

Hannah put her purse and notepad on the kitchen table before walking out to the screened back porch and down a short flight of steps to her favorite spot under a sprawling ancient magnolia tree. A brilliant scarlet cardinal flitted by and landed on an empty feeder. Mae cherished the birds, from the clamoring blue jays to the diminutive cocoa-brown house sparrows. Hannah located the five-gallon aluminum can where her mother stored the seed and filled all four feeders. Maybe the new owners would continue her mother's careful guardianship. Hannah sank down onto the second-to-last porch step and propped her head in her hands.

The screened door hinges creaked behind her. "Hey! Wondered where you were," Hal called out.

"Come sit." Hannah patted the stair beside her. "Helen here yet?"

Hal grunted as he lowered his lanky frame. "Nope. But she's on the way, just called me on the cell. Michael Jack's with her." Her brother surveyed the backyard. "I need to get over and mow pretty soon. The rain's making the weeds sprout."

"I can meet you one afternoon and help whip the yard into shape, before we list the house."

Hal nodded.

"Didn't this look different when we were kids?" Hannah asked. "I remember it being so . . . huge."

Hal pointed to a cluster of live oaks at the rear of the lot. "I had a tree fort right over there."

"No girls allowed," Hannah said in a snarky sing-song voice.

"God knows I had to have someplace to escape you women!"

Hannah snickered. "I used to sneak out there when you weren't home and sit in it. Just for spite."

"I knew you did."

Hannah punched him playfully in the arm. "Oh yeah? How's that?"

"Girl cooties all over the place. I had a special spray to rid my haven of them."

"What, like bug spray?"

"Lysol, or some other bathroom odor stuff. Whatever I could find. One time I used half a can of Ma-Mae's deodorant."

They shared the silence for a few moments before Hannah spoke. "Must be a boy thing. Josh has a little hidey-hole in his closet."

"I need to build that boy a tree house."

"He'd probably like that. Norman's a good man and a wonderful father, but heaven help us all if he so much as picks up a hammer without someone giving him directions."

Hal's handsome face lit up in a smile. "He can't be all bad. He's put up with you for all these years."

"Everyone has a cross to bear, I suppose." She stood and swatted the dirt from her pants. "We'd better go in and at least do a quick review of Ma-Mae's list. You know we'll have to deal with Helen's hysterics soon."

"Suzanne'll be by later. She had to run her mama over to Tallahassee."

"Anything wrong?"

Hal held the door open for her to pass. "Routine stuff. Ruthie takes a blood-thinner and they check her every so often. Where's Norman?"

Hannah felt the warmth rise. Again. So adolescent, to heat up at the mention of his name. What the heck. If she was lucky, maybe they'd do it again soon. For Christmas. Or Easter.

"He'll be here after lunch. The kids are off with their friends for spring break, so this really does work out to go ahead and do this now."

Hal paused before entering. "It's mighty strange to think of anyone else living in our house."

The sound of sniffling and loud nose-honking alerted Hannah to her sister's distress. She found Helen sitting cross-legged in the living room amidst a stack of plastic storage bins.

"Honey, maybe you should take a break for a while. It's not like we have to do this all in one day."

Helen wiped mascara sludge from beneath her eyes. "I can't help it. It's like she's already gone and we're picking through her belongings."

Hannah knelt. "I know, Sissy. It's hard for Hal and me too. I thought maybe this room and the storage closet would be easier for you than . . . the bedroom."

"I don't think I could take going through her clothes." Helen inhaled and exhaled, obviously willing her emotions to subside. "I was doing pretty well with the list, separating things out like she wants, until I found these." She motioned to three identical gray plastic bins. "The others are full of Christmas decorations and one box is nothing but outfits for Lucy Goosey. Lordy be, that statue surely has a load of clothes! A Santa cape and hat, a spring showers raincoat and tiny umbrella, an orange and yellow polka dot shorts suit and sunglasses. There must be over a dozen."

"I guess after we moved out and most of the grandkids were older, Ma-Mae poured all of her sewing skills into that yard goose. I found a tiny pink tutu and tiara in the sewing room. I'd never seen that outfit before. What's in these other boxes?"

Helen snapped the lid off one container. "Looks like she was busy compiling scrapbooks." She handed a large leather binder to Hannah. The first page, written in Mae's careful block printing, read: "This is your life, Hannah Mathers Olsen." Inside were photographs from black and white baby snapshots, up to grade school, high school, college, and finally, marriage and family.

"Mine and Hal's are basically the same." Helen ran her fingers through the piles of loose pictures. "The rest are various vacation and holiday photos." She dabbed fresh tears. "That's not all. She's also written little notebooks for all the grandkids." She fished in one of the bins. "Here's Michael Jack's."

"Grand-Mae Remembers," Hannah read the title aloud. She flipped through several pages of her mother's script. "This is amazing, Helen. Suppose it was to be for Christmas, or something? Our birthdays?"

"Could be. Maybe it was left here for us to find. You remember how it always delighted Ma-Mae to hide our gifts when we were kids."

Hal and Michael Jack walked into the living room. "I thought we'd run up to Bill's and pick up some lunch. My stomach's beginning to think my throat's been cut," Hal said.

Hannah stood and stretched. "Good idea, bro. I'm going to splurge on one of those wonderful gut-burgers—all the way, with cheese."

"Fries?"

"Might as well. And a large unsweetened tea with a couple of packages of sweetener in the pink pack."

"You're so much like Ma-Mae that way, Hannah," Helen said. "Eat all you want, by golly, but don't dare put real sugar in your tea." She turned to her brother. "I'll take a chef salad with ranch dressing on the side. And *sweet* tea for me."

The four of them sat on the front porch. Grease and catsup dribbled down Hannah's chin. "This is absolutely scrumptious."

"Mr. Bill uses real meat and slaps 'em up by hand," Hal said. "None of that pre-fab hockey-puck crap."

Michael Jack cleared his throat. "Um, I wanted to ask you all something."

"Sure, hon." Helen reached over and pushed a strand of her son's sandy brown hair from his eyes.

"How would y'all feel about me buying this place?"

Mae's three offspring stared at Michael Jack for a moment before his mother answered. "You'd want to live here? In Chattahoochee?"

Michael Jack nodded.

Hannah tilted her head to one side. "It's a bit of a commute to Tallahassee."

"It's only thirty-five minutes by the Interstate to my building. I could find someone to carpool with, like you do. A lot of people from over here work in Tallahassee."

"Wouldn't you much rather buy a little townhouse over there, or maybe a duplex without much yard to keep up?" Helen asked.

Michael Jack swabbed a thick home fry in a puddle of catsup. "I'm kind of tired of living over there. I mean, it was fine when I was twenty-one and hitting the clubs, not that I ever partied that much." He glanced at his mother. "I find myself wishing I could come home to somewhere a bit quieter and simpler."

Hal clamped a hand on his nephew's shoulder. "I can't speak for everyone, but I wouldn't have a problem with you buying the place."

"Ma-Mae will be thrilled," Hannah said. "If we didn't need the money to help pay for Rosemont, she'd probably just sign it over."

Michael Jack waved his hands. "I don't want that. I'll buy it, fair and square. I've got decent credit. I don't owe a dime to anyone, except for six more payments on my truck. I'm pretty sure I can get a mortgage."

"As far as I'm concerned, it's a done deal, baby," Helen said.

Michael Jack's face lit up. "Cool! I'll get busy."

"We'll have to get it appraised, son. Soon as we get things cleaned up a bit, we can move on this as fast as you'd like. It'll save us a tidy sum, not having to list with a realtor."

Suzanne's van pulled into the driveway and she bounded up to join them on the porch. "You save me a little bite?"

Hal passed his wife a white paper bag dappled with absorbed grease. "Got you a BLT and some home fries. They might be a bit cold by now."

Suzanne dug into the bag. "Doesn't matter one hair to me. I've never met a potato I didn't like." She took a bite of her sandwich and shared Hal's tea. "What's up? Y'all are all grinning like goats eating briars."

Chapter Twelve

Hannah glanced at the monthly newsletter for Mae's assisted living facility. The headline and accompanying photograph midway through the first page caught her attention.

"Welcome to Rosemont's Newest Resident, Miss Lucy Goosey Mathers."

In the photo, Lucy Goosey sported a fetching early spring sundress, completed by a silk rose-trimmed straw hat and purse.

"Lord have mercy!" Hannah thumped her coffee mug on the table and reached for the phone. "Hey, favorite sister-in-law," she said when Suzanne answered. "Did I wake you?"

"You kidding? I got up at chicken-thirty to bake brownies for my grandson to take to a little party at school."

"Have you gotten this month's *Rosemont Rap?*"

"I haven't seen it yet. Doesn't mean it's not here. Your brother brings in the mail and piles it on the kitchen counter. I haven't gone through it for a couple of days. Hold on."

Hannah heard the faint rustle of papers.

"Well, look at that! Ain't that Mae's yard goose?"

"One and the same."

Suzanne's bubbly laughter brought a smile to her sister-in-law's morning face. "Guess it's a good thing we gave Lucy to Rosemont. Says here they're planning a welcome party."

"Unreal." Hannah scanned the short article. "Lucy's going to be stationed at the front desk as the official greeter."

"That's rich. Those folks at Rosemont surely take any excuse to throw a party."

"Family and friends are invited. Wanna go?"

"Sure. I bet it'll be a hoot." Suzanne paused. "Why don't you phone up Helen and we'll make it a girl-thing? You know Hal and Norman would rather watch paint fade."

"Good idea. Helen's always accusing me of leaving her out of our social loop. I can't help it she lives an hour away."

"Heavens!" Suzanne said when she stepped into Rosemont's front hall. "Looks like the Easter Bunny stroked out."

Hannah and Helen stood side by side, their gazes roaming the room. Flower and pastel-painted egg garland draped the doorways, paper maché bunnies stood by several chairs, and straw sun bonnets trimmed with greenery and posies rested on most horizontal surfaces. Social director Catharen had hit her stride.

Mae rounded the corner and waved the group toward the hallway. "I waited and waited in my room until I was plumb worn out. When you girls didn't show up, I decided to traipse on down and see if you'd gone on to the party without me."

Helen glanced at her watch. "Ma-Mae, we're fifteen minutes early."

"Miss Esther—she's head of the kitchen staff and my personal favorite— told me she made petit fours shaped like little Easter eggs. We need to get up to the sunroom before they're all snatched up."

Mae walked a few paces ahead, joining a line of resident-powered walkers. "Y'all surely missed the excitement." She glanced back to as-sure they were tuned in. "Beulah Lambert lost her dang mind."

"How's that?" Helen asked.

Mae paused to wait for them to catch up. "She came charging down the hallway a couple of hours ago—up on second—a-carryin' on to beat the band. Half naked!"

Suzanne's lower jaw dropped. "Wha—"

"Screaming 'We're at war! We're at war!' at the top of her lungs. It took all of us aback. We were five minutes into Bingo and none of us had heard anything about a war. I had watched the midday news on WCTV, and I couldn't fathom how it could happen so fast."

Helen looked befuddled. "There is a war, Ma-Mae, in the Middle East. Nothing new."

Mae's voice grew intense. "Here's the thing. When the aide finally grabbed a'holt of Beulah's walker and put a halt to her headlong ram-page, he asked her what the Sam Hill she was talking about." Mae's eyes flashed. "Beulah hollered back at him, 'there's some fellow named Hitler and he's ripping a path through Europe!' "

"Lord help." Suzanne's perfectly-plucked eyebrows stood at attention.

"They had to call the doctor to order a calmative, and there's talk Beulah will be moved to the . . . third floor."

Mae's eyebrows lifted when she said "third floor." To the more mentally sound residents, the top story—a secured special needs unit for the memory-impaired—was the equivalent of an assisted living Alcatraz.

Mae continued, "And they're making sure she doesn't get the History Channel on her cable TV anymore."

Hannah sucked on her lower lip to avoid laughing. In reality, it wasn't funny.

"Poor dear," Helen said.

Suzanne cut her eyes at Hannah and winked.

"I hope my mind outlasts my body," Mae said, shaking her head. "This old age trip ain't for the faint of heart." She pushed her way into the waiting elevator and motioned for them to follow.

Catharen O'Kelly greeted the family at the entrance to the sunroom. The long rectangular hall, used for Bingo and social functions, was decorated in shades of lemon yellow, mint green and bright white. Windows ran the length of three walls with double French doors opening to an inner courtyard. In one corner, a thirty-gallon aquarium teemed with exotic fish. At the far end, an upright piano shared the space with a TV/DVD combination on a rolling cart.

"How'd you organize this so fast?" Helen asked Catharen. "We just brought Lucy by last weekend."

When Catharen smiled, twin dimples formed on her cheeks. "It was the most perfect timing. I wanted to have a spring party, but many of the residents are leaving with family for the holidays. So I tacked this event onto the Singing with Velma spot, already on the calendar." As the social director spoke, her hands carried on their own air dance. "Voilá! A party with live entertainment."

Mae pushed past the group and ambled to the food tables.

Suzanne picked up a small ceramic duckling. "Where'd you find these adorable decorations?"

"I'm a Dollar Store addict," Catharen confessed. "I have to work within a budget. I find some of the cutest things for next to nothing.

Y'all help yourself to the refreshments and sit wherever you please." She turned to greet another group of party attendees.

"Looks like your mama made a bee-line for the cake," Suzanne said.

Hannah spotted Mae at the far end of the sunroom surveying the confections. "Nothing wrong with Ma-Mae's appetite. That's for sure."

They joined the crowd in line for food. Lucy Goosey served as the centerpiece and guest of honor on the main table. A triple-tiered glass platter stood on either side, laden with cookies, brownies, fruit and the coveted Easter-themed petit fours.

Suzanne leaned over toward Hannah and said in a low voice, "Good thing you bleached the mold and bird poop off ole Lucy before you donated her."

Maxine pulled alongside with her walker. "Glad to see all you gals." She grabbed a plate and loaded up with five petit fours, three brownies, and two chocolate chip cookies. "Did Mae tell y'all about our plans for this here goose?"

Suzanne shook her head. "Just what we read in the little paper."

"We're going to donate stuff for her outfits. Doll hats, beads, that sort of thing. Then, Catharen's going to help us make up all sorts of little clothes in the arts and crafts hour each Thursday morning. By the time we're done, Miss Lucy Goosey will be a true fashion princess."

Helen smiled. "That's nice, Maxine. You want to sit with us?"

Maxine balanced her over-filled plate in the basket seat of her deluxe walker. "Thanks, honey. I'm waiting on my granddaughter to get here. If there're a couple of seats by y'all, I'll take them. If not, we can light most anywhere." She rested a fleshy hand on Helen's forearm. "Me and your mama spend lots of time together. This time is for family."

"How are all my grandbabies?" Mae asked when the three women joined her at a table.

Helen's expression grew wistful. "My boys aren't around much, anymore. I get them home for special occasions, but they've got their own lives. I may see more of Michael Jack if he ends up buying the house."

Mae beamed. "It would do my old heart good to know it's still in the family. I know it's no mansion, but your daddy and I managed to raise three children in it."

"My kids are on spring break," Hannah said. "Jonas is at the beach with a group from church, and Justine's at a river house on the Ochlocknee."

"You'd better start reining that gal in some, Hannah," Mae warned. "She's got a wild streak in her. Starting that trip up Fool's Hill, that's for sure!"

"I can handle her, Ma-Mae." Hannah took a sip of the punch and winced. "She's a good kid."

Mae shook a crumb-coated finger in the air. "She might be, but I'd still not give her so much leeway. Lots of meanness to get into, these days." She studied her youngest daughter's pinched expression. "You got the sweet punch by mistake, didn't you? The one made with the pink sweetener is on the opposite table. It's better for you." She took a huge bite of a petit four and licked the butter crème icing from her lips.

Velma Brackenburg settled onto the piano bench. The majority of her ample rear hung from the back of the seat. Her hair, sprayed to stiff curls, shone in a pastel shade of blue, and her fingers displayed so many rings, Hannah wondered how she could pound a single key.

"Good afternoon, everyone." Velma plunked out a few opening trills. "Let's lift up our voices!" As she played, flaps of flesh beneath her upper arms waved in a rhythm all their own.

"That— " Hannah whispered to Helen and Suzanne "—must be the famous yodeling Velma Ma-Mae's talked about."

Velma was blessed with the type of vocal cords that could have called up hogs from a ten-mile radius, or announced supper to the field hands toiling on the back forty acreage without benefit of a megaphone.

The entertainer ripped into a raucous rendition of "Camptown Races" followed by "Way Down Upon the Swanee River," then slowed it down for an impassioned rendition of "Beautiful Dreamer." As her pitch intensified, age-spotted hands around the sunroom reached up to adjust hearing aids.

Periodically Velma twanged a sour note, at times veering off key for a few bars before hemming the melody back into line. By the time she brought it home, the residents and guests appeared slightly dazed, as if they had stepped from a scary theme park ride.

Hannah imagined the scene:

Snaking lines of Rosemont's finest and their loved ones inch between the "you-are-just-minutes-away" signs. Blasts of air-conditioning from overhead keep fainting to a minimum. A cart shaped like a giant grand piano swishes into place and the air brakes hiss.

Hannah and her family settle in, secure the yellow woven seatbelts, and grab a padded lap bar. "Little Brown Jug" plays as they enter the darkness. The last thing Hannah recalls is the sound of yodeling and the squeal of an overworked hearing aid.

"Hannah? Hannah? HANNAH?!" Mae's voice snapped Hannah back to the sunroom. "I thought you gave up that day-dreaming when you were a teenager."

"Sorry." Hannah smiled sheepishly.

"You missed out on Lucy Goosey getting invited to join the Rosemont Charter of the Red Hat Society," Suzanne said.

"I thought a woman had to be over fifty to be a Red-hatter," Helen said.

"I'm sure that doesn't apply here, her not being human and all," Mae said. "We'll have to get her something to wear to the socials."

"Maybe it's like it is with dogs—you know, seven to our one," Suzanne added. "Lucy is fifty, if you count in cement yard goose years."

Hannah closed her eyes and rotated her head side to side. One day, her doctor would think she had the beginning of Parkinson's tremors because she had shaken her head in disbelief so often, it had become an unconscious habit.

Chapter Thirteen

Hannah stepped from the shower and grabbed a towel. After a quick sniff, she dropped it to the floor and snatched a laundered one from the cabinet over the commode. Slug stretched and yawned, then settled onto the toilet seat lid to keep his mistress company.

Nothing in the known world, other than a free week in Tahiti, could equal the feeling of a clean, de-haired body. Hannah's scrubbed skin tingled as she applied a layer of soothing aloe and shea butter lotion.

Being a card-carrying owl, Hannah shunned bright lights in the morning until after the first cup of strong coffee. A single-bulb night-light provided the only bathroom illumination. She reached for the roll-on container next to the sink and slathered its contents under her left armpit. The pungent locker-room scent of menthol reached her nose at about the same instant the burning sensation registered in her sleep-deprived brain.

"Shoot-fire!"

Hannah flipped on the light and squinted at the label. She fumbled for a washcloth. For the next few moments, she soaped and scrubbed vigorously. The white heat continued for a brief period before being replaced by intense cold. The sore muscle reacted exactly as advertised.

Hannah wrapped the damp towel around her body and snorted to the second bathroom. A blast of steamy air hit her in the face when she opened the door. "Was your back hurting again last night?" she called out over the roar of the shower.

"Yeah," Norman said. "Why?"

"You moved the Freeze-Out."

"Uh . . . yes . . . guess I did." He stuck his dripping wet head around one end of the shower curtain. "I got up in the night and put some on. Was that . . . a problem?"

"Not life or death. I mistook it for my roll-on deodorant, is all."

Norman flinched. "Sorry."

"Let me tell you, that stuff doesn't feel real special on raw armpit skin."

"Don't imagine it would."

Norman allowed the shower curtain to fall back into place. Hannah heard his muffled laughter as she shut the bathroom door. She paused a beat before she cracked the door, reached back in, and flushed the toilet, sending a blast of cold water into his hot shower.

The day could only get better. But it didn't. At work, everything she touched turned to a pile of poop, traffic held more than the normal maze of texting, lane-shifting, doddering misfits, and she broke a nail to the quick. By the time she crawled into bed at day's end, Hannah wanted to escape into a good, solid dream, preferably one involving someone bringing her mounds of imported chocolate truffles on a silver tray. A dream with respectful children, a healthy mother, and a husband who always put her first in his every thought and deed.

She'd settle for a few moments of peace and a Hershey's bar on a paper plate.

Hannah dreamed of antebellum mansions and mint juleps. She heard a telephone trill; strange, everything else about this dream predated electrical wiring. The ringing became more insistent, until she realized it emanated from the headset on her bedside table. She wrestled with the sheet, freed one hand, and answered.

Her brother said, "Pookie?"

She flipped on the small bedside lamp. Norman grunted, rolled over, and pulled the sheet over his head.

"Hated to call you up at such an ungodly hour, but you and Norman need to throw on some clothes and come over to the sheriff's office in Quincy."

Her fun-loving prankster brother was known for practical jokes, but this was a toe over the line. "Hal, what the—?"

"Don't panic, Sissy. Justine's okay. She's gotten herself in a little trouble."

Hannah flung off the covers and sat up on the edge of the bed. "Trouble? Trouble? What do you mean trouble? What kind of trouble?"

She could hear the muffled sound of her daughter blubbering and snuffling in the background.

"Justine and some of her friends drank a little hooch and went joy-riding down one of the dirt roads near the river. Their car hit a patch of pine saplings."

"Oh my God!" She turned to Norman and shoved his shoulder. "Wake up! Justine's been in a wreck!"

Hal's voice was gentle and coaxing. "Sissy . . . Sissy?"

"We're on the way, Hal. Is she hurt?"

"A little shook up. And more than a little crocked. They checked her over at the scene. Luckily, the driver wasn't going fast. Only one was taken over to Tallahassee."

Hannah held the headset between her shoulder and cheek and grabbed a pair of jeans and a T-shirt, then rummaged in the dresser for clean underwear. "We'll be there as soon as we can."

"Don't kill yourselves driving over," Hal said. "She's with me. She's safe. You stay that way too, hear?"

When Hannah and Norman entered the officer's break room at the Gadsden County Sheriff's Department, Justine lifted her red-rimmed gaze and blinked to focus. The flourescent lighting cast a faint green tinge on her skin. Her damp blonde hair hung in dirty strings.

"Hi, Mom. Dad." A cloud of putrid air hovered around her like an evil aura.

"You've been throwing up." Hannah hated herself for stating the obnoxiously obvious.

Hal clamped a hand on his niece's shoulder. "All over the passenger side of my county truck."

Hannah took in the sparse room. Empty. Either the others were on their shifts, or Hal had discreetly asked his fellow officers to allow them a little privacy.

"She'll clean it up, Hal. I'll see to it," Hannah said. "Who do we have to see to post bail or whatever?"

"She's not under arrest. Released to parental supervision."

Justine leaned to one side, over-corrected, and almost fell before her father reached out a steadying hand. "For now, let's get you on home, young lady." Norman held Justine by the shoulders and guided her toward the door. "Appreciate you, Hal."

Hannah's lips twisted. "Maybe a night in jail would do her some good."

Hal chuckled and rested his arm across his sister's shoulders. "We don't like to lock someone like Justine—someone with no priors—up with the real hard-core juvenile offenders. We've found it traumatizes them too much and doesn't have the desired results."

"So that's it?" Leftover adrenaline morphed Hannah's initial jolt of fear into parental annoyance.

"Not exactly. She'll have to go in front of the county judge. Then she'll have to undergo substance abuse counseling. After that, dependent on what the counselor advises, she'll either be exonerated, or have to do community service."

"That ought to scare some sense into her. She's always had a thing for authority figures. She has a fit when she sees a police cruiser in the rearview mirror."

Hal's expression darkened. "Be happy you weren't called to the ER. At least she's not hurt, except her pride. From what I've heard, the boy driving got off with a busted leg. If they'd been going a little faster or the trees had been bigger than saplings, we might not be having this discussion."

Hannah took a shaky breath. "Kind of puts it in perspective, huh?"

"Justine's not a bad kid, Sissy. You know that. It's going to be okay."

Hannah sighed so deeply, she feared her skin would cave in. "I know. This too shall pass. But why do all the little life lessons have to crowd in together?"

"Ah-hah! There you are, you little dickens." Mae plucked a blue puzzle piece from the cardboard lid and fit it into the shoreside scene. "That nearly-'bout does it for the sky, honey."

"Happy for you, Ma-Mae. This sand section is a total bi—"

Mae shook her finger. "Watch your language, young lady!"

Hannah huffed and raked one hand through her hair.

"You're a bit peevish this afternoon. Are you plugged up? I get a bit out of sorts when my bowels aren't regular. Do you need one of my little pink pills?"

"No. I'm fine in that department. Thank you."

"Something weighing heavy on your mind, hmm?" Mae's gaze bored into her. Hannah recalled the same piercing expression from her youth. When Ma-Mae looked at her that way, her mother already owned the details and it was up to Hannah to come clean.

"How'd you know?"

The squeals of a winning game show contestant sounded through the walls. Mae's next-door neighbor Nancy: hard of hearing and addicted to television.

"Nothing much gets by your old mama." Mae grinned. "Cynthia Jean's grandson was at that little folderol last Saturday night. Only, he had sense enough to con someone into taking him home before the cops were called. He was drunker than Cootie Brown. Poor boy puked for hours." Mae chuckled and took a sip of iced tea. "Reckon he's grounded for the next year, knowing his parents. His daddy's a deacon at the Baptist church."

Hannah located three puzzle pieces, but none fit snugly into the spot she was trying to fill. She squelched the urge to pound one of them into place.

Mae sucked air though her teeth. "Hate to say 'I told you so' . . . "

"So resist the urge."

Mae separated the tan and brown sections. "Here, baby. It's much easier to find what you're searching for if you get all the similar ones hemmed up in one place."

No matter how old Hannah was, she was forever a child in her mother's eyes. "Thank you, Ma-Mae."

"You want me to talk to my granddaughter?"

"If you want to. Don't know if she'll listen. Or if she does, if it will sink in. Justine's awfully hard-headed."

Mae passed her daughter a piece of the beach section and it fit perfectly. "So are you and you turned out pretty fair." She paused. "Can I tell you something without you getting all sullied up?"

"You're going to anyway." Hannah massaged her temples and wished Mae's TV remote could reach through the walls. *Mute. Mute. Mute!*

"Suppose I am." Mae nodded. "Younguns try their parents to see if they can get away with the devil. It's happened since Adam and Eve ate that apple and left the Garden. You wouldn't want a child who was a doormat. The trick is to keep 'em reined in enough so they don't kill their fool selves, while letting them try their wings."

"Easier said than done, Ma-Mae."

"Sugar plum," Mae said as she fit two more pieces into place. "Only bad things are easy."

Chapter Fourteen

Hannah closed her eyes and imagined a tropical cruise. The ship rocked gently. Overhead the skies were deep blue, marked by a few high clouds scudding on the trade winds. The sun caressed her oiled skin, the tension in her muscles eased, and she drifted into a blissful semi-slumber on a cushioned lounge.

"Baa-savis! Baa-savis!" an accented voice called out. It took a second for Hannah to translate: *Bar service!* She managed to lift one hand and the linen-crisp server appeared by her chair.

"Yes Miss?"

The title amused her. How many years had it been since anyone had referred to her as Miss instead of Mrs. or Ma'am or Madam?

"One of those frozen dessert coffee drinks, please. Don't spare the whipped cream."

"Yes Miss." He bowed and scurried off to the cabana bar.

She wondered what the peasants would be doing at this hour. Frying bacon and flipping eggs? Making the beds? Worrying about kids and an aging mother? Good thing she wasn't one of them.

"Mom," a young male voice called. "Mom? MOM!"

A female voice said, "She's coffee-tripping again."

The vestiges of the tropical fantasy faded and Hannah opened her eyes. She was back amongst reality, a peasant holding a spatula and an opened bag of ground coffee beans.

"Maybe you should see that shrink instead of me." Justine grabbed the spatula from her mother's hand and stirred the browning potatoes.

Jonas rummaged through the refrigerator's condiment section. "Mom, where's my catsup?"

Her son would eat catsup on cereal, if he could get away with it.

"You told me last night you were out, Jonas. I haven't been to the store yet."

He backed out of the refrigerator and shut the door. "This will go on your permanent record, Mom."

"Oh really?"

"Yep, and I'll take it into consideration when I choose a nursing home for you."

Justine stifled a snicker.

Jonas continued, "And I may choose not to feed you your applesauce."

He ducked to avoid the damp dish rag Hannah hurtled in his direction.

"Now you've done it!" Jonas stood with his arms akimbo. "I'll have to put in that call to child services."

When had her sweet son developed such a keen sense of humor?

"Fair enough," Hannah fired back, "but the next time you leave a pile of disgusting moldy wet towels in the bathroom, or I find even one half-eaten sandwich shoved underneath your bed, I'll make sure you attend college at the University of Florida."

His grin faded. Since Jonas and his father were die-hard Florida State fans, the mere mention of the rival school struck deep. Jonas grabbed his chest. "You wouldn't!"

Norman schlepped into the kitchen. "Morning, hon." He delivered a drive-by kiss on the way to the coffee maker. "Boy, did I ever sleep like a ton of bricks last night."

One side of his comb-over stood up, reminding Hannah of a rooster's headdress. She reached up and smoothed it down. "Snored like you were hauling them up a steep hill, too." Hannah turned to the stove and flipped a fried egg. "Gah! I hate it when I break the doggone yolk!"

"I'll eat it, Mom. I hate the runny junk anyways." Jonas loaded a plate with crisp hash browns and held it out for his mother.

"You're a good man, Jonas Olsen." She slapped the over-cooked egg atop his potatoes and added two strips of turkey bacon.

Justine poured a tall glass of orange juice and grabbed a piece of buttered toast.

"You want eggs, Jus?" Hannah asked.

"No time. Got to be over at Brit's."

"Where will you be today?"

Hannah stifled a grin as she witnessed the inner struggle reflected on her daughter's features. Since her brush with the law, Justine's polite party manners, usually reserved for complete strangers or peers, warred with her turbulent teenaged defiance.

"I'll be at Brit's until nine, when her mother will escort us to Governor's mall. We'll shop for a couple of hours or so. Then we'll grab lunch, maybe go to Target or Kohl's. Back at Brit's before six. Her mom has to be somewhere later."

Hannah turned back to the stove and cracked two eggs into the sizzling skillet, a smile curling the corners of her mouth. "A most gracious thank-you for your specific itinerary, Missy-Ma'am."

Justine finished the orange juice in several swigs, ate a couple of bites of toast, and wiped her lips. "See ya!"

Norman settled into a chair at the round oak table and flipped a paper napkin onto his lap. "Restriction surely isn't what it used to be."

Hannah loaded two plates and joined her son and husband. "She's been housebound for a couple of weeks now. She's done all the chores I assigned, plus attending the counseling sessions mandated by the judge. I thought a little reward of shopping, with adult supervision of course, wasn't out of line." She took a bite of hash browns. "Besides, she needs some summer tops, and I don't feel like getting back in the car and driving to Tallahassee. I have to see that section of road every day as it is."

Hannah crumbled turkey bacon and put a few pieces on a napkin on the floor beside her chair. Slug regarded her with his sleepy-eyed gaze of appreciation before hunkering down to eat.

"Brit has bird legs," Jonas said. A dribble of grease glistened at the corner of his mouth.

"She's a bit thin," Hannah said. "That's the way girls your sister's age want to look."

Jonas shrugged and took a swig of milk.

Hannah studied her son. "Since when have you started noticing the females in your world?"

"Oh Maa-umm."

"Good for you to see something besides that computer screen," Norman said.

"I didn't say I liked her. Gross." Jonas pinched his lips together. "She's just way skinny, is all I meant."

~~~

When Hannah turned into the Rosemont parking area, she braked sharply to avoid a cluster of emergency vehicles: two fire trucks, an ambulance and several police cruisers.

"What the—?" She circled in vain before accelerating to a nearby convenience store parking lot. Her hands shook as she jabbed the cell phone's quick-dial number for the front desk. "Beth? This is Hannah Olsen."

"Oh. Hi."

"What's going on? I pulled up and there were all these emergency people!"

"We've had a little fire," Beth said over the din of background noise.

"Wow. Serious?"

"Don't think so. It started in one of the AC units on the third floor. But the smoke came down the elevator shafts to the second floor."

"Where are the residents?"

Beth chuckled. "Most of them are standing here in the reception area. They were outside until the fire chief gave the 'all clear.' Now they're milling around, talking about the adventure."

"You must be having fun right about now."

"Yeah, you could say that," Beth said. "The rest are probably still out in the garden. That's where the second and third floors evacuate."

Hannah heard shuffling and bits of conversation.

"Your mom's down here in her robe. She was napping when the alarm sounded."

Hannah took a deep breath and released the tension in her shoulders. "Will you tell her I'll be by later? I have some papers for her to sign, but I think I'll wait until things calm down there."

"You should've seen us!" Mae swept her hands through the air. "It was like the fire drills in elementary school when we had to line up single file and go to a certain spot outside the building. Course back then, we would've been thrilled if the place burnt to the level ground."

Mae motioned to the white wicker chairs lining Rosemont's front porch. "Let's sit a spell outside. I was cooped up most of the day yesterday, 'cept for the fire alarm."

"They make you go through fire drills here?" Hannah asked.

"You bet. Some kind of safety rule, no doubt. My hall is to head out either the main lobby door or the emergency door at the end of the unit. There's an aide in charge of opening each exit. It's a good thing too, on account of that hall door is metal and heavy as the dickens. Suppose if push came to shove, me and the woman across the hall could manage to bully it open." Mae grinned. "Everyone toddled along like clockwork. The administration folks were real proud. Reckon they'll throw us a party."

"Not like you don't already have one a week."

They sat in silence for a moment before Hannah noticed a few white blooms on one of the trees by the parking lot. "Look, Ma-Mae. The Magnolias are starting to bloom."

"Bet that one at the house is full, too. That tree has to be over sixty years old by now. Surely hope my grandson doesn't get a wild hair to cut it down."

"Don't think he would. Michael Jack's terribly sentimental. He climbed that tree when he was a boy."

Mae clamped her hands together. "When's he moving in?"

"End of the month. The paper work's almost ready for the closing. Michael Jack's excited. He's making plans to refinish the wood floors and build extra shelves in the closets."

Mae rested one hand over her heart. "Does me a world of good, knowing he'll be there to love my house. Me and your daddy spent a lot of good years protected by those walls."

Hannah switched the subject. "You given any thought on where you might want to go on Mother's Day?"

"Doesn't much matter to me, sugar. Anywhere you kids take me is okay. I like to get out every now and then. I miss driving my car. But Lord knows, with my eyes like they are anymore, I surely wouldn't want to risk it."

Maxine pushed through the double doors. "Mind if I join y'all?"

"Got your name on it, right here." Mae patted the tropical-print cushion in the chair beside hers.

Maxine eased down with a grunt. "Whew! Took every bit of my wind to walk out here and sit down. That's pitiful, ain't it?"

"Just be glad you got that wind." Mae smiled.

"Did you hear? Barney's in the hospital," Maxine said.

"Lordy, no! What's up with him? Did you finally push him over the edge?"

Maxine smirked. "Of course not. It had nothing whatsoever to do with me. The old coot slipped and fell."

"Did he break anything?"

"Just bummed him up, from what his son told me."

Mae tsked. "Good thing he didn't go and break a hip. That's the start of the downward spiral on folks his age."

"Ma-Mae, isn't Mr. Barney younger than you?" Hannah asked.

Mae's penciled-in brows knit together. "Possibly. Hard to tell. All old men look alike to me."

Maxine held up one finger. "He's younger than both of us, Mae. His shakes make him look like he's older, is all."

"You are surely the voice of compassion today, Maxine," Mae said. "Since when do you take up for Barney?"

Maxine tilted her chin upward. "Me and Barney have come to an understanding."

"Is that so?"

Hannah allowed her mind to wander. The friendly chatter flowed around her.

"Rosemont's too small for us to continue on the way we were going," Maxine said. "We've declared a truce. Doesn't mean I'm going to sit next to him or idly pass the time of day. But at least we won't be firing up the artillery."

"That's Christian of you two," Mae said. "Don't you think so, Hannah?"

When her daughter failed to answer, Mae poked her in the side. "Wha—?"

"You and them daydreams of yours! One day, you gonna miss out on something worth hearing."

"Sorry." Hannah offered a sheepish smile. "It's such a nice afternoon. Guess I have a case of spring fever."

Maxine clucked. "Ain't a thing wrong with that kind of fever, honey. I've felt a twinge of it myself, lately. It was springtime when I first fell in love."

"Does tend to get the blood rising." Mae nodded.

Maxine turned to Hannah. "Did your Mama tell you about the mother/daughter tea next weekend?"

"Shoot!" Mae slapped her lap. "I'd forget to breathe, if my lungs didn't do it by themselves!"

"What tea?" Hannah asked.

"They're having a special tea in honor of Mother's Day next Saturday," Mae said. "I'd like you to be here, if you can. Ask Helen and Suzanne, and Justine if she'll come."

"We're supposed to dress up and wear hats," Maxine added.

"We used to wear white gloves to tea parties." Mae strummed her fingers over her hands as if she was donning the imagined accessory. "I had the prettiest pair with delicate handmade lace at the cuff and seed pearl buttons."

Hannah said, "The only gloves I own are heavy latex and they're bright blue."

Mae patted her daughter on the arm. "Might leave the gloves off, then."

Chapter Fifteen

The garden dining area at Good Eats was unusually calm. Hannah chose a table next to a bubbling wall fountain and wiped a few crumbs from the glass top. The lunch crowd had dwindled and a less frenzied group took its place: soccer moms, college students, and a scattering of briefcase-toting executives. The afternoon spread out before her. No work, no children, no mother. A few stolen hours to squander in any fashion she pleased.

Becky Weston rushed onto the patio and flung her arms around Hannah's neck, almost knocking her backward into a parlor palm. "Good gracious, woman! It's so good to see you!"

Becky slipped into the chair opposite Hannah, casting her hot pink, fur-trimmed purse to the faux brick floor. "I couldn't believe we were actually going to have lunch together. How long's it been?"

Before Hannah could mentally calculate, Becky answered, "Since before Christmas. I remember because we talked about that disastrous Thanksgiving dinner at my in-laws."

One good thing about her life-long friend: an uncomfortable lull in conversation was never an issue. On the occasions when Becky phoned, Hannah could wash dishes, vacuum, and clean both toilets while her vivacious friend babbled. As long as Hannah contributed an occasional grunt of acknowledgement, Becky could steer the cart all by herself.

Hannah studied her friend's features. The wrinkles around Becky's green eyes had deepened and the worry-crease between her brows seemed more pronounced. Becky's shoulder-length, coarse straight hair, once dark black, had morphed into a mostly gray mix of salt and pepper. She was what Ma-Mae referred to as a handsome woman: not pretty by conventional measure, yet pleasing in appearance.

Hannah ran her fingers through her own short brown hair. How did she look to someone who had not seen her in six months? Had the stress of being pulled in so many directions etched new crags into her once-smooth face?

"You look wonderful!" Becky continued without benefit of a reply. "Why the heck don't you ever age, dadgum you? I swear, if you hadn't been my best friend since grade school, I'd despise you, Hannah Mathers Olsen."

The off-hand compliment brought a slight smile to Hannah's face. "You obviously aren't looking closely then. That's the good thing about failing vision. The lines don't show up too well, unless you're wearing glasses. It's like having a soft-focus filter. But thanks for saying so, all the same."

Becky reached across the table and gave Hannah's hand a quick squeeze. "How's everything? I'm so sorry I haven't been in touch. Kids, job . . . " She flipped a manicured hand in the air. "Life."

Hannah exhaled. "Whatever happened to the times when we were carefree and young? Seems like there was nothing to worry us at all."

"We're the grown-ups now. That's what happened." Becky pursed her lips. "And it seriously sucks."

A pair of twenty-something women walked by, their tanned midriffs exposed. One wore a jeweled navel ring. Becky and Hannah watched them saunter past, then shook their heads.

"Did you order yet? I'm starved. Course, I'm always starved." Becky rummaged in her handbag and withdrew a wallet as pink as the purse.

"I was waiting on you before I ordered."

Becky jumped up. "I'll tell 'em. It's on me today." She threw up a hand before Hannah could protest. "Don't."

"All right. If you insist. Get me a regular-sized Greek salad and a large unsweet tea."

Becky returned shortly with two tall Styrofoam cups of mint-flavored iced tea and a cellophane-wrapped piece of homemade cake. "You should've been the one going to the counter. Hummingbird cake. Couldn't resist it. Love the cream cheese icing. You'll help me eat it so I only feel half as guilty, right?"

Hannah tore a pink packet of artificial sweetener and dumped the contents into her tea. "Of course. Like you had to even ask."

"No sugar in our tea," Becky said as she grabbed a packet of sweetener. "But by golly, we'll suck down a slab of cake the size of Texas."

"Ma-Mae says they cancel each other out." Hannah pointed one finger up. "And my mama's always right. About everything."

Becky stirred her tea with a straw and took a long sip. "How is Miz Mae?"

"Depends on which week you ask. Holding her own. We're in a lull right now. It's up and down."

"It's her age, H. My mom's doing the same thing, and she's a bit younger than yours."

Hannah's stomach started its familiar deep-pit burn. "Her last illness was pretty scary. I really didn't know if she wanted to make it."

"Must be difficult for her. I mean, I have aches and pains at my age. Imagine being in your eighties. I can see why, when you add a sickness into the mix, she might want to throw in the towel." Becky leaned closer. "How about you?"

"I'm as good as Zoloft can make me."

"Who isn't on something, anymore?" Becky's brows flicked up and down. "I take mine right along with my vitamins and hormones. The maintenance is a beach, the older I get."

"It's such a treat to see you in person. Feels like I haven't talked to you in years."

Becky rested her chin on her hands. "I've been thinking of having an affair." Her name sounded on the overhead speaker and Becky jumped up. "I'll go. You sit."

So like Becky to deliver such a dramatic declaration, then torment her by not being available for an immediate explanation.

Becky reappeared and doled out the food, napkins, and plastic utensils like a seasoned waitress. "Oops! Forgot the salt and pepper. Be back."

Hannah dribbled homemade creamy dressing over the best Greek salad in Tallahassee. Crisp Romaine lettuce topped by a mound of dilled potatoes, ripe tomato wedges, strips of sweet Vidalia onion and green pepper, two kinds of olives, feta cheese and anchovies. Hannah's mouth watered in anticipation.

"So," Hannah said around a mouthful when Becky returned, "tell."

Becky's expression: the picture of childlike innocence. "What?"

"An *affair*?"

Becky took a delicate bite of her cashew chicken salad sandwich and dabbed a dribble of mayonnaise from one corner of her mouth.

"Not *having* an affair. Just *considering* having one."

"Jeez, Beck! Who?"

"Haven't picked one out yet. Though, I'm thinking—younger." She nodded. "Definitely younger."

"Are you and Keith having—?"

"Problems?" Becky considered the question. "No, not really."

"Then why?"

Becky picked at a cashew that had fallen from her sandwich. "Maybe this is my midlife crisis."

Hannah noticed two more tanned skin-flashing women take a seat at the next table. Between cell phone calls and texting, the two continued to talk animatedly, their youthful, thin, sun-kissed arms gesturing with exuberance. Hannah forked a chunk of Hummingbird cake thick with icing and popped it into her mouth.

"Do you ever feel like you're invisible?" Becky asked.

"Not sure what you mean."

"*That's* what I mean." Becky pointed to the younger women, to herself and Hannah, then sliced a portion of cake and jammed her fork into it. "Exactly *that*. Like you don't really matter."

One of the canned-tan girls gave Hannah a bored once-over and resumed her animated conversation. Hannah recalled a favorite scene from the movie *Fried Green Tomatoes,* where actor Kathy Bates rammed the VW of a smart-aleck younger woman. *If only…*

Hannah's fork stopped midway between the paper plate and her mouth. "How depressing."

Becky stared at the women for a moment before turning her gaze to her friend. "I've felt it off and on since I turned forty and more often lately. It's like people look right through me." Her smile, wistful. "Remember when we were at FSU? We went out at least four nights a week. Not necessarily to party, just to see and be seen."

Becky picked idly at cake crumbs. "I can't even remember the names of all the boys I dated, much less the ones I slept with."

"That was you, Beck. I was much more reserved."

"The last of the Vestal Virgins. Of course. Pardon me! How could you and I be so close, yet so different?"

"Opposites attract, maybe?" Hannah considered 'fessing up about Marcus Motivano, and that she hadn't been an unsullied bride. No need to shatter Becky's image of her. Norman knew. Besides, times were different and that was all so many years ago.

"Now look at us," Becky said. "Two middle-aged old gals, married to men who fart and channel surf for fun, with kids who'd rather die a thousand deaths than agree with one word that comes from our mouths."

Hannah exhaled with a loud huff. "Wow. Thanks. I feel so much better about my life, now."

Becky leaned back and crossed her arms across her chest. "You're always the bright idea girl. Tell me. What can I do?"

"Take up a hobby?"

"Hobby." Becky's tone fell flat. "If I start to paint or knit or decoupage, I'll feel like I've gotten a new lease on life?"

"That wasn't exactly what I meant."

"I'm listening." Becky cocked her head to one side.

"It's not like all the rest of the married people our age are breeding like rabbits, Beck. Sex isn't exactly the main point in my life, for sure. I hardly have energy left after the kids and Ma-Mae. Norman only gets frisky about once a month, if that." The recent animal-like romp crossed her mind. She decided not to share. "Don't feel like everyone has this exciting sex life."

Becky chewed the end of her drink straw.

"Think about it," Hannah said. "Consider all you stand to lose if you have an affair. It might make you feel great for a while, but you're as steeped in Southern-fried guilt as I am. Pretty soon, you'd be more miserable than when you started."

"Probably." Becky inhaled and released the breath slowly.

Hannah continued, "There are other people in this equation. Keith, the kids. If they ever found out . . ."

"Hell to pay. I've thought about that." Becky worked the drinking straw up and down in the plastic lid. The thrusting movement brought a sting of warmth to Hannah's cheeks.

"When Ma-Mae gets down, she tries to learn something new. Swears by it, or she used to."

"My learning a couple of new sex positions isn't an option, I gather."

"Unless you plan to include your husband, no, I'd say it isn't." Hannah licked the last dollop of icing from her fork. "Can you believe me? I sound like some kind of morality teacher. Hard to believe I was a child of the seventies. Free love and all that."

"That whole thing was a crock. Love is never free."

"How profound."

Becky pushed her half-eaten sandwich aside. "I've got to come up with something new—some amazing activity—to make me feel alive again. Like I'm sexy and desirable. And it can't be illegal or immoral?"

"Pretty much."

Becky pursed her lips. "I may have to get back to you on this one."

Two days later when Hannah answered the phone, Becky's high-pitched voice resonated with excitement. "Belly dancing!"

"I don't follow," Hannah said. "And please don't holler. It hurts my ears."

"The answer to my little dilemma, H! Belly dancing."

"I suppose—"

"I've signed us both up. Beginner's lessons. Tuesday evenings at 7:30, at the Women's Club in Chattahoochee. I don't mind driving over."

"Beck, I—"

"You wanted to help me out? Here's your chance. Besides, it's great exercise. We don't have to buy any special equipment to start, and it's only eight bucks a lesson. If we hate it, we don't go back. There's not any kind of contract or anything. I checked."

A vision of the two of them twirling around in gauzy outfits and veils made Hannah giggle. Heaven help, they didn't have to wear a jewel in their navels.

"Admit it. You're as intrigued as I am. What do you say?"

Hannah considered. "Might be fun."

"Hey, invite Suzanne and maybe your sister. Helen might not want to drive over, but you could ask all the same."

No doubt Suzanne would take the opportunity to buy a new pair of shoes. "What the heck. Sure."

Becky squealed so loudly, Hannah had to hold the phone away from her tortured ear.

Chapter Sixteen

Hannah sat on the porch swing, a steaming cup of black coffee in hand, and searched the trees for the serenading songbird. She spotted it on one of the lower branches of a Japanese elm. To be such a drab gray and white fowl of average size, the mockingbird made up for its lack of flash with an amazing repertoire.

"Sing it, baby," she said aloud.

One mimicked call resembled the high-pitched chirp of the purple martins that often circled above the neighbor's yard. A cardinal's staccato call sounded briefly in the lineup, but the rest were indistinct to her untrained ear. Where had the little bird eavesdropped? How many miles of forests and rivers had it crossed to bring the faraway songs to her backyard?

If a huge celestial hand reached down and plucked her from the planet right at this moment, Hannah would have no reason to complain. She relished the juiciness of life, a rare moment of perfection. The gifts of being able to see the clear blue morning sky; hear the song of her favorite bird; smell the rich aroma of fresh coffee; feel the caress of the late spring breeze tickling the fine hair on her forearms—more than enough.

Belly dancing. I'm going to take up belly dancing. Lord help. Hannah smiled and took an appreciative sip of coffee.

Becky had always been the instigator. The Halloween when they toilet-papered old man Hardigan's yard—the cranky butt-hole. The summer they thumbed a ride to Lake Seminole, five miles out of town, and three miles over the Florida/Georgia line. The time they played Spin the Bottle at one of Becky's preteen birthday parties, and Hannah had ended up kissing Barry What's-his-name right on the lips. The senior prom, when Becky got so aggravated with her touchy-feely escort that she insisted Hannah accompany her home, all the way from the high school gymnasium on spiked heels that had already rubbed blisters the size of dimes on Hannah's feet.

Wasn't that what being a friend was all about, keeping each other's histories? Laughing and crying and growing older while providing an honest mirror? Swiveling one's ample hips to a Middle-Eastern beat?

Hannah's thoughts shifted to her family. Suzanne had devised the "share-the-mother-load" program after Mae had expressed her dismay at feeling like the rope in a tug-of-war contest. All of her children wished to spend time with her on Mother's Day, but the logistics often became so tangled, the joy ebbed from the occasion.

Hal and Suzanne had taken Mae to dinner and a movie the weekend before. Today was Hannah's sponsored trip for lunch, shopping, and pedicures. After Saturday's Mother-Daughter High Tea at Rosemont, Helen would load Mae up in her Lincoln Town Car for an overnighter with her family in Marianna. Helen had big plans to keep their mother for several days, but Hannah knew what would likely happen. Mae would become restless after one night away and insist Helen return her to Rosemont. Hannah wasn't certain whether it was the security of routine, or Mae's fear she might miss juicy tidbits of gossip. Either way, Mae rarely spent more than a day away from the group home.

Mae wore the red and purple outfit usually reserved for the Rosemont Red Hatters' Society. Her crimson straw hat sported an oversized purple bow and a silk rose. Completing the ensemble: matching earrings, a bangle bracelet, and a pin depicting a fat-butted woman in a purple and red dress.

"Do you like my fire-engine red tennis shoes?" Her mother pointed one foot out. "Maxine bought all of her best friends a pair at The Wal-Mart last week. She got the purple socks there too."

"You're festive, Ma-Mae."

"Ain't no reason to be drab just 'cause I'm a little old lady." Mae poked out her bottom lip.

"By all means. You look great in bright colors."

Mae scribbled her name and departure time on the resident sign-out sheet. "We'd best get on with our business if we don't want to miss our foot appointments. Where're you taking me, anyway?"

"I thought we'd ride up to Havana and have lunch. There's this little café that has wonderful food, and today's perfect for their patio."

"Good!" Mae clasped her hands. "I love those old-timey shops. I hope we can eat in time to poke around a little."

Hannah consulted her wristwatch. "Plenty of time. Won't take that long to get there and it only takes twenty minutes to drive to Tallahassee from Havana."

The small town of Havana, Florida, boasted two signal lights on the main thoroughfare. On either side of the street, old brick buildings held an array of antique and specialty shops. Two eateries catered to lunch patrons.

The Azalea Café entrance backed up to the one-way side street parallel to the busy main road. Masonry walls of the neighboring buildings provided a private garden dining area reminiscent of the New Orleans French Quarter. Thick ivy and waxy-leaved flowering jasmine vines covered the red bricks, and the overhanging branches of two Bradford Pear trees cast dappled shade over the cobblestone pavers.

"How's this table?" Hannah asked.

"Suits me fine." Mae lowered herself into a wrought iron chair. "Order for me, honey. You know what I like. Just make sure to get me a big iced tea. It's early enough in the day, it won't keep me up tonight."

"I brought you the pink sweetener you like," Hannah said when she placed two tall glasses, utensils, and napkins on the linen-cloaked table.

"We'll save our calories for dessert." Mae gave a conspiratorial wink.

Hannah nodded. "I ordered a piece of homemade applesauce cake. Figured we could split it. But I can always get two."

Mae patted her stomach. "Lord, no. My pants are getting tight across the waist."

In a few minutes, a young man delivered two plates of dilled chicken salad sandwiches and spring greens with ranch dressing. "Enjoy, ladies."

The gentle breeze rocked the wind chimes in an overhead branch. In the distance, a train whistle blew.

"Listen to that." Mae closed her eyes. "That's one thing I miss about home. I could sit out on my porch of an evening and hear the lonesome cries of the trains coming into River Junction Station."

Mae opened her eyes and looked at her daughter. "It's things like that, that make me homesick."

"I'm sorry, Ma-Mae. I know you must miss the house."

"It's the past I miss, honey." Mae picked up a dill pickle spear and took a bite. "Like this pickle, here. Reminds me of when your daddy took up pickle-making. Those were the best darn pickles. This one comes closer than any I've had in a while. All crispy and full of flavor. Not rubbery like the ones you buy in the store."

"Memories are a good thing."

"And they get more and more precious, the older I get." Mae chuckled. "I can recall things that happened fifty years back, better than I can yesterday."

"That's normal, isn't it?"

"For someone my age, I reckon it is. I don't believe it's the Old-timer's Disease, just yet. I still know my name and all that. One good thing about it: I can't stay angry for very long. I can't remember what I was worked up about!"

Hannah and her mother laughed.

"That can't be a bad thing, Ma-Mae."

"If it's something I want to stay upset about, I have to write it down. That way I can remind myself to get fussed up."

Leave it to her organized mother to make a list of things to stay pissed about.

The waiter delivered a generous piece of cake with two forks. "You ladies let me know if you need anything now."

"You tell the cooks I surely did enjoy my lunch," Mae said. "Don't know when I've had a better pickle, like the ones my dear husband used to make. You tell 'em that, will you? This is my Mother's Day outing, and I'm enjoying it like I was the Queen of Sheba." She motioned across the table. "This here is my baby daughter Hannah, and she's the apple of my eye. She's a mama too, and she gave me two of the most wonderful grandkids a woman could ever ask for. We're from over Chattahoochee way and . . ."

The waiter listened patiently to Mae's life history before politely excusing himself back to work.

"Nice young man. Be sure to tip him big." Mae dug into the cake with zeal, then gestured with her fork. "Take a bite of this, honey. Lord, I reckon I could eat cow crap if they put cream cheese icing on top."

"Me too." Hannah knew this would be a day she'd save in memory, savoring it like the taste of fresh-baked applesauce cake.

"I'm glad we're doing all our walking first before we get our ped-die-cures. I wouldn't want to ruin our happy feet." White flecks of icing dotted Mae's grin.

The waiter reappeared. "Here are a couple of pickles for you to take home." He set a small bag in front of Mae. "Have a great Mother's Day."

Mae's eyes lit up. "I surely will, son. I surely will."

Score one for me, Hannah thought. My mama's happy.

Chapter Seventeen

The muffled blend of voices and her sister-in-law's distinctive laughter sounded through the closed door of Room 104. Hannah rapped the family-code knock—"shave and a haircut, two bits"—five staccato taps and two longer ones.

"I'm coming!" Helen's voice called out, so like Mae's.

Helen tapped the face of her watch after she opened the door. "How is it you're the last to arrive, even though you live the closest?"

"Am I *that* late?" Hannah stepped into her mother's apartment.

"You're just not on *Helen-time*," Mae said. "She likes to get here ahead of when she's due. I was buck-naked when she knocked on my door."

Hannah shot a sly *nah-nah* wink at Helen. "I stopped by the pharmacy for that arthritis joint cream you needed, Ma-Mae. That and every time I started to walk out my door, the phone rang. None of the calls were for me, of course. Justine should have a phone surgically implanted. You'd think, with her cell phone, we wouldn't have half the boys in town calling the land line."

"Probably the ones she doesn't like well enough to give her personal number," Suzanne said. "My boys weren't that bad about sitting on the phone, but the girls used to call them all the time."

"Women didn't call men in my day." Mae harrumphed. "It's those *walking phones* that have ruined young people. Now they can go anywhere with a receiver up to their ear."

Hannah gestured toward a vase of roses, ferns and assorted lilies. "What beautiful flowers!"

"Helen brought those. They liven up the place." Mae rocked back and forth several times before managing to stand. "We best get on down to the dining hall and pick our seats. They won't have us at our regular tables this afternoon."

They joined the train of walker-pushing residents and family members in the hall. By the time the group reached the double doorway, the dining room was half-filled. The usual long rows of tables had been separated into more intimate groups of four to six.

"Get that one right there by the piano," Mae instructed. "It's the closest to the buffet."

White linen table cloths were decorated with porcelain cups and matching saucers filled with blooming annuals. A china tea cup rimmed in gold sat at each place, with purple and yellow pansy-print napkins.

"Isn't this pretty?" Mae clasped her hands together. "It's like we're in England at some fancy-pants high tea with the Queen Mum."

Hannah spotted Maxine at a nearby table and waved. As she glanced around the room, several familiar residents smiled greetings.

"I don't see that little Barney fellow anywhere," Suzanne hesitated, then added, "I suppose the men wouldn't be invited to a mother-daughter tea."

"He's at the V.A. hospital down in Lake City," Mae said.

"I hate to hear that," Hannah said. "Is he very sick?"

"I don't know all the details," Mae answered. "I think they're doing some extra 'thur-a-pee' for his Parkinson's. Maxine would know. Her fingers are smack dab on the pulse of Rosemont. That's a fact."

Servers meandered through the room with silver teapots, dispensing hot water into the china cups. A plate on each table held an assortment of teas, lemon slices, creamer and sweeteners.

Helen dipped an herbal mint tea bag into her cup. "This is such a nice way for us girls to celebrate Mother's Day."

Mae said in a lowered voice, "You won't bee-lieve where the men voted unanimously to go for Father's Day."

The three of them leaned in.

Mae's eyes sparkled. "Catharen's driving them to Hooters for dinner."

The shared mental image of the Rosemont transport van pulling into the Hooters Restaurant parking lot sent the four of them into spasms of laughter.

Mae snapped her napkin flat and smoothed it onto her lap. "I don't think they're going there for the food."

"For heaven's sake, Ma-Mae," Hannah managed between gasps. "What was your first clue?"

Catharen O'Kelly stopped by the table. "You ladies sound like you're having fun. What's got you so tickled?"

Mae's eyebrows flickered up and down. "Nothing special."

The social director flashed a smile before drifting off to visit the adjacent tables. In a few minutes, she motioned for the first groups to line up at the buffet. Assorted scones, cookies, cakes and finger sandwiches accompanied a platter of fresh fruit with honey-yogurt dip.

As her family returned to the table with loaded plates, Hannah spotted Maxine gesturing for her. "Be right back."

"Honey, would you escort me through the line? My daughter couldn't make it today." Maxine used the edge of the table to help her stand.

Hannah held out one arm. "I'd be honored."

"The way they got these tables set up, makes it impossible for me to get my walker through very easily. Appreciate your help."

"I don't mind at all. Besides, I'm much cuter than your walker." Hannah grinned.

"If only I could get you to shut up for a moment's peace." Maxine winked. "I'm just pulling your leg. I love to carry on with you. You're like your mama—full of the devil and not afraid to let him come out every now and again."

"Thanks for the compliment, I think."

They shuffled slowly toward the buffet.

"Ma-Mae told me that Barney's at the V.A. Hospital."

Maxine nodded. "That he is."

"Will he be back?"

"I'm not so sure he will." She grunted. "Good riddance, far as I see it. He's much too fresh with us women. Always saying things not appropriate and making suggestions."

"I kind of liked him."

"You wouldn't after you got pinched, poked and patted a few dozen times."

Maxine grabbed a china plate from a stack and heaped it with cookies, cakes and sandwiches. "It got to be tiresome. I even heard that he was taking Viagra. Don't that just beat all?"

After she helped Maxine to her seat, Hannah returned to the family.

"I cleaned out my closet yesterday," Suzanne said. "I couldn't believe how many pairs of shoes I have."

"I'd guess forty," Mae said.

Hannah slipped into her chair. "Has to be at least eighty or ninety."

Helen sipped her tea, then dabbed her lips demurely. "Oh you're kidding, Hannah. How could one woman have so many?"

Suzanne grinned. "I had one hundred pairs, counting the boots."

"You told me not long ago that it was closer to eighty," Hannah said.

"I was delusional, I reckon." Suzanne threw her head back and laughed. "I got to pitching shoes over my shoulder into the hallway—the ones I didn't wear anymore—and I still had a gobacious amount left. When I turned around, there were over forty pair in the discard pile and I still had plenty in the keeper pile."

Helen asked, "What're you going to do with the rejects? You're not going to throw them out!"

"Oh, no. I'll find something to do with them all."

"What size are they?" Helen's eyes lit up.

"Six and a half."

Helen laced her hands together. "My exact size."

"Stop by the house when you and Mae leave today and I'll let you take them on home to Marianna with you. I got 'em all boxed up in the carport. What you don't want, give to someone who needs them."

Hannah's bottom lip poked out. "Too bad I wear a nine and a half."

Mae patted Hannah's hand. "You can't help God gave you feet the size of water skis, honey-pot. You're taller than your sister. I reckon if you didn't have such big feet to balance out your height, you'd fall on your face. Besides, we love you just the way you are."

Hannah smirked. "I'd surely hate to be perfect."

The din of female voices and laughter—young and old—flowed around the room like background music.

"Why didn't you invite your mama to come along this afternoon?" Mae asked Suzanne.

Suzanne's features darkened slightly. "Mama's not been feeling up to snuff. She gets winded walking across the room. Not only that, she's anxious about being away from the house for more than a half-hour or so."

"Maybe she needs a good cleaning out," Mae said.

Ah, yes. Ma-Mae's answer to everything: proper bowel regularity. The world—heck, the universe—would be a much happier, gentler place if it wasn't so full of crap.

Hannah smiled when they entered the public boat launch area. The Apalachicola River flowed beneath the ruins of the Old Victory Bridge and its modern replacement, widening as it passed Chattahoochee Park. Rows of pick-up trucks hooked to empty trailers lined the cement parking lot, attesting to the number of hopeful anglers already on the water.

Diamonds and gold never really appealed to Hannah in the way they did some women. Other than her wedding ring set with its small chip of a stone, a durable watch, and plain gold earrings, she rarely wore jewelry. All she really desired— when asked for a wish list—was a neat house, a clean car, and a little leisure time.

Norman pulled the boat trailer into position. "All right, son. Let's get her ready to float."

Justine and Hannah transferred a packed cooler and two bulky beach bags to the boat while Norman and Jonas lowered the motor and unhooked the ratchet-ties securing the bow and stern. Jonas held the bow rope and walked alongside as his father backed the trailer into the water. He signaled when the boat floated clear, and Norman drove up the ramp to locate a parking spot.

Hannah's eyes watered slightly as she watched her son guide the boat and tether it to a floating dock. What happened to her little boy and who was this lanky muscled young man who had taken his place?

Many times, she'd heard her mother's lament about time's swift passage. It seemed like yesterday when she, Hal, and Helen had played mud pies and built tree forts in the Mathers backyard. Now, Ma-Mae commented she was surprised to see a wrinkled old woman staring back at her when she looked in a mirror. Hannah understood.

"Yo! Mom! Hop in! Earth to Mom!" Jonas's voice snapped her from her reverie. He extended a hand and steadied her as she boarded, then helped his sister do the same.

Norman loped down the dock, the orange boater's safe box in

hand, and vaulted into the boat. "Wait'll I crank her up, son. She's been sitting awhile. The battery's charged up, but we'd best make sure she's going to run before you shove us off."

The powerful Mercury 160 roared to life in a cloud of exhaust, then Norman throttled it back to an even idle. "Like a charm."

Jonas flipped the tether rope onto the bow, gave the boat a firm shove, then jumped aboard.

"Can't believe this is the first time we've had 'er in the water this year." Norman steered around two bass boats and aimed downstream.

Hannah tied a scarf over her hair. "We've had a pretty cool spring. Now that Ma-Mae's better, we can go more often."

Norman pulled his favorite baseball cap on and secured it to his collar with an elastic clip. No matter how many caps Hannah and the kids gave him, he deferred to the sweat-stained faded yellow *Two Egg, Florida* hat he had picked up several years prior at a convenience store west of town. In the hat, with his nose ghost-white with sun-screen, out-dated over-sized sunglasses, mismatched T-shirt and cut-off shorts, Norman was the poster-boy for Nerds of America. Hannah swallowed hard around the lump of emotion in her throat. Nerd or not, she loved the man.

For the first couple of miles, the river flowed straight and wide. Past the train trestle overpass, it narrowed and began the first of many long, gentle curves.

"Want to drive, son?" Norman asked.

On a land vehicle, Hannah would have instantly grown white-knuckled at the suggestion. But in the Florida Panhandle, knowing how to operate a boat felt as natural as learning to walk and talk. The nautical basic training extended to women too. Both Hannah and Justine knew rudimentary driving and docking skills. In case of an emergency, having more than one available skipper was not only prudent, but necessary.

Norman slowed the motor and the boat wallowed in its own re-bound wake as it idled in neutral. Jonas switched places with his father and rested one hand on the throttle and the other on the wheel.

"Ease it into gear like I showed you last year. That's right. Go ahead and give her a little more."

Jonas followed his father's instructions carefully.

"Okay, you're up on plane, so trim your motor back down a bit. That lowers the bow so it doesn't bounce up and down."

Jonas grinned, his dark hair whipping away from his face.

Hannah recalled the rush of emotions from her youth. Like so many local families, both she and Norman had spent the better part of the seemingly endless summers boating on the Apalachicola.

"You want to see if the big sandbar's taken?" Norman called out over the roar of the outboard motor.

"Okay by me," Hannah called back. "Did we bring the skis?"

"Should be on board where we packed them end of last season," he said.

Since the river provided passage for barges ferrying goods from the Gulf of Mexico upstream to inland ports beyond the Jim Woodruff Dam, the Army Corps of Engineers regularly dredged the channels, creating wide sandbars, a boon for pleasure boaters. Talk abounded about returning the waterway to its natural state, a proposal Hannah found agreeable. It would mean no beaches, but sometimes nature had to win out.

After they passed the third set of granite jetties, the first large sandbar came into view. One boat was pulled to the shore.

"Plenty of room," Norman said. "This all right with you folks?"

Jonas pulled back on the throttle.

"Tilt the motor up a little so the prop will clear the shallows." Norman signaled Jonas. "Perfect. Shift to neutral. Let the momentum take her in. Slow. Slow."

Justine crouched on the bow with the tether rope, then vaulted easily into the shallow water and pulled the boat onto the sand.

"Good, Son. Cut the engine." Norman jumped out and secured the anchor line. "All right, kids!"

Hannah grabbed a beach bag and hopped overboard onto the warm sand. "Let's set up underneath the willows." She pointed to a clump of trees lining the beach.

Jonas stood beside her. "You sit down, Mom. We're supposed to do all this. For Mother's Day."

Hannah crossed her arms over her chest. "I'll pretend y'all are my personal slaves for the day." She unfolded a towel and flopped down. "Okay. I'm ready for you to wait on me hand and foot. Attend to my every want and need."

Justine walked by, carrying the loaded picnic basket. "Don't get carried away, Mom."

"What did you kids pack for lunch?" Norman asked.

"You mean, you didn't have a hand in this?" Hannah asked.

Jonas thought the microwave was God's gift to cooking, while Justine generally tried her level best to avoid the kitchen, zipping through long enough to grab a soft drink or a bag of chips.

"I was in charge of the boat: the equipment, gas and oil. Your son and daughter insisted on providing the picnic."

Hannah imagined the menu: Cheez Whiz and saltine crackers, a half-full bag of corn chips, maybe a few now-cold microwave pizza rolls. Hannah's stomach lurched. The price of motherhood. She could tough it out for one meal. A container of antacids waited in the medicine cabinet at home.

"I know what you're thinking," Justine said. "I can cook if I want to. Remember the lasagna?"

And Donald Trump could possibly darn his own socks. But did he? Hannah suppressed the urge to laugh at her daughter, standing there so puffed up and indignant with her hip cocked to one side and her hands propped on her slender waist.

"That was frozen. All you had to do was shove it in the oven," Jonas mumbled low enough that his sister didn't hear.

"You can do anything you set your mind to, sweetie." Hannah said. Ma-Mae's old adage came in handy.

Justine nodded once and fired orders to her brother. A faded quilt served as an oversized ground cover. Justine removed several plastic snap-lid containers from the cooler, then arranged floral-printed paper plates, napkins, iced-tea-filled cups, and plastic cutlery in the middle of the quilt. The finishing touch, a single rose bud atop a pastel greeting card.

Jonas bowed. "You first, Mom."

Hannah's eyes widened when she beheld the offerings: wrapped sandwiches of pineapple, cucumber, or ham and cheese, dill pickle spears, green and black olives, grapes, Granny Smith apples and a tomato/feta cheese/artichoke pasta salad. In lieu of the usual potato chips, bags of pretzel pieces in cool ranch and honey mustard flavors.

"Wow!" Hannah looked up at her children. "Obviously someone has been busy."

Jonas beamed. "I made the sandwiches."

"And the salad?" Justine pointed to herself. "That would be—me."

"My daughter? The one who can barely boil water without scorching it?"

Justine nodded. "Really, I made it. At Brittany's. It's her mom's recipe. Simple. Just macaroni—cooked first, of course. A can of drained diced tomatoes, some crumbed feta cheese, and chopped-up canned artichoke hearts. Oh, and a little extra-virgin olive oil."

"Somebody pinch me." Hannah glanced at Norman. "You had absolutely no part in this?"

"Other than doling out the cash for the groceries, no."

Jonas handed her a plate. "You going to eat or what?"

Later, Hannah lolled on the quilt, content with a full stomach. Norman pulled one of the kids while the other watched the skier for hand signals. Jonas fell five times before successfully balancing on the slalom. His sister, a natural water skier since her preteens, effortlessly negotiated the river.

The sun popped from behind the high puffy clouds, sending penetrating warmth through her skin. Here on the old river's banks Hannah felt a connection with its ancient native inhabitants. Along the water's edge, small pottery shards could still be found partially buried in the sand, a testament to man's impermanence and the unrelenting passage of time.

Hannah closed her eyes and drifted. The hum of passing boat motors and muffled laughter from her husband and children accompanied the breeze whispering through the river willows. Nostalgia washed over her in a velvet ripple.

Her father's boat, *The Three Amigos*—after Helen, Hal, and Hannah—had been a twenty-two foot cabin cruiser built by her father and longtime friends Sam Blount and Dan Davis. On weekends not spent fishing or skiing, the Mathers family joined members of a loose-knit boating club, the Chattahoochee River Rats, for overnight sandbar campouts.

Peace and stillness were what she remembered most. Far removed from electric lighting, televisions, and automotive traffic, the only sounds came from nature: the serenade of peeper frogs, crickets, and bullfrogs, the occasional grunt of a bull gator, and the gentle lap of water on the anchored boats.

Mornings brought boiled coffee, fried eggs, and country bacon cooked over a charcoal fire pit. For the duration, the men took charge of food preparation duties. The women visited, played with the children, and enjoyed the welcomed role reversal.

Unlike her father's lumbering cabin cruiser, the Olsen family's craft was a swift combination ski/pleasure boat with a glossy finish that glittered garnet and gold in the sunlight. The outboard motor sported a dinner-plate-sized Seminole head sticker, demonstrating the family's allegiance: the Florida State Seminoles.

When Norman's mother Grace had passed away, she had endowed her estate to her two sons with one stipulation: they should use the monies from the sale of the house and land to buy something each had always wanted. Norman's brother Nathan used his for a down payment on a small cottage on the Wakulla River south of Tallahassee. Norman shopped for the boat of his dreams.

Since the craft had been compliments of his deceased father's careful financial planning and his mother's last wishes, Norman named the boat the *Savin' Grace*. At first, he toyed with the title *Amazing Grace*, but decided against it. Every now and then, Norman skipped church and slipped off to fish, and he worried the church-hymn name might demonstrate a conflict of interest.

From the first crisp mornings of spring until the frosts of fall, the *Savin' Grace* rarely sat idle. Every Saturday, other than an occasional sacrifice for a round of golf, Norman woke early, often abducting his son for a day of fresh water fishing.

As the fading sun cast long shadows across the sandbar, the family reluctantly loaded the boat for the trip home. When they passed the final jetty, Norman cut the engine back to a slower pace. "Since we're not in a huge hurry to get back, let's 'Cadillac along' for a while, shall we?"

Norman's expression brought to mind a long, pink boat of a car, its purpose to see and be seen rather than move at any great speed. Justine dozed on the bow, her tanned lithe body stretched across a line of cushions. Other than the times she had skied, Justine had seemed a bit preoccupied. Hannah fell into her habit of worrying, then forced herself to resume peaceful, happy thoughts. Teenagers wore angst like designer fashions, especially the female of the species.

Jonas took the opportunity to cast a trolling line behind the boat. Any fish would be released, as Norman had designated the day off-limits for scaling and cleaning bream, bass or river catfish. At the helm, her husband wore an expression of complete contentment. In his world of male responsibilities, the river was the one place he held a modicum of control. He didn't have to voice this; Hannah knew it intuitively.

Hannah closed her eyes and inhaled the aroma of the Apalachicola: a blend of rich earth, vegetation, and the fleeting scent of fresh water fish lurking in the shady water beneath overhanging tree branches. Her family had given her the perfect gift for Mother's Day: peace wrapped in love.

God help, it might last a few days.

JUSTINE'S PASTA SALAD

1, 13.5 oz. box of pasta (shells, rotini or elbows)
1, 15 oz. can of diced, stewed tomatoes, drained
1/2 cup crumbled feta cheese
1 can artichoke hearts in water, drained and cut into small bites
3 Tbsp extra virgin olive oil
Salt and pepper to taste
Dash of garlic powder

Cook and drain pasta according to package directions. Place in a large bowl. Add drained diced stewed tomatoes, crumbled feta cheese, diced artichoke hearts, and the olive oil. Toss to mix. Add salt and pepper, and a dash of garlic powder, to taste.

May be served warm or cold. For variation, toss in a cup of cooked, cubed chicken breast.

Chapter Eighteen

"Still can't believe you talked me into this," Hannah said in a low voice.

Around them, women of all shapes, sizes and ages stretched in preparation for the belly dancing class. A few wore brilliantly-colored hip scarves festooned with reflective bangles.

Becky leaned over and attempted to touch her toes. "Man, am I ever out of shape." She grabbed Hannah's shoulder and gave it a playful shake. "C'mon H, this will be a blast. Good exercise, learn something new, challenge your body and mind. Ching, ching!" She touched her middle fingers to her thumbs, clanging imaginary finger cymbals. "Besides, you're helping me stave off my midlife crisis, remember?"

"I'm honored to serve so noble a purpose in your life, Beck."

Suzanne bustled into the Women's Club ballroom and flung her hot pink purse to the floor in one corner. "Hope I didn't miss anything. I was tied up with that brother of yours."

"What's he done now?" Hannah asked.

"He's making redneck wind chimes."

Becky lifted one eyebrow. "What?"

Suzanne stretched before answering. "Something he saw at the Madhatter's Festival down by the river a couple of years back. He's making a bunch to sell."

"My brother, into arts and crafts?" *Speaking of a midlife crisis . . .*

"Not much art to it," Suzanne said. "Flattened beer cans strung on fishing line, hanging from a piece of scrap wood, with metal washers between to make 'em clang in the wind. They raise holy Hades in a stiff breeze."

Hannah shook her head. "For Pete's sake."

"We don't even drink beer. That's the sad part. Now, I'll drink the heck out of the Sangria I make, but I've never been much of a beer fan. Bloats me." Suzanne slipped her pink flower-festooned slides off and threw them to her growing pile. "Hal buys the cheapest brand and pours the booze down the drain."

Becky asked, "How, exactly, did his newfound passion make you run late?"

"Hal lined up a bunch of cans and I drove across them with the van. He's tried it several ways, and the tires do the best job. When you smash them with a hammer, the label crumbles and flakes off." Suzanne flashed a smile. "All that back and forth gets downright time consuming."

"No wonder people from up North think we're interbred cretins," Hannah said.

"You best learn to get past it, Sister-in-law. Hal's making you an extra big set for Christmas."

"Oh good," Hannah said. "I'll finally be able to compete with Mrs. Keats's yard two doors down."

Becky tapped her chin with one finger. "Don't know about that, H. Last time I was in Chattahoochee, I noticed she had added a manatee and two leaping dolphins to her front flower bed."

"Obviously you haven't seen the five-foot chainsaw grizzly bear under the oak tree in her side yard," Hannah said.

Suzanne laughed. "I've always thought half of the nuts in Chattahoochee weren't locked up."

"Easy, Sis," Hannah chided. "Need I remind you that you married one of us and that he is, even as we speak, turning trash into treasure?"

"Never said I didn't *like* colorful folks," Suzanne said.

A raven-haired woman shimmied by wearing a purple spangled hip scarf.

"Eww!" Suzanne's eyes sparkled like a kid's at an ice cream truck. "I want one of those things with the jangles across the behind." She glanced down at her bare feet. "And I'll have to buy me a pair of those little ballet slippers."

Hannah patted her sister-in-law on the shoulder. "Heaven forbid, you without the proper foot wear."

The instructor clapped her hands. "Let's spread out a bit. Give yourselves at least an arm's width in all directions." Deep dimples flanked her wide smile. "For those of you who don't know me, I'm Amy Vanguard. Teacher for Middle Eastern dance."

"Suppose that's the politically correct way to say belly dancing?" Suzanne whispered.

"Now," the instructor motioned toward her left, "I see a few of my more advanced ladies. I want y'all to cluster over on this side." Her gaze roamed the room and rested on the three of them. "Ah, my newbies. Y'all move on up here so I can keep an eye on your form."

Becky leaned close to Hannah. "There goes being a good back-row Baptist."

They shuffled to spots directly in front of the teacher. For the next few minutes, Amy led a series of stretches, then reviewed proper posture. "Get in the habit of tucking your pelvis forward a bit. Prevents lower back strain. Don't slump! Shoulders back!"

Hannah felt as if she had landed in belly dancing boot camp, except the highly-polished wood floors of the Women's Club hall didn't resemble a military facility.

Amy demonstrated a few basic arm, hip, shoulder, and hand movements.

"I feel sexier already." Becky grinned and swiveled.

Hannah focused on raising and dropping her right hip while holding her arms at shoulder height. "Maybe you can go home and demonstrate for your husband."

Becky cut her eyes at Hannah. "As long as there's not a ball game on. When it's game time, I could strut by wearing a loincloth, sporting a bone through my nose and he wouldn't pay any mind, except to tell me to quit blocking the dadgum TV."

Amy shimmied and talked at the same time. "I see some really good hip movement out there!" The next series involved stepping from side to side to the count of eight, then four, then two, all while rotating the shoulders front to back.

"I get my feet going okay," Suzanne said. "Then my shoulders don't move right."

"Don't think about what you're doing," Amy suggested. "Just move to the beat."

After a few intermittent stretches, Amy dug around in a small silk pouch and removed two small metal discs. "These are zills."

"Seals?" Suzanne asked.

"Zills. Z-I-L-L-S. Like dills, only with a Z." The teacher slipped the attached elastic bands around the third finger and thumb on each hand, then clanged a rhythm to match the music. The ladies in the advanced section scuttled to their duffel bags and returned, zill-clad and ready for action. Amy rotated to a spot in front of them and demonstrated the complex set of short and long beats.

"I really want some of those," Suzanne said.

"Looks deceptively easy, doesn't it?" Amy talked effortlessly while her fingers carried on in their own nervous fashion.

Hannah felt the stir of something primordial: the urge to fling back her head and let out one of those trilling vocalizations she had heard from the women in movies set in the Middle East. If she could add intense sunlight and waves of undulating heat, there was no telling how wild and demented she might become. Would Norman wear sheik's robes, if she asked him nicely? The notion caused her to laugh out loud.

"Having fun?" Amy said, fingers flying and everything from the waist down moving.

Hannah nodded. "I may not be able to get out of bed by morning, but who cares?"

"Okay! Time to work with the veils." Amy dropped the zills back in their silk pouch, then passed out several long, filmy lengths of fabric to the students who hadn't brought their own. "Let's form a large circle."

Amy demonstrated the proper way to hold the material between the second and middle fingers. When she cued the music, the students walked briskly in a circle. The gauzy veils rippled in multicolored wakes behind them.

"Here's a little move I like to call the washing machine." Amy twirled her veil around in front of her, then back, in one fluid motion. After several spastic attempts, the newbies managed a reasonable imitation. "Next week, we'll incorporate the veil into our routine."

"That ought to really trip me up," Hannah said. "I can barely chew gum and walk at the same time."

An hour and a half later, after numerous twitches and swivels, the three newbie dancers walked out to the dimly lit parking lot. Other than a distant dog barking and the muffled sound of canned television laughter from a nearby house, the street had settled into the solitude Hannah enjoyed. Forget big city life.

"I'm taking a handful of Advil before I hit the bed," Becky said. "I can already tell my hips are going to be sore tomorrow."

"I'm slathering mine with Bengay when I get home," Hannah added.

"I hear y'all. I'm whipped," Suzanne said. "And I still have to stop by the store on the way home." She turned to leave.

"Why don't you go tomorrow, Sis?" Hannah called. "What do you need that's so important?"

Suzanne stopped and spun around. "Ice cream and Preparation H."

Becky bent double with laughter.

"What a combination." Hannah shook her head.

Suzanne propped her hands on her hips. "I'm craving ice cream, and my butt is hurting. Okay?"

Becky gasped for air. "Are we three pathetic old broads, or what?"

Hannah agreed. "You ought to see me getting ready for bed. I have a nose strip on to keep me from snoring and a mouth guard so I don't grind my teeth. Good thing I'm married to Norman. He doesn't seem to mind. Otherwise, I would be lucky to have sex again in this lifetime."

Becky rested one finger on her chin. "That's an idea, H. If I swipe a thick slash of black eyeliner under my eyes and put on a pair of shoulder pads—along with the outfit you described— I'll bet it would make Keith hot! I'd look like a linebacker. He loves anything to do with football."

Chapter Nineteen

When Hannah entered the kitchen, she noticed her daughter wiping away a tear. Since the drinking incident, their relationship had shifted slightly in a positive direction. How long the open communication lines would last was anyone's guess. At least for the moment, Hannah felt comfortable inquiring into her teenage daughter's affairs.

She poured a cup of steaming coffee and joined Justine at the kitchen table. "You okay?"

Justine tucked a strand of blonde hair behind one ear and sniffed. "I guess."

"Anything you want to talk about?"

Justine's petite shoulders rose and fell. The trick was to draw her daughter into sharing intimate feelings without triggering the protective shields.

"Everything seems to be going better for you." Hannah tried for a casual tone. "Since the meeting with the judge, I mean. I'm proud of the way you've handled yourself, Jus. It's a sign of maturity when you take responsibility for your actions."

Justine sipped from a glass of Diet Coke. "I suppose."

"Is it . . . boy troubles?"

"As if." Justine slumped back in the chair. "The guys in this town aren't worth wasting tears over, Mom. I can't wait until I leave for college!"

Hannah chuckled. "I remember feeling much the same way. Then, lo and behold, I married your hometown-boy father and moved back."

"Like, I see that happening to me. Really."

"If it's not recent legal issues or men, what has you so upset that you're crying so early in the day? Only if you want to share . . . "

Justine's blue eyes glistened. "It's Grand-Mae."

"She said something to upset you?"

"Sorta."

Hannah rested one hand on her daughter's shoulder. "You have to remember, honey. Your grandmother is from another generation. Her way of thinking may seem old-fashioned, but she means well."

"It's not that."

Hannah willed herself to wait patiently without prodding.

"I went by to see her on the way home from class yesterday."

"That's wonderful, Jus. It means a great deal to her when you kids visit."

"We were having a pretty good time for a while. She had this puzzle of the beach and I was helping her. She didn't want me to do the sky, so I did the sides all around."

Hannah smiled and nodded.

"She started talking about dying." Justine's eyes brimmed. "All this stuff about the funeral and preacher. Even how she wants socks on her feet and no shoes. It was so creepy, and weird."

Hannah rose to refresh her coffee while she gathered her thoughts. When she returned to the table, she took a moment before she spoke. "I can't tell you how many times she's told me the same things. She wants the green nightgown and matching robe. It's kind of an aqua color and is hanging in the back of her closet. She wants the First Baptist preacher to perform the service. She doesn't want to be carted to the church, then out to the cemetery, just straight to the grave. The casket will be open during the viewing and visitation, then closed for the funeral. She'd like a few flowers, but wants money donations for the Baptist Children's Society, too. Her wedding ring and her gold cross necklace for jewelry. Her little white Bible with the gold lettering in her hands. Oh, and a clean embroidered hankie, though I can't imagine why."

Justine turned to face her mother. "Yeah. All of that."

"It's her way of trying to prepare us," Hannah said. "Suzanne says her mother does the same thing."

"I don't like it!"

"Neither do I, Jus. But it obviously serves some deeper purpose for your grandmother."

Justine wiped her nose with her sleeve.

Hannah started to scold her, hand her a tissue, then thought better of it. "I've learned to listen when she talks about death. I think it makes it easier for her, and maybe takes away some of her fear. Besides if she tells me exactly what she wants, I won't have to wonder when the time comes. And it will come."

"I don't wanna think about that."

Slug wove between their feet, begging for something, anything. Hannah shook a couple of kitty nibbles from the treat jar and made him "sit pretty" before she yielded the chicken liver nugget to his paws.

"No one does. Death is as much a part of life as birth. And unless we die before your grandmother, we'll have to experience her leaving."

Justine smiled weakly. "I wish we could all live forever."

"Know what your grandmother tells me when I say that?"

"What?" Justine sniffled.

"It would get mighty doggone crowded down here."

Mae and Hannah sat on Rosemont's long shaded front porch where residents, family members and friends talked and laughed, soothed by the gentle evening breeze.

Mae removed a pearl and diamond ring. "Try this on."

Hannah slipped the ring onto her finger.

"You must be my exact size," her mother said. "Fits you like a glove."

"I discovered that when the jeweler measured you for the family birthstone band we gave you for Christmas. Remember?"

"I reckon." She motioned to Hannah's hand. "You can give it back now."

What was this all about? She waited for Mae to reveal her thoughts.

"I want you to have this pearl ring, baby. Helen can have my little diamond earrings your daddy gave me for our fiftieth anniversary." She waved her hand through the air. "Helen wears so many rings already; I can't imagine she could find a finger to fit one on. I don't know how she can stand to wear all those. It would drive me crazy."

Sweet Jesus wept. Can I really stand to have this discussion again? Hannah's spirits sank.

Her mother's blue eyes studied the distant line of trees surrounding the far end of the parking lot. "I'm still using them right now. Didn't say you girls could have them right away."

Adele, a resident in her sixties, pushed through the double entrance doors, followed by her son and daughter-in-law. The stroke that had confined her to a wheelchair had also destroyed her hearing. Mae was one of the residents Adele counted as a friend. Many afternoons, when Hannah stopped by, she found the two immersed in their improvised form of conversation. Mae scribbled on a notepad and Adele replied in a loud voice, almost a shout.

"Hello, Mae!" Adele called out. "Aren't we so lucky? We have such good families who love us!" Her smile, wide and genuine.

Mae nodded and said slowly, "Yes, we do."

"I love your mother," Adele directed to Hannah. "She has a heart the size of a volcano."

Adele pointed to a group of vacant chairs and her son and his wife settled in.

"She can't hear, but she can read lips a little," Mae explained to Hannah. "She's one of the sweetest folks I know."

"She obviously thinks a lot of you."

"Most won't take the time and effort to talk to her." Mae shook her head. "She's a very intelligent woman. Had that stroke, now she needs help to get by. We talk about all sorts of things. I enjoy her. I really do."

Hannah studied her mother's profile. "Ma-Mae, are you feeling okay?"

"I'm a little tired."

"You seem to be talking a lot, here lately, about funerals and last wishes." She poked her mother gently on the arm. "You planning on leaving me soon?"

"No. Not necessarily."

"Something's bothering you."

Her mother took a deep breath. Today, the dark circles beneath Mae's eyes seemed more pronounced. "A woman died in her sleep last night. They found her when she didn't show up for breakfast."

"Oh."

Mae turned to face her. "Some days, I feel like this place is one big holding pen. A train station on the last leg of the journey. But you never know when your ticket will be collected."

"Oh, Ma-Mae." Hannah searched for soothing words. Sadly, her mother's interpretation held more than a hint of truth.

"I'm on borrowed time. Bible says we're due three score and ten years. That's seventy, and I've seen that age come and go."

Blue jays fussed in a crape myrtle next to the porch. Such pretty birds. Such big mouths.

"Sometimes, Ma-Mae, after watching your struggles, I'm tempted to take out a contract on myself, let some thug clip me, when I reach about eighty."

Without hesitation, her mother answered, "You might check with some of your friends, honey. Maybe y'all can get a group rate."

Hannah and her mother giggled. One trait she had inherited from her mother, before old age and ill health turned Mae periodically sour: the inability to stay serious for too long.

Adele's son John listened to their conversation. He leaned over and said, "Not that I'm trying to butt in, Miz Mae, but—we just got in from a memorial service for a friend down in south Florida. I graduated with her. She died last week—forty-seven years old. None of us have any time guaranteed, and death is not only for you seniors."

His wife Bethany jotted down the ongoing conversation for her mother-in-law.

Adele's eyes watered. "I don't understand that. Why would God take someone so young? Why not me?"

The elderly gentleman to their right spoke up. "He knows what He's doing."

John glanced from his mother to the group. "That's what they tell us. Not that I'm being morbid, but it was a serious lesson about not taking my time for granted."

Mae shook her finger. "That's why I eat all the chocolate I can get my hands on."

Chapter Twenty

"Did you get your invitation?" Helen's voice jiggled with excitement.

Hannah took a quick sip of coffee and pushed the porch swing into a gentle sway. "Mail hasn't run yet today, Helen. What invitation?"

"To the social event of the season!"

"Which is—?"

Her sister paused a beat. "Michael Jack's Memorial Day shindig."

"Really?"

"Yep. He's inviting the whole family." Her sister hesitated. "He's probably going to hand-deliver yours."

"Is it a cookout? Do we bring food?"

Helen mumbled something. "Says right here to bring a covered dish. The main course and drinks are provided."

"I'll make that mandarin salad, unless you want to."

"Go ahead. I'll come up with something. Maybe one of Ma-Mae's recipes. She'll like that." Helen paused. "Have you talked to her lately?"

"Only every day, Sissy."

"She seemed kind of depressed last time I saw her."

"Mother's Day? She was so happy about traveling over to your house, I can't imagine."

"She was—though she didn't stay but the one night." Helen blew out a breath. "She didn't seem real . . . connected. I don't know how to explain it. Kind of detached."

"She goes through these spells, Helen."

"Maybe this party will lift her spirits. We get to see what Michael Jack's done with the home place. He's been working like a dog."

Walking onto the front porch of the family home on Satsuma Road, Hannah had the surreal sensation of stepping into a dream: one where she had been many times, yet never. The wooden front porch shone with a fresh coat of dark green paint to match the window shutters. White metal pedestal planters supported lush Boston ferns, and pots of flowering annuals in sherbet shades hung along the eaves. Two cushioned pine rocking chairs stood on one end; a porch swing occupied the other. The refinished front door held a bronze kick plate and matching hardware, with a wreath of red, white, and blue carnations.

"Looks like your nephew's been busy." Norman pushed the brass bell.

Clad in a flag-themed Polo shirt and white cargo shorts, Michael Jack held the door open for his casserole-bearing relatives. "Come on in! Y'all are the first to arrive."

"I beat my sister?" Hannah held one hand to her heart. "I'm going to have the big one."

"Mom's on her way," Michael Jack said. "And in a full blown snit. Tommy and his family can't come, and she just found out that Jimmy and a couple of his kids have bad head colds. She's not pleased that she and Dad are the only representatives of my immediate family."

"I'm sorry they can't make it." Hannah kissed her nephew on the cheek. "I haven't seen those boys in years, it seems. I know Ma-Mae'll be disappointed."

Michael Jack swatted the air. "Their loss. Are my two cousins coming? And where is Grand-Mae? Not sick, I hope."

"Justine's driving them all over," Norman answered. "Heaven forbid she pass up an opportunity to get behind the wheel."

"I recall those days." Michael Jack led them into the dining room where a long decorated table waited. "Now I'd just as soon pay someone to drive me around."

"Call Justine." Hannah sat the chilled bowl of mandarin salad down. "She'll be glad to help out."

Norman slid a casserole dish onto a trivet. "When she starts paying for her own gas and insurance, the blush will fade from the rose, I'm sure."

Hannah made an effort not to downright gape at the changes in her childhood home. The original hardwood floors glistened. The walls were painted a soothing shade of creamy mocha. When she stepped into the small kitchen, Hannah noted white and black tile checkerboard flooring instead of stained linoleum, and cabinets painted white with new silver hardware. The toaster and canister set, bright red. Very retro.

"I'll replace the countertops as soon as I gather more resources,"

Michael Jack said. "Can I get y'all a drink? I have tea, coffee, bottled water and soda."

Hannah nodded. "Tea for me. Norman likes his Diet Coke."

A petite young Asian woman slipped through the door leading from the hall. Michael Jack held out a hand and drew her affectionately to his side. "Aunt Hannah, Uncle Norman, I'd like you to meet my fiancée, Mili Wah."

Hannah ventured a quick glance at her husband. Helen was going to poop a brick. Her confirmed bachelor son had chosen a bride of foreign descent. Though Helen swore on her sense of fairness and lack of bigotry, she often fell short when it came to her immediate family.

"Pleased," Norman said. "Um, what was your name again?"

Mili smiled shyly. *Me and Lee.* Mili." To Hannah's surprise, the young woman's voice held no hint of foreign dialect.

Hannah grasped Mili's tiny hand. "Welcome to the family." She winked at her nephew. "Did you prepare her for this bunch of nutcases?"

"Figured I'd let her judge for herself." Michael Jack's brown eyes glistened when he looked at Mili. "We met online in a chat room. Never in a million years did I think I would find someone like her."

"You haven't introduced her to the rest of the family?" Hannah said.

"Only Uncle Hal. Mili's been helping me with the remodel. He dropped by one day last week when she was here."

Hannah made a mental note to slap her brother silly for holding out. "Hal didn't mention it."

Michael Jack grinned. "I asked him not to. I wanted it to be a surprise."

Hal and Suzanne were the next to arrive. Suzanne bustled in, sat the covered dish container down, and dug in her oversized woven grass purse. "Wait till you see!" She extracted a small crimson velvet pouch. "I bought my zills last night!"

Hannah's eyebrows knit together. "When? I didn't see you shopping."

"After you and Becky left. I stayed behind for a few minutes to go over that snake arms movement." Suzanne turned toward the rest of the group and explained, "We're taking this belly dancing class and learning all kinds of different undulations. I do fine with my right arm, but let me try the same with my left, and honey hush! I can't even pick my nose with my left hand without cramming my finger clean to my brain, much less move it in time to the music."

When their laughter died down, she continued. "Anywho, I went ahead and bought a set of these student zills. They were only twelve bucks."

Hannah poked out her bottom lip. "I'm jealous."

"You ought to see the cats hightail it when I clang them."

Michael Jack said, "Those are little finger cymbals, right?"

"They're called zills, like in dills, but with a z." Suzanne stuck out her hand toward Mili, then thought better of it and gave her a quick wind-deleting hug. "You must be Michael Jack's intended. Hal told me all about meeting you. I'm Suzanne."

"My honor." Mili clasped one hand to her chest. Probably trying to get air back into her lungs.

"Place is really coming along, Michael Jack." Hal looked around. "Helen's not here yet?"

"No," Hannah answered. "Can you wrap your mind around that?"

By the time Helen and Charlie arrived, the family had relocated to the shaded backyard beneath a large Southern Magnolia tree, where they sipped iced drinks and watched Michael Jack operate his new stainless steel gas grill. The tantalizing aroma of barbequing chicken and pork ribs floated in the late spring breeze.

"Hey, everybody!" Helen descended the stairs leading from the screened back porch. "Sorry we're late."

Charlie, her paunchy balding husband, stepped down beside her. "Helen had a cooking emergency."

"Disaster was more like it." Helen accepted a tall glass of iced tea from Hannah. "My lemon cheesecake looks like one of those Bloomin' Onions they fry up at the fair. It was pretty as a magazine cover picture when I took it from the spring form pan, then this itty-bitty crack appeared on one side. Before you could scat a cat— poof! It fell all to pieces."

Hannah rested a hand on her sister's shoulder. "I'm sure it will still taste good, Sissy."

"I wanted it to be perfect. The more I tried to fix it, the worse it got." Helen focused her attention on her son. "I'm so sorry about those brothers of yours, Michael Jack. Sickness happens and I don't fault Jimmy for that. But I reminded Tommy a half a dozen times about today."

Michael Jack used a pair of tongs to flip chicken pieces on the grill. "It's okay, Mom. Really."

Helen's gaze rested on Mili. "Here I am running my motor mouth. Are you one of my son's friends from Tallahassee?"

Michael Jack wiped his hands on his white cook's apron and held out his hand to Mili. "Mom, Dad. This is Mili Wah. My fiancée."

Hannah fought back a chuckle. The expression on Helen's features flickered from shock to dismay before recovering to mild surprise. "Fiancée?"

Michael Jack hugged Mili to his side and they gazed into each other's eyes for a moment before he answered. "Yes."

Charlie stepped forward and pumped Mili's hand. "Well, how about that! Pleased to meet you, young lady."

"Yes. Pleased." Helen's voice sounded weak as she offered her hand.

"Yoo-dee-hoo!" The sound of Mae's voice calling from the top of the stairs broke the tension. "Is this my old house? Could it be?" Mae threw her head back and laughed. "Can we crash this little bash?"

Chapter Twenty-one

Hannah admired the wood plank floors and high ceilings of the Fort Braden Community Center, eleven miles west of Tallahassee. The massive old red brick building, once a public school, now served as a civic hub and host for the Hafla/Luau event. She closed her eyes, imagining the shuffle of children's feet down the long hallways and the familiar blended aroma of chalk dust and Murphy's Oil soap, a scent so distinctively academic, she wondered if all American school buildings smelled the same.

Hannah liked the idea of "repurposing"—the coined word popular with the recycle-and-reuse crowd. She had spent her life being repurposed: suckling baby to headstrong child; school girl and daughter to wife and mother; carefree college coed to careworn caretaker. *Maybe I'll get a tattoo,* she thought, *a nice tri-color recycle sign on my behind.*

The auditorium held rows of metal folding chairs, with vendors in the rear. Over-sized pillows rested along one wall, with a young magenta-haired henna artist ready to embellish temporary body decorations. Dancers strolled the hallways bedecked in vivid costumes: the bright floral prints of the Polynesian performers, the ruffled gowns of the Spanish troupes, and Middle Eastern costumes similar to hers.

Suzanne appeared and deposited a dripping umbrella and a duffel bag beside Hannah's chair. "I'm shopping right off, before all the good stuff's gone."

Becky arrived a few minutes later. "Did I miss anything? I got caught in a downpour."

"They don't start dancing until twelve," Hannah said, glancing at her watch.

The exotic scent of curry wafted through the air. Hannah felt a sudden urgent craving for peanut butter. Weird, she didn't eat it that often, and it smelled nothing like curry.

"I'll shop later. I want to see how the dance troupe puts it all together." Becky plopped down and patted the seat next to hers. "Catch me up on everything. We hardly had a chance to talk in class."

"I can't get over what happened at the Memorial Day party." Hannah sat down. "Unbelievable."

Becky handed her a cold bottled water from a small cooler. "Do tell."

"First of all, Michael Jack, you know my sister's youngest son? He's engaged."

"I always wondered about him. He's always been so bookish. When did he find time to pursue a woman?"

"He met her on the Internet."

Becky's eyebrows shot up. "Another computer geek?"

"Suppose so. She and Michael Jack launched into a couple of high-techie type discussions before Helen told them to talk so the rest of us could understand."

"You're a computer expert. That should've been right up your alley."

"Not compared to those two." Hannah took a sip of water. "The part that was so interesting is that she, Mili, is Chinese."

"That surely sent your sister over the edge." Becky smiled. "Helen never has been one to be very diverse. Not to dis' your sister, but—"

"True though."

"How'd your mother react?"

"Ma-Mae warmed right up to Mili. Drew her into a corner and started talking like they had known each other for years. By the time the party ended, Mili had promised to cook dinner for Ma-Mae sometime soon. You know how mama loves any kind of Asian food."

"Isn't that something, your mama being more open-minded than your sister."

Hannah nodded. "I asked Ma-Mae about it later. She told me that when you get to be her age, you pay a lot less attention to the outside than the inside."

Becky glanced around the auditorium. "Where's Suzanne?"

"Shopping. Where else?" Hannah motioned to the far end of the room.

The corners of Becky's lips curled up. "Keith gave me a hundred dollar bill. Told me to buy us a new outfit."

"Things have heated up a bit?"

"He even so much as hears one ring of my zills and he turns into a hitching post." She giggled. "Good place to hang my veil."

Hannah's lips twitched. "I'm pleased things are working out, Beck."

"I'm just pleased they're still working, period."

The sound of wind echoed through the building. "Man, did it ever rain on us driving over," Hannah commented. "It really hit us right around the Quincy exit off I-10."

"Worst of it is supposed to blow through by tonight, from what they said on the weather channel."

"I feel for those poor folks in Pensacola," Hannah said. "They got slammed end of last hurricane season too."

Becky agreed. "At least Arlene's a tropical storm and not a full-fledged hurricane."

"Still, sixty-mile-per-hour winds aren't anything to sneeze at. One of my co-worker's cousins lives over near Pensacola, and she's just now completed the repairs to her house. She was one of the lucky ones who had most of hers left standing."

"Be glad the brunt of it isn't headed our way," Becky said. "We dodged the bullet this time around."

"They say this season's going to be active. Twelve or more."

Becky snorted. "Keith lives for a good natural disaster. He bought a generator the size of my car."

"We have one too. And enough tarps to cover half of Gadsden County. And duct tape, though I'm not sure why Norman needs seven rolls, two in a fetching purple camo-print."

Suzanne slipped into the seat next to them and dropped several packages on the polished wooden floor. "All that spending has worn me out."

"What'd you get?" Becky lunged for the bags.

"Don't you touch! There may be something in there you don't need to see." Suzanne rummaged in the wrappings and extracted a turquoise silk veil.

Hannah ran her fingers through the rich material. "Feels like warm honey."

"Wait till you get a load of this." Suzanne removed a clear plastic bag. "This is the hip scarf to match." Gold bangles rippled with each movement. Strips of metallic thread ran between woven stripes of turquoise, purple and deep blue.

"That's about the most beautiful thing I've ever laid eyes on," Becky said.

Suzanne motioned to one of the vendors' tables. "Each one's a little different, so you don't have to worry about being a copy-cat." She winked. "I'm sure you can find Keith's favorite color somewhere in that big pile."

Hannah reached a hand over and shushed them. "They're getting ready to start."

Billowy Indian-print material and tropical silk orchids and ferns decorated the raised stage. Two silk palm trees held strings of white lights and inflated tropical fish. Netting draped the performance area: Sheik's lair meets Hawaiian vacation.

The Butterfly Rainbow Dancers, the children's troupe, performed the first three sets. The audience oohed and ahhed. Then the adults took the stage. Following the Flamenco artists and two Polynesian troupes, the Middle Eastern groups undulated.

"I recognize some of those moves," Suzanne said in an excited whisper.

"We'll be up there, this time next year," Becky said.

A far deeper meaning dawned on Hannah as she watched women and men of all ages and body shapes move in time to the tribal beat. The performers seemed comfortable with their bodies, releasing to the music and joy of the dance. She wondered if her mother and father had ever danced together. Must've, what with the popularity of Big Band music during their younger years. The thought of her parents doing the Jitterbug made her smile. A brief memory like the whiff of a long-faded perfume teased her mind: Her mother and father gazing into each other's eyes, arms intertwined, swaying in the kitchen, her father humming a wordless tune.

"I want one of those shiny outfits." Becky's eyes twinkled.

"I priced them," Suzanne said. "Two hundred and fifty dollars for the bra, harem pants, vest and matching scarf."

Becky beamed. "Keith did want me to come home with some-thing pretty."

"Pick one of them up, Beck," Suzanne said. "Weighs a ton! Better make sure your hips are ready to take the strain."

"If I come out wearing that outfit," Becky said with a wink and nod. "I won't have to move around much."

Summer in the Florida Panhandle arrived with an almost audible groan. The humidity hovered as close to a hundred percent as possible without turning to liquid. Hannah cussed her hair. Even the short bob—thank heaven for Mandy at the Triple C—failed to tame her unruly waves. Wisps of hair stuck out at bizarre angles the moment she stepped into the moisture-saturated air.

As a formal proclamation of the season, Rosemont's official greeter, Lucy Goosey, showed out in an eye-popping yellow and orange polka dot bikini with coordinating head scarf, beach pail and shovel, and terry cloth towel. A small mesh carry-all at her side held tanning products, a copy of *Bird Talk* magazine, rhinestone-studded sunglasses, and a vintage transistor radio.

Beth glanced up from her computer screen. "Morning, Hannah."

"To you, too. I see Lucy's heading for the coast."

"That cement bird owns more outfits than you and me put together." Beth chuckled. "She has three swimsuits. The residents made them in Catharen's craft class." Beth handed her the sign-in booklet. "One is a saucy little purple strapless number with a heart-shaped peephole on the behind."

Hannah scribbled her name and date on the roster. "Lord help."

"Your mama's seemed a bit down the last few days." As Rosemont's front desk commandeer, Beth possessed a sixth sense when it came to the residents.

"My dad passed away in July of ninety-three. She gets a bit more melancholy starting around mid-June."

"Usually, she'll stop by and talk to me in the mornings on her way back from breakfast. Tell me some joke or story she's heard." Beth waved a hand through the air. "Don't mind me. I worry about my people."

When Mae failed to answer after the second set of knocks, Hannah dug in her purse for the extra room keys. As she fit the key into the lock, the doorknob turned.

"I heard you," Mae said. "I'm not motivating very fast this morning."

"Do you feel bad?" Hannah asked as she stepped into the room.

Mae shrugged. "My get-up-and-go has got up and went. I didn't sleep so well."

"I have those restless nights every now and then. Keep waking up and checking the clock every hour or so, just to see if it's still working." Hannah plopped down on her mother's bed.

"I wake up, all anxious about things." Mae trundled to the restroom. "Let me put on some rouge and a little lipstick so I don't look half dead, then I'll be ready to go."

"What's worrying you, Ma-Mae?"

"Nothing. Everything." She pursed her lips and applied a ring of deep red lipstick, then blotted with a sheet of toilet paper. "I wake up and wonder: why, what, when, and where."

"I don't follow."

"Why I'm still here, what I'm supposed to be doing, when I'll finally get to leave, and where I'll go when I do."

"Sounds pretty heavy."

"Enough to weigh an old lady down." Mae heaved a sigh so prolonged, Hannah was surprised her mother's lungs could hold so much air. "You know how I get in the summer."

"Same as me."

"It's like the air presses down and I can't catch a good breath. My patience is about as long as my pecker." Mae offered a weak smile. "And that ain't long at all since the Good Lord didn't give me one."

"I can't get cool at night. If I throw off the covers, I shiver. But then I can't stand to have the sheets touch me, either."

Mae patted her daughter on the shoulder. "It's the change, sugar. I used to have the worst hot flashes when I was your age. Lord have mercy! I could have the oscillating fan blowing a gale right on me and still be flat-out burning up."

Hannah nodded emphatically. "Yeah, that's exactly it. I'm on fire from within."

"Get you an ice bag and take it to bed. I used to sit one right square in the middle of my chest. Wash your feet with a cool wet rag before you turn in. That helps."

"Thanks, Ma-Mae."

At times, the reversed mother-daughter role stood aside and a comfortable female camaraderie took its place. Just two women discussing life's trials and travails.

"Where are we bound for?" Mae handed a small leather purse to Hannah and grabbed her cane and room keys.

"Nowhere special. Just lunch. You in the mood for anything in particular?"

"I don't have much of an appetite when it's hot weather. Maybe a salad—one with everything on it, meat and all."

Hannah followed her mother into the hallway and closed the door behind them. "After we stop at the Dollar Store, we can ride over to Quincy. I hear there's a new little café on the square across from the county courthouse."

As Hannah steered from the Rosemont parking lot, Mae said, "I worry about running you ragged."

"Why's that?"

"You're always dashing to and fro, dragging me around to the store and doctor's appointments and such." She turned away and stared out the passenger window. "I hate to be a burden."

"You're not. I enjoy our time together."

The realization sunk in, spreading like ripples from a pebble cast in smooth water. In spite of the stress and constant niggling worry that accompanied her like a second skin, Hannah truly treasured time with her mother. The image of an overturned hourglass popped into her mind, its finite crystals pouring continually downward.

Chapter Twenty-two

Justine slammed the back door so hard the decorative plates on the wall rattled. She scurried through the kitchen, leaving a wake of discarded items: backpack, purse, hot pink flower-studded sandals.

"Hi honey," Hannah called out to no response. "Due to lack of interest, today's parent-child goodwill program has been canceled," she announced aloud to the dead air. A fog of peachy aroma lingered: Justine's bath and body signature scent.

Hannah praised God on a daily basis for sending her and Norman only one angst-ridden hormonal girl child. Jonas would submit his own unique set of issues as he crept into his late teens, but he'd have to stretch to equal his sister in the intensity of mood swings.

Jonas shuffled in from baseball practice, dropped his glove, bat, and duffel on the floor, then rummaged in the refrigerator.

"There's a bowl of fresh pasta salad if you need something to hold you until dinner."

He backed out of the frigid air, his arms filled with a loaf of bread, deli packages, and condiments. "S'kay, Mom."

Hannah sipped from a diet cola and tended to the simmering pot of meat sauce on the stove. "I'll have the spaghetti ready in a bit."

"No sweat. I can eat again."

If Jonas kept consuming food at his current rate, she and Norman would need to peddle their souls on a street corner to supplement the grocery budget allotment. Again she praised God, this time for sending only one bottomless-pit boy child.

Jonas slathered enough mayonnaise on the wheat bread for four sandwiches, added three slices of Colby cheese, a mound of sliced turkey breast, lettuce, two thick slices of tomato, and half a jar of dill pickles. He smashed the towering creation with both hands to a more manageable height.

"I don't know how you're going to fit that in, hon," Hannah said.

"You always said I have a big mouth."

"Must take after your father."

"Uh-huh." Jonas grabbed a glass, added ice, and poured it full of sweet tea.

"What's up with your sister? She seems a bit unsettled."

"And that's new?" Jonas asked.

The pungent odor of stale boy-sweat hit Hannah's nostrils and overrode the earlier peach scent. Motherhood came with an array of sensory delights. Dirty diapers and throw-up were only the beginning.

"Probably the usual, Mom. Fighting with Brittany." Jonas crammed in a huge wedge of sandwich and attempted to chew.

"Jeez, son. Don't take such outlandish bites! You'll choke."

When he had enough clearance to speak, he continued, "Heard Jus screeching on the phone last night. Not that I'm trying to rat on her or anything."

"Our secret. I don't mean to put you in a bad position. Really. I'd like to help out if she's in some kind of trouble."

He wiped a glob of mayonnaise from his chin. "Jus was crying. Told Brit that 'she was going to tell someone about her little problem.' "

Hannah's chest constricted. *Little problem?* Boys? Fashion? Or something more ominous or life-changing? She closed her eyes. *God forbid, not pregnancy.*

On the short trip down the hallway to Justine's room, Hannah felt the same mix of emotions as she did with her elderly mother: a mish-mash of intense love, protectiveness, anxiety and temerity. Both were basically good, kind people. Shining through Justine's center-of-the-known-universe teen vantage point, Hannah glimpsed moments of compassion and empathy. Her elderly mother's world view had narrowed as well, but Mae still managed reserves of selflessness and concern for the people in her orbit.

Justine's door exhibited a road sign replica announcing **Private! Posted! Keep out! Violators will be shot!** Or at least verbally castrated, Hannah thought. She tapped on the closed door.

"What?!" Justine's stern voice called.

"Honey, may I come in?"

Justine cracked the door and peered out, her eyes red-rimmed and puffy. "Mom, I really don't—"

"Please, Jus. Pacify me, will you?"

Justine swung the door open, then plopped down cross-legged in the middle of the bed.

Over the years, her daughter's lair had morphed from the lace and frills of girlhood to a blend of bright colors and geometric shapes. A few vestiges of the sweet tow-headed child remained: a worn Raggedy Ann doll, a fuzzy chenille teddy bear missing one button eye, and a milky-white bubble glass lamp with a dingle-ball-trimmed shade.

"Whatsup?" Justine asked.

Hannah settled onto a cushioned stool next to the vanity. "Same old. I'm not here invading your space to talk about me." When Justine failed to take the lead, Hannah continued, "You've been moping around the house for the past few days. I'm concerned. We all are."

Tears welled in her daughter's blue eyes. Justine's gaze dropped to the clenched hands in her lap.

"I try to stay clear of your affairs, Jus. You have to learn to handle things—problems—on your own. I encourage that . . . It's just . . . " Hannah groped for the words to penetrate Justine's fortifications. "When I notice you not eating and staying closed up in this room for hours . . . " She studied her daughter for a moment. "Are you sick, honey? Or, is it Shaun?"

Justine flicked her eyes up then down. "Shaun? That was so forever ago."

Hannah fought the urge to smile. "It's hard for me to keep up. Sorry." She reached over and gently tucked a stray hank of hair away from Justine's eyes. "Share with me? Maybe I can help."

Hannah waited while Justine wiped her eyes and blew her nose.

"She's dying, Mom, and I can't do a thing to stop her!" Justine hung her head and buried her face in her hands. Her thin shoulders shook slightly.

Hannah slid onto the bed and enfolded Justine in her arms until the sobbing quieted.

"I can't take it. I just can't take it," Justine said in a shaky voice.

"You and I talked about this. Grand-Mae doesn't mean to upset you when she talks about death."

"No, not Grand-Mae. Brittany."

Hannah pushed back and studied her daughter's face. "Is she sick?"

Justine nodded. Her crystal dangling earrings tinkled like fairy music. "Sort of."

"Does her mother know?" Hannah asked in a soft voice.

Surely someone in town would have mentioned a child's grave illness. Secrets in a small community were rare.

Justine's expression darkened. "She doesn't have a clue."

"Drugs?"

Justine scowled. "No, Mom! Not drugs! Gah, why is it that all adults think drugs are the root of all?"

"They are, a lot of the time."

"She's puking." Justine's lips curled in disgust. "It's so sick!"

"Stomach problems?"

"No. No. She's doing it on purpose. You know, to stay thin."

"Ah-ha! There you are, you little dickens." Mae plucked a blue puzzle piece and fit it easily into a section of sky.

Hannah snorted. "How can you always find the right one when all of them look the dadgum same?"

"Attention to detail, sugar-pot. And patience—something you are sometimes in short supply of." She reached over and patted her daughter's hand.

Hannah continued to rummage through the puzzle box lid.

"What's eating at you, honey?"

Hannah glanced up. "What do you mean?"

"Something's playing on your mind this morning."

"And you can tell this . . . how?"

"You get a deep crease betwixt your eyes." Mae touched a spot between Hannah's eyebrows. "Right here. Furrows up when you're mulling over a problem. Been that way since you were a child. Best be mindful of it, lest you forge a permanent worry line there."

Hannah massaged her forehead with two fingers.

Mae plugged another section of sky into place. "I sleep with a piece of scotch tape between my brows."

"What's that supposed to do?"

"Keeps me from frowning in my sleep," Mae said.

"I see."

Mae studied her daughter. "You going to tell me what's causing you to screw up your face? Norman? Or is Justine cutting the fool again? Teenagers can be such a trial."

"No, none of that. Everything's even keel, for now."

Mae's left eyebrow shot up. Hannah knew she might as well give it up when the question-mark brow appeared.

Hannah massaged her cramped neck muscles with one hand. "I'm trying to decide whether or not to interfere in someone's business."

"Uh-huh." Mae continued to work on the puzzle. When it came to waiting out a confession, her mother possessed boundless endurance.

"Do you remember Justine's friend Brittany?"

"The Rodgers girl? Been a while since I've seen her, not since her daddy passed some years back. Your father and I attended the funeral." Mae rested a finger on her chin. "Little slip of a girl, wormy-looking."

"She's Justine's best friend."

"Seems like I recall my grandbaby mentioning her before."

"Justine confided something to me. I'm trying to decide if I should break her confidence and interfere, or not."

"Is she in a *family way*?"

"No, no." Hannah paused. What harm could talking to her mother do? "Justine told me that Brittany's bulimic."

"That throwing-up condition, right?"

Hannah studied a puzzle piece, frowned, then pitched it back into the box. "It's caused quite a rift between them. Justine's beside herself with worry. I'm at a loss."

Mae sat back and crossed her arms across her chest. "Some things are best left alone—like marital problems, for instance. I've gotten caught up in other couples' affairs of the heart a time or two, and let me tell you, I learned that lesson the hard way." She paused before adding, "But when it comes to something that's life-threatening, especially when it involves a child, I'd have to find some way to step in."

"How? My relationship with Justine's improved. She comes and talks to me now. I don't want to ruin that."

"Sometimes sugar, all you have to do is plant a seed and let it grow. Just because you happen to drop by and visit with Brittany's mama, and happen to mention how thin Brittany's become—"

"Visit? With Missy Rodgers? That in itself would seem forced. She and I are two different breeds, Ma-Mae."

Mae rested a hand on Hannah's shoulder. "You're a bright gal. You'll figure a way around it. After all, what's more important? You feeling a little sheepish, or a young woman dying because no one said a word?"

HANNAH'S TANGY SPINACH SALAD

1 bag fresh spinach, washed and drained
1/2 large red onion, thinly sliced
1 can mandarin oranges, drained
1 cup toasted, slivered almonds (toast raw slivered almonds under oven broiler until lightly browned)
1 pkg. feta cheese, crumbled
1/2 cup golden raisins or dried cranberries
Honey and bacon French dressing

Toss all ingredients together. Top with commercial honey and bacon French dressing.
Serve chilled.

Chapter Twenty-three

Hannah hesitated for a moment in front of Missy Rodgers's perfect fortress, a basket of muffins hanging from one arm. How long had it been since she had stepped inside the restored Victorian home of Chattahoochee's reigning volunteer queen? Five years? Ten? Dimly, she recalled a PTA planning meeting for one of Justine's elementary school functions. Naturally, Missy Rodgers had been the chairperson.

The porch provided a good measure of the owner's decorating skills. Matching rattan swings lined with plush pillows. Verdant ferns at precise intervals and terra cotta pots filled with colorful blooming annuals. Concrete statues of lop-eared rabbits crouching beside two white rocking chairs. Hannah could envision a covey of Southern belles milling in the cool shade in frilly hoop skirts, sipping mint juleps, batting their eyelashes at fawning suitors.

Missy Rodgers answered the door after the second set of musical chimes. She wore the latest summer fashion: lime green crop pants with a coordinating wispy form-fitting blouse. Her fingers and toes glistened with hot pink polish in a shade matching her lips.

"Hannah Olsen!" She swung the screen door open wide. "I was so pleased and surprised when you called. Do come in."

Missy ushered her into a formal front parlor: a room that continued the illusion of the bygone glory days of Dixie. The high ceilings provided adequate space for large oak antiques that would've overpowered most modern homes. Cabbage roses in sherbet shades filled crystal vases. The Victorian furniture appeared about as comfortable as a bed of prickly pears.

"I made some fresh mint tea. Would you join me for a glass?"

"Sounds great. I'll never turn down tea." Hannah handed over the basket. "These are for you and Brittany."

Missy smiled to reveal even white teeth. "How thoughtful. Banana nut muffins. It's been positively ages since I've had one of these." Her petite hand fluttered at her throat like a butterfly moth caught in a screen. "My recipes are so complicated and call for such exotic ingredients. I can't recall the last time I made something so ordinary, yet so good. Thank you."

Was there a back-door compliment in there somewhere? Hannah forced her lips to lift. "My pleasure. But I can't take credit for baking them. I bought them uptown at the Borrowed Thyme Bakery."

"Well, it's the thought that counts, right? I have, upon occasion, purchased Mr. Joe's cakes and pies. When I was in a pinch."

A smirk tried to fight its way to the corners of Hannah's lips.

"I'll just pop a couple of these in my convection oven and warm them up a bit. We can have one with our tea. With butter, of course. I never use margarine, do you?" Her button nose crinkled as if she had detected a foul scent. "Come on back to the kitchen."

Hannah followed Missy down a long hallway plastered with family photographs, past an ornate mahogany staircase, and into a large airy kitchen at the rear of the house. Except for a few tasteful touches of lemon yellow and blue, the room was bright white. Hannah couldn't imagine facing such blinding gaiety first thing every morning.

Missy motioned to a round oak table surrounded with cushioned chairs. "Make yourself comfortable." She wrapped two muffins in a damp clean cloth and popped it into the over-the-stove microwave/convection oven, then poured two glasses of iced tea and added sprigs of fresh peppermint.

A few moments later, Missy sat the warmed muffins on the table on two china saucers along with several pats of butter. Hannah noted how the blue in the plates matched the linen napkins. *Of course.* In her house, a person would be lucky to get a couple of paper towels and flimsy Dollar Store plastic plates.

"This really is a pleasure, you popping by." Missy took a delicate sip of tea. Her eyebrows raised slightly in a question.

Time to make up a lie, and make it up quick. Missy Rodgers was not someone you visited for sport. "Are you chairing the Relay for Life?" Hannah asked.

"I have for the past five seasons. It's a wonderful opportunity to raise money for a worthy cause." She nipped a minute piece of muffin and chewed.

"My office would like to enter a team this year."

"That's all well and good, Hannah. But the relay was held a few weeks back."

She really must start keeping up better. "I know. I meant for the next one."

"It never hurts to plan ahead, I suppose. Tell you what I'll do. I'll put you on my mailing list. I generally start sending out information after the first of the year. That way, you'll have oodles of time to gather your people."

Hannah sipped her tea, a perfect brewed blend with the extra punch of cool mint. "That'll work."

"I've been meaning to apologize for that bit of unpleasantness with the girls," Missy said. "I've thoroughly chastised my relations for their lack of supervision."

"Teenagers will be teenagers. We've dealt with Justine. The run-in with the authorities scared her so witless, maybe she'll think twice before she drinks like that again."

"Brittany has been on restriction since that night." When Missy frowned, only her lips showed dismay. The flesh between her thin arched brows and around her mouth remained smooth. Botox, or did her mastery of perfection include a moratorium against damaging facial expressions?

"Justine has done her time—not only from Norman and me, but with the county too. I don't see any sense in running it into the ground."

"You must raise your daughter as you see fit. Since Andrew passed, I've had to navigate the shoals of parenthood alone." Missy nibbled a muffin. At this rate, she'd finish one by Christmas.

Hannah bit her lower lip. How much more of Missy could she take without blowing a blood vessel? "I'm sure it's not easy these days." Hannah hesitated. "I do worry about Brittany, to be honest."

Missy set her iced tea glass down and dabbed the moisture from her lips. "Why's that? Is she making herself a nuisance?"

"Not at all. She's like another member of the family, practically. She's just so . . . thin."

"All of the women in my family are dainty," Missy countered. "We're lucky to reach a hundred pounds. The only time I went a little over was in my last month of pregnancy."

Hannah flashed back to her final trimesters with both Justine and Jonas. They could've strapped on ropes and floated her in the Macy's parade. "I think girls our daughter's age see those models in magazines and try to starve themselves half to death. Do you think she might be doing that?"

"I see to it that Brittany has a balanced diet," Missy replied. "My daughter has a high metabolism. I'm the same way. I could eat that entire basket of muffins and not gain an ounce. I've never been one to lean to excess though. It's a blessing, really."

Shoot me now. Hannah polished off the rest of her muffin in one bite. "Guess I'm being overprotective. She looks a little pale and—" Hannah searched for a reasonable substitute for *emaciated.*

"She's had a few female problems, hormonal." Missy offered a pinched smile. "It is nice of you to be concerned, but I'm well aware of my daughter's health." She stood and began to clear the dishes. "You'll forgive me, Hannah. I have a garden club meeting this afternoon. I haven't completed my notes yet. I'm presenting a talk on herbs. Do you garden?"

The volunteer tomatoes that had sprouted by the compost bin probably didn't count. "No time now, what with my mom and the family, and work."

"Shame. It's really very soothing to the soul."

Hannah stood to leave.

"Thank you again for the muffins. Do stop by more often. We should talk more, Hannah. Our daughters surely do."

As she walked the few blocks back to her house, Hannah mulled over the conversation. Good thing she hadn't taken the whole dozen muffins. At the Olsen house, they'd be eaten and enjoyed. She had made no inroads into Missy Rodgers's faultless force field. An offbeat Southernism of her mother's popped into her mind: "there's more than one way to skin a cat."

Dr. Emery pushed his rolling stool away from the dental chair and stood up. "I'm happy to report: no cavities, gums look healthy, no more cracked teeth. Congratulations!"

"No offense, folks, but I'd much rather come only for my regular cleanings." Hannah sat up and swung her legs to the side of the dental chair. "Before I leave, may I speak with you about something?"

"Of course." Dr. Emery settled back into his chair and handed Hannah's chart to the hygienist. "Want to step into my private office?"

"No, that's okay. I was going to phone you, but I realized I had this appointment. I've been reading up on anorexia and bulimia, and I have a few questions."

Her dentist's brows furrowed. "Not Justine, I hope."

"Oh, no. She's fine, except for the hourly teenaged crisis. I'm concerned for her best friend. She's not your patient, by the way." Hannah continued, "The article I read on the Internet mentioned something about dental problems relating to bulimia."

"Depends on how long the behavior's been going on. I've seen cases where a good deal of chemical erosion has occurred to the enamel as a result of frequent exposure to stomach acids."

"If a patient came in and you noticed this, would you consult with the parent?"

"Depends. Is this patient a minor?"

Hannah nodded.

"In that case, yes. The new privacy rules prohibit us from disclosing information without written consent, even to family members. But in the case of a child under eighteen, we're allowed to talk with the parent or legal guardian."

"I see." Hannah gathered her purse and keys. "If I spoke with her dentist and told him my concerns, he could follow up?"

"Legally, ethically, he or she can not discuss a patient with you, Hannah. Not unless the parent has given the okay, or she is your child."

"The dentist could listen, though."

He tilted his head. "I don't see why not."

Hannah smiled. "Perfect."

Chapter Twenty-four

The aura of the previous night's dream lingered as Hannah sipped her second cup of black coffee. She had felt the inner flame ignite early in the previous evening, and had tried to convince Norman the air conditioner wasn't working properly. By bedtime, so many fans blew on her body, she almost needed tie-down straps to remain fixed to the mattress. She still craved peanut butter and felt seriously horny. Bizarre.

During her fitful sleep, her first love had dropped in for a visit. Marcus Motivano: a tall, wavy-haired, mustached young man with dark smoldering eyes. Even now, Hannah wanted to moan then cry.

Her freshman year of college had found Hannah Mathers a save-yourself-for-marriage, dewy innocent: the sort of girl who took men at face value and believed all people good and honest. Hard-knock 101 taught her a life lesson, with Marcus as the masterful mentor. Following eight months of unrelenting charm, he succeeded in bedding Sweet Hannah Mathers. The entire sexual act had happened so fast, Hannah recalled few details. She vaguely remembered wondering: *Is that it? Is that what everyone is so hyped up about?* Marcus had rolled over promptly and fallen asleep. Two weeks later, he unceremoniously ditched Hannah for a blonde bubble-headed bimbo with breasts the size of his libido.

Hannah shut down. Dated, yet never allowed one man to tip-toe close. For years, throughout college and the first part of her career, she developed male acquaintances—some, she would consider friends—but none broached the ice fields.

Until Hometown Norman.

Plain, milk-toast, dependable-as-an-old-Volvo Norman. So unassuming and non-threatening—a protective, brotherly type of man. Like a creamy rich piece of dark chocolate with a mocha filling, Norman sheltered a core so profoundly sweet, Hannah slipped and fell in love. Not frantic, heart-wrenching anguish, but the steady Sunday-morning-in-curlers kind of devotion. No matter how many cellulite thigh dimples Hannah counted, Norman only saw a beautiful wife and mother.

Sex with Norman astounded her. So, the female was supposed to benefit from the act? Imagine! Regardless of time's passage, Norman remained a considerate lover. Slowly, he unearthed Hannah's buried anger and replaced it with an easy contentment. True, the frequency and intensity had waned in the past few years, but all the talk shows attested to the normality of that.

Why, after all the years—loving husband, stable life, and two mostly-obedient children— did her unconscious mind periodically revisit Marcus Motivano? He appeared casually in a fleeting dream, never aged past twenty-three, where they would linger over drinks like dear old friends. A sexual undercurrent rippled beneath the surface of the discourse: a subtle flirtation, an invitation to replay the scratched, warped, and out-of-date vinyl recording.

Hannah despised loose ends. Mind-numbing work projects were completed. Refrigerated leftovers, purged when they turned into Petri projects. Dishes didn't stand in unwashed stacks. Dust bunnies never grew to the size of volleyballs. If a thing was important enough to deserve time, then it would be hand-held to the bitter end. She counted less than five-fingers' worth of loose ends in her life. Marcus topped the hit parade.

Initially, the infrequent forays into the past had left her with a vague haze of cheater's guilt. But she couldn't reign over slumber any more than she could stunt the persistent crop of whiskers sprouting from her chin.

Once, a few years back, she had toyed with contacting Marcus, and located his current address and phone number using the Internet. What could she say if she called? *Hi, remember me? I'm the virgin from Chattahoochee—the one you pumped and dumped eons ago.*

She imagined an innocent conversation over coffee at a truck stop off the Interstate. Like her, Marcus would be older, but much more tattered, with wisps of gray in his wavy dark hair. If he still had any. What if he didn't recall the pivotal event of her young life? Hannah might leave the encounter convinced the whole affair had been ill-advised, and all that rich, righteous indignation would have to disappear.

Hannah tapped her fingernails on the sides of her cup. Would her life have turned out differently if the Southern Don Juan had married her? Absolutely. No doubt, she would have a set of dark-haired children with soulful eyes. Judging by Marcus's limited fidelity, the union would've crumbled, leaving her a bitter single parent.

Hannah shuddered, then glanced heavenward. "Thank you, thank you, thank you," she mouthed.

"It's way hot in here," Justine commented when she appeared for her customary breakfast of buttered toast and coffee. "I started to sweat the minute I got out of the shower."

"Tell your father." Hannah motioned to the back of the *Tallahassee Democrat*.

"You women are wearing me out," Norman's voice sounded from behind the daily paper. "I'll call someone to check out the AC unit. Probably needs juicing up with Freon."

"I think it's more than that, hon." Hannah dabbed perspiration from her upper lip. "We had it serviced the end of last summer. It shouldn't be on the fritz again."

Norman snapped the paper closed and folded it beside his plate. "Could be that it's so hot and humid that it's struggling to keep up."

Hannah frowned at the two pieces of toast she had overcooked to charcoal. "That would describe me."

"Until we win the lottery and buy a second home in the mountains, we're stuck here for the summers," Norman said with a weak smile.

"It's even hot up there, from what the Weather Channel says. If I got in a car right now and started to drive, I might not stop until I hit Canada." Hannah started to shave the blackened toast with a knife blade, then gave in and pitched them into the trash. "I'll have more out in a couple of minutes, Jus."

Norman gathered his dishes and took them to the sink. Hannah smiled. Now if she could get him to consistently put down the toilet lid.

"I'll call the serviceman and plan on leaving early from work," he said. "Someone will have to let him in the house."

Hannah faked a bow in her husband's direction. "Bless you, Norman Olsen."

"Just kiss the ring, and back from the room." Norman grinned.

She wanted to take him. Right there. On the kitchen floor. What the heck had gotten into her?

Jonas slipped into a chair with a loaded cereal bowl. A wave of milk and Cheerios washed over one side. "Dog-gone!"

"If you didn't try to fit an entire box into one bowl, you wouldn't have a problem, piglet," Justine said.

Jonas stuck out his tongue. "Better to eat like a pig than look like one."

Hannah signaled for a time out. "Too early for this, kids."

"Just sharing the love, Mom," Jonas said around a mouth full of cereal and sliced bananas.

Maxine pushed her ruby-red walker to the front desk at Rosemont. "Y'all need to check on Sarah Gordon in 201. She didn't come down for lunch and she was pale as rice pudding this morning at breakfast."

Beth scribbled a note. "Thank you, Miz Maxine. I'll page Lora and ask her to look in on her."

Maxine nodded, then turned to face Hannah. "Afternoon. You seen your mother?"

"I'm on my way down to her room right now."

Maxine's features darkened. "She's not content today."

"That so?"

"She was in a high rolling boil at lunch. Never seen her in such a frizzle." She released the brake lever on the walker. "Guess you'll find out soon enough."

"Appreciate the heads-up, Miz Maxine."

Hannah felt her stomach lurch. "Thank the heavens above for Zoloft," she muttered as she walked down the long carpeted hall to room 104.

The blare of the evening news sounded through the thick door. Since there was no way her mother would hear her knock, Hannah fished in her purse for the room key. She rapped as she unlocked the door. "It's just me, Ma-Mae!"

The whoosh of a toilet flushing answered her call. The bathroom door swung open and Mae emerged, dressed only in her bra and panties.

"Good Lord All-mighty!" Mae clutched her chest. "You scared me half to death! I swannee, you're going to give me a heart attack one of these days, slipping in like you do."

"Maybe if you'd turn the television volume down, you'd hear me knocking." She picked up the remote from the bedside table and punched the mute button. "Whew, that's better. Couldn't even hear myself think."

"There's a purpose in everything the good Lord does, even taking away a person's hearing when she's older. Reckon He figures I'll be better off not to hear most of what's going on around me." Mae made her way through the room to the closet where she picked out a long-sleeved pink pull-over top and tan pants.

"Kind of warm for long sleeves, don't you think?" The thought of wearing a thermal knit top brought a flush to Hannah's skin.

"Thin blood," Mae said. "I'm going down to watch a show in the living room. They keep it cold enough down there to hang meat."

"I always found it perfectly comfortable." Hannah plopped into the cushioned rocker.

"You have one of your long days?"

"I didn't get a lot of sleep last night." Hannah thumbed through an old *Rosemont Rap*. "Our air conditioner is on the fritz."

"I can't abide sleeping in a hot room either, even with my thin blood. In the dead of the winter, I turn the heat way down before I crawl underneath the covers."

"Norman called the repairman today, or he was supposed to. I'll wring his neck if he forgot."

"You can always come bunk in with me, sugar. My air's working fine."

Hannah smiled at the mental image of the two of them piled in the queen-sized bed. Her mother snored loud enough to wake the dead, or at least annoy them terribly.

"Thank you Ma-Mae. I'll get by." She closed her eyes and rocked gently.

"Suit yourself." Mae pulled the shirt over her head. "You get me an appointment for my nails and toes? My poor feet are beginning to feel a bit neglected."

"Melody at the Triple C has you set up for a mani-pedi, tomorrow at three. I'm taking the afternoon off, so I'll be here by two, the latest."

Mae sat down and worked the pants on, one leg at a time. "What about my hair?"

Hannah opened her eyes. "Hair?"

"I need a cut and set. I know I can get the woman here to do it, but I haven't gotten around to seeing her this week."

"I'll call in the morning and see if Mandy or Wanda can work you in. Why all this push to beautify?"

Mae stood and wiggled the pants to her waist. "I got a call from your uncle in Macon. My baby sister Dot's coming down from Maryland, and they're going to drive down for an over-nighter."

Hannah searched her recent memory. "I don't recall them calling me."

"They might not have. I gave them the number of a nice motel over by the Interstate not too far from our exit."

"They probably could've stayed with some of the family. We don't have a lot of space, but Hal and Suzanne have a guest room."

Mae wagged her finger. "You know your Aunt Dorothy, honey. She'll bring a month's worth of outfits, several pairs of shoes, and Lord only knows how many bags of makeup and such."

The Triple C Day Spa and Salon was its usual fizz of activity when Hannah and Mae entered the formal front parlor. Elvina Houston glanced up from the appointment book and held up a just-a-minute finger.

"Still seems strange not to see Piddie Longman at that desk," Mae said in a low voice. "Some folks, you expect to live on forever." Her expression grew wistful. "But she died at almost a hundred, so I suppose she came close."

Elvina set the phone headset down. "Sorry. Sometimes, folks want to blather on and on—Lordy, I reckon some of these women around here have tongues that are loose on both ends, cause they sure wag a lot."

"Not that you or I would know a thing about that affliction," Mae said.

Elvina winked. "One of the privileges of aging, far as I can see." She glanced to one of the long color-coded columns and ran a tapered nail down its length. "You're in with Melody for a mani-pedi, then I've managed to squeeze you in with Wanda for a cut and style." She looked up. "I know you generally see Mandy, but she's slammed full. The Miss Lake Seminole contest is coming up, and the girls are starting to come in for her to experiment with fancy up-do's."

"Fourth of July." Hannah sighed. "I can't believe we're halfway through this year already."

"Two more weeks." Elvina tapped the small calendar cube beside the appointment book.

"Time speeds to a gallop, the older you get," Mae said. "Come on back to the salon and visit if you're a mind to, Elvina."

Elvina stuck a sharpened pencil behind one ear. "I've got to place an order for the stylists, then I will. Y'all make yourselves at home. Melody's ready for you, Mae. Hannah, there's a fresh pot of coffee in the kitchen. And some blueberry muffins from the Borrowed Thyme Bakery and Eatery. Evelyn Fletcher brought them in fresh this morning. Sure am glad her husband learned to cook." She lowered her voice so it wouldn't carry to Evelyn's sewing room. "Keeps us from having to suffer through Evelyn's culinary disasters, bless her heart. My friend Piddie Longman used to swear that Evelyn's bad cooking kept her regular."

Three of the professional hair dryers hummed at one end of the large hair salon. Mandy waved when she saw Hannah and Mae reflected in her station's mirror. "Y'all find a seat where you can. We're hopping today."

Delilah O'Donnell— budding beauty star and first cousin to Ladonna O'Donnell, local model—held up a hand mirror to study the back of her hairdo.

"How's your mama getting along, little Miss Delilah?" Mae asked as she made her way to Melody's nail care station.

"Okay," the teen answered.

"You helping her out since she got home from the hospital?"

Delilah lowered the mirror. "Yes ma'am. Daddy's making me cook and clean until she's able."

"Takes a good six weeks after surgery for a person to gain energy," Mae said. "With your mama being a young woman, she'll bounce back pretty fast. Be sure to tell her I asked 'bout her, will you?"

"Yes 'um." Delilah plucked at a curl. "I want to have some little flowers in my hair too, Mandy."

"Might want to wait till right before the contest, hon." Mandy gestured with a rat-tail comb. "Unless you use silk flowers and manage to sleep sitting up."

Delilah's tanned shoulders rose and fell.

Melody studied Mae's hands. "You have the prettiest, best-shaped fingers I believe I've ever seen."

Mae beamed. "I could've been one of them hand models, if I would've started earlier."

"You have a particular color in mind?" Melody wiped the old polish with a cotton ball dipped in remover.

"Scarlet. Same for my toes. Old women need to wear bright colors."

"How many girls in the pageant this year?" Hannah asked Delilah as she settled into a director's chair with a fresh cup of black coffee.

"Ten, I think. I don't know how many in the Little Miss Seminole Contest."

"What's your talent act?" Mandy asked.

"Fire batons," the teen answered.

"That's always such a spectacle," Melody said. "I'd be scared out of my wits. I've heard of twirlers catching their hair on fire."

Mandy's eyebrows rose. "As much spray as you use, Mel, you'd be a flaming torch they'd see all the way to the space station."

"I can't stand to have fly-aways." Melody smoothed one side of her curly style. "Besides, that's what hair spray's *for.*"

Mae's fingertips soaked in a crystal bowl of warm sudsy water. "I believe if your hair tried to fly, it'd have to be powered by a set of jet engines."

A titter of laughter rippled through the salon. Hannah smiled and took a sip of the rich, espresso-blend coffee. She lived for the volley of words between women-friends. She glanced around the hair salon with its aged plank flooring and high ceilings and tried to envision the mansion as the Witherspoon family home. The tall windows looked out over an expansive garden framed with Magnolias and pines. Would this have been a sitting room?

Mandy tilted her head to one side and rested her hands on Delilah's shoulders. "I worry about you young women. All of you try to be so pencil thin."

"It's not healthy," Jolene Waters added from her position beneath the bonnet of her dryer. "You seen the Rodgers girl lately?"

Hannah snapped to attention. "Brittany?"

"She's thin as a rail," Jolene continued. "Looks like a concentration camp victim. She and her mama came into the Dragonfly Florist to order an arrangement for the First Baptist sanctuary for next Sunday. Child looked like she could barely put one foot ahead of the other."

Hannah felt resolve harden inside of her like two-day-old cathead biscuits.

Wanda Orenstein Green bustled into the salon and crammed a pocketbook the size of a carpetbag beneath the cabinet at her stylist station. "Hey, youse guys."

"You really have to learn to say *y'all,* Wanda Jean. We're going to work the New Jersey out of you yet," Mandy kidded her coworker.

Wanda's impish green eyes sparkled in contrast to her red hair. "You got me to eat grits. What more do you want?"

"Did you get Pinky taken care of?" Melody asked.

"I left him passed out cold on the sofa."

Mae looked up from admiring the freshly-painted nails on her left hand. "What's ailing your husband? I hadn't heard about him feeling poorly."

"He's fine." Wanda flipped her hand. "I took him over to Talla-hassee for a colonoscopy. Routine stuff. You know how they nail you with all kinds of tests after a certain age. They gave him a sedative beforehand and he's so susceptible to medication. He only takes those herbal remedies he mixes up when he's under the weather."

"Good thing he's having himself checked out." Wanda spritzed Delilah's style with holding spray. "I still shudder when I think about what Hattie Davis went through. She was barely forty when she had her colon cancer."

Elvina appeared at the arched doorway dividing the front parlor from the stylist salon. She eased into an empty chair and rested the phone headset on her lap. "What did I miss?"

"We've already raked half of Gadsden County over the coals, El-vina. Where have you been?" Mandy asked.

Elvina sniffed. "Some of us have to work for a living."

MAE'S PEA-PICKIN' CAKE

1 box yellow butter cake mix
4 eggs
1/2 cup cooking oil
1 small can mandarin oranges, undrained

Preheat oven to 350°
Mix all ingredients and bake in three round layers for 20 minutes.
Frost when completely cool.

FROSTING:

I large can crushed pineapple, undrained
1 pkg. vanilla instant pudding mix
1 large container whipped topping

Mix pineapple and pudding mix. Add whipped topping and fold together.

Use this between layers, and on top and sides of cake.

This cake must be refrigerated.

Chapter Twenty-five

Hannah turned into the Holiday Inn parking lot and lucked into a shady spot beneath a large live oak. Her mother's family had arrived the afternoon prior and swiped Mae from Rosemont for a mini-vacation. Since Mae had shared the hotel room with her Aunt Dot, Hannah doubted either had slept. Each time the two sisters reunited, they morphed into the schoolgirls they had once been—giggling and talking into the wee hours.

Hannah followed her Uncle Toby's instructions, located one of the adjoining rooms, and rapped on the door.

"Here she is!" Her uncle threw open the door and smashed her to his chest. "Glad you could join us for breakfast."

Suzanne wasn't the only one from a family of intense huggers. Hannah took in a breath. "Wouldn't miss it."

Dorothy and Pauline took turns hugging her and lavishing praise. Good thing Hannah wasn't a stand-offish sort who shunned body contact.

"You never change one little bit," Dorothy said. "You have the Brown-family skin. We Brown gals don't show our ages."

"Till we hit about seventy-five," Mae added. "Then it's downhill all the way."

Dorothy checked her lipstick in a compact mirror. "Speak for yourself, Mae. I have friends who believe I've had work done, on account of my unlined face."

Toby offered one of two upholstered chairs. "Sit down Hannah and tell us all about yourself, the kids. Your cousins all said to tell you hello. They're busy with family and work; they couldn't come down in the middle of the week. But we'd love for you and Norman and the kids to come up. You could bring Mae up for a couple of weeks, and we'd bring her back. We've got a big house right on a little lake with plenty of room."

Hannah fondly remembered summer vacations spent with her

Uncle Toby and Aunt Pauline in Macon, Georgia. Toby and Pauline's house hosted a constant frenzy of activity with four girls and three boys at various levels of maturity. When she visited, Hannah nestled into the midst of bunk-bed space and shared bathrooms. Aunt Dorothy, Mae's younger sister, lived in Pennsylvania. Though her visits to the South were infrequent, Hannah adored the sweet-natured woman with a soft, bosomy embrace and features similar to her mother's.

"Maybe in the fall," Mae said.

Right, Hannah thought. Since you won't leave Rosemont for over twenty-four hours.

Uncle Toby turned to Hannah. "We were pleased to see Lucy Goosey had found a new home."

Aunt Pauline laughed. "I have a yard goose too, but never have taken the time to make it any clothes."

"Shame on you, Pauline." Mae wagged her finger at her sister-in-law. "If I'd known your goose was buck naked, I would've sent a couple of outfits your way." She glanced down to her arthritis-gnarled fingers. "Was a time I could do fine tailoring, but not anymore. Some of the ladies at Rosemont have taken it upon themselves to take care of Lucy's wardrobe."

"Have you seen her little dress?" Aunt Dot asked Hannah.

Hannah threw a questioning look toward her mother. "The bathing suit's gone already?"

"Lucy's switched to a fetching red, white, and blue ensemble complete with a sun bonnet and matching parasol for the Fourth," Mae flipped back.

Hannah threw up her hands. "Heaven forbid that cement goose had to wear an outfit longer than a couple of days."

"I think it's plainly adorable," Dorothy said. "And it gives them something to do, there at Mae's place."

"Are we going to get to see your kids?" Pauline asked.

"Justine and Jonas are meeting us for dinner, along with Norman of course. Luckily, my son didn't have a baseball game tonight. The only way he'd miss one of them is if he was unconscious."

Toby leaned forward and slapped his knees. "I don't know about you ladies, but my stomach's touching my backbone. What say we take this discussion and have it over coffee and breakfast."

Hannah turned to her mother. "Did they get your meds together for you?"

"Lora put them in my little pill box. Now where did I put it last night, sister?"

Aunt Dot hopped up and rummaged in Mae's purse. "I could've sworn you put it in here, Mae. Where else would it be?"

For the next few minutes, they tore the room apart searching for her mother's morning medications.

Mae rested her hands on her hips, patted her pants with a curious expression, then pulled a small gilded box from her pocket. "Well, look here. I had them all along."

"I dearly love these Country Cracker Restaurants." Dorothy settled into a gingham-cushioned booth. "We don't have these up north in Pennsylvania."

"She's gotten a fair share of them this past week," Toby commented. "We've eaten out in the one close to our house most every morning since her feet hit Southern dirt."

The morning crowd swelled in number around them. Hannah watched platters of fried eggs, red-eye gravy, and biscuits pass by and wondered how much collective fat filled the restaurant.

Dorothy snapped a cotton napkin and laid it across her lap. "I take advantage of it as I can, brother of mine. I can't get decent grits unless I make them at home." She wagged her finger. "Don't you forget my barbeque before I fly home."

Pauline looked up from the brown paper menu. "We'll get takeout from Johnson's when we get back to Macon, Dot. His is the best in Georgia."

"Wish y'all could stay on a few days," Mae said.

Dorothy patted her elder sister's hand. "I'd love it too, Mae. I'm only down for a week, and I still have a few old friends to catch up with back in Macon."

The conversation turned from current events, grandchildren and great grandchildren, to reminiscing. Hannah had noticed the same trend the past few times the uncles and aunts reunited.

"Remember the time Auntie Mamie brought you, me, and Caroline those dolls?" Dot asked Mae.

"Prettiest things." The skin around Mae's blue-gray eyes crinkled when she smiled. "Hand-made down to the little pantaloons. She even painted their porcelain faces. I was named after her—Auntie Mamie. Only, Mama called me *Mae* instead of adding the *me*."

"The hands and feet were porcelain too, as I recall." Dorothy's features morphed into a sneer. "I hated my doll."

"Whatever for, Aunt Dot?"

"I was the baby, you see, so Auntie Mamie made Caroline and Mae's dolls twice the size of mine." Dorothy focused on the menu. "Guess I was envious."

"Wish I'd have kept that doll-baby," Mae said. "Don't even know what went with mine."

"I burned mine up in the oven," Dorothy said.

The white-aproned waitress appeared, took their breakfast orders, and filled coffee mugs before skittering off.

Mae slapped the table with one hand. "Lordy! I had nearly forgotten about that. Mama was mad as a wet hen and tore your little tail up."

Dorothy turned to face Hannah. "I recall opening the oven door— it was a big clunky cast iron model—and shoving that little doll inside. Pretty soon, the whole kitchen filled with smoke. Stunk to high heaven."

Toby added, "I remember you on the front steps beating the doll in the head with a hammer." The group laughed.

"Have mercy, Aunt Dot. Nowadays, they'd send you straight to a counselor because they'd worry you were a budding serial killer."

Dorothy grunted. "I don't remember any hammer, Toby." She turned to Mae. "You and Caroline would never let me play with your dolls after that."

Hannah grinned. "Gee, I wonder why." *Will this be me and my siblings in a few years?* While her aunts and mother reminisced, Hannah thought for a moment about parents and children. How Mae had been young once, with an entire life that did not include Hannah. An epiphany lurked, but she didn't allow it to develop. Maybe later when she had time. Right.

The beyond-cheerful waitress arrived with breakfast-laden platters.

"Nothing short of an act of Congress is going to keep me from having one of these." Hannah picked a plump biscuit.

Mae shoved a bowl toward her daughter. "Slather it with some of this sausage gravy. If you're going to feel guilty later, might as well have something worth the effort."

Chapter Twenty-six

Becky tied a double knot in her turquoise hip scarf. "There. Maybe it won't try to fall to my knees tonight." She shimmied a few times to check the fit.

"If you had more hips for it to hang onto, you wouldn't have issues," Suzanne said. "Reckon we'll play the zills tonight? That's my favorite thing."

Hannah took a big swill of bottled water and glanced around the Women's Club hall at the other dancers donning their costumes. "Amy said we're learning something new this class."

"Speaking of learning something new," Becky said. "You'll never bee-lieve what my husband signed up for."

Hannah and Suzanne leaned in.

Becky beamed. "Middle Eastern drumming lessons."

"Never pictured Keith as a musician." Hannah paused. "No offense, Beck."

"None taken. He's absolutely not." Becky's smile turned evil. "But he does have awesome rhythm."

Suzanne huffed. "Oh, good Lord."

Becky tilted her head to one side and gyrated, sending ripples through the scarf's bangles. "It's a fact."

"Okay. Enough!" Hannah threw up her hands in surrender. "But drumming?"

"Keith wants to accompany me. If he sticks with it, I'll buy him a dumbek for Christmas—with inlaid mother-of-pearl like the one Amy's husband played at the Hafla."

"Somehow, I don't think it would fly with Norman," Hannah said, tying on her new scarlet hip scarf. Her belly seemed a bit swollen, so she loosened the knot. No more biscuits or desserts for her for a while.

Suzanne laughed. "It'll be a hard frost in Jamaica before your brother does it either."

They took their places in the line-up.

"Never did ask—what did y'all end up doing for Father's Day?" Becky leaned over for a slow cat-like stretch.

"Cologne and chocolate cake," Suzanne said. "Hal's an easy man to please."

"Long as he has you, sis dear, he'll be happy. I sent Norman off for a day on the river with Jonas. Then we had a fish fry on Sunday afternoon to reap the rewards of their hard work. Justine made a strawberry refrigerator pie."

"I performed a *special dance* for Keith." Becky's left eyebrow flicked upward as she air-quoted. "That and a new dress shirt and pair of khaki slacks. The man would rather wear rags than set foot in a clothing store."

"You're riding this belly dancing wave till it hits the shore, aren't you hon?" Suzanne kidded.

"You bet. Hey, how'd the family cookout go yesterday?" Becky asked.

"It was like a mini-reunion. Ma-Mae really enjoyed it." Hannah looked thoughtful. "Uncle Toby and I talked."

Suzanne said, "I saw y'all over to the side in an intense conversation."

"Uncle Toby told me he understands now, why Ma-Mae's at Rosemont."

"I figured a couple of days with her, and they'd see," Suzanne said.

"From what I can gather, he and the family had serious reservations about Ma-Mae moving, though she told them it was her idea. He sees it's a good thing. She's happy and well taken-care-of. She has friends to do things with, and places to be. Before, she just sat in front of the television."

"It's really up to you, Hal, and Helen, as to how you see fit to care for your mama," Suzanne said.

"True," Hannah said. "Still, it made me feel better that he understood we weren't shoving Ma-Mae out of her house for selfish reasons."

A slow middle-eastern beat, a beledi, sounded. Amy clapped and motioned to the group. "Let's warm up!" The instructor swiveled her shoulders, then the movement flowed effortlessly down to her waist and hips.

"I wish I could work it like she does," Suzanne said.

"Tonight," Amy said, "We'll learn to wrap our veils and then, in a series of magical moves, to unwrap them from our bodies."

Becky's smile switched on her deep dimples. "Oh, goody. Like unwrapping a gift."

"Mind out of the gutter, Beck. Mind out of the gutter." Hannah thought of Norman unpeeling her like a ripe banana and her face flushed. She pushed down the racy vision and attempted to stretch and chastise herself simultaneously.

Hannah seldom experienced Monday-itis. Tuesdays proved to be her most aggravating day of the week. The last Tuesday of June started out with her carpool traveling through the kind of thunderstorm the South is famous for: jabs of lightning and sheets of water that could send a motorist hydroplaning into a ditch. By the time Hannah pulled into the parking garage, her fingers clamped around the steering wheel like eagle claws on a fresh kill.

Two conference calls followed a drawn-out interdivision meeting that accomplished next to nothing other than making the work pile up on her already crowded desk. She had just sat down to sort through two days' worth of office email when the phone rang.

"Hon?"

Her heart rate accelerated. Rarely did she and her husband phone each other during work hours. "Norman? What's wrong . . . Ma-Mae?"

"Your mother's fine, far as I know." He paused. "Don't get all upset, now."

A conversation beginning with a disclaimer: not good. "Tell me—"

"Jonas has broken his arm."

"What! How? When? Where?" She sounded a bit like her high school journalism teacher coaching the makings of an investigative piece.

"Calm down, hon. I've taken care of things. The nurse called from the teen center. Seems Jonas was horsing around and fell down a set of steps, first thing."

Hannah forced herself to release the breath she held.

"I picked him up and carried him around to the Walk-in Clinic. Simple fracture in the forearm close to the wrist—the radius, Doc said. Anyway, he has a nice navy blue cast on it for the next six weeks.

Doc doesn't think it should give him any trouble."

"Which arm?"

"Left."

"Thank goodness it wasn't his right," Hannah said. "Jonas can't even scribble with his left hand." She did a quick calculation. "He'll be out of the cast before school starts back."

"Good point."

Hannah coaxed her shoulders to relax. "So, where are my two boys now?"

"On the way to get a bite to eat. I'll take the rest of the day off. Family sick leave. I'm rarely out, so they shouldn't complain."

"Thanks, sweetie. We're swamped and two people have called in sick this morning. That's on top of the ones who are already on vacation." She hesitated. "Is he in pain?"

"Not too bad," Norman assured. "They gave him a couple of extra-strength Tylenols at the Walk-in."

She heard her son's voice in the background.

"Let me speak to him, Norman, please."

"Hi, Mom."

"Are you sure you're okay, baby boy?"

"It's just a broken arm. No big deal."

"Love you, Jonas."

"You too, Mom."

Norman spoke again, "We're stopping at Bill's for burgers."

Ah, the gobacious gut-spreader special: Bill's quarter-pound, real beef burger, loaded, slathered with mayonnaise and oozing with juice. Beside it on the platter, a towering mound of crispy seasoned home-fried potatoes. For dessert, a piece of Julie's blackberry cobbler with a double scoop of vanilla ice cream. Hannah's stomach rumbled. "Wish I was there with you."

"We'll make it a point to think of you. Hey, you want I should cook dinner?"

Grilled, no doubt. Norman lived for the thrill of cooking over an open brazier fire. He rarely touched a stove.

"I'll take you up on that, Norman Olsen. There're chicken breast fillets in the freezer. That and a salad should suffice. Remember, we're supposed to be cutting back on the night meal."

After she hung up, Hannah sat back and sipped the now-cold dregs of her third cup of coffee. Madeline, one of her coworkers, stuck her head around the cubicle divider. "Everything okay? I couldn't help over-hearing."

"My son has a broken arm," Hannah said. "But fixable."

Madeline nodded. "Life's an uphill hike sometimes."

Another thunderstorm announced its intentions with a white blaze of lightning, followed by a deafening boom. The overhead lights flickered twice before the room fell into darkness.

"Ain't it though," Hannah replied to the dim outline of her co-worker. "Uphill and I'm wearing high-heeled sandals."

"Doesn't that dang bird just beat all?" Maxine commented from her seat next to the front desk.

Hannah signed the Rosemont visitor's log. "I'd like to be half that prepared for a good time."

Someone had added a few finishing touches to Lucy Goosey's Fourth of July ensemble. A small red and white checkered cloth-lined picnic basket stood beside her, packed with bottled water and a sack of mixed bird seed. A goose-sized lounge chair fashioned from plastic straws and striped material, folded for easy transport, leaned next to a small cardboard box painted to resemble a cooler.

"How's your belly dancing class coming?" Beth asked.

"Loads of fun. Don't even think about the fact that it's exercise."

"You going to paste a jewel in your navel and come do a dance for us?" Maxine asked.

Hannah laughed. "Don't know if you'll catch me baring my middle any time soon, Miz Maxine."

"We're an appreciative audience. Half of us can't see the broad side of a barn and the other half are deaf as a stick." Maxine flashed a dimpled smile. "Bet you're a sight."

"That's a good way to put it."

Beth said, "Your mother and Miz Harrison are excited about the outing today."

"They surely are," Maxine confirmed. "It's all they could talk about over breakfast. I'm proud to see your mama has taken her under her wing. Josephine's having a hard time adjusting."

Hannah asked, "Hasn't she been here the same amount of time as Ma-Mae?"

Beth nodded. "Yes."

"That son of hers hardly ever visits." Maxine huffed. "He's too busy with work to pay his mother much mind. The other son lives clean out on the west coast. She might as well not have any kids, the attention they pay her."

"Your mother said she's adopted Miz Harrison," Beth added. "It's very sweet. You don't see one without the other."

Maxine stood slowly and leaned on her walker for support. "Your mama gets Josephine out and marches her around the building most every day, weather permitting."

Mae always took in strays: people or animals. Hannah recalled a steady stream of orphans: baby squirrels, rabbits, dogs, cats, snakes, turtles, and once, a nanny goat. Several times, the family had shared the cramped house on Satsuma Road with down-on-their-luck drifters. Not once had Mae's kindness been repaid with hate.

Beth motioned toward the elevators. "You might check up in Miz Harrison's room, Hannah. Your mother was helping her get ready. Miz Josephine moves pretty slowly in the mornings."

"Don't we all?" Maxine turned and pushed her walker toward one of the long halls.

"She's in room . . . ?"

"Two-fifty-four," Beth answered without hesitation. "Take a left from the elevator and then around the corner. About half-way down, on the right."

"Thanks." Hannah caught up with Maxine before calling for the elevator. "I'll see what I can work out with the dancing as soon as we learn enough to piece a routine together."

"You do that. We'll even make Lucy a belly-dancing costume."

Two voices answered in unison when she knocked on the magnolia-decorated door on the second floor. Hannah entered to find Josephine Harrison seated on a small wooden chair with Mae hovering behind her, comb in hand.

"Hi, sugar! Didn't know your old mama could fashion hair, did you?" Mae winked.

"Nothing you do surprises me, Ma-Mae."

Hannah glanced around the room. Unlike her mother's, Josephine's space showed little decoration. Except for stacks of books, the room looked utilitarian and sparse.

"Josie has the prettiest hair. It's like spun silver. She gets this one flat place in the back where she wallows around on the pillow."

"Really, Mae." Josephine dabbed dots of cologne on her wrists. "You make me sound like some old hog. I don't wallow!"

"Well, missy, if you don't wallow, how you reckon your hair sticks out like a scared porcupine every morning?"

Hannah pushed aside a stack of novels and sat on the edge of Josephine's single bed. "Looks like you two are almost ready to go."

Josephine nodded. "It's taken us a couple of hours and more than a few curse words, but we're about as ready as two old women can get."

Her mother asked, "Where's your sister?"

"Helen's meeting us in Havana."

"How'll she ever find us? We're bound to be wandering around in the antique stores." Mae shellacked Josephine's hair with spray.

"Havana's not that big, Ma-Mae. I'll have my cell phone on."

Josephine stood slowly, then balanced on the back of the chair. "Let me use the restroom before we go."

"She's got another of her kidney infections," Mae said after her friend closed the bathroom door. "I try to get her to drink more water, but that woman is used to going like a house afire once she gets started. By midday, she's worn herself slap out. She's got to learn to pace herself. At our age, life's more a marathon than a sprint."

Mae's metaphors were so on target.

"God provided me a lesson with her, He did." Mae motioned toward the bathroom.

"How's that?"

"When I first met Josie, I thought she was plain cathead crazy. Judged her wrong. She wasn't oriented to life here at the Mont."

Mae recapped the hairspray and stored it in a small cabinet by the closet. "Smart as a whip, that woman. Keeps busy on her computer, and she's even writing a book. She wants to start up a memoir-writing class. I think that's a fine idea, don't you?"

"I'd love it if you recorded some of your memories. Helen and

Hal would too."

Mae checked her lipstick in the mirror. "Reckon it's best I write them down before I don't have good sense."

Josephine stepped from the bathroom. "Is there room to take my walker, Hannah? I can use a cane, if need be. But I can move much faster and easier with my walker."

"Hannah's got one of those suvs," Mae told Josephine.

Her mother refused to call the vehicle by its initials—SUV—preferring to pronounce the acronym as a word. Hannah had heard the term so often, it seemed normal.

Chapter Twenty-seven

The main street in Havana streamed with cars and transport trucks making their way north toward the Alabama line. Once Hannah turned onto a side street, the traffic disappeared.

"Use the handicapped permit, sugar, so Josie won't have to walk too far." Mae pointed to a vacant space in front of the Art Gallery.

"Any place special you ladies want to visit?" Hannah asked as she retrieved Josephine's walker from the rear compartment.

"I think Josie might like the Lazy River General Store," Mae said.

"My uncle owned a hardware store down near Crystal River when I was a little girl, but it was more like a general store." Josephine smiled behind her dark sunglasses. "Folks came by as much to visit as they did to buy. The men would gather at the counter and talk and talk."

"Hardware stores are to men what beauty parlors are to women," Mae commented. "You could spend a couple of hours at the Triple C and learn anything about anybody."

"Not that most of it would be accurate." Hannah walked ahead a few paces and held open the country store's door.

"Speculation is the gravy of society," Mae said.

Rena waved from behind the wooden counter. Though the shop's proprietor was close to Hannah in age, she appeared years younger. Even when Rena's features relaxed, the corners of her lips turned slightly upward, the kind of demeanor her mother labeled approachable.

"Look, Mae! Cherry licorice!" Josephine pointed to a glass jar filled with long braided ropes of the deep red chewy candy. "I haven't had that in years."

"I'm addicted to it," Rena said. "If I don't watch myself, I'll eat up the inventory."

When the cell phone in Hannah's purse trilled, she stepped outside to get a better signal and a little privacy.

"Sister?" Helen asked.

"Where are you?"

"Just now passing Quincy," Helen said. "Got a late start. What kind of mood is Ma-Mae in today? She was melancholy when I talked to her last night."

A semi rumbled by and Hannah waited for a moment to answer. "You know how she gets in July. That's one of the reasons I wanted to get her out today."

"I'll find you. Gotta hang up and drive. These country roads are narrow as the dickens."

Two hours later, after taking in a watercolor exhibit at the Art Gallery and wandering through shops of assorted antiques, Helen, Hannah and the two seniors stopped for lunch at the Azalea Café.

"What did you like best, Miz Josie?" Helen asked.

"The old books especially, but I liked it all. Funny, the things I remember from childhood are now antique collectables."

Mae reached over and patted her friend's hand. "We're antiques too, gal. They just can't figure a way to sit us on a shelf."

Hannah sat back and enjoyed the women's easy camaraderie. She noted the similarities between Helen and Ma-Mae: how they both listened intently; the way they made the speaker feel like she marked the center of the world; the softness around their mouths and eyes that hinted at depths of empathy.

" . . . and Hannah, didn't you tell me—" Mae stopped. "You with us, sugar?" Then to Josephine, "When Hannah's got that goofy look on her face, she's gone off to somewhere else. Probably gets that from me. I used to daydream a lot when I was her age."

The front doorbell chimed. Odd. Most visitors to the Olsen home came to the carport door. Other than a polite knock, callers didn't bother to formally announce themselves. That was reserved for postal workers, pushy salespeople, and the occasional Jehovah's Witness. Since none of those would call on a Sunday, Hannah was hard-pressed to guess at the identity of person on the finger-end of the bell.

When Hannah opened the door, Missy Rodgers squinted and shaded her eyes from the glare of the summer sun. "This isn't a bad time, is it?"

Oh great. The one person in the entire universe I'd rather not see at this moment. Hannah glanced down at her outfit: the rattiest, most-faded shorts in her wardrobe, a yellowed-with-wear T-shirt. Add to that: no makeup and left-over-from-church hair. "Why, no! Come on in."

Missy brushed by her, a cloud of floral perfume in her wake. "I just popped these blonde brownies from the oven. Thought your family might enjoy a few." She carried a lacquered white wicker basket, lined with a pastel paisley-printed napkin, topped with a perfect pink bow. The aroma of hot sugar and spices lifted into the air.

"How thoughtful of you, Missy. Norman and the kids aren't here—they rode over to Quincy to Wal-Mart—but I'll make sure to save them a bite." She tabbed mentally through the refrigerator contents. "Can I offer you a glass of tea? Or I have soda, and . . . maybe some lemonade."

"Tea would be wonderful." Missy dabbed the glistening perspiration from her upper lip. "Silly me, I walked over here. I don't know what I was thinking, in this heat."

Not to mention, the fact that Missy wore a dress, pumps and pantyhose. You could torture political prisoners with an outfit like that, given the humidity and ninety-plus temperature.

"Please, have a seat. I'll get you a tall glass with plenty of ice."

Hannah dialed the ceiling fan up a notch on her way to the kitchen. The last thing she needed was Missy Rodgers passing out in her living room.

"I can't believe anyone bakes this time of year," Hannah commented as she handed a frosted glass to her guest. "If it can't be warmed in the microwave or cooked on the grill outside, we don't eat it."

"I don't know what came over me this morning. I got up in a baking mood. I've already cooked three batches of cookies, a cake, bread, and these brownies." Missy took a long drink of tea.

"It was nice of you to think of us." Hannah stretched to find some common ground for conversation. Other than their daughters' friendship, what did they share?

"Actually, I came to apologize." Missy's blue-eyed gaze rested on her.

"Apologize? For what?"

Missy sat the tea glass on a coaster and folded her hands primly in her lap. "I was somewhat abrupt with you when you last visited my home. I didn't want you to think unkindly of me."

"Not at all," Hannah said. "Suppose Justine stays over there with Brittany so much, I figured I could barge in without proper warning. The blame, if any, is on me."

"Oh, but you're always welcome." Missy hesitated. "I don't have many callers, other than the charity committee members."

Was the Queen of Southern Etiquette's veneer showing a hairline crack? With her money and societal position, it was hard to imagine Missy Rodgers lacking for company. "You always seem so . . . busy."

Missy fidgeted with one of her diamond and emerald rings. "I keep myself that way on purpose. It fills the time. Sometimes, being a single parent . . . " Her gaze dropped to her lap.

"It must have been difficult, not having your husband to lean on. I don't know, some days, how I would handle things without Norman."

"Brittany's an absolute angel; she's always been an easy child. Well, there was that one river-party incident. But she is a teenager. I guess I should expect a bit of foolishness. None of us were innocent at that age." She offered a weak smile.

"My kids are pretty good, too. I don't expect perfection. Heaven knows, Norman and I aren't perfect. You do your best."

"Your husband seems to be such a nice, family man."

Hannah nodded. "He is. I'm fortunate. I fuss about his golf and the way he's sometimes a bit of a slob—leaving his shoes and clothes cast off around the house. And he leaves the toothpaste lid off, most of the time. Little things, but all in all, I can't complain."

Missy's eyes watered slightly. "My Andrew was a bit . . . demanding."

Hannah searched her memory for any hint of the person Andrew Rodgers had been. Other than seeing him at a few school functions, she had little recollection of the man. Clean cut, dark hair, nicely dressed. She could barely recall his features.

"Andrew was a good provider. He left Brittany and me . . . " Her voice faltered. "To be honest, Hannah, I don't miss him at all."

This was turning out to be the most interesting Sunday afternoon, full of true confessions from Chattahoochee's eminent ice queen. Hannah had no idea why she'd been singled out to supply the counselor's couch. "I suppose it's true, what they say about time healing all wounds."

"He controlled everything we did." Missy's expression hardened. "Everything. Down to how the towels were hung in the bathrooms. He didn't allow Brittany to ever look like she had any soil on her clothing. She was the perfect little girl, always trying so very hard to please her daddy."

Heavy stuff. What exactly could she say? "I take it, you don't mind being—"

"— alone?" Missy supplied the word. "I have my daughter. And my charity work." She shook her head. "I don't know if I ever want to be involved *that* way again."

Hannah fiddled with a hangnail. The clock ticked.

"Gosh, listen to me. I didn't intend to come over here and rattle on so." Missy reached over and touched Hannah's hand. "Thank you for being concerned enough about Brittany to come by. She's fine, really. Your Justine is such a good friend to her. If only . . . "

Hannah leaned forward.

Missy's expression grew wistful. "We should all be so fortunate to have one true friend."

Chapter Twenty-eight

The morning of the Fourth of July left no doubt in Hannah's mind that summer had settled in with hellish gusto. By midday, heat waves shimmered from every horizontal surface. The Olsens' backyard bloomed with holes excavated in Snooker's earthen attempts to stay cool. Slug refused to step outdoors for any reason, content to view the birdfeeders from a window ledge. People and animals alike moved like chilled syrup. To do otherwise would've been a down payment on disaster.

Mae stepped from Hal and Suzanne's back door and propped her hands on her ample hips. "This pool sure is a welcome sight!" She motioned to her hips. "You should've seen me trying to wriggle into this bathing costume. Feel like I've poked myself into a sausage casing. I really have to stop eating that good food at the Mont."

"You say that every time something is the least bit tight." Hannah helped steady her mother as she ambled toward the pool steps.

Suzanne floated in the pool's shallow end on a water-lounger. "Today isn't the day to start up a diet. We've got tons of food. And you can't leave it behind for Hal and me."

The pool-side picnic was Southern-mandated for the Independence celebration. The in-ground pool sparkled next to a long covered porch. Hal's pride, a stainless steel gas grill, stood ready for action.

Hal dozed on a float in the deep end, too tempting to his baby sister. She stripped off her bathing suit cover-up and took a few steps back to get a running start.

"Cow-a-bunga!" The cannonball Hannah executed sent sprays high into the air and the wake scuttled her brother.

Hal's head popped up from the water's surface. "Of course you know this means WAR?!"

Hannah giggled like a teenager. "Ya think?"

A slam-dunk game of cat and mouse ensued. Suzanne slipped from her floating lounger and headed for the steps. "I'm not going to get caught up in all this business. I just colored my hair."

"You kids, calm down now!" Mae called out.

Hannah and Hal dunked each other one last time before obeying their matriarch's orders.

Justine lifted her head from the pillowed lounge and peered at her mother and uncle from beneath a straw visor. "Nice to hear someone else get fussed at, for a change."

Jonas, lying on the chaise near hers, chuckled.

"When you reckon Helen and Charlie will be here?" Mae slipped inch by inch into the cool water, alternately grimacing and hissing.

"Any time now," Suzanne said. "She was taking the beans from the oven when she called, and then they were on the way."

"And Michael Jack? He bringing Mili with him?" Mae asked.

"Far as I know." Suzanne wrapped in a beach towel. "I'm going to bring out some drinks. Anyone want anything special?"

Hannah pointed to a large red cooler. "Why don't you put yours with ours. That way, you don't have to go in and out."

In the shallow end, Mae huffed and puffed.

"Ma-Mae, you act like getting wet is about to kill you," Hannah said.

"I can't go barreling in like you and Hal do. It might stop my heart," Mae said. "You do it your way and I'll do it mine, thank you very much."

Hal used a beach towel to dry off. "I'm going to pick up Suzanne's mother."

"Tell Ruthie to bring her bathing suit," Mae said.

"I doubt she'll get in the water, Ma-Mae. Ruthie's only gotten in this pool twice in all the years Suzanne's had it."

Helen and Charlie stepped through one of the double gates. "Yoo-hoo! We're here!"

"Helen, you'd be late for your own funeral." Mae tsk-ed.

"I was way-ting on my beans," Helen fired back. "You know full well, I like to be early."

Charlie cradled a watermelon. "Lady was selling these beside the road for two dollars apiece. Said they were real sweet."

Suzanne stepped from the house, her arms full of soda cans. "Hey, y'all. I'll hug when I get my arms free." Michael Jack and Mili arrived and Suzanne directed everyone to drinks and places to store the casseroles and chilled food.

"Too bad your younguns can't join us, Suzanne," Mae said.

"They're at their in-laws." Suzanne ushered Mili and Helen inside.

Mae nodded. "Reckon it gets that-a-way, after a fashion. Rare to get everyone in one place at a time."

A few minutes went by before Hal returned with Suzanne's elderly mother. He helped Ruthie into a chair, provided a cool drink, and jumped into the pool.

Mae pointed toward the water lounge. "Reckon I could ride that thing?"

"Don't see why not." Hannah pulled the float toward her mother.

"Hold 'er steady, daughter." Mae backed up.

Each time the duo came close to taming the wild-stallion pool lounge, it spit them out in a whirlpool of thrashing arms and legs.

"It's like trying to ride a rotten banana peel!" Mae said between attempts. "Hal, help your sister hold this doggone thing still."

With Hal on one side and Hannah on the other, they finally managed to plop their elderly mother squarely into the middle. Mae's smile: triumphant. "There's nothing my kids can't do if they put their minds to it," she proclaimed.

Helen stepped from the back door and propped her hands on her hips, laughing. "Y'all just beat all I've ever seen."

"Oh I don't know, Helen." Hal lurched from the pool and grabbed his older sister. "I think you in the drink would beat even us."

"Don't you dare, Hal Mathers! I swannee!"

"Hold your breath, Sister," Hal warned.

"Oh, shoot!" Helen grabbed her nose with one hand and the two plummeted into the water. Seconds later, their heads bobbed up.

"You've always been such a little shit." Helen fought the laughter threatening her bruised attitude.

Mae splashed water in her eldest daughter's direction. "Mind your potty-mouth."

"Are we going to act like that when we get old?" Justine asked.

Jonas plucked the MP3 player's earphones from his ears. "You say something?"

"Never freakin' mind." Justine turned over to tan her back.

"Hey, I got a new redneck thing for y'all," Charlie called out. "You might be a redneck if—" One of the family's favorite games: spotting distinctive Southern behaviors, based on comedian Jeff Foxworthy's claim to fame. "—if you keep a spoon stored in your mayonnaise jar." Charlie delivered the punch line with a wide grin. "I found one in ours this morning."

Hannah closed her eyes, her body bouncing with laughter. In that moment—hearing the distinctive chortles from each of them—the collected tension from being a mother, wife, and caretaker faded and love for her family took over, a white-hot emotion so intense it sent a prickle through the fine blonde hairs on her forearms.

A couple of hours later, Suzanne sat the chilled watermelon in the middle of a patio table. Mili followed with a butcher knife, a handful of napkins, forks and a box of salt.

"You best go wake up those two sleeping beauties," Suzanne told Hal. "Especially your mama. If she sleeps through the melon, she'll be mad as a mule chewing bumblebees."

Hannah laughed. Where did her sister-in-law come up with her expressions?

Following the bountiful meal of baked ham, barbequed pork ribs, potato salad, coleslaw, deviled eggs, baked beans and corn on the cob, the family matriarchs had retired inside to air-conditioned bedrooms. The rest of the clan had alternately swam and lolled around the pool, too full to do much else.

As soon as Mae and Ruthie joined the group, the age-old family dispute started: Watermelon—salt versus no salt.

Helen: "Yuck! I can't abide salt on watermelon."

Norman: "You don't have to shake any on your slice, Helen dear. Some of us think it's better that way."

Charlie: "I like it with salt. Brings out the sweetness."

Hannah: "That never made a dab of sense. Salt on something sweet to make it sweeter?"

Michael Jack: "I'm with you guys. Pour the salt to it."

Mae: "Salt's for homegrown tomatoes and fried eggs, not watermelon."

Ruthie: "My blood pressure won't allow for salt."

Mili: "Must be a guy thing. I never put salt on melon."

Does everyone beat a subject to death quite like my family? Hannah wondered. The same debate raged every time someone showed up for a summer function with a ripe melon.

Mae glanced up. "Hey, don't you kids want some? It's going fast!"

Justine shook her head, but Jonas jumped up, grabbed a huge salted slice and returned to his lounge.

"First time I've seen that girl without a cell phone glued to one ear," Helen said.

Hannah flicked flat black seeds from her slice with the tip of a knife. "She doesn't bother turning it on when she and Brittany are quarreling." Hannah glanced over toward Justine. "Jus had planned on watching the pageant. This morning at breakfast, she asked to come over here with us instead."

"It'll pass," Mae said. Pink watermelon juice glistened on her lips. "Younguns her age can fight like starved dogs over a pot roast one minute and swear undying faith the next."

Michael Jack asked, "Y'all still plan on going down to the lake, right?"

"Of course." Hannah rested one hand on Norman's knee. "One of our first dates was to the Lake Seminole fireworks."

Norman winked. "That night was lit up in more ways than one."

"I'll be, Norman." Suzanne's eyes shone with fun. "Who ever took you for such a romantic?"

You don't know the half of it, Hannah thought. Lately, she craved Norman almost as much as peanut butter.

HELEN'S MIXED-UP BAKED BEANS

3 slices bacon, cut into bite size pieces
1 medium onion, diced
1/2 lb lean ground beef
1 tablespoon Worcestershire sauce
1/2 cup dark brown sugar
3/4 cup ketchup
1 (16 ounce) can kidney beans, rinsed and drained
1 (16 ounce) can lima beans, rinsed and drained
1 (16 ounce) can pork and beans (okay to use the vegetarian kind)
Sauté bacon, onion, and ground beef. Drain off grease and add rest of
ingredients. Pour into casserole dish (a lasagna pan works well). Bake
at 350° for 1 hour, uncovered.

Chapter Twenty-nine

Hannah followed Hal's official Gadsden County Sheriff's Office truck in the family motorcade. He motioned to a spot reserved for handicapped access, perfect for the two elderly women. Jonas hopped from the Olsens' SUV as soon as it pulled to a stop.

"Son?" Hannah crooked her finger. "C'mere."

Jonas turned in mid-stride.

"I don't mind you hanging around with your friends, but I need you to promise me something. Do not, under any circumstances, leave the immediate area unless you check first with either your father or me. Clear?" Hannah used her stern-mom face.

"Yes 'um."

"When the fireworks are over, meet us right here. Do not make us have to come hunting for you in this crowd. Got it?"

Jonas's head bobbed, his eyes searching the gathering.

Hannah could recall a time when parents didn't have to worry about letting their children run wild, but meanness and crime had seeped into even the remote corners of the South. Hannah gave him a nod. "Okay, then."

She would've kissed him on the cheek, but heaven forbid she show that type of affection in public. People might see! Hannah longed for the cuddly little ragamuffin who had always reached up for hugs and sugar-smacks.

Justine said, "I'm going to find out how the pageant went. 'kay?"

"Same goes for you. Be back here before it's time to pack up and leave."

Twilight shadows cast by the light of a full moon cloaked the expectant crowd gathered on the banks of Lake Seminole. A paved path off the main road led to the east bank landing, where a team of pyrotechnicians readied the staging area. Next to the lake, food and drink vendors blended with a mixture of people from three surrounding Florida counties and parts of southern Georgia.

"There's a perfect spot right there, Norman." Mae pointed. "Ruthie won't have so far to walk afterwards."

Norman popped the hatch on the SUV to unload the chairs. The family had just settled in for the show when Justine appeared, her face flushed.

"Something awful has happened!" She gasped for air. "Brittany . . ."

Hannah stood. "Slow down. Breathe!"

Justine leaned over and put her hands on her knees, panting as if she had completed a marathon.

". . . passed out during her talent presentation . . . took her off in an ambulance."

"Where'd they take her?" Hannah asked.

Justine wiped sweat from her face and shook her head.

"Where's her mother?"

"Dunno. With her, I guess. She was supposed to be down here."

"I can find out," Hal volunteered before jogging into the crowd.

Justine cried. "Oh, Mom. I was so mean to her. What if . . . "

Hannah wrapped one arm around her daughter's shoulders. "Let's not jump to any terrible conclusions."

Hal appeared. "She's been taken over to Tallahassee General. Fellow I talked to said heat stroke, maybe. Her mom followed the ambulance over."

Justine wrung her hands. "Can I go to her? I can drive if—"

"Not at night, and on a holiday, you're not," Norman said. "Too many drunks and fools on the highways."

"I'll go with you." Hannah turned to her husband. "Can you get Ma-Mae and Jonas on home after the fireworks?"

"Sure."

"Good. Thanks. I'll drive Justine over to TGH."

"You sure, hon?" Norman asked.

"Missy's all alone, Norman."

"Be careful." Norman kissed his wife. "Keep your cell phone on. Call me as soon as you have any news."

"Mom. Where are you going?" Justine asked when Hannah raced through Chattahoochee and turned down Bonita Street instead of heading to the Interstate.

"You have a key to Brittany's, don't you?"

Justine's blonde brows knit together. "I know where she hides the spare. Why?"

"Because we're going to stop by and pack up a few things for them."

"Mom, no! We have to get to Tallahassee right away!"

Hannah parked the SUV in the Rodgers's driveway. "This will only take five minutes, tops. Trust me, Jus. If they admit Brit, which is very likely, her mom will stay with her tonight. Neither have any clothes or toiletries with them. I've been through this scenario with your Grand-Mae more times than I want to count."

"If you think—"

"I do think. Now, go into Brittany's room, find a bag, and pack up undies, a couple of nightshirts, socks, maybe a pair of jeans and a T-shirt. Then grab what she'll need from the bathroom: shampoo, deodorant, toothpaste, brush and comb—those sort of things. I'll take care of Missy's bag."

"Won't they get kind of pissed at us for going through their stuff?" Justine asked as she reached beneath one of the pottery planters for the front door key. "I mean, Brit's still mad with me, and well . . . you and Mrs. Rodgers aren't exactly friends."

"We can deal with that later, honey." Hannah pushed through the ornate wooden front door. "They can both get glad in the same panties they got mad in."

Hannah pursed her lips when she saw the perfection of Missy Rodgers's private space. The underwear drawer looked like a store display with small wooden dividers between the rows of folded bras and panties. The other drawers and master bathroom mirrored the same careful organization. She was unprepared for what lay behind the bi-fold closet doors.

"Jeez-o-pete!" Hannah let out a long whistle.

A category 5 hurricane would have left a neater aftermath. It was like finally making it to the Garden of Eden and finding weeds a mile high. Hannah's mouth dropped open and stayed in that position until the initial shock waned.

Hangers crammed the double rods. Wrinkled clothes hung haphazardly from bent wire and clear plastic department-store hangers. Soiled clothing crowded the floor, allowing a path barely wide enough to gain entrance. At least sixty pairs of shoes lay in heaps underneath the suspended rods, many missing mates. The closet made Hannah feel closer to Missy than all the well-meant home-baked muffins and polite conversation in the South.

"Bless you, Missy Rodgers. You are human, after all."

"Were you and Brit disagreeing about her eating issues again?"

The dim glow of the interior dash lights illuminated Justine's anxious features. On the Interstate, holiday traffic flowed in thick strings. Justine nodded and sniffed.

"Want to talk about it?"

"It got real ugly, Mom. It all started because Brit wanted to bleach her teeth for the pageant. God only knows why. They practically glow in the dark now."

Hannah pulled a tissue from the console box and handed it to her daughter.

"After that last time, I had decided not to get involved with it, at all. Brit was barely speaking to me as it was." Justine turned to face her. "You should've seen her in the bathing suit she bought for the competition. Her bones were sticking out all over. It's like . . . she's a skeleton!" Justine huffed. "She believes she's fat. Can you imagine?"

"From what I've read, anorexia goes hand in hand with a poor self image. You were saying—something about her teeth?"

"Oh yeah. So she went to Dr. Payne's office uptown to see about the bleaching. She was going to get started before the contest. The dentist told her the enamel on her teeth was all screwed up. He started asking her all these questions, then he called Mrs. Rodgers after the appointment."

Hannah felt a twinge of guilt about her brief conversation with Missy and Brittany's dentist. Obviously, he had been listening. "How did you figure into this whole affair?"

"I was over there when her mom came home and confronted her." Justine's voice trembled. "Brit made up this stupid story about how it was some toothpaste she was using and how Dr. Payne was full of crap."

Hannah pursed her lips. "Missy, of course, believed her daughter."

"Not totally. She wanted to, I could tell. But it was such a bold-faced lie!" Justine wiped her eyes and blew her nose. "I couldn't take it anymore. I told Mrs. Rodgers everything. How Brit had been eating then throwing up for months."

"Brittany was upset."

"You could say that. She screamed at me. It was awful. Told me to get out and never come back. Like, as in e-ver!"

Hannah reached over and rested a hand on Justine's thin shoulder.

"Brittany will never forgive me. And now . . . " Justine dissolved once more into tears.

"And now, you and I will do our best to support them in any way they will allow."

The waiting area at the Tallahassee General Hospital ER teemed with people. Hannah figured the holiday magnified the numbers, adding in a mix of fireworks injuries and misfortune brought on by too much free time and not enough good sense. Hannah and Justine waited in line at the reception desk.

"Let me do the talking," Hannah said in a low voice. "With all those new privacy rules, I might have to tell a little white lie to find out anything."

"Justified deception," Justine said. "How come I can't get away with that?"

"Ground me later."

"May I help you?" the nurse asked.

"Please. They brought my niece in earlier. Brittany Rodgers. Is she still in the ER, can you tell me?"

The nurse tapped on a computer keypad. "She's in room six."

"May I go back?"

The nurse glanced from Hannah to Justine, then handed over a visitor's pass. "If there are more than two of you with your niece, one of you must wait here. We have to leave room for the staff to operate."

"My sister's with her. I'll check in, see if she needs a break. I promise, one of us will come right back out."

The nurse hit the lock release and Hannah and Justine walked quickly down a long hallway leading to the treatment rooms.

"This is a lot bigger than before," Justine said.

"Oh, that's right. You weren't over here last time we brought your Grand-Mae over." She motioned ahead. "There's room six."

When they entered, Missy glanced up. Missy's eyes were red-rimmed and her usually perfect hair, disheveled. On the gurney, Brittany slept, a spidery network of wires attached to her arms and chest. Hannah gasped involuntarily. Justine's best friend's skin appeared ashen, her withered body barely making a ripple in the stiff white sheets.

"Hannah. Justine . . . " Missy's voice sounded ragged with emotion.

Hannah crossed the small room and hugged her, while Justine stepped toward the bed and gently grasped Brittany's hand.

"We came right over as soon as we heard," Hannah handed Missy a soft cloth hankie from her purse. Ma-Mae would have been proud.

"I'm so glad you're here. You don't know . . . "

"The doctors— what do they say?" Hannah kept her voice calm.

Missy's weary eyes watered. "Can we talk outside?" She glanced toward her daughter.

"Justine, will you stay with Brittany a few minutes?" Hannah asked.

"If you need me. If they come to move her . . . " Missy's hands smoothed one corner of the sheet, flitting like dying moths.

"I'll text Mom's cell. Don't worry, Mrs. Rodgers." Justine pulled up a plastic-backed chair and settled in by the bedside.

Hannah searched the busy waiting area and motioned to a quiet corner near a parlor palm. A TV monitor tuned to CNN yammered on about a tropical wave, churning off the coast of Africa. "Go sit down. I'll get us both a cup of coffee." Hannah paused in front of the monitor. If this one found its way into the Gulf of Mexico . . . She stopped herself from speculating and found the coffee vending machine.

When she returned with two Styrofoam cups of coffee, Missy offered a weak smile. "I can't imagine why you came, Hannah. Neither you nor Justine have had the kindest treatment from us lately."

"Sometimes people do things that are out of character, Missy. We wouldn't be worth anything if we couldn't overlook and forgive."

Missy picked at the cup clutched in her hands. Miniature dots of the plastic foam stuck to her fingers. "I still can't believe all of this."

"Do they know what happened?"

"Heat, combined with dehydration and . . . malnutrition." Missy's hands shook as she took a sip of the steaming black coffee. "You tried to tell me. So did Justine—"

"As a parent, it's hard to see. We're all blind when it's someone close to us."

Fresh tears popped into the corners of Missy's eyes. "She was starving herself to death. Killing herself, one little bit at a time. And I flatly denied it." She squeezed her eyes shut. "God, what kind of a mother am I, to stand by and watch my child wither away in front of my eyes?"

Hannah rubbed Missy's shoulder. "I've seen how you dote on Brittany. It would be clear to anyone what she means to you." She hesitated, reaching for the words. "What's important now is getting her the help she needs."

"The ER physician mentioned something about programs for people with Brittany's disorder. He said someone from the counseling department would come by when she's out of immediate danger." Her voice grew strong with resolve. "She will get better."

"Yes she will."

"They're admitting her into intensive care, probably for a couple of days. Her heart—" Missy took a deep breath and exhaled slowly. "—her heart is very weak."

"She's young. She'll pull through."

Missy's blue eyes sought hers. "I have to believe that."

They sat for a few moments. The drama of other people's interrupted lives flowed around them.

"Justine and I stopped by your house and packed some things for both of you."

"Oh."

"It was presumptuous of us," Hannah said. "But I knew you'd be staying over here until she's better."

Missy leaned over and hugged her hard. "You truly are a friend, Hannah."

"If anyone asks, I'm your sister." Hannah held up her index finger and thumb. "A teensy fib to get me into the back."

"Since I've never had one and always wanted one, it's perfectly okay by me." The corners of her lips twitched upward. "I would consider it an honor." A horrified expression washed across Missy's petite features. "Oh . . . no. "

"What?"

"You saw my closet." Missy's gaze darted around the waiting area as if she expected a news team to materialize.

"We'll consider it a family secret."

Chapter Thirty

Hannah watched the latest report on the Weather Channel. The fourth named hurricane of the season bowled a path into the Gulf of Mexico and turned north. Not good for the Florida Panhandle. With Norman and Jonas securing the Olsens' house, Justine and Hannah turned their attention to the Rodgers's home, shifting plants beneath the porch and furniture to the front parlor. At Rosemont, Lucy Goosey donned a red rain slicker and matching bonnet. At her webbed feet sat a bag packed with a miniature flashlight, water, and AAA batteries. An airline ticket to Toronto protruded from her jacket pocket; the goose wasn't taking any chances. She was much too highfaluting to flap her cement wings and flee under her own power.

"Y'all ready for the storm?" Beth asked when Hannah entered the lobby.

"As ready as we can get. Norman bought a generator last year after Ivan left us without power. It's not that we can't get along without electricity, but I'd hate to lose a freezer full of meat and vegetables. Not to mention all the fish Norman and Jonas have frozen."

"We have generators ready too." Beth pointed to a rolling suitcase beside her chair. "I'll be right here. We stay fully-staffed during hurricanes."

Hannah glanced around. "This place is a fortress."

"A couple of years ago, we had evacuees from an assisted living facility in Panama City here. They camped out in our dining room on cots."

Hannah imagined the chaos. "Nice of you to take them in."

"Judging from the news reports, you won't be able to find a motel room for miles."

"Our house is brick," Hannah said. "As long as the roof survives, we're good. This far from the coast, it's tornadoes I worry about most."

Beth nodded. "My father lost one of his barns that way. Picked it up and slammed it down a few miles off. They found things hanging from the trees afterwards."

Hannah signed in and turned toward the hallway. Mae was in a high rolling boil when Hannah entered her room. "Ma-Mae? Your door wasn't locked."

A mountain of clothing and an opened suitcase littered Mae's bed. "Reckon I forgot to turn the latch. I'm in a rush, I tell you, an absolute rush!"

Hannah deposited her purse on the rocker and stood with her hands on her hips, watching her mother shuffle aimlessly from one point to another. "What are you trying to do?"

Mae paused long enough to fire her daughter a dagger-look. "Pack an evacuation bag!"

"Um . . . why?"

"They told us to pack one—just in case—with a change of clothes, toiletries, and some money." She dug in the bedside table's drawer. "And a flashlight."

"I don't think you'll be going anywhere but here, Ma-Mae."

"If that storm heads in our direction, Lord only knows where I'll end up."

"Want to come to our house?"

Mae shot Hannah an incredulous look. "Why would I do that?"

"I don't know . . . you're worried, and you could be with us?"

Mae dismissed the idea with a swipe of one hand. "The nurses have all my medicines, and I'll be with my friends, and besides you hardly cook anymore."

"Thanks for the vote of confidence."

Mae stepped over and rested a hand on Hannah's shoulder. "Don't get all sullied up. It's nothing personal against you and Norman. But I'd rather take my chances with the Rosemont crew."

"Maybe you could throw us a line if you see us floating by."

"You're funny with your ways sometimes, child." She kissed Hannah on the cheek. "If you want to help me, get this blasted bag packed. I can't think straight long enough to decide what to take."

"I can do that."

"Good. I don't want to miss the '50s party up in the sunroom at three. Then that singing fellow, Randy, is coming to play for us at four. He bangs on a guitar and bellows this one song about a purple cow that tears me up every single time."

A row of flashlights with new batteries lined the kitchen counter. Both bathtubs and a large plastic jug held water.

Hannah clapped. "Okay, troops! Let's review our battle plan one more time." She pointed to Jonas.

"Get Snooker on the leash and rendezvous in the hallway," he said.

"Check! You sure you can perform your designated duties with the use of one arm?"

Jonas nodded emphatically.

"And Justine?"

"Mom, we've been over this twice already. Aren't you being a little, like, anal?"

"Humor me, will you?"

Justine puffed out a breath. "Cram Slug in the cat carrier and meet you guys in the hall."

"Check! Norman?"

"Run around like a banshee and totally lose it." Norman looked amused with himself.

Hannah's left eyebrow lifted. "How can I expect the kids to take this seriously if you don't?"

Norman's shoulders rose and fell. "Sorry, hon. Okay, I should come running from wherever I am, make sure I have my cell phone in my pocket, and meet y'all in the hall."

"Very good."

Jonas grabbed the notepad from his mother's hands and stood military straight. "And you, Master Sergeant, what's your duty?"

Hannah saluted and snapped a crisp reply, "Grab the comforter from the daybed in the study and meet the squad in the hall, Sir!"

"From the sound of it," Norman said, "the storm's aiming away from us, toward Pensacola and Mobile. I doubt we'll get much more than rain and a little wind."

"Tornadoes spawn in those outer feeder bands," Hannah stated, "waiting to reap destruction."

"You've been watching way too much Weather Channel, Mom," Justine said.

"It's a category 4, at one hundred and thirty-five mile-an-hour sustained winds and the pressure has fallen several millibars in the past hour. The storm's strengthening."

Justine's lip crimped on one side. "Like I said . . ."

Outside, blue skies held a few scattered clouds scudding on a mild, warm breeze. When she stepped onto the back deck, Hannah noted the eerie silence. Animals always seemed to know when to shut up and hunker down.

Jonas stood beside her. "Where do the birds and squirrels go during a hurricane?"

"I imagine the squirrels hide away, somehow. If I was a bird, I'd fly to where it felt safe."

"Remember last year after Ivan when Snooker found the three baby squirrels?"

A dog that normally chased and tormented squirrels, Snooker had tenderly carried them one by one to place them on the deck, unharmed save a ropey layer of saliva. The newborns looked like little hairless rats, their eyes not yet open. Hannah and Jonas packed them in soft cloth in a shoebox and took them to St. Francis Wildlife Association, where they joined forty-plus orphaned squirrels.

Hannah patted him with affection. "You and I will make sure to check around and see if any of the babies got knocked from the nests, when it's safe for us to come out."

Hannah and her family camped out in the den, glued to the storm updates. Overnight, the hurricane turned north and aimed toward the heart of the Florida Panhandle. In Chattahoochee, a hundred miles from the massive storm's center, fierce winds whipped the treetops, sending an ominous keening through the air.

"They always have some poor reporter standing in the wind and sheeting rain. I feel sorry for those weather people." Norman grabbed a handful of popcorn. "Remember that one storm a few years back— was it Andrew?— where Dan Rather was hanging onto a pole for dear life?"

"His hair was longer then," Hannah said. "I remember it blowing straight out to one side."

Jonas's eyes lit up. "I think it'd be cool to be there in the middle of it all. I wanna be a storm chaser."

The power flickered. The Olsens gasped. The power stayed on.

Slug slept in Jonas's lap, oblivious to the excitement. Snooker took turns begging for treats and cleaning up anything dropped on the carpet. A loud crack sounded outside, followed by a jarring thud in the back of the house. The family jumped up. Snooker barked. Slug's coat puffed up to full volume, then he dove beneath the couch. Everyone talked at once and the family emergency plan bit the dust.

"You and the kids stand back!" Norman's voice stopped them dead. The lights went out. Norman dug in his pocket for a small flashlight and followed the beam down the hall. The sound of dripping water and wind sounded from Jonas's bedroom. Regardless of Norman's warning, the others crept behind.

Jonas and Justine huddled behind their mother. "See anything, honey?" Hannah asked.

Norman blew out his breath in a long whistle. A large oak tree branch protruded through the ceiling like King Arthur's sword. Rainwater sluiced down the bark and puddled on the carpet.

A second crash jarred the house, this one from the opposite end. Snooker took off into the dark, barking. "That sounded like it came from the backyard," Norman said.

The group scurried to the large window over the kitchen sink, led by Norman the Fearless.

"Can't tell for sure, but I think something hit the fence." He trained the beam of a larger flashlight to the far corner of the yard. "Probably the tree that got struck by lightning end of last summer." Norman sighed. "I was going to have it cut, anyway. Nature saved me the trouble."

"Snooker, good boy. Hush now," Justine soothed.

"What'll we do about that huge freakin' tree in my room?" Jonas asked.

"Nothing for now," Norman said. "I'll get a tarp up there soon as I can. Meanwhile, we'll drag a couple of mattresses into the living room." He checked his watch. "I'll give it an hour before I crank up the generator for the fridge and freezer. In the morning, I'll call Hal over with his chain saw as soon as the worst of the storm's over."

Jonas's eyes twinkled in the flashlight's illumination. "Cool."

Men and their beloved power tools. Hannah shook her head. *What the heck. We need a new roof anyway. It's only money.*

Mae answered the phone after four rings.

"Mom? You okay? I've been calling all morning. "

"Why wouldn't I be?"

"No reason, I mean, I know it didn't get too bad here."

Mae sniffed. "Are you all right? Your voice sounds strained."

"I'm fine," Hannah said. "We lost power for a bit and we have some limbs down." No need to bring up the oak tree in Jonas's room, the pine that had taken out a good portion of the fence, or the untimely demise of Mrs. Keats's cement yard manatee, two doors down. "What've you been doing?"

"This and that. They plan things for us here. I've been up in Josie's room talking a blue streak."

"You weren't upset?"

"Why would I be upset?"

"The hurricane, Ma-Mae."

Her mother hesitated. Hannah could envision her walking over to the window to peer outside. "Oh. That. Well, it's nearly passed now, hasn't it?"

"Yes."

"I'm going to sit in the living room for a while. They're showing some Disney flick. Was there something you needed?"

"Suppose not. I'll stop by to see you on the way home from work tomorrow."

"I might not be in my room. You'll have to find me."

Hannah smiled. "I'll hunt you down. Don't worry."

"Goodbye, then. Remember Ma-Mae loves you."

The disconnect click sounded on Mae's end.

Hannah cradled the silent phone set in her hand. "Night, Ma-Mae. I love you, too."

Chapter Thirty-one

"You've outdone yourself, this time," Suzanne walked around Becky and gave a low whistle.

"Did you make that outfit?" Hannah asked.

Unlike her mother, Hannah viewed sewing as a tedious, time-warping, energy-sucking black hole. Hannah's deluxe Singer machine stood idle, providing convenient overflow for Norman's papers and flux from other areas of the house.

Becky beamed. "Sewed every little dangle on by hand."

Scarlet rhinestones covered the bra top, with longer hanging strands at the midriff. The harem pants were filmy silver chiffon with an overlaying handkerchief-hem tribal skirt and hip belt. On Becky's feet, ballet slippers sparkled with the same red faceted stones. Wristlets and a headband in glittery silver completed the ensemble.

"You look like an Arabian Nights' MTV parody," Hannah said.

"Wait!" Becky dug in her gym bag and pulled out a scarlet silk veil edged in silver thread.

Suzanne ran her fingers over the buttery material. "Dang, woman!"

The instructor walked in and stopped when she spotted the costume. "Woo! You're a diva."

Becky smiled seductively and swiveled in a wide hip circle. "You like?"

"With that outfit, you'll have some rich sheik's Mercedes parked in front of your tent by nightfall," Amy said.

"My sheik drives a Dodge Hemi pick-up." Becky's eyes twinkled. "You've given me a great idea for this weekend." She fanned her hands through the air. "Our bedroom set up to look like a desert oasis tent. Pillows, billowy draperies hanging from the ceiling, low lighting . . . "

Amy laughed. "You go girl!" At her signal, the class lined up in three rows, many wiggling in anticipation of the music. "Tonight, we'll do a quick review of the moves we've learned so far. Then, I'll teach you a new rhythm for the zills."

"Love those," Hannah said. "Can't move and play them at the same time, but I love them anyway."

"That'll come." Amy swiveled a few times, then led them through the warm-up moves. "Would you like to learn to *zaghareet?*" Twin dimples formed at the corners of her wide smile.

"Zah-what?" Suzanne asked.

Amy placed her hand in front of her mouth and emitted a loud high-pitched trill. "That's what they refer to as zaghareeting." She demonstrated the quick tongue movements. "It's *lah-lah-lah*—done really fast."

The students echoed.

"Sounds like some kind of demented banshee call to me," Suzanne commented.

"Now, place your hand demurely over your mouth and do it. That muffles the sound." Amy continued, "This is a *woman thing*, sometimes used as a greeting. Or to say 'hey, look at me', or 'hey, look at you!' "

"I've heard it before in movies," Hannah said. "And at the Hafla."

"If you're somewhere and there's a belly dancer performing, and you'd like to cheer her on, you can do a more subdued zaghareet. This tells her that you know something about her moves—a form of praise and appreciation for her dancing."

"I feel like I'm dripping in culture each time I leave this class," Becky said.

An hour and a half later, the three tired dancers made their way to their cars. Becky waved goodbye from her parking spot, then Hannah and Suzanne walked together to their vehicles.

"I like the shimmy movements," Suzanne said. "Feels like I get a good workout."

"I always have to go home and ice my butt." Hannah laughed. "By the way, Norman called me on the cell as I was on my way to class. Said you and Hal are taking Ma-Mae out to eat on Friday night."

"Uh-huh." Suzanne hit a button on the van's keyless remote. "We're leaving Sunday on vacation, remember? Branson, Missouri, for a week. Your brother's particularly excited about seeing the musical shows."

"Oh yeah, I knew it was coming up soon. Anyway, Ma-Mae's a bit confused. She wants us to go with you on Friday too. I've told her at least three times this week that I'll be in Jacksonville for a training meeting, not home until Saturday afternoon sometime."

Suzanne pitched the gym bag into the passenger seat. "My mama's the same way. It really is like second childhood. You think about it. When your kids were little, you'd tell them the same thing over and over and over until you turned blue in the face. Still, they wouldn't get it. Unless," she held up her index finger, "it was something they really focused on long enough for it to stick—like going to Disney World or getting ice cream. Then, they'd remind you fifty jillion times a day."

"You're right."

"Then, as it continues— this whole circle of life thing— people get to the point where they're dependent for everything again. Wearing diapers, maybe not being able to communicate, or walk, or even eat."

Hannah located her keys in the duffel bag. "The idea of having a hit man take me out when I get to that point sounds better and better every day."

"Maybe there's a lesson in all of this, about living in the moment. No past, no future, only the now. No worries."

"Except the worries are still there," Hannah said. "You pass them along to your adult children."

When Hannah walked in from the seminar, she found Jonas hunkered over the kitchen table. "Hey, baby." She pecked him on the head and parked the rolling suitcase by the table.

"Mom. How was—?"

"In a minute!" she called over her shoulder as she tore a path to the bathroom.

When she walked back into the kitchen, she noticed the object of her son's intense focus: a length of bent wire. "Sugar, exactly what are you trying to do?" She grabbed a bottle of peach/mango flavored water from the refrigerator and plopped down opposite him.

He held up the barely recognizable clothes hanger. "Voila!"

"I give up. This new miracle of youthful ingenuity is—?"

He wedged the hooked end of the hanger between the skin and the cast on his left arm, and slid it in and out. "SCSD—Sub-cast scratching device. Neat, huh?"

"Clever." Hannah scanned the kitchen. A few dirty glasses, chip crumbs, a skillet with congealed grease on the stove. All in all, not too bad. "But a bit risky, don't you think?"

Jonas's dark brows furrowed. "No. Why?"

"If you nick the skin, you could get an infection and that wouldn't be good. The wound can't get air and there'll be no way to put any ointment or a bandage over it."

Jonas poked out his bottom lip: the same gesture he had used since early childhood when considering a perplexing problem. "Good catch, Mom. Back to the drawing board." He extracted the scratching tool and studied the hooked end. "I can cover this with a cushioning layer of . . . something."

"I'm sure you'll work it out." She ruffled his thick brown hair. "How have things been? Anything new to report?"

"Gah, Mom. You weren't gone that long. Not like things happen around here at killer speed. Dad's in town getting a haircut. Um . . . oh, and Mrs. Rodgers came by and told Justine that Brittany's breaking out of the hospital this week."

"Good! On both accounts. Your father needed to clean up a bit, and I'm proud Brittany's improved."

"Brit's going to a place for crazy chicks who don't eat. I don't remember."

"Some kind of treatment center?" Hannah asked.

Jonas shrugged. "Dunno."

"Anything else?"

"Dad and I caught ten bream this morning—we went at the crack of dawn. I helped clean them, and we froze 'em in baggies."

More fish. My freezer is practically an aquatic morgue now. "The river wasn't too high, then."

"Way up over the banks. Muddy as all get out. We went to Lake Talquin instead."

"And your sister. Did she tag along?"

He fixed her with a serious expression. "Get real."

Right. What was I thinking? Justine touch bait or a fish? "What did she do with herself?"

Justine swished into the kitchen. "*Herself* was a perfect angel, thank you very much." She pecked her mother on the cheek.

"Well?"

"Well, what? I stayed home. Except I did go visit Grand-Mae like you asked."

"And?" Why did she always feel as if she teased bits and pieces of conversation through fine mesh with a pair of tweezers?

"She's in a class-A funk. I took her out for ice cream. Even that didn't help."

Hannah took a deep breath. Since the hurricane excitement, Mae's mood had once again turned sour. How Pollyanna-ish, to think her mother would somehow forget to be depressed and miraculously change for the better over a weekend.

"What's for dinner?" Jonas asked.

"Whatever you order. I'm not cooking after driving in from Jacksonville."

The kids exchanged knowing looks. "Pizza okay?" Justine asked.

"Only if you get hand-tossed. I hate the thin kind. Tastes like ketchup on potato chips. Add extra sauce and cheese. I don't much care about the rest. Get a lot of meat for your father."

Justine tapped the memorized number for the local pizza delivery business. "It's going to cost, with all the extra stuff."

"Everything has a cost," Hannah said.

Chapter Thirty-two

An insistent ringing jarred Hannah from sleep. For a moment, she didn't know where she was—still in the Jacksonville hotel room or at home. She snaked one hand toward the house phone, checked it, then tapped with the same hand to locate her cell phone buried beneath a mound of newspapers on the bedside table.

Mae's voice said, "Hannah? You are coming by the Mont this morning, aren't you?"

"Yes." *Don't I always?* Hannah heard the disconnect click on the other end.

Norman rolled over and opened one eye. "Problem?"

"Dunno."

"Want me to go?"

Hannah scrubbed the sleep from her eyes. "Nah. You pull breakfast duty."

Hannah located her mother in Rosemont's sunroom, sitting alone by the aquarium.

"Morning." Hannah kissed her mother on the cheek before settling onto a chair. The light-filled room with its yellow and green-printed cushions, airy wicker furnishings and leafy plants provided a direct contrast to her mother's glum demeanor.

Mae glanced down at her watch. "Almost *not* morning, now."

"I was exhausted from the drive home yesterday. I couldn't get going, not even for church."

Her mother's blue-gray eyes stared across the room at nothing in particular.

"Not feeling well today, Ma-Mae?"

"Burdened." Mae faced her. "We need to talk."

Please. Not funeral plans. Not today. Hannah closed her eyes for a moment, took a deep breath and focused. "What's on your mind?"

"I've been carrying around a secret all these years. Not my secret.

More, your daddy's secret. But it fell to me, after he passed."

A female resident stopped her walker in the hall outside long enough to sense the privacy of their meeting before moving away.

"That was Ethel Price. Glad she didn't stop. She can talk a blue streak. Says the same thing over and over until you want to choke the life from her." Mae paused before continuing, "Josie says I need to tell you this, honey. I don't see as it matters much now, but she's a firm believer in unloading one's trespasses before traveling on Home. The baggage can slow a person down, Josie says."

"Ma-Mae, I—"

Mae held up her hand. "Just listen. May not make a never-mind, but still I'd like to get it out in the open."

"If it's that important to you."

"It's about that Motivano boy." Mae tapped a finger to her temple. "Try as I may, I can't seem to call up his first name."

"Marcus," Hannah supplied.

"That's it! Couldn't remember that to save my soul. Marcus Motivano."

Hannah felt the muscles around her lips pull taut. "What about him?"

"Your father did something he wasn't particularly proud of at the time." Mae reached over and grasped her daughter's hand. "But maybe now, with you having children of your own, you can understand why he did it."

Hannah's skin prickled.

"Did you ever wonder why that boy seemed to up and vanish—" Mae snapped her fingers. "—like that?"

Hannah nodded.

"Your daddy ran him off."

"What?"

"That's right. You were out of town. Something or other . . . some trip with your school friends . . . ?"

"That was years ago. I don't know." Hannah said.

"Marcus came calling at the house. He seemed to be as fond of your daddy and me as he was of you." Mae smiled. "Loved my lemon pie."

Mae licked her lips, as if the tartness had stained them over the years. "Your daddy, he smelled a rat. Thought the boy was way too charming and all. He had a little daddy-to-son chat with him."

"Oh?"

"Yep. Surely did. Told him you were a good girl, the kind who'd make any man a faithful and loving wife and mother. Told him you weren't to be played with and tossed aside. He was trying to ferret out the boy's true intentions. Whether they were honorable, or not."

Mae paused to catch her breath. "Your daddy was as crushed and heartbroken as you when Marcus stopped coming around. Then we found out he had taken up with some floozy. Remember how your daddy refused to hear his name even mentioned in our house?"

Hannah's gaze fell to her lap. She picked at a ragged cuticle until it pearled with blood.

"Your daddy was torn up. Knew he'd caused your loss, in a way. He was terribly disappointed in Marcus too. That boy had betrayed all of us. Not just you. Many a night, I saw your daddy walk the halls, tormenting himself with what-ifs." Mae searched her daughter's face.

The gurgling of the fish tank aerator filled the silence. Hannah grabbed a used tissue from her purse, wrapped her wounded cuticle, and pressed to staunch the bleeding. "Why didn't Pop ever tell me?" She asked in a soft voice.

Mae's lips drew into a bittersweet smile. "He was afraid, baby."

"Why?"

"You were so jewel-eyed over that boy. Your daddy was scared you'd turn against us and run after Marcus. Your daddy loved you better than life itself. Deep down, he felt he did right by interfering. Still and all, he was terrified of losing your love and respect if he confessed to meddling in your private affairs."

Hannah willed herself to take a deep breath and exhale slowly. "It was probably a good decision, not to tell me. I was so stupid-in-love. I've thought about that time in my life a lot." She managed a flicker of a smile, remembering the recent sheet-churning dreams. "I never understood how Marcus could just drop me. I thought I wasn't pretty enough, smart enough, good enough—"

"Wasn't you that was no good, sugar." Mae fiddled with her plain gold wedding band. "Your daddy wasn't easily swayed by a smile or smooth style. Marcus even had me bamboozled. Your daddy looked clean through him and didn't much care for what he saw."

"I'm glad you told me, Ma-Mae. I don't blame Pop. Not at all. I would do the same thing to protect one of my kids."

Mae gave Hannah's hand a gentle squeeze. "I'm so happy you aren't angry."

"Time for us to let it go, eh?" Hannah leaned over and kissed her mother's powdered cheek.

"Good as gone." Mae whisked a hand through the air. "My friend Josie was right. I feel like I've dropped a lead weight." One of her eyebrows elevated slightly. "Can I ask you something else, then we'll leave it behind for good?"

"Sure."

"Did that boy talk you out of your panties?"

"Ma-Mae!"

Her mother jabbed her in the side. "C'mon. We're both grown women now."

Hannah tilted her head back and laughed. "Once. Nothing to describe in juicy detail, since there were so few details to the whole thing."

Mae's eyes narrowed. "I thought so!"

"Takes two, remember."

"Still and all. A pox on him!"

Chapter Thirty-three

"How will I make it through work? I barely have the energy to breathe." Hannah raked her hand through her hair.

"Don't you know what today is?" Norman asked.

Hannah sighed. "Wednesday?"

Norman peered at her over his morning paper. "July 20."

Happy occasions like birthdays and anniversaries, Hannah managed to record on the official refrigerator calendar, and in her day-planner and computer at work. She had never been one to count sad dates. Norman was the one who recalled those numeric details.

Hannah joined Norman at the table with a hot cup of black coffee. She had no appetite for breakfast. "Okay. . . "

"Today is the eighth anniversary of when your father died."

Hannah sat back and curled her fingers around the warm mug. "That's right."

"You always feel this way starting in mid-July. Just like your mother."

"Really. Do I?"

"Yes, hon." Norman snapped the paper closed. "You worry about Mae and how she gets in the summer, but you do it too."

Hannah reached over and gently rubbed the soft black hairs on the back of his hand. "What would I do without you, Norman Olsen?"

Grieving, Hannah thought, seemed to operate on a preset time schedule: two to three days of intense sorrow followed by no more than a couple of weeks of numb inactivity. By six weeks, the bereaved was expected to bounce back into the ongoing push of daily demands. In six months, hardly anyone mentioned the deceased or asked about any leftover sorrow of those left behind.

When her father, J.B. Mathers had died, Hannah had taken one week away from work. The call came on a Wednesday before lunch break. She remembered it as if it were yesterday.

Her mother's voice, shaky with emotion, said, "Sugar, it's your daddy."

A twisting sensation started in her stomach. His heart, again? "Are y'all at the ER?"

Silence then, "No, baby. He . . . he's passed."

Hannah couldn't grasp the idea. "Pop?"

"He was working on the boat motor. I told him it was too hot out." Mae's voice faltered. "I made lemonade and when I took it out to him . . . "

The sound of sniffling and short staccato breaths echoed from the other end.

Hannah's stunned brain kicked into emergency mode. "I'll be home as soon as possible. I need to call Hal and Helen."

"Your brother's here. He's called your sister."

The day turned gray-blue: the drive home, crying so hard she could barely see the dotted white highway center lines. Some other part of her consciousness took control and helped her to arrive safely in Chattahoochee. She and Hal met with the funeral director. Helen stayed with Mae.

The casket display area still hovered in Hannah's memory, a surreal sales lot of caskets in different designs, colors, and prices in a thickly carpeted room. The lighting, soft and rose-tinted, floated from frosted-shade pole lamps. Ethereal music wafted from a hidden speaker.

Hal, now the official patriarch, had handled the financial arrangements while Hannah debated over the style of casket, finally choosing a navy metallic model with burnished pewter trim. Blue was Pop's favorite color.

At the visitation, Hannah responded as heartfelt condolences ebbed and flowed around her in a garbled rush. Later at the Mathers home, supplies and food poured in: cakes, pies, casseroles, cold cuts, coffee and tea, paper goods, cases of soft drinks, and platters of country-fried chicken. Though grateful, the family picked absently at the food. Hannah recalled Piddie Longman's red velvet cake, rich and sweet with mounds of cream cheese icing: the only flavors that managed to revive her stunned senses.

After the funeral, the crowds diminished. The front doorbell fell

silent. Only close friends and the immediate neighbors entered un-
obtrusively through the unlocked back door to offer support. Her father's muddy worn work boots stood in the garage. His jacket hung
on a peg. His woody scent lingered in every nook. The memory of
his laughter and generous spirit hovered at every turn. Some people,
Hannah believed, left larger holes in the universe than others when
they crossed over.

She would have it all to go through again. Death, cloaked in shadows, waited patiently with his curved harvesting scythe.

Hannah heard the sound of someone clearing her throat and
glanced up from the computer screen. Suzanne, resplendent in an
orange floral-print sundress with matching sandals and handbag,
stood in the threshold of Hannah's Tallahassee office cubicle. "Hey-
ho, sister-in-law of mine."

"Hey, yourself!" Hannah pushed away from her desk and stretched.
"Have a seat." She cleared a stack of papers from a chair.

"Looks like you're up to your armpits."

"Is there any other way?" Hannah said. "What brings you to the
big city, Sis?"

"Shopping." Suzanne grinned. "Is there anything else?"

"Don't tell me. You bought a new outfit a couple of weeks ago and
you don't have exactly the right shade of shoes to match."

"I didn't come for shoes today, smarty pants, if you must know.
I'm looking for something for Mama's birthday. Lord help me, I don't
have an earthly clue what to get her."

"After a certain age what can a person want, or need, for that
matter?"

"Exactly." Suzanne finger-combed her blonde curls. "I decided to
stop in and see if maybe you might do lunch with me."

Hannah glanced at her cluttered desk. "Wish I could."

"Sure you can. This will be right here when you get back."

"That's what I know."

Suzanne pursed her lips and tilted her head to one side. "Besides,
you need to take a little fun break."

"You've been talking to Norman."

Suzanne's brows knit together. "I know how you are, Hannah. Your brother's the same way."

Hannah crossed her hands over her chest. "Oh, and how's that?"

"Y'all both try so hard to pull off this tough exterior, but I know you."

"I don't have a clue— "

"The anniversary of your daddy's death, that's what. You think the people around you don't notice how you've both fallen into a deep funk?"

Hannah slumped in her chair.

"No use rolling around in it by yourself. I'm here to help."

"What about Hal?"

"Don't you worry about your brother. I'm here, right now, right here, to see to you." Suzanne snuggled her purse beneath one arm and stood. "So, what'll it be? You best take me up on buying lunch. This gift horse might trot on back to the barn if you don't."

Hannah put her computer into hibernation mode. "What the heck? I hardly ever take an actual lunch break. I'm overdue."

Suzanne swept her arm in an arc. "After you, darlin'. I'll even let you pick the place. I have to tell you though; I'd be happy if it's not a five-star joint. Not that you're not worth it, but I'd like to have the money to get home."

"With those legs and that outfit, you wouldn't have any trouble hitching a ride."

The phone trilled the instant Hannah entered the house. She deposited her purse and laptop computer on the kitchen table and dashed to the portable phone dock.

"Hannah?" Helen asked.

"Hi, Sissy."

"You sound out of breath."

"Just walked in the door. What's up?"

"Have you talked to Ma-Mae today?"

Hannah reached into the refrigerator for a bottle of water. "Not yet. I wanted to come home and throw a salad together for dinner. I'll go by later. Why?"

"I just spoke with her. She sounded . . . happy."

Hannah took a large swig of water and wiped the dribble from her lips. "And this is a problem?" From the edge in her sister's voice, she knew Helen was pacing, probably twisting a tissue in her hands.

"You do know what day it is, don't you?" Helen asked.

"Even though you think I'm somewhat spacey, I do realize Pop died eight years ago today."

"You don't tend to remember dates, is all."

"Norman reminded me at breakfast."

"Don't you find it upsetting that Ma-Mae is happy?"

"When she's usually morose? Yeah. It's different. But keeping with a lot of changes I've noticed in her lately, not surprising."

"She doesn't remember, is that what you're saying?" Helen continued without benefit of a response. "How could she forget? How is that possible after all the years they were married?"

"It's not that she's forgotten Pop, Sissy. She misses him very much." Hannah considered telling her sister about Mae missing her birthday back in March, then decided against it.

Helen sniffled on the other end.

"Suzanne and I had lunch today," Hannah said. "We talked about how Ma-Mae's been lately. She said something that helped me to understand."

"Oh?"

"Ma-Mae's living more and more in the present. She recalls the past, no problem there. She remembers bits and pieces of things coming up too, especially if she writes them down on her calendar. But like a child, she's absorbed with whatever's happening at the moment. It's a natural part of all of this aging business."

Helen blew her nose and snuffled. "Makes a certain amount of sense."

"Suzanne's seen the same pattern in her mother. She's only a few months younger than Ma-Mae." Hannah paused. "We're all kind of feeling our way along with this. Too bad we can't dash out to the bookstore and buy a manual."

Hannah wedged the phone between her ear and shoulder and searched the refrigerator for anything remotely resembling salad materials. A cucumber turned to mush in her hands and she pitched it into the garbage.

"There's only you and me and Hal now, to mark Pop's date," Helen said. "How sad."

Hannah heard the sound of muffled weeping, again. "Sissy, I know it's hard. There are days when I come home from Rosemont crying my eyes out. Other days, I laugh hysterically at something she's said or done. We've got to get through it somehow . . . together."

"And one day, we'll mark the date for Ma-Mae too, won't we?" Another round of sobbing came from her sister.

Hannah's eyes watered. "I'm afraid so." Hannah shared the hiss of dead air for a moment. "That any of us think we have another day promised, is a bit presumptuous. We have to take it a little bit at a time."

"Yes." Her sister's voice sounded weak.

"What are you doing on Sunday?" Hannah dumped the salad veggies into a colander and blasted it with cool water.

"Church. Dinner. The usual. Why?"

"Tallahassee Little Theatre is putting on a comedy with Southern characters. Why don't we take Ma-Mae? She loves the theatre. I can call ahead and reserve tickets. I'll call Suzanne and see if she wants to go along and take her mother. Kind of a girls' day out. What do you say?"

Helen's voice brightened. "I'll have to skip church. But what the heck? Hell won't freeze over if I'm not there one Sunday. Think Ma-Mae will go for it?"

"Are you kidding? Our mother is always ready to go."

Chapter Thirty-four

"Oh, good!" Mae said when she answered Hannah's knock. "You're here in time for Singing and Pizza with Randy."

"I can't stay long, Ma-Mae. I still have to catch up on the laundry." Hannah dropped several plastic grocery bags onto the bed. The weariness she felt so often, especially lately, threatened to shut her down.

"Housework is the nearest thing to perpetual motion the Good Lord ever invented. You can spare an hour." Mae slipped the room key fob around her neck and grabbed her cane. "C'mon. I don't want to be late."

What the heck? Hannah gathered her remaining energy and fell into step beside her mother. *Maybe I can put my head down on one of the tables and catch a nap.*

In the dining room, residents gathered, some sipping lemonade, as the one-man band set up. Along with a pearl-inlaid, six-string Gibson folk guitar, Randy had a harmonica mounted on a holder circling his neck and a foot-controlled top-hat cymbal. Hannah followed Mae to the table where her friend Josie waited.

Randy smiled out at the crowd. "Howdy folks."

"You're late," one woman commented.

"Was I?" Randy checked his watch. "I had to change out a broken G string."

"He was on time," Catharen said as she passed out slices of hot cheese pizza from a rolling cart. "We got seated a bit early because we returned sooner than usual from our afternoon drive."

Randy settled onto a stool and adjusted a worn copy of *Best Loved Songs of the American People* on the tripod stand. A straw hat with a rainbow-colored brim sat on his head. His smile flashed with the easy familiarity of a traveling troubadour.

"Whew! It's hot enough outside to barbeque the road kill." He chuckled and fine-tuned the strings one by one. "Did the hurricane take off part of your roof? I couldn't help but notice the crew when I pulled in."

"No," a woman in the front answered. "They're putting on new shingles. But not because of the storm."

"This place is solid as a castle," Mae said in a loud voice. "We can barely tell when it's bad weather outside."

Randy winked. "I know where I'm coming next time we have one of our big blows."

"Bring your pillow," Catharen said. "We'll find you a place."

"He can stay in my room," Maxine called out.

A titter of laughter rippled through the room.

The troubadour grinned. "Well now, Miz Maxine. I'll consider that a red-carpet invite."

The musician began with "Swing Low, Sweet Chariot," then moved to jazzy versions of "Blue Suede Shoes" and "Buffalo Gals." His repertoire ranged from folk favorites to old spirituals to comic pieces. Between songs, he kept up a running line of jokes and commentary.

"Play that Purple Cow song!" Mae called out.

"Only if our favorite social director will do the dance," Randy said.

Catharen, always the good sport, scuttled to the front of the room. "Hit it!"

While Randy strummed and sang a tune about a purple cow who thought she was a chicken, Catharen strutted between the tables, doing her best to cluck in time. The harder the residents clapped and laughed, the louder she crooned.

"She beats all I've ever seen," Mae commented. "I've never known anyone who enjoys her job as much as that woman."

Hannah felt her spirits lift. For all of their physical, and sometimes mental, limitations, most of the seniors managed a cheerful outlook, enjoying each other and everyone who cared enough to join them.

Randy completed the set with "Good Night Ladies." He walked around the room, speaking one-on-one with the Rosemont residents before packing up his equipment and swinging his guitar case over his shoulder. He tipped his hat and waved then ambled slowly down the hallway.

What kind of music will be featured at the facility when I'm Ma-

Mae's age? Hannah wondered. Old Doobie Brothers or disco tunes? Perhaps a few Eagles favorites? She envisioned her and Norman swing-dancing with their walkers.

"You still up for the play tomorrow?" Hannah asked Mae as they joined the residents leaving the dining hall.

"Bet your bottom dollar I am. I'm heading up to the Reminiscing Session in the sunroom. Want to come?"

"Really, Ma-Mae. I need to—"

Mae stepped into line in front of the elevators. "Go on then. You best find time for a nap. You look a little pale." As the elevator doors closed, her mother blew her an air kiss and sang, "Thaaaanks . . . for the mem-mor-ries."

Cicadas were the devil's spawn; Hannah grew more convinced of it every summer. The insects' high-pitched keening rose and fell in undulating waves, loud enough to be heard over the roar of two fans and the air conditioner. Between periods of blessed calm, her stressed eardrums echoed, only to be accosted anew by the swell of yet another round of cicada love ballads. Even the crickets packed up their little carpetbags and went looking for new digs.

Would they summon the fellows in the crisp starched jackets if she ran into the middle of the yard and hollered "shut up! shut up! shut up!" at the top of her lungs? Hannah envisioned a T-shirt with the silhouette of a cicada printed on the front, a large cross-hatched circle stamped on top. She would own one in every color.

Hannah was entertaining the notion of cicadas for target practice when she heard the bang of the kitchen door.

"Hello, sister!" Helen dashed by. "Be right back!" She returned shortly. "Lord help me, I can barely go an hour without a potty break. I hate to drink anything if I'm traveling, or I'll have to pull off to pee."

"It's part of being middle-aged," Hannah said. "Bladder the size of a field pea."

"Ma-Mae riding with us?"

Hannah nodded. "Soon as Suzanne and her mama get here, we'll pick her up. You know Ma-Mae. She's been sitting on go since breakfast. She's already called three times."

"Our mama has always loved the theatre. Me, too."

"Mom?" Justine walked into the kitchen, wrapped in a pink chenille robe. "Okay if I wear jeans?"

"Sure. Tallahassee Little Theatre has always been kind of casual, especially for the Sunday matinee." When her daughter left the room, Hannah said, "Justine decided to join us. Can you believe it?"

"Maybe there's hope." Helen pulled out a kitchen table chair and sat down. "She always has been mature for her age. Other than the one incident, you have to admit, she's not been a hard child."

"Especially when I hear about other parents dealing with drugs and, heaven forbid, early pregnancy or STDs." Or having a child with bulimia. Missy's daughter could actually die.

"Whatever happened to the days when the worst thing a child could do was sneak a cigarette behind the school, or drink a beer?" Helen checked her watch for the second time since she arrived.

Hannah dug in her purse for the car keys. "Changing times—not for the better sometimes. I was playing with Barbie dolls at the age when some of these girls are beginning to have sex."

Suzanne stepped through the back door following a courtesy knock. "Mama's in the van with the air conditioner running. She's not feeling very spry today."

"The heat," Helen said. "Zaps it right out of me, too. I hardly go out of the house this time of year." She glanced in Hannah's direction. "Probably the reason you've been so tired lately."

Suzanne smiled. "Glad you made an exception and came out, for the likes of us."

"Figured y'all needed someone along to provide a little class," Helen said.

Hannah's eyebrows shot up. *My sister, making a joke? Pinch me.*

Over the years, Hannah had attended many quality musical, dramatic, and comedic performances in the single-story brick building on Thomasville Road. As the family entered the cool semi-darkness, a sense of anticipation washed over her.

"We're right up front," Suzanne glanced at her ticket. "Great seats, Hannah!"

"I tried to pick a spot where Ma-Mae and Ruthie wouldn't have to climb stairs or crawl over people," Hannah said.

They settled into thick-cushioned chairs.

"The theatre." Mae's gray-blue eyes twinkled. "Something about it all unfolding in front of you makes you feel a part of the action in a way a television can't."

Suzanne helped her mother get seated. "I wish we could have popcorn."

"That would be rich," Helen said, "hearing a poor actor try to deliver his lines with someone smacking and crunching behind you."

Suzanne wiggled into her cushion. "I just love popcorn, is all."

The lights flickered three times, the signal for the audience to quiet.

During the second act, Suzanne and her mother slipped from their seats and exited toward the lobby. When they failed to return, Hannah waited until a pause in the action to seek them out. She found her sister-in-law hovering over Ruthie, who was seated in a folding chair.

"You guys okay?" Hannah asked in a low voice.

"Mama's not feeling well."

Ruthie's round face appeared pale and a fine line of sweat beads trailed across her upper lip. "I'm all right. You two go on back in."

Suzanne shot a look to Hannah. "Says her chest is hurting."

"I get this way sometimes," Ruthie managed between gasps.

"I think you're having one of your anxiety attacks, Mama." Suzanne said. Then to Hannah, "She's gotten to where she has these whenever we're anywhere except my house or hers. I knew better than to come over here."

Hannah frowned. "I don't know, Sis. Her color doesn't look right. Maybe we ought to take her to the hospital and let them check her over."

"It's the heat. That's all." Ruthie slapped the air with one hand.

Suzanne propped her hands on her hips. "Mama, maybe Hannah's right. I'd hate to ignore this and have it turn out to be something else."

"Whatever you think best." Ruthie's words sounded strained and breathy.

"I'll go motion for the rest." Hannah turned to leave.

Suzanne grabbed her sleeve. "Mae has looked forward to this since you first mentioned it. I'll take Mama on around to the ER at Tallahassee General. You know how hospitals are. It'll be a while before they decide what's to be done, if anything."

Hannah hesitated. "I hate for you to be alone."

"I'll call your brother, if need be. Now get back inside." Suzanne pointed.

"We're only five minutes away. I'll turn my cell on vibrate. If you need anything, call."

"Will do." Suzanne tipped her head. "C'mon, Mama. Let's get a move on."

Ruthie stood slowly, wobbled slightly before she balanced, and ambled toward the door. Suzanne turned to her sister-in-law and whispered behind her hand, "I know it's one of her spells."

Chapter Thirty-five

"Hey Miss! It's just me!" Hannah called as she helped herself to a cup of fresh coffee. She spotted the unwashed dishes in the sink: yet another sign of Missy Rodgers's transition to the world of imperfect humans.

At some point, Hannah and Missy Rodgers had morphed into back-door friends. Neither bothered to ring the doorbell, and each knew the spare key hidey-hole in the rare event the rear entrance was locked.

Missy appeared in a cotton robe, her hair gathered in a haphazard ponytail. "Hey, you." She motioned to the refrigerator. "Got some of Joe Fletcher's sweet potato biscuits, if you want to reheat one. I'd go with the toaster oven. The microwave makes them gummy."

"Coffee's enough. Thanks. I'm trying to cut back." Hannah huffed. "Can you fathom me drinking coffee when it's already in the high eighties outside? It's going to be close to the hundred degree mark again, today. God help us."

Missy bustled around the kitchen, depositing dishes in the washer and wiping down the countertops before pouring a cup and joining Hannah at the table.

"It's never too hot for good coffee. I keep on drinking it and turn the thermostat down. I dread to see my electric bill." She sipped. "So tell me about Miz Ruthie."

"How did you know? I mean, it just happened yesterday afternoon."

"The Triple C. I treated myself to a manicure. How else?"

"Ah, the hair salon hotline."

"So tell," Missy said. "Mandy and Melody didn't have all the details."

"Ruthie started having problems. Suzanne took her to the ER, and we followed after the play was over—at Suzanne's insistence. I sent Helen, Justine, and Ma-Mae on home after they dropped me off at the hospital. They admitted Ruthie to the cardiac care unit for observation."

"She had a heart attack?"

"Angina. But the tests showed damage from previous attacks: the silent ones—you know where there aren't strong symptoms. Or Ruthie ignored them." Hannah pursed her lips. "She's functioning with about forty percent of her heart. They found blockages too."

"Will she have surgery?"

Hannah shook her head. "The doctors think she wouldn't survive the operation."

"How very sad. I know your sister-in-law is frantic."

"Suzanne's holding up, all in all. It's been one thing after another for the past few years, with her mom's health issues and all."

"I'll call and have Jake make a nice cut flower arrangement as soon as Ruthie comes home."

"Put my name on the card, and I'll split the cost with you." Hannah eyed the plate of russet-colored biscuits and willed herself to ignore them.

"I just remembered." Missy jumped up, removed a stack of cookies from a Ziploc baggie, popped them into the microwave for a few seconds and sat the warmed plate on the table.

Hannah scowled. "Missy." The aroma of cinnamon brought water to her mouth.

"Don't worry. I made them with Splenda. Still some calories, but sugar-free."

"In that case." Hannah bit into a warm oatmeal cookie and groaned. "Wow. Good." She imagined two fat cookies with a mound of peanut butter in-between. What a weird obsession.

"Aren't they? I might not have a problem convincing Brittany to eat them."

"How is she?"

"She's put on six pounds!" Missy beamed. "I'm so proud of her. They're doing this Cognitive Behavioral Therapy, where she delves into the reasons behind her eating disorder. She has to eat six times a day; they monitor her daily intake and weight. Brittany wrestles with her issues, as do I. We're both in counseling. Sometimes together, sometimes separate."

"That's good. I mean—about Brit's improving."

"She'll be home in time for school in the fall, if she continues to do well. That'll bring a new set of challenges: being with her friends, and struggling to fit in without feeling ashamed."

"Justine misses her terribly."

"Brit lives for your daughter's cards and letters. I appreciate her . . ." Missy's eyes watered. "and you. You've been such a good friend."

Hannah gave Missy's hand a quick squeeze, then poured a second cup of coffee from the insulated carafe. "I can't tell you how exciting it is to come in this house and see dirty dishes in the sink." She took a long, pleasurable swill of the rich Kona blend. One sure thing about her newfound friend: Missy didn't scrimp when it came to primo coffee beans.

"Something about having a child in crisis makes a person let go." Missy picked absently at the cookie crumbs trapped in the placemat's fringe. "Not that I want to develop into a complete slob, but it feels okay to relax a bit."

"You've been around me too much, Miss. My free and easy brand of housekeeping has rubbed off on you."

Missy swished the notion aside. "Your house looks fine. A little mussed at times. But inviting. The kind of home a person feels welcome to come right in and plop down."

"You might have to push aside a fat cat or a pile of discarded kids' clothing to find a seat, but yes, I suppose that's the decorator look I was striving for."

Missy glanced around the kitchen. "It's not just the house. I've let other things slide."

Hannah took in Missy's wispy, off-center ponytail. "Your 'do hasn't been so rigid lately."

"It's too much of an effort." Missy plucked at a strand of hair. "Besides, who the hell cares if every single hair on my head is in place?"

Hannah reeled. Had Missy Rodgers just cursed? Lord help.

Missy stood and removed the saucer to the sink. "I'm sure my hair and makeup are the least of the world's concerns." She turned and faced Hannah, her expression serious. "I've dropped some of my volunteer duties."

Hannah choked on a swallow, nearly sending a spray of coffee from her nostrils. "No way!"

"Surely did. Except for the Relay for Life. I'm still head chairper-

son for that. But the others? I spent the better part of an evening calling around and excusing myself from so much heavy responsibility. I
probably didn't make any friends."

Hannah reached over and held the back of her hand to Missy's
forehead.

"No, I'm not feverish. I just stopped."

"Good for you, kiddo." Hannah slapped her on the back. "Proud
of you."

Missy glowed with the praise. "Thank you, Hannah. Really."

"So what now, former Queen-of-All-There-Is?"

Missy propped her chin on her hands. "Don't know. Depends on
how things go when Brittany comes home. I may get a part-time job,
or start a small business of some sort."

"Business?"

"Some crazy ideas I have floating around. Nothing concrete. You'll
be the first to know. I promise."

Hannah polished off the last bite of cookie. "Better be. If I hear
it over a hair cut at the Triple C, I'll be really chapped."

Hannah stopped cold when she spotted Lucy Goosey's latest ensemble. Obviously tired of the summer beach scene, Lucy had dressed
for a night on the town. A shimmery, form-fitting, black gown draped
over one shoulder and fell in a pool at her webbed feet. A string of
pearls surrounded her arched neck. Blue shadow highlighted the area
above her eyes, and her cheeks were dotted with deep red blush. Small
pearl studs, glued on due to Lucy's lack of earlobes, completed the
understated elegance. A satin beaded clutch purse leaned at her side,
stuffed with theatre tickets, a lace handkerchief (of course), and formal long white evening gloves.

"Puts on the dog, doesn't she?" Beth asked.

"Sad to think this goose has more of a social life than I do," Hannah said. *Even odds, my mom supplied the hankie.*

"Than all of us put together." Beth smoothed a wrinkle in Lucy's
dress. "It's rumored she'll be taking a cruise in October."

"Really?"

"I saw a little sailor's hat Miz Maxine made. She wouldn't tell me
about the complete outfit, but I'm sure it'll be rich."

"And where is Lucy going, exactly?"

"Canada," Maxine answered from behind them. "She has tickets to leave the third weekend in October with a prominent cruise line. Seven day round-trip. She'll fly first class to New York, where she will meet the ship, then on to ports in Boston, Rhode Island, Bar Harbor, and Canada. She may spend a few days in New York when she returns, to shop and take in a couple of Broadway shows."

"How fortunate for her," Hannah said. "I'm sure the leaves will be in full color."

"Do geese have problems with sea sickness?" Beth asked.

Maxine waved a jeweled finger. "Good point, Beth. One we had not considered. I'll be sure she has some Dramamine packed."

Hannah and Beth exchanged amused glances. Lucy Goosey's life had taken a turn for the better since moving to Rosemont.

"I was heading down to see your mother," Maxine said.

Hannah gestured. "Walk with me, then."

"I've heard some distressing news." Maxine shook her head slowly. "I hate to tell Mae, but I have to."

"Can you share with me?"

"It's about Barney."

Hannah stopped and turned to face Maxine. "Is he back from the VA hospital?"

Maxine's eyes watered. "I'm afraid not."

"He didn't—"

Maxine patted Hannah on the arm. "Oh, no. He's still alive. He's just not ever coming back to Rosemont."

"Oh."

"His family had to move him into a nursing facility down south near Tampa."

"I'm sorry to hear that. Miz Maxine, excuse me for saying so, but didn't you and Barney have your issues?"

"We did." Maxine's lips twisted.

"It's just . . . you seem so unsettled by this. I'd think you might be glad he wasn't returning."

"You must realize, Hannah. Rosemont's one big family. For some who don't have relatives or folks who come to see them, Rosemont is their *only* family." Maxine turned and pushed her walker slowly forward. "Just because you don't like something about your family, you still miss them when they're not around."

"You think this will upset my mother, obviously."

"I do. Your mother is so tender-hearted. She takes to everyone like they were her long-lost cousins. Mae might not have approved of Barney, but she still took the time to befriend him, probably more than any of us did." Maxine stopped and stared down the hallway. "Especially me. I was pretty mean to that old fart."

"We all say and do things we'd like to take back, Miz Maxine. Don't be so hard on yourself."

"Ah . . . well." Maxine rolled forward a few inches, then paused to face Hannah again. "Your mother is fairly satisfied. I want you to know that."

"Sometimes it's hard to tell."

Maxine rested a gnarled hand on Hannah's arm. "Don't allow yourself to become unsettled. Understand, we oldsters have good and bad days, like everyone else. Half the time, I don't even recall having a bad day, by the next morning." She tapped her forehead. "Less gray matter to cloud."

Suzanne's Fancy Green Rice

2 Tbsp. oil
1 cup raw, long-grained rice (not converted)
1/4 cup finely chopped onion
2 green chilies, chopped
6 green onions, finely chopped
1 clove garlic, peeled and minced
1/4 tsp. salt
1/4 tsp. ground cumin
1 and 3/4 cup chicken broth
1 and 1/2 cup shredded Monterey Jack cheese
1/3 tsp. dried coriander

Preheat oven to 350°. Heat oil over medium heat in a skillet or sauce-pan. Add rice and cook, stirring until rice turns opaque, about two minutes. Add white onion, sauté 1 minute. Add chopped chilies, green onion, garlic, salt, cumin and sauté 20 seconds. Add chicken broth. Mix. Heat over high heat to boiling, then reduce heat to low. Cover and simmer about 15 minutes until rice is almost tender.
Remove from heat. Add 1 cup of the cheese and the coriander. Toss to mix. Put in a greased, 1 and 1/2 quart casserole dish and top with remaining cheese. Bake, uncovered for 15 minutes.

Chapter Thirty-six

"Tonight," Amy announced with her usual effervescent enthusiasm, "we'll put it all together." She adjusted her deep purple hip scarf and gave a few trial shakes. "The moves we've learned so far are fun, but we can't stand around and do hip drops for hours on end. The folks in the audience would fall over from boredom."

"Audience?" Suzanne said in a low voice. "You expect us to be able to dance in front of people?"

"You may decide to perform with the troupe," Amy said.

Becky tied a bright scarlet, gold-trimmed hip belt around her harem pants. "I think it'll be a hoot. By the time I learn a routine, Keith'll be good enough to join the drummers. I hope."

"I only want to work off some of this flab." Hannah retied her belt twice before she was satisfied. Her belly pouched out. *No more cookies for you, Hannah dear. Not even Missy's low calorie ones.*

After warm-up stretches, Amy demonstrated the first series of movements in a choreographed routine named "Dancing Hips." "We'll add in the zills as soon as we get the sequencing down."

"I do okay until I try to sashay around *and* play those zills." Hannah flailed her arms. "Ka-ray-zee klutz-o, as Jonas puts it."

"Oh, poo!" Becky said. "Remember when we first learned this snake-arms move? How we looked like we were having seizures? Now all three of us can do it like we were born in the sands of Arabia."

Amy agreed. "You three are doing well. Give yourselves a little credit. You've only been taking lessons for a couple of months. I've been dancing for seven years, and most of these intermediate students have been with me for at least a year. By the time the Hafla rolls around next spring, you'll be on stage."

"Heaven knows, Amy. If you believe in us that much, we'll give it all we've got." Suzanne accented her statement with a rolling hip swivel.

The instructor drilled the first eight movements until perspiration glistened on the students' faces. At the end of class, Suzanne folded her hip belt into her duffel bag. "Man, do I feel wiped out."

"I hear you," Becky said. "I've lost eight pounds already. I dance two hours a day."

"You've lost weight, and your mind," Hannah commented.

Becky ignored the jab. "How're y'all's mamas?"

Suzanne lifted one shoulder and let it fall. "Mine barely leaves the house. Says she's short of breath most of the time. Understandable, with her heart condition."

"I hate it that they can't do anything for her," Becky said.

"I don't think she would go for it, even if they offered. She told me she didn't want to see any more doctors or have any more tests. Period, the end. I guess she's made up her mind that the Good Lord will determine when she's ready to check out."

Becky turned to Hannah. "And Mae?"

Hannah blew out a long breath. "Up and down. Things I think for certain would depress her don't. Then she'll get all worked up about something from years past that I'm sure everyone but her has forgotten."

"Mama's the same, reviewing things and processing them all over again." Suzanne's lips turned downward slightly. "They say people's lives pass before them right before they die, but I believe it begins earlier. Especially when you're old like Mae and my mama."

"Lots of time to sit around and think," Becky added. "My mom's right there, too."

Hannah picked up her bag and swung the strap over one shoulder. "Ma-Mae said the oddest thing yesterday. I'm still rolling it over in my mind. She was reliving something from four years ago, worrying and carrying on like it was recent. She felt like folks were gossiping about her. I kept asking her who had brought it up to start with. Thought maybe one of her friends had dropped by for a visit and passed along some idle talk. You know what she told me?"

Becky and Suzanne leaned in.

"She said it was 'coming in from the air.' "

Becky's eyebrows arched. "Like a radio show?"

"Something like that, I suppose," Hannah said.

Suzanne threw her arm across her sister-in-law's shoulder. "I wouldn't worry too much about it, Hannah. They say odd things at times. Makes sense to them, but not to the rest of us. She's probably remembering little snippets, popping into her mind at random."

"Maybe. "

"I look at it this way. Life is this mystery story. You get a few clues along the way. Some red herrings to throw you off the trail to truth. But, you don't get the big picture of how it all comes together until—" Suzanne raised both hands, palms up.

"—until the end," Hannah supplied.

The phone rang at six o'clock on Sunday morning. Hannah's pulse quickened as she grappled for the phone.

"Hannah?" Her mother said.

"Ma-Mae? What's wrong?"

"I'm feeling a little puny this morning."

"Your stomach? What?"

"The nurse doesn't seem overly concerned. She asked if I wanted her to call you earlier when she came to check me out."

"You hurting anywhere?" Hannah pushed off the covers and sat up.

"Just not up to par. I told the nurse not to bother you, that I would call you myself later on. I knew you'd break your neck getting here. And there's no reason. I need a day of lying around in bed."

"Good day for that. Supposed to rain, pretty much, off and on all day. I'm going to do the same. Some laundry, get ready for the work week. I don't even know if I'll make it to church this morning. I'll be here if you need me. You'll call, right?"

"You don't worry. They sent my breakfast down."

"She okay?" Norman asked after Hannah hung up.

Hannah lay back and nestled into the crook of his arm. "Says she's feeling bad."

"You want to get dressed and ride to Rosemont?"

"I'll go over later. It'll make her mad if I go running over there now."

Norman gently ran his fingers through his wife's hair and massaged her scalp. "I know you're concerned, hon. Wish I knew how to help."

Hannah hugged closer to her husband. "You do help, by being beside me."

Slug bounded onto the bed, landing between them. He yowled twice before hunkering down in the middle of Norman's chest. "You need to put this feline on a diet. I can barely breathe."

Hannah scratched Slug under the chin and his purr-motor roared. "He's only trying to love you some."

Norman huffed. "A man should be so lucky."

"Norman?"

"Hmm?"

"I'm sorry I haven't been very physical lately."

"It's okay."

"It's not that I don't absolutely adore you. The past couple of months have been really good with us. I just . . . I don't have much energy by the time we're alone."

"We've been under a lot of strain, Hannah."

"I'm so afraid, sometimes, that you'll get fed up and go find another woman."

"Oh please!"

Hannah traced a finger along his chin. "I'm not meeting your needs. My wifely duty . . . "

"I don't want anyone else, Hannah Olsen." He kissed her lightly on the forehead. "Don't concern yourself with my needs. Life isn't all about sex. After all, I still have two perfectly good hands."

Hannah swatted him on the chest. "Norman!"

"They worked fine back in college before I married the love of my life."

Hannah laughed and snuggled into the security of his arms.

Soon after her morning coffee, Hannah initiated a cleaning binge. She excised three bags of clothing from the master bedroom closet, then barreled into Jonas's and Justine's rooms. If it hadn't touched human skin in two years, it went into the charity pile.

She moved into the study and filled trash bags with papers, paid bills, magazines, advertisements, and assorted riff-raff, bound for the garbage or shredder.

Norman escaped to his workshop with orders to clean and pitch. Justine exercised the vacuum, and Jonas herded dust bunnies. By the time lunch rolled around, the exhausted family—reeking of lemon-fresh cleansers and sweat—gathered in the kitchen for warmed-over lasagna.

"Don't you all feel better?" Hannah asked as she handed out paper plates and napkins.

Her family stared at her.

"Sure, Mom," Jonas finally replied.

Hannah walked into Rosemont later, feeling tired yet accomplished. Instead of disturbing Mae with a knock, Hannah used her key. "Ma-Mae?" she called in a soft voice as she entered.

"Come on in."

Hannah dropped her purse and keys on a chair and sat on the side of her mother's bed. "How are you?"

"Better." Mae rose up and plumped her pillows. "Josie brought me a bowl of soup."

"I thought the dining room staff usually did that when you weren't well."

"They do. Good about it. But you know Josie has that rolling walker with the little tray."

"You are better?" Hannah noted the sallow cast to her mother's skin. The tang of camphor reached her nose. Besides laxatives, Mae believed mentholated chest rub cured every ill.

"I had a case of the stomach sours. Never did upchuck, but I was nauseous all the same. Didn't eat much—just drank—until the soup. And Josie brought me a nice slice of pound cake."

"I've been worried."

"That's why I didn't let the staff call you. No use you running over here every time I toot. I raised three children and nursed a husband with a heart condition. Reckon I can get through a stomach ache."

Hannah removed the dish tray and sat it on the bureau.

"Leave that. Someone from the kitchen will be by to fetch it later," Mae said. "There is one thing you can do for me. The three-way light in my pole lamp's blown. I thought I had a spare, but I've searched high and low."

"I'll buy a couple tomorrow. You okay until then?"

Mae motioned to the bedside table light. "Got this one here. I'll live."

Norman snored: a soft, snorting noise with an even rhythm that usually lulled her to sleep. Not tonight. Tonight was a hot flash/worry night. One minute she shucked the covers and the next she dove beneath, shivering.

Hannah took the opportunity to stress about everything and anything: the kids, the glitch-infested software program at work, the extra pounds around her midsection, Suzanne's mother's heart condition, the spittle bug infestation in the front lawn, Ma-Mae's declining health.

She finally moved to the couch. Slug joined her. He bathed for fifteen minutes, then settled beside her, purring. Two hours later, exhausted, she finally drifted off.

In the dream, Randy the one-man band played to a room of Rosemont residents. His folksy voice crooned, "He's got the whole world in his hands." Hannah looked around her at all the hands, clapping along and gesturing to the old spiritual song in the manner learned in elementary school.

Something about those elderly hands—hands that had held babies, wiped feverish brows, comforted lovers—filled her with a deep peace.

Chapter Thirty-seven

Hannah caught a whiff of her underarms as she waited in line at Chattahoochee Drugs, her mother's favorite hemorrhoid ointment in one hand and a bottle of antacid in the other.

"Jeez," she muttered, clamping her arms to her sides. *How is this? I've been in an air-conditioned cubicle all day. I layered on deodorant and a topcoat of powder.*

Hannah envisioned contented bacteria festering in the dark moisture of her armpits. A sulfurous haze hung over their cozy little neighborhood. No Irish garden, dew-drop, linen-fresh concoction could smother them. Like cockroaches, bacteria were indestructible, bound for eventual world domination.

Hannah longed for the cool, dry breezes of fall—and a tepid, sudsy shower.

"What's the matter, sugar? You look like you sucked a sour lemon," Mae commented when Hannah returned to the idling SUV.

"I stink! That's what's the matter." Hannah shoved the gear shift into reverse and backed out of the parking spot.

"Now that you bring it up . . . "

"Why didn't you tell me?"

Mae slapped her hands in her lap. "How in Sam Hill do you say something like that?"

"You say, 'Gee, my sweet daughter, you smell ripe. You need to wash your pits.' That's what you say."

"That would be plain rude."

Hannah looked away from the road long enough to shoot her mother a smoldering glance. "So if I had a piece of spinach stuck between my front teeth, you wouldn't tell me?"

"More than likely, I'd stick my fingernail between my teeth and nod and hope you'd get the message."

"Ma-Mae, when I was growing up, you didn't hesitate for one

split second to tell me if a dress was too short, or that my makeup was too heavy."

"That was different. A parent's role is to guide."

Hannah chuckled. "Excuse me. When did you stop being the parent?"

"When you grew up and became the mother."

They rode in silence until Hannah made the turn into the Rosemont parking lot.

"Am I being too bossy, Ma-Mae?"

Mae tried twice to unfasten the seatbelt clasp before allowing Hannah to assist her. "Who says I don't want to be bossed around a bit, huh? I don't want to make all the decisions anymore, or worry so much about little details." She winked. "Besides, you're so good at it."

"I should be. I learned at the feet of a master."

"Maybe so." Mae steadied her cane before getting out. "But this master is tired and retired."

"Must run in the family."

Hannah jerked so hard when she heard the deep male voice, her coffee sloshed onto her lap. "Hal!" She stood up and flapped the moisture from her shorts. The porch swing pitched and yawed. "You scared the daylights out of me!"

"Sorry, sis. I thought you heard me slam the patio door."

Hannah steadied the porch swing, sat down, and dabbed a napkin over the trickles of coffee trailing down her thighs. "If I wasn't awake before, I surely am now."

Hal sat beside her on the swing. "You were in a heavy conversation with someone." He fanned one hand through the air. "Out there."

"I know it sounds crazy, but I was talking to Pop."

"Suzanne's always catching me. Especially when I'm working out how to build something, it helps me to explain it to Pop, even if he's not technically here. I always ran things by him before."

Hannah reached over and tousled his hair. "Got fresh coffee on, if you want a cup."

"I've had three already. At this rate, I won't slow down till midnight. But thanks. You know I'd help myself, anyway."

Hannah nodded, then asked, "Think Helen does it too, the whole talking to Pop thing?"

"Knowing Helen—she probably emails him too."

She took a long sip of coffee. "You think I'm bossy, Hal?"

"Is this one of those loaded female questions where there's no right answer—like, 'does this outfit make my butt look fat?'"

"No. Legit. Do I?"

"You can be . . . somewhat forceful at times." He held up both hands. "Not an awful quality, necessarily."

"Ma-Mae has started referring to me as *her mother*."

"I've heard her say that. I thought she might be imagining a ghostly visit from Grandma, until I figured out she meant you."

Hannah turned to face him. "Really?"

"It's not a bad thing. Not like she's upset or anything."

"I've tried so hard to let her hang onto whatever shreds of independence she can. Her judgment isn't so hot anymore. I don't pull rank unless I think she's doing something that might prove harmful."

"Don't sweat it." Hal leaned back and slipped his arm across his sister's shoulders. "Each of us has a role. I'm *the man*." He flicked his fingers in mock quotations. "She looks to me when it comes to business dealings—the sale of the house, for instance."

A brilliant red male cardinal swooped to one of the bird feeders, squabbled with a blue jay over dominance, scattered seeds until he found one that suited him, then flew off.

"I take care of her checkbook and pay bills, and she still thinks you're in control of the finances," Hannah said.

"I'm a substitute for Pop, I guess. The male figure head, the monarch. You know, like in England. But the real leader is the prime minister—you."

"Glad you've worked this all out, your majesty." Hannah dipped her head. "What about our sister? Where does she fit in to this hierarchy?"

"Helen is . . . " He thought for a moment. "the ambassador. Kind of a counselor/good will type. You know she can cry at the drop of a hat. Always thought she would've made a good soap opera actress. Too much empathy for her own good. I think Ma-Mae reaches out for Helen when she needs someone to ease a burden of the heart."

"She talks to me all the time, Hal. You saying I don't treat her with compassion?"

"No, no." Hal shook his head. "Not what I meant at all. Ma-Mae can talk to either of us. We get things done, take action. She tells Helen about stuff when she needs someone to feel with her, emote, carry on. Clear as mud?"

"About that."

"We're lucky all three of us share this, Hannah. Suzanne has to be everything to her mama. It's a tremendous strain."

"I thank my lucky stars every day." She leaned over and kissed him on the cheek. "Did you just stop by to offer words of wisdom?"

Hal pulled a measuring tape reel from his jean pocket. "I came to get a rough idea of how much pressure-treated lumber Norman and I need for your deck extension."

"Thought y'all weren't starting that until the weather cooled off."

"We can knock this project out in a weekend, if it'll stop raining long enough. Suzanne's put in for a gazebo, so Norman and I can start that project as soon as your deck's finished. My dear wife read some article in *Southern Living* about outdoor living rooms and decided we couldn't live without one. She has the big ideas, and I get to hammer them together."

Hal thumped his forehead with the heel of his hand. "Man! I'd forget my head if it wasn't tied on! Suzanne wanted me to invite y'all to our church this Sunday. They're having a special Parents' Appreciation Day and a big dinner on the grounds. We thought Ma-Mae would really enjoy it. She knows a lot of folks over our way. Suzanne's mama will be there. She really likes Ma-Mae. If you don't want to go, I'll drive over and pick up Ma-Mae."

"Who in their right mind would miss an old-fashioned dinner on the grounds? All the cooks break out their best recipes."

"Suzanne meant to tell you at dance class. Guess she got too busy sashaying around."

Hannah grinned. "She's really into this belly dancing thing. I'm sure you enjoy it too."

The male cardinal returned, this time booting a female of his species from the feeder. Why did everything in nature seem like a struggle?

"If most men were honest, who wouldn't like feeling like a sultan.

I'm a sensitive type of oasis king. I'll go with whatever role she wants me to play." Hal smiled. "Long as I can choose jeans and a four-wheel drive pickup over robes and a camel."

Chapter Thirty-eight

"Why isn't Justine coming with us?" Norman asked as he steered the SUV through Rosemont's parking lot.

Hannah studied her reflection in the passenger side vanity mirror and dabbed her lipstick with a tissue. "It's kind of a moral high ground, from what I could understand. Brittany's coming home next weekend."

"In honor of that, Justine can't eat?"

"She said she couldn't support the epitome of gluttony when her best friend is struggling to eat at all."

"Jus is a nut case," Jonas commented from the back seat.

Hannah turned around. "Not kind of you to say about your sister, Jonas. She has the right to her opinion, no matter how odd it may seem."

"She was afraid I'd touch her with my alien feeler." Jonas waved his withered, now-cast-free arm in the air.

Hannah smiled. It was hard to be stern with her son for very long.

"You should've seen it when they first took the cast off, Mom. The skin was all creepy, and boy did it stink!"

"Spare me the details, son." Hannah pulled a frown.

"I wish it would stay all skinny like this forever. It's pretty radical."

"It won't." Norman glanced in the rearview mirror. "The muscles have atrophied from lack of use. Pretty soon, it'll look like nothing ever happened."

"Bummer."

"You want me to go in and get Ma-Mae?" Norman asked Hannah when they pulled to the covered front entrance.

Hannah slid from her seat. "Y'all keep the car cool. She should be ready to go."

When Hannah unlocked and entered Mae's room, her mother was still in her purple velour robe.

Mae's brow wrinkled. "What are you doing here? You should be at work."

"It's Sunday, Ma-Mae. We're all going over to Hal and Suzanne's church. I called to remind you last night."

Mae trundled to the bulletin board that held her calendar and traced the grid with one finger. "Oh. Here it is." She threw up her hands. "Reckon I'm not going. I don't have on the right clothes for church."

Hannah took a deep breath and exhaled slowly. "Let me tell Norman and Jonas to come in and wait in the living room. I'll help you get dressed."

"Do we have time? Am I going to be late?"

Hannah checked her watch. "You've had your bath?"

"I could do a quick whore bath."

Hannah stifled a smile at her mother's terminology for bathing only the essential parts. A whore bath before church. What a concept.

When Hannah returned from the parking lot, outfits dotted the bed and Mae struggled to coax a pair of support hose over her damp feet and legs.

"I was up, helping our new table mate," Mae explained as she inched the thick hosiery up her calves. "Reckon that's why I wasn't dressed."

Hannah let the statement pass without challenge. One day, she might need fabrications to bolster her own tattered tether to reality. "This purple pantsuit is pretty, Ma-Mae."

Mae bounced three times, stood, then teetered for a moment before leaning to pull up the hose. As much as Hannah was tempted to butt in, she hung back.

"I positively hate putting on hose," Hannah said, removing Mae's pantsuit from its tubular plastic hanger.

"Don't know one woman who doesn't." Mae wiggled the pants up and over her distended stomach. "But they keep my legs from swelling up so bad." She frowned. "I'll be dog-goned!"

"What?"

"I've got to pee." Mae shuffled to the bathroom.

At this rate, we'll be lucky to make it in time for the after-service dinner, Hannah thought.

The toilet flushed and Mae emerged. "Help me with my top. Mind my 'do. I just had it fixed yesterday."

Hannah worked the tunic over her mother's sprayed-stiff hair.

"That new woman that sits with us at mealtime, she's from Ft. Lauderdale," Mae said.

Hannah straightened her mother's collar. "That right?"

"She's having a time fitting in. Don't know why she didn't move into a place like the Mont down there." Mae sat down with a grunt.

"Does she have any family?"

"One son. Lives over near Quincy." Mae motioned to the closet. "Look in there and hand me the navy sandals. They don't worry my bunions."

"I can understand why he'd want to have her up here. Close by."

Mae slipped the leather sandals on and secured the Velcro straps across the insteps. "She came down for breakfast this morning and left before she could eat."

"Wasn't she feeling well?"

"That wasn't it." Mae rose and gestured toward the bathroom vanity. "Let me put on a dab of lipstick so I won't look like death warmed over."

Hannah stood behind her mother with a hair pick and attempted to fluff the flattened spot where sleep had crushed her hairstyle.

"It was crazy down there in the dining hall this morning," Mae continued. "Folks asking for things the cooks didn't have. People sniping for no reason. Some days are like that with us old folks." She puckered and applied a thick layer of rose-tinted lipstick, then smack-kissed most of it off on a tissue. "The servers didn't get her order fast enough. Then when it came, something was missing. She got up and left!"

"Close your eyes." Hannah spritzed hairspray across Mae's curls. "There. I'm no stylist, but it'll do."

"I'll need a wrap, baby."

"It's in the nineties outside. I hardly think—"

Mae pushed past her daughter and rummaged through the hanging clothes to locate a soft white shawl. "I'll take this thing Helen gave me for Christmas last year. Gets cold in the sanctuary. You'll understand one day when your blood gets old and thin."

"I'm the opposite. Hot most of the time."

Mae scanned the room. "Do I need my glasses?"

"Sunshades. It's overcast, but bright." Hannah handed Mae her neck key fob. "Ready?"

"As I ever will be." She reached up and felt her earlobes. "Damnation! Forgot my earbobs!"

Hannah felt a grin tempt the corners of her mouth. *Damnation:* the one curse word somewhat condoned by Mae Mathers. If it was good enough to be printed in the Bible, it was fair game.

Mae rooted around in a small velvet case, then snapped a pair of pearl studs in place. "Now we can go."

As they walked down the corridor, Mae continued her narrative. "I took the woman's breakfast up to her."

"That was nice of you."

"From talking to her, I gathered she doesn't feel 'good enough,' like folks are looking down on her." Mae shook her head. "I told her a little story. Think it made her feel better. She ate some of her eggs and a slice of toast. Remember that seafood shack we used to eat at down in Eastpoint?" Mae asked.

Ah, the story about the handmade sign with the worn cliché. Hannah thought about putting a stop to it, but decided to listen, again. As if she hadn't heard it a million times.

"Try as I may, I can't remember the name of the place, right on the water off Highway 98. It got blown down in one of the hurricanes. We would sit and watch the oystermen coming in after a long day on the Gulf. There was a plaque hanging beside the checkout counter. I can see it plain as yesterday. Had a cartoon of a bedraggled fellow, a bum—patches on his knees and elbows. He was smiling to beat the band. Know what it read?"

"What?"

"I know I'm somebody, 'cause God don't make junk."

Chapter Thirty-nine

A sensation floated over Hannah as she drifted between sleep and wakefulness, her hand loosely clasping Norman's: her father's large hand—rough, calloused, strong—folding around hers. She tried to grasp the feeling, but it faded.

Hannah often looked at family photos, straining to call up snippets of her father's physical presence. As the years passed, the memories slipped into obscurity. Only through Hal, the sole male Mathis offspring, could she glimpse reflections of her father's ambling walk, broad shoulders, and belly-shaking laughter.

Norman's chest rose and fell in an easy rhythm. He ignored the clock radio's insistent intrusion and Hannah slapped the snooze button. Even on hot-flash nights when she whipped the sheets to a damp froth, Norman slept peacefully, dadgum him. She snuggled closer to her husband, chasing a vague fear with the comfort of human touch. His heartbeat, even and strong, provided a reassuring mantra.

Hannah's thoughts crept to Mae. What small tidbits would she recall about her mother? The softness of Mae's wrinkled cheeks. Her baby-fine, angel-white hair. The way her blue-gray eyes twinkled when she acted mischievous. Her child-like laughter.

Possessions—cars, houses, money, jewelry, clothes— meant nothing in the end. The legacy lay in the remembrances of loved ones and friends, and in the small, seemingly insignificant acts of everyday goodness.

The clock radio jarred her reverie again. Just as well. No need to delve so deeply into the meaning of life before a shower and a cup of strong coffee.

Hannah fumbled with the toggle switch, kissed Norman on the cheek, and stumbled to the bathroom. She showered in the dim illumination of the night-light. How in the world did those morning-people bounce straight from sleep to chirping and flinging open blinds?

Rivulets of warm water trickled to either side of her belly like a raging river avoiding a boulder. She glanced down and frowned. Salads only for her for a while. Even her most forgiving pants failed to meet at the waistband. She soaped, rinsed, and dried off without looking too long at any one body part.

Other than the rhythmic ticking of the kitchen clock, the house was silent. Jonas and Justine slept, enjoying one last week of freedom before the start of the fall school term. Jonas would be the first to appear, usually about the time Hannah left for work. Forget seeing her daughter until after ten, at least. If sleep truly equaled beauty, Justine was drop-dead gorgeous. Norman stayed in bed until the last possible moment, easy for a man. He could shower, dress, and grab coffee in less than thirty minutes.

In the kitchen, Slug twirled in languid circles at her feet until she filled his bowl. She mixed Snooker's dry kibble with a splash of warm water, added a dog biscuit and carried it to the deck with her coffee and a day-old cinnamon roll. She ate on the swing, accompanied by the smack and slap of Snooker's lips and tongue. Delicate, he wasn't.

Moisture clung to every surface and swirled in pools of mist beneath the trees. Hannah longed for the first indications of fall: small changes in the way the air felt on the fine hairs on her forearms; a certain scent carrying the promise of the final harvest; the edginess of animals preparing for the dead season.

Each year as the summer dragged on, weighing human and animals down to a miserable crawl, the thought of relocating teased the back of her mind. Yet when ice storms and blizzards screeched the northern states to a housebound halt, Hannah reaffirmed her Southern roots. She could barbeque in the backyard in a light jacket while some poor fellow shoveled his walkway for the third time in a week.

Life: a series of tradeoffs. Hannah studied the half-eaten cinnamon roll and wondered how it would taste slathered with peanut butter.

"Sweet Jesus wept," Becky whispered, her eyes wide. "Look who just strolled in."

Missy Rodgers spotted the group of women across the dance studio, waved and walked to join them. "Hey!" She smiled and plopped a quilted bag on the floor. "Hope y'all don't mind me joining the class. Hannah has talked about it in such glowing terms."

Hannah, the first to recover, said, "Of course not."

Missy glanced at Becky's ornate ensemble, then down to her own black tights and tank top. "I didn't know what to wear."

"What you have on is fine," Suzanne said, digging in her bag. "Here, tie this on." She handed Missy a mint green chiffon scarf trimmed with rows of silver dangles.

"Isn't this the prettiest thing?" Missy tied the scarf around her waist and gave a few experimental shakes. Anyone who knew the Majesty-of-the-Volunteer-Squad would not have recognized Missy as the same uptight, ultra-perfect housewife and mother. Her hair was drawn back in a loose ponytail. Even her scrubbed-clean facial features, formerly frozen into an insincere facsimile of a smile and lacquered with makeup, seemed relaxed.

"I thought you'd be busy getting ready for Brittany's homecoming," Hannah commented as they lined up.

"One can only mop the floor and polish the furniture so many times," Missy said. "My counselor highly recommended I do something just for me. I'm so stuck in a rut and . . . well, bored."

"Didn't think you lit in any one place long enough to be bored," Becky said. "You're on the social page of the paper practically every week."

"Everything I do is for someone else, not that volunteering is a bad thing. I need something to call my own."

Hannah nodded. "We women tend to define ourselves in terms of our families."

Suzanne leaned over and stretched. "I thought we weren't allowed to get all profound during official dance-and-fun time."

"Point taken." Hannah motioned to a spot beside her. "You can be up here on the front row next to me if you'd like, Missy. It's easier to see what the instructor's doing."

Amy bustled through the door, a rolling case trailing behind. "Hey, everyone." She stopped in front of Missy. "Eww! A newbie!"

Missy blinked. "Did I need to let you know ahead of time that I wanted to come?"

"Not at all. We'll get you caught up." Amy tied on a black and silver hip scarf and loaded the CD player. "Let's stretch out the wrinkles."

"I took dancing in college," Missy reached overhead with both arms.

Becky said, "It'll take a bite out of your behind, the first couple of classes. After that, you'll be fine."

By the end of the class, Missy had mastered the basic hip movements. Afterwards, the group stood in a cluster in the parking lot, exchanging a few last minute comments.

"You know, Missy. You're not half as bad as I always thought," Suzanne said. "If I didn't like you so much better, I'd almost hate you for how good you are already at this dancing thing."

"I'm a long, long way from perfection," Missy said.

Becky slapped Missy playfully on the back. "Thank God for that. Perfect people are so annoying."

Hannah felt a glow of pride for her new friend.

"I have an idea," Missy said. "Why don't you all come over this weekend? I'll throw together some munchies and we can review the moves."

"Isn't Brittany due home?" Suzanne asked.

"Yes. But I don't want her to feel as if she's under a spotlight. If it's only the two of us cooped up together, I'll hover. I know how I am." Missy turned to Hannah. "Maybe Justine can come over. She and Brittany could spend some time catching up on their girl talk. Saturday about two?"

"It could work. Norman and Jonas will probably take the boat out, if the weather's good."

"Saturday's okay," Becky added. "I have plans on Sunday."

"I'm in," Suzanne said. "I don't practice at home enough as it is. Hal can amuse himself for one afternoon."

Missy clasped her hands together. "Wonderful! Now I have to find some of that music like Amy plays in class."

Becky held out both arms. "Got that covered. I went online and bought out the entire Middle Eastern Dance section."

"That's what I've always liked about you, Beck," Hannah said. "Your over-the-top enthusiasm."

"Better *en-thused* than *re-fused*." Becky threw over her shoulder as she walked toward her car.

The phone rang at 6 a.m. as Hannah settled down with her first cup of coffee and the Saturday *Tallahassee Democrat*.

Her mother said, "Did I wake you?"

"No, Ma-Mae. What's up?"

"I know we're supposed to have a girls' morning out, but I'm having trouble with my bowels. I got that puffy feeling like my stomach is all swelled up." Mae sighed. "I've been on the move so much, I've let myself get off schedule."

"Haven't been drinking your water, have you?"

"I forget."

"Why don't you ask them to make sure you have some prunes along with breakfast? You've always maintained that helped you."

"Good idea, sugar. I'll mention it to Miz Leah. She caters to me, you know. For now, I'll take one of my little pink pills and hope for the best."

Do other people have in-depth discussions about irregularity first thing in the morning? Hannah wondered. "Can I bring you anything?"

"I'm okay for now. I don't think I want to be far from a bathroom when the medicine starts to work. Maybe you can stop in later on. If I feel better, we can go for a frozen yogurt."

"Call me if you need me," Hannah said. "I may break down and do a little weeding this morning, but I'll have the phone out here with me."

"Love you a bushel and a peck and a hug around the neck."

Hannah smiled at her mother's little ditty. "Love you, too, Ma-Mae"

Chapter Forty

Missy Rodgers answered the door wearing a sweeping black skirt and matching tank top, overlaid with a scarlet hip scarf. Her hair, tied up on the crest of her head, sported multi-colored strips of material.

"You're really going all out." Hannah smiled. "It took me four lessons before I committed to buying a hip scarf."

"I've wanted to get back into some kind of dance, ever since college. But my dear departed husband didn't think it was comely for a married housewife." Missy crossed her eyes and stuck out her tongue like a petulant two-year-old, then laughed. "C'mon in. I'm making fresh peach daiquiris."

"Sounds like you're going to an awful amount of trouble."

"Not really." Missy gave a dismissive wave. "I bought a bushel of Georgia peaches yesterday at the fruit stand. I'll freeze some, but the rest will ripen faster than Brittany and I can eat them."

Missy spun and bustled off toward the kitchen, Hannah in her wake. Suzanne and Becky sat at the round oak table, eating crackers and gourmet cheese.

"About time you got here," Becky said.

Hannah pulled up a chair. "I stopped to check on Ma-Mae."

"How is she?" Suzanne asked.

"Not such a good day."

"Too bad she's not here. Missy could fix her up with one of those concoctions she's churning," Suzanne said. "Judging by the rum she's adding, we'll do good to stand up, much less wiggle."

"I made a virgin batch too," Missy said. "And I didn't put *that* much rum in." She glanced at Hannah. "I know we have to teach our kids about the danger of alcohol consumption, but I believe they have to learn about responsible drinking by adults too."

Hannah held up a stop-hand. "I'm not judging, Missy. Relax. Norman and I have an occasional beer or glass of wine."

Brittany and Justine appeared.

"Mom, we're going to ride up to the lake," Brittany said.

"Fine, honey. Be sure to take plenty to drink. It's really hot outside."

"I've got bottled water in the car." Justine held her hand out to her mother, palm up. Hannah dug in her purse for a couple of bills and handed them over.

"Be home before too late, please," Missy called after the departing teens. "I'm making your favorite supper."

"Brittany looks pretty good," Hannah commented after they heard the front door slam.

Missy poured four tall insulated tumblers full of the sherbet-toned frozen mixture. "She's put on seven and a half pounds. But it'll be an ongoing trial to keep her from regressing. The counselor says this is the difficult part, when she rejoins her peers."

"Knowing my daughter, she'll keep a close eye on her," Hannah said.

"A fact I am greatly appreciative of." Missy delivered the mint-garnished daiquiris to the table.

"Sure am glad you're not giving up totally on your 'hostess-with-the-mostest' role," Hannah said.

Missy smiled and took a delicate sip before answering. "Entertaining is the heart of me. I see no reason to quit now."

"I bet each ounce of this wonderful drink has about a thousand calories," Suzanne said.

"Probably." Missy made an amused sound. "I plan to make y'all dance till you drop, so there shouldn't be a problem working it off."

Becky laughed. "Why do I get the feeling that all that volunteer energy you've shucked off is going to land on us?"

Missy raised one eyebrow. "It has to go somewhere."

Suzanne followed her sister-in-law to her car. "What's up with you?"

"I'm pretty whipped. All that swiveling."

"You seem kind of washed out."

Hannah frowned. "A little." The slight rum-buzz had faded.

"Anything I can help with?" Suzanne leaned against the side of Hannah's SUV.

Hannah felt the burn of impending tears. "Not really. Same old. I've been so tired lately. I can't seem to get enough rest."

"When was your last period?"

Hannah thought for a moment. "Two, three months ago maybe? No real schedule. I never know."

"Probably a huge part of how you feel. The whole hormonal switch-off thing."

Hannah leaned against Suzanne's van. She found support wherever she could, lately. Exhausted because she couldn't sleep. Crying jags. Laughing jags. Jags for no good reason. Tears welled in her eyes. At least her eyes weren't dry.

"I'm coming over and we're going to talk," Suzanne said.

"Don't feel like you have to do that, Sis. I'm always leaning on you."

"You've been there for me. You forget all *those* times."

A few minutes later, the two women settled onto Hannah's porch swing with tall glasses of iced tea. Snooker greeted them with knee licks before flopping down on the deck and promptly going to sleep. Hannah sometimes wished she was a dog, or better yet a cat. Fed, watered, able to play or snooze at will.

"It's Mae, isn't it?" Suzanne asked.

"Primarily, I guess . . . I feel like such a broken record."

Suzanne nodded. "I get so tired of hearing myself talk about the same things over and over. It's a wonder your poor brother doesn't go stark raving mad."

"If he's like most men, and I know he is, he only hears about half of what you're saying anyway."

"True. True," Suzanne agreed. "He'll at least grunt every now and then. Sometimes, he gives some pretty good advice." Suzanne kicked her feet to put the swing in gentle motion. "What is it with your mama today?"

"Nothing new, really. She wasn't feeling well. Irregularity issues."

"Nine times out of ten, it's either her bowels or kidneys, like my mama."

"When she feels bad, she gets down mentally. Starts wondering why she's still here. She's been having nightmares." Hannah held the frosty tea glass to her forehead and rolled it back and forth. Maybe I'll move to Siberia for a few years, she thought.

"What's she dreaming about?"

"I don't think she remembers. Just that she wakes up in a cold sweat. She's dreamed a lot, especially in the last couple of weeks, about Pop. That upsets her because she's 'dreaming of the dead.' I've tried to explain to her that isn't necessarily a bad thing. They were together so many years; it's only natural for her to dream about him. I do."

"You came away sad again, after talking to her?"

Hannah nodded.

"Don't take this like I'm raining down on you, Hannah, but you have to develop the ability to let Mae's stuff roll off you better. If not, you'll go plain cathead crazy."

"I'm there already." *Maybe I'd feel better if I did get up and pitch a fit. Flail my arms, jerk and jive, let a little drool drip down my chin.*

"Old people have good and bad days, like the rest of us," Suzanne continued. "Mae's body's wearing out and she hurts. It's enough to make anyone feel blue. Plus, your daddy's gone. My mama misses my daddy something fierce. No amount of me loving her up is going to change that."

"I know all of these things on a conscious level, Sis."

"You are by nature, a caring type of person, Hannah." Suzanne's gaze filled with concern. "Your mama raised you up to be that way. But you have to figure out in your mind some way to listen without soaking it all inside."

Snooker jerked awake and dashed off, barking. From zero to murder-the-squirrel mode.

Hannah watched her dog circle an oak tree. The squirrel climbed to a safe level and chattered. "I already take Zoloft, for heaven's sake."

"All that drug does is help take off the edge. But you have to settle in your own mind. If I had a magic wand, I'd clobber both of us over the head with it. It's not like I'm the expert of the world. You'll more than likely take my words and spit them right back at me when I get myself loaded down." Snooker returned, panting, and flopped down. Suzanne petted him with the tips of her toes.

Hannah took a deep breath. "I have these awful thoughts, sometimes. I hate to admit them to anyone."

"You wish Mae would die before it gets any worse for either of you," Suzanne said, her voice soft.

Hannah turned to face her sister-in-law. "Do you—?"

"Yes. And if most people in this situation were honest with themselves, they struggle with the same thought."

"How unbelievably awful of me." Hannah swiped her sweaty bangs away from her forehead. "I'm wishing for my mother to die. What kind of a person does that?"

"You aren't wishing her dead. You're hoping for her passage to be free of pain and that slow, steady loss. You want her to be able to skip the lingering-on." Suzanne snapped her fingers in irritation. "Dang it! I can talk till I'm blue, and still not find the right words to say what I truly mean."

Hannah bumped her playfully on the shoulder. "If you're at a loss for words, Sis, this must be pretty hard to figure out."

"I have a hankering for ice cream, all of a sudden." Suzanne moistened her lips.

"Sounds like my craving for peanut butter. I can't seem to get enough. As to ice cream, I have some low-carb stuff in the freezer if the kids haven't eaten it all."

Suzanne stood so suddenly, Snooker scrambled to his feet and regarded her with wide eyes. "Uh-uh. That fake stuff isn't going to cut it. I need a double dip of rocky road fudge in an old-fashioned crispy cone. I want to wallow in it and lick the dribbles off my fingers. Nothing short of that is going to soothe what ails us both. We can get you some with peanut butter in it, I'm sure."

"I'll drive."

No matter how hard she tried, Hannah couldn't figure out her husband's ongoing passion for power tools. Not only did Norman own every kind of cutting, measuring and drilling device, his shed bulged with yard-related gadgets. And he wasn't especially handy with them.

The latest acquisition was an electric-powered pressure washer. As soon as he cut off the price tag, he took great pains blasting the front sidewalk until his hands could barely form a fist around the control nozzle. Not deterred, he figured a way to tie the release handle so that it didn't require a heavy squeeze. Next, he moved to the driveway. The reflected glare from the newly-cleaned cement hurt Hannah's eyes, even through celebrity-dark sunglasses. An entire Saturday spent washing away grime and mold. Norman, in power-tool heaven.

Today, though it was Sunday, Norman and his assistant Jonas had awakened early. They roamed the property, searching for anything that would stay still long enough to hose down. Snooker cowered beneath the deck, afraid of the bath of a lifetime.

Justine sat at the kitchen table, her head bent low over a bowl of soggy cereal. Between her elderly mother and teenaged daughter, the family mood swings seldom slowed to a complete halt.

"Bad morning?" Hannah popped a cinnamon roll into the microwave and topped off her coffee.

Justine poked out her lips and shrugged. "I guess."

"Want to talk about it?"

"Don't know what good it would do."

Hannah slid into a chair with her cup and saucer. "Might not. Then again, it might. Only if you want." Never, ever sound or look too interested in a teenager's affairs; she had learned from experience.

"It's just . . . Brittany."

"I thought you two had a pretty good day yesterday. You didn't get in from the lake until almost dark."

"We had an okay time." Justine stirred the spoon around, creating a miniature wave of milk and toasted oats.

From outside, Hannah heard the low-pitched rumble of the machine. Judging from the direction, she guessed the deck was under attack. Poor Snooker. He was probably pacing the back fence line by now. "Did you have an argument?"

"Not really."

If discussions with Mae were like walking in a minefield, talking with Justine reminded Hannah of trying to land a hundred-pound grouper on a bream pole: inch by careful inch, cringing lest the line snap.

"Brit's changed."

"She kind of had to, don't you think?" Hannah asked.

Another exaggerated shrug. "Guess."

"What's your perception of things, Jus? Has she changed for the better? Or are you worried?"

"She . . . oh, I don't know really." Justine flipped her long hair from one shoulder to the other. "She's more blunt, or something. I can't explain it."

"Give me an example."

"Well, like, Brit always asked me what she ought to wear. All the time. She never picked out anything. And yesterday she was ready when I got there. She kind of got all huffy when I gave her a hard time about it. It was so weird. Like, it's so not Brit."

"Are you upset about her changing or that you aren't the one telling her what to do?"

Justine's brows knit together. "I don't get it."

"I'm going through something similar with your Grand-Mae. I see things I want her to do, or ways I think she should act. When she doesn't follow along, it frustrates me to no end."

"Okay . . ."

"I had to realize that, for all of my good intentions, Ma-Mae has the right to live her life without me controlling it totally. Our relationship has shifted. I have to step in and take over in some areas where she's no longer able, but she still has some independence that I don't need to take away. The hardest part is figuring out exactly when to intervene and when to step aside."

"You think I'm trying to rule Brit?"

"I don't know, honey. Are you?"

Justine considered. "She's always wanted me to tell her how to, like, be."

"But not now?"

Justine nodded. "She's not the same since she went into that place."

Hannah heard Snooker yelp. Should she stage an intervention? Scared dog versus troubled daughter willing to talk. Daughter won.

"The way she was before wasn't working for her, Jus. If Brittany had kept going like that, she would've died. She nearly succeeded in destroying herself."

"So now, I just stand back and . . . what?"

"Be her friend. Like you always have." Hannah stood and refilled her coffee. "Friendships change. Relationships change. Whether or not you choose to change along with Brittany is up to you."

"I don't know how to act around her anymore, Mom. It feels so strange."

"And it will. For a while. Until the two of you settle into new roles. Is she worth the effort?"

Justine pursed her lips. "Um, yeah."

A stack of dishes teetered in the sink. Bits of dried egg. Toast edges. Coffee grounds. A rubber band? Clean kitchen versus conversation with daughter. Daughter won. Hannah took her fresh cup of coffee and sat down.

"You solved the dilemma, then. If it's worth your time and energy to maintain a close friendship with Brittany, you'll find a way." Hannah slid the bowl of soggy uneaten cereal away from Justine. "Why don't I make you some French toast?"

"With lots of cinnamon sugar?"

Hannah tousled Justine's hair. "As much as it takes to turn your pouty lips upward."

She and Justine cleaned the breakfast dishes, then Hannah curtailed Norman and Jonas's pressure-washing rampage to get ready for Sunday School and church. After two unsuccessful attempts at donning pantyhose over sweat-dampened skin, Hannah wadded them into a tight ball and slung them into the wastebasket. Good riddance. At least she didn't pitch them from a car window this time.

"Looks like I wear pants today," she grumbled. Another challenge: finding a pair she could button.

The phone rang. Her mother's voice. "Are you on the way out to work? Did I wake you?"

Hannah closed her eyes and fought a wave of bone-weariness. "No, Ma-Mae. It's Sunday. I'm getting ready for church. What's up?"

"I forgot to tell you about today. My mind's not good."

Understatement. "What about today?" Hannah glanced at the digital clock radio on the bedside table.

"Family Appreciation Day. Eleven to one."

Responsibility sat squarely on her chest, making it hard to breathe. "I wish you would've told me before the last minute. You know I've tried to attend every function they've had there since you moved in. I can't make this one."

"Well . . . " The disappointment in her mother's tone was unmistakable. "It's my fault. I didn't tell you. It's . . . all right."

"Please try to understand, Ma-Mae. I'm supposed to be at church in fifteen minutes, after which we're going over to Quincy to eat a quick lunch and buy groceries for the week. If I don't, I'll have to shop after work one afternoon. Then, I need to come home and make sure everything's ready for the kids to start school tomorrow."

"You're busy with your family. I know."

"I'll come by later in the evening to visit for a bit. Is that okay?"

"I reckon."

Hannah hung up and the guilt oozed into every pore. She ticked through the family roster. Hal and Suzanne: at the coast for a much-needed weekend respite. Helen? No way could she make it on such short notice. The image of her mother sitting alone and neglected amongst a herd of visiting other-people's relatives flashed in her imagination.

Michael Jack answered on the third ring. His voice: groggy with sleep.

"Hi, sweetie. This is your favorite auntie calling."

"Hey." He yawned. "What's up?"

"I know it's early and Sunday, but do you and Mili have any pressing plans for today?"

He mumbled a muffled question before answering. "Just hanging out. Too hot to do much of anything."

"In that case, I need a huge family favor."

Josephine Harrison rolled her walker up to the front desk where Hannah stood, signing the visitor's roster. "Good evening, Hannah."

"Hi, Miz Josie."

"Have you seen your mother?"

"I just came from her room. She's settling in for the night."

Josie's eyes sought hers. "She thinks the world of you. You're a good daughter."

"I try to be. Sometimes I fall short. I hated missing the family thing today."

"Your nephew and his intended sat at our table. Nice young couple. Your mother had a good time introducing them around."

Hannah smiled. "I'm so glad Michael Jack and Mili could come. Did your son make it?"

Josie's eyes watered slightly. "He intended to. But, no."

"I'm sorry."

The older woman dropped her head slightly. "I have your mother, and we manage to have an enjoyable time." When Josie paused, Hannah sensed her indecision. "Mae is slowing down. You know that, don't you?"

Hannah's chest felt tight. "Yes."

"Here lately, she doesn't get out to as many things."

"I've mentioned it to her nurse practitioner. I don't really know what else to do."

Josie fiddled with a stack of newspapers in her walker's basket. "Can't be helped. Natural part of it all. I suppose."

"Thank you, Miz Josie, for being concerned. And for being Ma-Mae's friend."

Josephine smiled. "Wish I had met her years ago. We have so much catching up to do and so little time left to accomplish it."

MICHAEL JACK'S HOMEMADE BARBEQUE SAUCE

1- 32 ounce bottle of catsup
1/2 cup water
1/2 cup white vinegar
1 lemon, rind and all, cut in half
1 Tbsp. sugar
1 /2 tsp. crushed red pepper (Italian-style) or 1 tsp. red pepper
Salt and pepper to taste.

Combine all ingredients in a small saucepot and simmer over low.
Reserve a little sauce to use at table. The rest is for the meat.
Apply generously to chicken, beef, or pork after meat has mostly
cooked on grill.

Chapter Forty-one

Insomnia: Hannah's latest delightful hobby. It required no special tools, cost no money, and could be accomplished on any flat surface. Hannah noticed everything. Norman's nose whistle blew as long and lonesome as the midnight train out of River Junction. Slug's nightly cat bath sounded like wet noodles slapping against her pillow. The ever-present and maddening screech of the cicadas echoed in her ears.

She checked the digital display and calculated how few hours remained before the alarm. Finally, she got up and grumbled all the way to the couch in the family room. The nubby fabric pricked her skin, so she dragged a sheet from the linen closet.

Hannah reclined with a sigh. She noticed the loud tick-tock of the mantel clock, the faint drip of the kitchen faucet, and the rock-bump of the slightly off-balance ceiling fan. She stuffed wads of cotton into her ears. Her own exhausted heart beat thumped.

Thoroughly chapped, Hannah rose, located a novel, and flipped on the pole light. She read three pages before the letters melted together and dripped off the page.

With her eyes held purposely half-closed, she rose and padded down the hall. The bed was soft. The linens were cool. She slipped into place beside her husband and closed her eyes. At four in the morning, she finally fell asleep.

"I would sell my soul for some sleep," Hannah told her nurse practitioner several days into the insomniac's marathon.

Kimberly Grant scribbled onto Hannah's chart. "You're not alone. Too bad we can't hook up all of the women of a certain age and let them talk to each other in the wee hours."

"Kind of a hot-flash hotline chat room."

Kimberly glanced up. "If you could figure a commercial angle on that idea, you'd make a fortune."

"Am I finally cracking up, or what?"

"Not at all." Kimberly rolled her chair closer to the cushioned exam table. "You have teenaged children. That alone is enough to rob you of sleep. Not only that, but you're helping your elderly mother through a difficult part of her life." The nurse practitioner paused. "What are you doing for you, Hannah? For recreation, for exercise?"

"Belly dancing."

Kimberly grinned. "Always thought that sounded like fun."

"It is. For at least two hours a week, my mind is not on anything but trying not to look like a complete klutz."

"It's a good thing, having a hobby. I knit," Kimberly said. "What about the rest of the week? Any other forms of exercise?"

"Most days, I'm too exhausted to do much of anything except throw together a meal and flop down on the couch."

"Maybe you and your husband could start walking a little."

"It's been so doggone hot. Even at nine o'clock, it's too humid to do much outside."

Kimberly nodded. "Do you know anyone in Chattahoochee with a pool? That way, you could get some movement in and remain cool."

Hannah said, "My brother and sister-in-law have one. Good idea. I'll talk to Suzanne."

"How about your diet? Are you getting proper nutrition?"

"Pretty healthy. Mostly salads this time of year. Too dang hot to eat heavy." Hannah considered. "I do like my ice cream, though. Justine sees to it that I always buy the low-carb kind, so it's not quite as bad. Girl's got to have some vices." *Like my morning cinnamon rolls.*

"If a bowl of ice cream is the worst thing you do, you're okay. Now, the rest of my suggestions. Avoid alcohol and caffeine as much as possible, especially close to bedtime. Your exercise shouldn't be within two hours of sleep. Your body needs time to wind down."

Kimberly slid the wheeled stool to a low countertop desk. "I'll get you a prescription for a mild sleep aid. It's useful when you really need a good night's rest and you haven't been able to accomplish it on your own."

"You know how I feel about taking drugs. But after three consecutive nights without sleep, I start to see things. Thanks for listening to my litany."

"That's what I'm here for. I'll write the orders for some blood work to make sure your aches and pains aren't related to the beginnings of some type of auto-immune issue." She consulted the chart. "It's been almost a year since we checked your cholesterol level. Might as well add that in. Means you'll have to fast before the test. Also, I'll check your hormone levels. Chances are, some of your symptoms are related to perimenopause. When you add the stress into the mix, it really raises the bar."

"I heard that."

"When was your last period?" Kimberly asked.

"Over two months ago maybe? I sometimes skip a few months, then back to regular."

The nurse practitioner referred to Hannah's chart. "What are you using for birth control?"

"Lack of sex?" Hannah chuckled. "I can only stand human contact for so long before I get hot, and not in a pleasant, arousing sort of way."

"Still, it's a time when pregnancy can occur. Easy to let your guard down." Kim jotted a note on the chart. "Unless you plan on extending your family, be aware."

"The only pitter-patter of little feet in my house is either the cat, the dog, or me getting up for the zillionth time to pee in the middle of the night."   .

Missy Rodgers stopped in mid-stride, a plate heaping with home-made cinnamon rolls in her hand. "Are you sick or something? I can't believe you're turning these down! I just now pulled them from the oven. I even slathered on extra powdered sugar icing, the way you like them."

Hannah's mouth watered. "I'm taking that cereal challenge. The one where I eat cereal for two meals a day, then one normal meal. It's supposed to help me lose a jeans size in two weeks."

"You're not that overweight, Hannah."

"I've put on weight, enough to make my clothes feel uncomfortable. I can't afford—I won't afford— a new wardrobe." Hannah continued after a sip of coffee, "All this has magically appeared since Ma-Mae . . ." Hannah sat her mug down. "I can't blame this on her. I do a lot of nervous eating when I'm stressed."

"I'm the opposite. I lose my appetite. Still, it isn't good either way.

My clothes hang on me anymore. I only have a few pants that fit."

"Tell you what, Miss. Follow me around for a few weeks. Every time I start to snack between meals, I'll hand it to you and make you eat it. That way, I lose and you gain. Deal?"

If Missy didn't sit the plate out of range soon, Hannah knew she would cave. "Please, Miss. Back away with the buns."

"Well, all right." Missy sat the plate on top of the stove and covered it with a sheet of waxed paper. "If you change your mind . . . "

"It wouldn't take much. Believe me." Hannah switched the subject. "How are things with Brittany?"

Missy poured herself a cup of coffee. "Warm-up?"

Hannah raised her mug for a refill. "Rules don't apply to coffee. Thank goodness."

"It's been challenging." Missy eased into a chair and propped her elbows on the table, the steaming mug grasped in her hands. "I have to lock the scales up."

"Really?"

Missy clicked her tongue. "She would weigh herself twenty times a day if I didn't. The counselor recommended that she only weigh in once a week, on a certain day. Still . . . " Her face echoed her weariness. "It's a fight to keep her believing in herself. She looks into the mirror and sees rolls of fat, when in reality, she's still far from a normal weight for someone her age and height. Each ounce she gains is a small victory."

"Justine told me Brit's enjoying cooking."

Missy offered a slight smile. "She's very creative with dishes. We cull through Cooking Light Magazine for good recipes." She took a sip of coffee. "I doubt she'll ever be one to overindulge in sweets, but she seems to like the idea of making healthy dishes. The meals she has concocted have been very tasty, with an interesting combination of flavors and colors."

"Chip off the old Martha Stewart/Missy Rodgers block, eh?"

Missy laughed. "If you saw the dust in my living room, you might rethink your opinion of me. I can't recall when I've cleaned the baseboards."

Hannah slapped her friend playfully on the arm. "Welcome to the human race. It's not pretty, well-organized, or, for the most part, clean."

"I suppose. Hey, can you have fruit on your diet?"

"That is the one thing allowed for snacks."

"I have a few ripe Georgia peaches left. They're Albertas, the sweet big ones. What say I cut up a couple and put a dollop of low-carb ice cream on top?"

The diet did allow milk. And ice cream was frozen milk.

Chapter Forty-two

On the nineteenth day of August, a day so infernal even the cicadas were too flaccid to sing, Hannah coined the perfect phrase to describe the weather: *the Lord Have Mercy! Heat.* People dashed from air-conditioned homes to cars to shops and back, seldom pausing long enough to dry the sweat-beads from their upper lips. Neighbors ceased hanging over the hedges to discuss daily events. The sidewalks buckled, ladies lost high heel tips in the soggy asphalt, and the postal workers wore short pants. If terrorists could have found a way to contaminate the iced tea, the majority of Southerners would've dropped dead.

At Rosemont, Lucy Goosey wore a pair of pink gingham hot pants with a matching bandeau top. A beribboned sunbonnet shaded her beak, and a pair of child-sized hot pink flip-flops rested beside her webbed feet. Around her neck, a single strand of seed pearls provided the only adornment. A scandalous amount of cement was exposed, but no one seemed to mind. It was too darned hot for any goose, living or stone, to bow to a code of modesty. How Hannah had been talked into a Wal-Mart run on the most hellish day of the year was a mystery.

"You and your mama off to play?" Beth asked.

Hannah moaned. "I'm taking her and Josie shopping."

"In this heat?" Beth shook her head. "You're a brave woman, Hannah Olsen."

"Ain't I, though?"

"No need to bother to sign in," Beth said. "Remind them to sign out, okay?"

Josie Harrison wheeled around the corner. "Good morning! Your mother and I have been really looking forward to this."

"I'll get Ma-Mae. Why don't you go ahead and sign out?" Hannah walked down the hall and tapped on her mother's door, then used her key when there was no answer. "Ma-Mae?"

The silence echoed. Hannah's heart beat accelerated slightly. A thin band of light showed beneath the closed bathroom door. She tapped. Again, no answer.

She held her breath as she pushed the door open. The room was empty. Hannah locked up and walked back toward the lobby. "Have you seen my mother by any chance?" She asked one of the aides in the hallway.

"Just passed her, heading toward the dining room."

Hannah found Mae hunkered down at a table, scribbling on a slip of paper. Hannah released the tension from her shoulders. "What cha doing?"

"Oh, hi baby. I'm leaving a note for Maxine. She'll wonder why both of us are gone at lunch."

Hannah picked the two ladies up under the covered porch, helped them fasten seat belts, and stored Josie's walker and her mother's cane in the back.

"Y'all have your lists?" Hannah asked as she turned from Rosemont's parking lot.

"Surely do. We sat up half the night making sure we had everything written down, didn't we Josie?"

"The nurse didn't bring my ten o'clock medication," Josie said.

Hannah slowed. "Do we need to go back and get it?"

"It keeps her from having those shakes so bad," Mae said.

"We'd better return," Josie said. "I'm so sorry."

"Not a problem." Hannah executed a U-turn.

"Maybe I should get the two-o'clock medication, too." Josie wrung her hands.

"Good idea. We may not be back by then." Hannah pulled the SUV beneath the shaded walkway. "Y'all stay put. I'll get the pills and some water for you to take them with."

Hannah pulled into traffic for the second time. "Let's try this again, shall we?"

Josie reached over and patted her on the arm. "Thank you. I told the nurse this morning that we were going out, but I forgot to check with her again. I know that was a lot of trouble."

"Not at all. You didn't even stomp a hole in the floorboard like

Ma-Mae would've when I flipped that U-turn."

"Don't get all smarty," her mother commented from the back seat.

"I've thought seriously about writing the car company and telling them what a great vehicle they made. As many times as Ma-Mae has applied the fake brakes on that side, the floor is still intact." Hannah winked at her mother's reflection in the rearview mirror.

"Hannah's passable," Mae said. "She obeys the speed limit, for the most part. Good thing we're going to the Wal-Mart in Marianna. Those fools over in Tallahassee tend to make her forget her religion and she cusses like a sailor man."

Hannah glanced at her mother in the rear-view mirror. "Stretching things a bit, aren't you?"

"Not particularly. Just be glad there's no sink in this car. On several occasions, you would've gotten your mouth washed out with soap."

Josie laughed. "You two are the most fun when you get to going at each other."

"This is mild." Hannah said as she merged onto the Interstate.

"I still don't know why Helen couldn't meet us," Mae commented.

"Something about a retirement party thing she's in charge of. I didn't half listen, to tell the truth. She was going on and on about some guy, knowing full well and good I wouldn't know him from Dick's hat band."

"Your sister has always been so involved in the social whirl of Marianna," Mae said. "Suppose we can overlook her not being able to drop and run like we can."

More like run and then drop, Hannah thought.

When they reached the shopping center parking lot, Hannah snagged the last handicapped-reserved spot.

"Don't forget to hang the little ditty on the mirror like you did last time," Mae said as she opened the back door. "If I hadn't sweet-talked that policeman, you'd have paid a steep fine."

As soon as the three entered the double automatic doors, Mae made tracks to the scooter shopping carts, motioning for Josie. "You know how to drive one of these?" Mae asked her friend.

"I'll just use my walker and take it slow."

"Nah, sit yourself down." Mae waved to her daughter. "Hannah, fold up the walker and put it in the back rack there." Then, to Josie. "It's as easy as falling off a log. If you can drive a car, you can surely run one of these babies."

After Mae's brief in-service training, the two seniors pulled away from the entrance lobby. The only thing the entire scenario lacked was the fire of a starting pistol.

Hannah hustled behind them. "Jeez-O-Pete!" She managed between gasps. "Do you have to go full throttle?"

"I like the rush of wind in my hair," Mae called over her shoulder, slowing for a few feet. She took off again, her daughter jogging behind. Fellow shoppers ducked into the safety of the aisles as Mae and Josie flew past.

"Didn't you miss the turn for the mini-pad aisle, Mae?" Josie called out.

Hannah watched in awe as her elderly mother executed a fast U-turn around a center display of stacked cat litter bags.

"Why didn't she just stop and put it into reverse?" Josie asked when Hannah finally stepped alongside.

"And take the fun out of giving me angina?"

Josie giggled and throttled. Hannah threw up her hands and rolled her eyes in benefit of several shoppers who had stopped to gawk. Mae had stopped mid-aisle, jabbing with her cane to jostle a package of panty liners from the shelf.

"Here, let me get them before you pull the whole lot down on your head." Hannah tossed the pink plastic bag in her mother's wire basket. "Having fun?"

"Absolutely. Get me two bags. I like to stay dainty. These hot days make me sweat more. God knows, I don't want to smell. Old people often smell, you know." Mae looked around. "Where'd you leave Josie?"

Hannah's gaze scanned the aisle. "I thought she was right behind me."

"We'd best go find her."

"She can't leave the building, Ma-Mae. I don't see—" Hannah stood with her hands propped on her hips, watching her mother zoom away. "If I survive today, it will be a dadgum miracle."

The threesome occupied a booth at Ruby Tuesday Restaurant.

While the seniors chatted, Hannah took a moment to enjoy sitting down. The soles of her feet throbbed and burned.

"That was some Mr. Toad's wild ride, wasn't it, Josie?" Mae clapped her hands.

Josie peered over the top of her menu. "I kind of felt bad for that one woman you ran into the toilet paper display."

"She had a soft landing." Mae shook her finger. "Folks need to yield right-of-way."

Hannah looked at her mother. "I didn't see any road signs in the store. How, exactly, do you determine that?"

"Age always trumps," Mae announced. "Now, what are we going to eat today?"

"I'm going for this Mexican salad," Josie said.

"The black beans will gas you up, Jo."

"Suppose you're right." Josephine lowered her menu. "What would you suggest?"

"A big old beef burger, loaded, with melted cheddar cheese and a mound of curly fries." Mae ran her fingernail down the laminated page. "And for dessert, one of those brownie and ice cream concoctions."

"Ma-Mae! For heaven's sake," Hannah said. "That's a lot of food."

"What's it going to do, kill me?" Mae winked across the table at her friend. "I'm way too old to die young, right Jo?"

Josie closed the menu and rested her folded hands on the edge of the table. "That logic defies me, Mae. But I'll have the same."

Hannah frowned. The menu was filled with low-calorie, carbohydrate-reduced fare. After four days, the cereal diet was beginning to wear on her nerves. Besides, if she had survived chasing two old women around a shopping center the size of a football field, she had worked off breakfast.

Hannah flicked a packet of artificial sweetener, then tore off a corner and poured it into her tea. "I'm adding bacon to mine."

Chapter Forty-three

The call came at 7 a.m. as Hannah prepared to leave the house to pick up her fellow car-pool members.

"Hannah?" Lora Strong, the charge nurse. Not a good sign.

She dropped her purse and briefcase on the kitchen table. "Yes?"

"I'm sorry to tell you, your mother is not well. We've called for an ambulance."

"Oh, God. What?"

"When she didn't come down for breakfast, her friend Mrs. Harrison went to see about her. She found her on the floor and immediately alerted the staff."

"I'm on my way."

"Justine!" Hannah yelled. "Jonas!"

The kids appeared at the door, curious expressions on their faces.

"Something's happened to Grand-Mae. Call your father and have him meet me at Rosemont."

"I'll come with you," Justine said.

"No, honey. You and your brother eat breakfast. Then, I need you to go ahead and get Jonas to school. Leave your cell on. Tell your teachers what's going on. I'll text you as soon as I know anything."

Justine rushed over and kissed her mother on the cheek. "Sure, Mom. You okay to drive?"

"I'll be fine. Call your father for me." She snatched up her purse, frantically dialing the cell phone number of one of the carpool members as she rushed into the garage.

A parked ambulance sat in front of Rosemont, lights blinking and engine idling; this time, she hadn't beaten them. Hannah's stomach rolled as she swung the SUV into the first vacant spot and dashed inside.

"The paramedics are with your mother," Beth said, waving her past the front desk.

A flurry of activity greeted her in the hallway. Maxine and Josephine stood to one side, their walkers pulled out of the line of emergency workers. Several staff members parted to allow Hannah to pass. Inside room 104, two paramedics were busy strapping her mother onto the gurney, taking vital signs, and communicating in medical lingo Hannah only understood in part.

Hannah waited, numb, by one wall. Her brain struggled to equate the pale woman on the gurney with the vital, funny senior who had terrorized the department store shoppers mere hours before.

"Are you her daughter?" The male paramedic asked.

"Yes."

"From her records, we see that her doctor has privileges at Tallahassee General. We're en route, if you would like to follow."

"Ma-Mae?" Hannah stepped to the gurney and asked in a quiet voice, "Can you hear me?"

Mae's eyelids fluttered. She mumbled unintelligible words. Her face drooped on one side and a fine line of saliva leaked from her parted lips.

Dear God, no. Not a stroke. Please.

Norman's voice sounded from the hall as Hannah trailed the gurney from the room. Beth rested a hand on Hannah's arm. "I'll see to it that her room's locked up tight. Don't concern yourself with anything here."

Norman fell into step beside his wife and cradled his arm around her shoulder. "Let's leave your car here, hon. Pick it up later."

Hannah was vaguely aware of the murmured well-wishes of her mother's friends and the Rosemont staff as they left the building.

"Norman, I'm texting Justine. Stop by the school."

"You sure?"

Tears coursed down her cheeks. "They need to be with us. I just *feel* it." She dug in her purse for a handkerchief.

Norman tapped the Bluetooth clinging to his left ear and spoke a command for the autodial. "I'm calling your brother again. He was on his way home to get Suzanne. They can pick up Justine and Jonas. One of you needs to be over in the ER when your mother arrives."

"Oh." Hannah closed her eyes. "I completely forgot . . . Helen."

"She and Charlie are already on the road. I'll call them next and tell them to go straight to Tallahassee."

Hannah rested one hand on her husband's thigh. "What would I do without you? I can't seem to think straight."

On a level deeper than she could put into words, Hannah understood. All the fear and anticipation, the intense worry, had culminated into this final set of disjointed moments.

This is it.

Mae seemed diminished by the fluorescent lighting of the ER. Hannah and Norman stood to one side watching as various monitors were attached. Without its customary animation, Mae's face appeared waxen and lifeless. Judging by the amount of intense attention from the nurses and emergency physician, her condition was grave.

A few minutes after the rest of the family arrived, a doctor in crisp green scrubs called the adults into a small conference room. The physician motioned for the family to be seated around the oval table.

"Mrs. Mathers has suffered a cerebrovascular accident, a stroke. The next few hours are critical. We'll be moving her to the Neurointensive Care Unit as soon as she's stable."

"Is she going to . . . die?" Helen clung to her husband.

"It is a possibility. However, I have seen patients of advanced age pull through. Unfortunately, your mother also has a multiple fracture of the neck of her right femur."

"Her hip?" Hal asked.

"Yes." The doctor paused. "This complicates things considerably. Once she's clear of danger from the stroke, the hip will have to be repaired surgically."

"She's eighty-five, Doctor," Hannah said.

"Can't she be confined to a wheel chair and not put her through surgery?" Helen asked.

"I'm afraid not. It's not that simple. The break necessitates some kind of repair, as the tissue will suffer necrosis otherwise." The doctor cleared his throat once before continuing. "Your mother has an advanced directive in her file. You are aware of this?"

One by one, Mae's three children nodded.

"We'll do everything within our power to help your mother. Often, with patients of her age, one event can lead to what we refer to as a cascading effect. Under the intense strain after severe injury, systems may start to shut down. When this happens, you, as her children, face some hard decisions. Would she want to be on dialysis if her kidneys cease to function, for example?"

"Ma-Mae, my mother, was very adamant about that sort of thing," Hannah said, glancing at her sister and brother. "She didn't want to be kept alive with all kinds of wires and hoses running from her. She told me just a few days ago. Used those exact words."

The doctor nodded. "The advanced directive covers a checklist of all types of scenarios. But I still like to talk to the family up front. This can be a very confusing time. A difficult time." He stood to leave. "We have an excellent counseling staff. We're all here to help you through this."

After the emergency room physician left, Hal voiced the thought common to all. "Sounds like we have a long road ahead."

Hannah closed her eyes and muttered the one word her mother found most common and low, never to be included in a perfect daughter's speech: What her kids referred to as the "F-Bomb."

Word of the family's crisis spread quickly in Chattahoochee. Friends and neighbors stepped in to share the burden. As soon as Elvina Houston caught wind of Mae's hospitalization, she fried the phone lines at home and the Triple C. With help from the Internet, Elvina added the extra punch of international entreaties to the heavens.

Missy and Brittany Rodgers immediately took the reins at the Olsen house, bringing in armloads of groceries and supplies, cooking meals, and cleaning the house from one end to the other. On the few occasions Hannah dashed home for fresh clothing, she found the furniture dust-free, the carpets vacuumed, the animals spoiled rotten and the bathrooms glistening, with a faint aura of bleach.

In the Tallahassee General Neurological Intensive Care Waiting Area, a soft touch brushed Hannah's arm. She opened her eyes slowly to find Becky, Suzanne, and Missy hovering over her.

"Hey you," her sister-in-law said.

Hannah sat up and stretched, feeling the dull ache of too little sleep over the past two days. "Hey." She rubbed her eyes and blinked to focus. "What's going on? I must've fallen asleep for a moment."

"How, I don't know." Becky motioned to the line of vinyl padded chairs serving as a make-shift cot.

"Doesn't look very comfortable," Missy said. "You don't even have a pillow, you poor thing."

Hannah massaged her shoulder and winced. "I must've been using my arm, judging from the way it feels."

Becky sat down beside her. "We're here to take over for a bit." She handed Hannah a set of keys. "You know where I live, five minutes from here, down Centerville. There're clean sheets on the bed and anything you need in the guest bath."

"I don't want to leave Ma-Mae. Norman's coming over with the kids—"

Suzanne sat on the other side of Hannah. "Hon, we're here. Hal's parking the van, and Helen'll be over later this afternoon. Don't you think we'll be watching over Mae?"

"Well . . ."

"You need some rest, Hannah." Missy knelt in front of her. "And I'm not talking about a half hour slumped over in a chair."

"That's right," Suzanne agreed. "When they move her into a room, given that it's a private one, we can have a cot brought in. Even then, we can take shifts staying with her. In the meantime, you're going to get sick if you don't sleep."

Hannah raked her fingers through her limp hair. "I could use a shower."

Suzanne winked at Becky and Missy. "We weren't going to mention it, hon. But now that you bring it up, you're starting to look a bit like a street person."

"You will call me if anything happens?" Hannah grabbed her purse and a small duffel bag that held a few toiletries.

"Of course." Suzanne helped Hannah to stand and steered her gently toward the door. "Now go!"

Following a long, hot shower, Hannah eased between the cool sheets. The room was mercifully dark, cold and quiet. For a few moments, she reviewed the events of the past forty-eight hours, the anxiety, the fear. Then she fell into a deep, dreamless sleep.

Until the trill of her cell phone jarred her awake.

Chapter Forty-four

Hannah recalled scattered, random details of the day her mother died.

The world turned gray and her eyes—tired and burning—couldn't hold a sharp focus through the haze of tears. Small things caught her attention. The way the peppering rain sent domes of bubbles dancing in the puddles next to the intersection in front of the hospital as Norman turned into the gush of five o'clock traffic. How the worry lines around Mae's eyes and lips disappeared after her spirit lifted away. The sound of that one final breath. The warmth of Norman's arms cocooned around her. The feather-light touch of her daughter's hand in hers, and Jonas's dark eyelashes beaded with tears. How the family pulled together as if by some unseen magnetic force: never far from touching, reaching for words of comfort.

"She looked better yesterday," Hal said for the fourth or fifth time. "I figured she was turning the corner. She seemed like she might be . . ."

Suzanne caressed his face in a gesture so caring, Hannah had to look away to staunch another round of shuddering cries.

"It happens that way, sometimes," Suzanne said in a soft voice. "God's little gift. A tiny piece of grace when things look a little brighter."

Hal's hands—usually busy, moving—were folded, still, in his lap.

Hannah didn't correct her brother. Had she survived, Mae would have been paralyzed on one side. The cruel reality of impending surgery, the loss of independence, the necessity for a nursing home rather than the freedom and camaraderie of Rosemont: All had loomed in Mae's future.

"It was her kidneys," Hal said. "She always had trouble with them."

Suzanne wrapped her arms around him from behind. "I know, baby. You all did everything you could. The doctors did too. Sometimes, a person's body can't go on anymore."

Hal's head bowed forward. Hannah knew without looking; her brother was crying again.

Helen had been led away soon after Mae's death, too overcome to remain in the room. Charlie cuddled her like a small child and nodded to Hal and Hannah. Later, she would participate in the planning, the ceremony, and the expected social graces. But for now, Helen would retreat with her boys and her husband to gather strength.

"Sweetheart, we need to go on home now," Norman said to his wife. "There are calls to make."

Hannah's logical mind refused to work. "What about Ma-Mae?"

"I've contacted Joseph Burns. He's on his way over to get her." Norman chose his words carefully. "He's a very good man, Hannah. He will take tender care of Mae. She picked him, herself, remember?"

"Can we stay, Norman? Can we stay until he gets here?"

"Of course. I'll send the kids on home with Hal and Suzanne. You and I will sit with Mae, if that's what you wish."

Her eyes met his. "It is. It really is. She wouldn't leave *me* all alone."

Elvina Houston slipped quietly from the Olsens' back door and ambled across the deck. "Morning, Glory." She offered a small smile. "Your daughter told me I'd find you out here. Mind if I sit a spell?"

Hannah gave a slight nod and the thin old woman with the beehive hairdo eased down onto a padded deck chair.

"There's a little something in the air this morning, don't you think? Oh, I know the heat will build later on and the thunderstorms will come, but . . . " Elvina lifted her chin like an animal testing the wind for scent. "I can feel a touch of fall in the air."

"Won't be too soon for me." Hannah wondered if her voice sounded as flat to others as it did to her.

"I reckon even folks who like the heat have had enough this summer. Been a rough one." Elvina folded her hands in her lap. "I brought over some of Joe Fletcher's fresh-baked sweet potato biscuits. He usually doesn't make them until Saturday, but he stirred up a batch special for y'all this morning. He threw in a few cathead biscuits too, for those who'd rather have those."

"Thank you, Elvina. I'm sure that'll make the kids especially happy."

Elvina tilted her head and studied Hannah. "How about you? You been able to eat anything, gal?"

Hannah cradled her coffee mug as if it held secret comfort. "Everything seems to make me nauseated. *This* is breakfast."

"Grief can rob you of an appetite. That's for sure." Elvina said. "I'm bringing over a big pot of chicken 'n' dumplings later. Piddie Longman's recipe. Do you remember her?"

"Who *didn't* know Piddie?" Hannah fondly recalled the beehive-haired jolly senior. "You two were good friends."

"Surely were. The best. For over forty years, wasn't a day that passed I didn't talk to her at least once."

"I know that's the one thing that will hit me hard, after all of this . . . " Hannah circled the air with one hand. "I'm so accustomed to talking to Ma-Mae about everything. We spoke on the phone every day, and I stopped by Rosemont several times a week on my way home from work. Not to mention all the time we spent doing girlie stuff." Her throat constricted with emotion. "I didn't even get to say good-bye. To tell her how much I love her. I kept praying she would open her eyes, just once more."

"Oh, sugar. She knew. Every time you took her out, every time you made sure she had what she needed, you told her. That's worth more than words." Elvina patted Hannah on the arm with one liver-spotted hand. "I'll share with you what my counselor told me after Piddie died." The old woman settled back into her chair. "I was lower than a snake's belly after Piddie passed. I suffer from depression, anyway. Have for years, on and off. Piddie leaving near 'bout killed me. I had all these folks around, but still felt so alone. My counselor suggested I keep on talking to Piddie." She smiled. "Thought they'd lock me up in the 'hooch uptown for certain if I tried it, but it surely helped.

"Every morning, first thing, I go out to this little cement sitting bench beside the Piddie Davis Longman Memorial Garden. That's where Piddie's ashes were scattered behind the Triple C. It's a daisy patch: a pretty, peaceful spot. Piddie told us exactly how she wanted it done. Anyway, I sit there and have a one-sided conversation with her. Tell her all about my aches and pains, the goings-on in town, or whatever comes to mind. Somehow, doing that eases my wounded soul a little. I like to think of my friend floating down to sit beside me on that bench." She winked. "Taking time out from her heavenly duties, and all."

"Sounds interesting."

"Everyone finds a way to grieve. Reckon that's mine."

The two women shared the silence for a moment before Elvina spoke again. "I dropped by the Dragonfly Florist. Jake's busy on Mae's floral drape. You did a good job of picking out the colors. He's doing it up right. He has a pile of arrangement orders a mile high too. There'll be a passel of blooms at the ceremony."

Hannah nodded. "Helen and I met with Jake. He gets all the credit for everything. He asked a few questions, then said he would take care of it."

"That's Jake Witherspoon for you. Finer man you won't meet." Elvina paused. "I've set up the church ladies in shifts to help with feeding your family and any friends coming in. Don't feel like you have to lift a finger."

"I never understood before, how much it helps to have all of you taking care of things. My energy level is . . . " Hannah's shoulders rose and fell. "Kaput."

"Let the mundane household stuff be the least of your worries, gal. Leave that to us. And if there is anything you think of you need help with, all you have to do is say so."

Hannah offered a weak smile. "Thank you, Elvina. Really."

"Something else I need to talk over with you, then I'll leave you to your thoughts. I know y'all cleaned out your Mama's little house awhile back. I'm sure you're grateful for that, at this point. But her room at Rosemont?"

Hannah blew out a long breath. "I suppose next week we'll have to deal with it."

"I have a suggestion," Elvina said. "You and your siblings can ponder on it and let me know later. Lucille Jackson—that's the wife of Reverend Thurston Jackson of the Morningside AME church—reminded me of something. They run an outreach program for displaced families: domestic violence victims, folks that have lost everything in house fires, what-all. I can have them show up on the day y'all meet up to clean out the room, with boxes to take away anything your family might not want or need."

"I'll talk it over with Hal and Helen, but it sounds okay to me, Elvina. I'd rather her things go to good use."

"Mandy wanted me to tell you not to fret about your mama's hair.

She knows exactly how Mae liked it styled. Rest assured, she'll get it right. Stephanie said she'd fit you into her schedule—Norman too, for that matter—if you feel a little massage would help your feelings. If she can't for some reason, I can talk to Hattie Davis. She still does a few, part-time."

Hannah answered with a slight tilt of her head. Breathing took such effort. Too many words jostled for attention.

Elvina hesitated before speaking. "I didn't spend as much time around your mama as I would've liked. The times I stopped by Rosemont to call on someone else, Mae was so helpful and positive. And always, we would pass the time when she came into the salon. Funny thing: I did have a nice chat with her not long ago."

"Oh?"

"I stopped by to leave a bottle of this special face cream Stephanie had ordered for Maxine. She and your mama were sitting on the porch out front. We got to talking about old age and its trials and tribulations. It's a common subject with us seniors. Your mama said there were only two things she was afraid of about the whole thing. You know what they were?"

Hannah moved her head from side to side.

"Mae was afraid of dying alone, and of living so long she became a burden. She didn't want to linger and linger, and get more and more sick and dependent." Elvina smiled. "Y'all were all around her when she passed, from what I understand. How lucky to have all the ones you love by your bedside. And she didn't go through a long period of grave illness before the good Lord took her Home. Reckon Mae never realized her two worst fears."

"Ma-Mae talked to me a lot about things—funeral plans, what to bury her in— but she never said anything about being afraid."

"Every one of us has a little bit of fear, Hannah. Only natural, no matter how strong our faith. Perhaps we don't so much worry about when it's going to happen, but how."

Elvina slapped her lap and stood. "I have to get a move on. Feel free to phone me at the Triple C or at home if you need me. I left both numbers on the side of your refrigerator." She bumped her forehead with the palm of one hand. "Lawsy! I almost forgot. I put clean sheets on my guest room bed. It's just me and Buster—my old Tomcat—at my house. I heard Norman say his brother Nathan and his wife are coming up from Tampa. They can have their own bathroom, on account of I have two. No need in anyone staying in no motel."

"Thank you, Elvina, for everything. I don't know how we can ever repay your kindness."

"No debt between friends. One day someone will be doing this all for me. I'd like to think I'll live forever, but reckon I'll move on one day." She pointed a finger heavenward. "Hopefully up!"

Chapter Forty-five

"You feel like having a little breakfast, hon?" Norman asked.

The morning of Mae's graveside service had dawned gray and overcast. Hannah awakened with a slight headache and swollen eyes.

"Just coffee, please." Her hand moved instinctively to cradle the roundness of her belly. Something nudged at the edge of her awareness, but slipped away as Norman bent down and kissed Hannah lightly on the forehead. "Stay in bed. I'll bring you a cup. And a piece of toast. You need something in your stomach."

Since the service was scheduled for eleven o'clock, family members agreed to meet at the Olsens' house to form a procession to New Hope Cemetery seven miles west of Chattahoochee. Hannah was applying a second layer of makeup over the deep blue circles beneath her eyes when Hal tapped on the bedroom door and entered.

"Hey, Pookie." He planted a kiss on her cheek. "How're you doing?" His voice shook with emotion.

"About as good as you, from the sound of it."

Hal sat on the edge of the bed. "Seems unreal."

She swiveled around to face her brother. "I've tried to prepare myself for this day—knew it would come. But now that it's here . . ."

Hal nodded. "Yeah."

"Have Helen and Charlie gotten here yet?"

"Nope. But they will be soon. I'm sure Charlie's keeping everyone on task."

Hannah scanned her lipstick shades, decided on a muted peach. "Helen's a mess. I think she's taking it the hardest of all."

"You expected any less?" Hal said. "She falls apart when a butterfly hits the grill of her car."

Hannah smiled weakly. "She *is* sensitive."

"That's our sister."

She leaned forward and applied a thin sheen of lipstick, blotted. "I'm numb. Empty." Her gaze lifted to her brother's reflection in her vanity mirror.

Hal's eyes watered. He straightened his tie. "Know what you mean."

"Did anyone talk to the Rosemont folks?"

Hal ran his fingers through his thinning hair. "Elvina Houston called Suzanne yesterday. Told her they're bringing a small group of Ma-Mae's closest friends on the Rosemont bus."

"I'm glad. Especially Josie and Maxine." Hannah raked a comb through her brush to dislodge a mat of hair. "It's going to feel really strange, not having Ma-Mae to take care of. Particularly the last three years, I've been focused on that."

Hal rose and enveloped his sister in a warm hug. "You still have Helen and me to watch over, Pookie, if you need to continue the tradition."

A large group of mourners spread out at the periphery of the dark green Memorial Memories tent. Hannah's gaze rested on the flower-adorned closed coffin as the immediate family filed into the first row of velvet-draped chairs. A centipede trailing along on the dried grass in front of her feet caught her attention.

"Let us pray," the preacher said.

Hannah bowed her head, but kept her narrowed eyes trained on the meandering creature. Each section moved independently, yet its entire body rippled in a perfect rhythm to move it forward.

As she watched the centipede traverse the ground beneath the funeral tent, Hannah's mind drew parallels. Like the insect's segmented body, her life was a string of separate parts: woman, daughter, wife, mother, sister, friend. Similarly, the different decades had brought distinct scenarios into play: kindergarten, grade and high school, college, marriage, children. And now, the latest bit-part: shouldering the mantle of the wise, older generation.

She allowed her mind to travel back to cherished memories of her parents. Her mother's easy laughter. Her father's strength. Scenes blinked past. Long hot summers, frosty pitchers of lemonade, and hand-churned ice cream. Skinned knees and tears. Homemade birthday cakes and party hats. Ma-Mae ordering the red-faced siblings to separate corners when their rivalry became too intense. Warm, breast-y hugs and butterfly kisses. "Sleep tight. Don't let the bed-bugs bite." "Now I lay me down to sleep. I pray the Lord my soul to keep. And should I die before I wake. I pray the Lord my soul to take."

Without glancing around, Hannah felt the compassionate cloak of family and friends. Missy Rodgers would be there to share her sorrow, returning the favor of friendship. Becky and the belly-dancing girls. Neighbors, church members. Her extended family of coworkers would reach out too. Suzanne sniffled beside her. Soon, Hannah could comfort her sister-in-law as she traveled the same path with her own mother. Helen and Hal would each grieve in their separate fashions, but Hannah sensed the underlying solidity of the family. For a time, Hannah's children might break away from their self-centered universes to orbit their mother, as Helen's children would for their mother. And Norman. Always steady, faithful Norman.

She glanced at Hal and vowed to spend extra sister-time with him. Heaped on her brother's sadness was his daughter's failure to show for the visitation or funeral. Hal hadn't acknowledged Natalie's slight, but it no doubt bruised him. Even Norman's brother Nathan had taken time from his busy schedule to drive up for the ceremony.

Rifts formed during grief took longer to heal, and Hannah knew Natalie had cut Hal to the middle. Yet time would pass. Life would proceed.

Norman reached over and enfolded her hand in his and gave it a gentle squeeze.

She became aware of the preacher's voice as he tied up the loose ends of the memorial service and led the final prayer. Just as Ma-Mae asked: "Make it short and sweet, then get on with it."

The crowd of supporters left. Her brother, sister, and their families headed to their homes. Nathan and Cindy visited before leaving for south Florida, with plans for the brothers to meet soon at Nathan's river house. Hannah's kids drifted off to their individual purposes. Elvina stopped calling once an hour. Norman hovered, his concern bordering on irritation. Between it all, final repairs to the house moved along, though Jonas seemed content to camp out in the living room.

"If you don't mind, I think I'll go rest." Hannah yawned.

Norman cradled her shoulders and guided her to their bedroom. "Go ahead, hon. If anyone stops by, I'll deal with them."

Hannah curled into a fetal position and stared into the dust channel formed by the sunbeam filtering through the blinds. Slug jumped onto the bed and snuggled as close to Hannah's heart as possible. She didn't remember closing her eyes.

As if viewing the scene from above, Hannah saw herself standing on a downtown street corner, maybe the intersection of Park and North Monroe in Tallahassee. A delivery-type truck pulled to a stop in front of her and two of the rear side panels flipped outward—one of those rolling food vans. A woman in her mid-forties stuck her head from one of the windows and smiled. A wave of shock and enchantment stunned Hannah. The lady looked exactly like a younger version of the Mae that Hannah had seen in family photos.

"Hi, gal. I was in the neighborhood and decided to drop by."

Hannah's voice wouldn't cooperate.

"Not like you to be at a loss for words, sugar plum." The young Mae looked Hannah up and down, then threw her arms open. "How do you like it? My new business venture. I'm running my own rolling bakery."

"Whu . . . wh . . .?"

"Thought I'd stop by and say howdy," Mae said. "I'm busy as a bee in a tar bucket. Moving on. Moss ain't growing on my backside."

"But you're—"

"Dead? Kaput? Passed over? Gone on to my ree-ward?" Mae tilted her head. "Doesn't mean I don't have things to do. You should taste my cinnamon rolls. They are to die for."

Hannah laughed at the pun. "So to speak."

Mae busied herself arranging a platter of cathead biscuits. "I came to tell you I'm okay. Better'n okay. Don't go looking for me, now. Don't waste your time on that nonsense. Don't ask the Angel of Lost Things to hunt me down. I'm not lost, not even misplaced. I'm exactly where I'm supposed to be and you'll see soon enough."

The scent of warm sugar and cinnamon wafted to Hannah's nose and she took a deep breath. The dream broke its hold and her eyes opened. For a moment, grief threatened to steal the sense of peace she had felt on the street corner, then she realized the aroma was real.

Somewhere on The Other Side, a younger version of Mae Mathers delivered hot bakery goods. Somewhere on this side, a loved one—Justine?—stood in her kitchen, cooking up comfort.

Chapter Forty-six

Two weeks crept by. The paperwork surrounding a family death loomed in loosely organized piles in the study. On the kitchen counter, empty casserole dishes awaited return to their generous owners. Boxes containing Mae's personal belongings from Rosemont leaned against one wall in the garage.

Hannah was more than ready to go back to work.

On the first day, she chose to drive to Tallahassee alone. Though she liked her carpool members, she wasn't ready for the well-intentioned questions and social niceties. Tears hovered, a blink away. All she needed to unleash a fresh barrage was for someone to be solicitous. As long as she could hole up with the computer and submerge herself in minutiae, she could maintain a level of composure.

Two o'clock came. Hannah's stomach growled. Not only had she not stopped to take a bathroom break—unusual for her, anymore— she had not eaten since the piece of dry wheat toast and coffee at six. Her spirit was numb, but her body still required fuel. If only she had a huge jar of peanut butter. She imagined licking a spooned glob like a double-dip ice cream cone. What the heck was that all about? Peanut butter: the new comfort food. She hadn't eaten as much extra crunchy since before Jonas was born.

Hannah pushed away from her desk and walked to the office lounge. On the bottom shelf of the cramped refrigerator, she located a carton of peach yogurt near its expiration date. She sat, spoon in hand, dipping mindlessly into the container, when it occurred to her: she felt delightfully comfortable and relaxed. Maybe the time off, regardless of the reason, had been good for her.

Hannah reached down and patted the front of her blouse over her heart. With a startled expression, she slid her hand to her waist and down the side of one hip.

"Oh good Lord," she whispered.

No small wonder she felt so comfy. She took a quick inventory.

Pants and a blouse. Shoes and earrings. Rings and watch. No bra and no panties.

What if the seams don't hold up all day? Hannah vibrated with the effort to stifle the merriment building inside like a shaken cola. *What if I have a wreck on the way home? Not only will I not be wearing clean underwear, I won't be wearing any at all!*

Hannah's face colored crimson from holding her breath. When she finally exhaled, she erupted into a full-blown, belly-laugh marathon. She held her sides. She rocked back and forth. She snorted.

Her coworker Madeline appeared at the lounge door. "Hannah? You okay? I could hear you from way down the hall."

"Whoo. Whoo. Whoo . . . " Hannah tried to reel in the out-of-control conniption fit.

Madeline smiled. "What in the devil has you so tickled?"

Hannah dabbed yogurt from the corners of her mouth, shook her head and held up a stop-hand.

Her coworker pulled up a chair and sat down. "I'll wait. Has to be good to have you going like this."

Hannah took deep breaths in through her nose and exhaled slowly through her mouth, closing her eyes. After a few moments, she felt composed enough to speak. "You know how I told you not to worry about me coming back to work so soon?"

Madeline nodded.

"How I was okay. Had it together and all?"

Madeline's right eyebrow rose.

"I thought I was."

Madeline leaned over and rested her hand over Hannah's. "You need a few more days off. It's okay. This place won't fall apart if you need to take time for yourself."

Hannah jerked sharply. "Dang! Now I have the hiccups."

"Take a really deep breath, put your head between your legs and count to twenty-five," Madeline said. "Then sit back up and exhale very slowly."

Hannah followed the instructions. "Wow. I've never tried that before." She took a shaky breath and continued, "Work is fine. Actually, it's good for me to think of something else. It's just—" Hannah covered her mouth like a four-year-old with a secret.

Madeline leaned forward. "What?"

"I just now discovered," Hannah lowered her voice to a whisper, "I don't have on a stitch of underwear."

Madeline's lips twitched. When Hannah started anew, her co-worker joined in, until their combined laughter echoed down the hall.

Hannah pulled into New Hope Cemetery and negotiated the narrow sandy lane between rows of marble headstones, finally stopping at the Mathis family plot. She allowed the engine to idle for a few moments before switching the key off and getting out. The occasional whoosh of a passing car sounded in the distance. The cry of a red-tailed hawk riding the thermals high above and the whisper of a gentle breeze through the pine trees added to the sense of repose. Her parents' final resting place seemed cloaked in a reverent silence.

Hannah crouched, then sat cross-legged on the sun-browned grass in front of the granite-edged plot. The wilted floral arrangements had been replaced with silk flowers in weighted pots. She picked a dried stalk of Bahia grass and chewed on one end. Her left hand held a soft white handkerchief edged in pale green lace: part of Mae's collection, now hers. Not common like a paper tissue. Perfect for tears. She finally had that detail right.

"Hi, Ma-Mae." Her gaze slid to her father's side of the plot. "Pop." She felt the push of tears behind her eyes.

"I dropped by Rosemont yesterday to say hello to your buddies, Ma-Mae. They really miss you." She chuckled. "You wouldn't believe that dadgum Lucy Goosey. She's all decked out in mourning attire—black with sensible pearls—and you'll love this, a nice white linen hankie. A true lady. Maxine's wondering how long they need to keep her in black. Couldn't help her on that one, as I have no clue as to the official mourning period for geese.

"Michael Jack and Mili have set a wedding date in late March. Thank goodness, not during the summer. Missy's redecorated. Got rid of those horrible couches. Helen's . . . Helen's just Helen. She'll be okay eventually. Let's see . . . Hal's building a potting shed for me."

She scanned her brain for any newsy tidbits. "Guess I don't have to cram it all in at once, huh?"

Hannah felt her spirits lift. "You always told me to keep my sense of humor intact, no matter what. I had to stop by on the way home and tell you and Pop a good tale on your baby daughter." She ran her hand down her side and felt the absence of a panty line. "You'll be so proud."

Hannah looked to the sky and smiled. "I can finally say that as of today, I am officially cathead crazy."

It dawned on Hannah, sitting in this place of solitude and final rest. Until now, she had thought peace to be her ultimate goal, her fondest wish.

Slivers of tranquility might tuck into unexpected spots, but her life was about broken arms, runny noses, bear hugs, and belly laughs. About a sweet, sometimes clueless man with comb-over hair, about flawed friends, inconsistent teenagers, dirty dishes, and refrigerator leftovers sprouting fur. About noise and hormones and unexpected delights.

Hannah moved one hand to cup her rounded belly—something so new, she still marveled it could be true. Marveled that she—someone who prided herself on being reasonably intelligent and observant—had been so distracted as to shrug off the telltale signs. Soon as she got home, she'd tell Norman and the kids. For now, Hannah Olsen and her third child shared the secret.

"I'm pregnant, Ma-Mae. I know it's a girl. And I'm naming her Joy."

Peace could wait. She had too much living to do in the meantime.

About the Author

Rhett DeVane is the author of three published mainstream fiction novels: *The Madhatter's Guide to Chocolate, Up the Devil's Belly,*
and *Mama's Comfort Food.* She is coauthor
of two novels: *Evenings on Dark Island* with
Larry Rock and *Accidental Ambition* with
Robert W. McKnight.

Rhett is a true Southerner, born and raised
in the Florida panhandle. For the past thirty-
plus years, Rhett has made her home in Tal-
lahassee, Florida, located in Florida's Big Bend area, where she is a
practicing dental hygienist. Rhett uses a portion of her book royalties
to support charitable causes.

A Few Words from Rhett

Ironic, how some of life's best gifts flow from times of the great-
est stress or hardship. For the final five years of my mother's earthly
existence, I grew to know her as a person, beyond her roles of provider and nurturer for her family. Her sense of humor and compassion
shone through the most difficult physical and emotional challenges.
Yet, there were instances when both of us stomped all over each other's
last nerve. We kissed and made up, then pressed on.

Other than the Bible's commandment to "honor thy father and thy
mother," no clever handbooks guided me and my siblings. Bookstores
held rows of manuals on childbirth and rearing, weight control, self-
awareness, and spirituality. Where were the tomes on navigating end
of life legal and medical issues, choosing care options, and balancing
responsibilities while managing some level of personal peace and sanity?

Cathead Crazy showcases one woman's bumpy journey. But it
could be anyone's. The anecdotes are based on truth, either personal or
those shared with me by others. Though Mae has many of my mother's

traits, Hannah's mother is much more cantankerous. Nor did I have two teenaged kids to add to the mix. Fiction demands drama, so I went all-out to torment Hannah. Poor dear.

In our reality, my family faced the sudden death of my sister Melody, six months before my mother made her own transition. I couldn't put readers or myself through that; I barely made it the first time. Both women are reportedly doing well on the Other Side (as my brother and I have been shown in dreams); my mother drives a bakery food truck and my sister sings to those nearing death. They stay busy. No huge surprise.

Statistics show that over 10 million Americans are part of the sandwich generation, caring for both children and elderly family members. This group falls between ages thirty-four and fifty-four and are of all cultures and ethnicities. Caretaking brings a crash course in legal matters, financial concerns, difficult medical decisions, and questions about housing. Add to that, finding time for the caretaker to rejuvenate before his or her own health and relationships suffer. Wow.

High time to open up, talk about this time of life, and help each other.

Discussion Points

1. Hannah acts out a fantasy in the first chapter, until she succumbs to reality. What kind of escape valve/fantasy do you have?

2. Hannah's sister-in-law Suzanne offers wisdom and support. What friend/family member supports you in times of crisis or stress? What is her/his strongest quality?

3. On several occasions, Hannah experiences a role reversal with her elderly mother Mae. When and how has this manifested in your life?

4. Mae's compassion shines through, in spite of her declining health. Where do you find instances of this in *Cathead Crazy*?

5. Hannah longs for peace, yet finds only glimmers of tranquility. Is there something you have hoped for, only to find it elusive or that you might not truly desire it?

6. Did your impression of Hannah's husband Norman shift as the story unfolded, and why?

7. Lucy Goosey is a Mathers family heirloom of sorts. What things are valuable in your family, regardless of their true worth?

8. Mae repeatedly reviews her end of life wishes. Do you notice this tendency within your family, or with yourself?

9. What kind of living arrangements do you feel most beneficial for someone who can no longer live alone? Is this something you and your family discuss?

10. Missy Rodgers seems to possess the "perfect" life until the façade crumbles. Are there people in your life that you put on this pedestal, and why?

11. What does Hannah's response to Missy and Brittany's crisis show you about Hannah's nature?

12. What does this end-of-life journey teach Hannah about herself, her mother, and her family of origin?

13. The worst happens and Hannah lives through it. When has a similar scenario occurred in your life? How has it changed you and your relationships with your family and friends?

14 Mae was adamant about her final wishes, in terms of life-prolonging measures and burial plans. How do you think this "last act" in our lives might be scripted to allow a more gentle, peaceful passing? Do you and your family/friends discuss end of life issues?

15. Mae insists on cloth handkerchiefs, especially for drying tears. What practices/customs have been handed down in your family?

Recipe Index

You might also enjoy these titles
By Wild Women Writers

Mama's Comfort Food
By Rhett DeVane

Karen Fletcher, alias Mary Elizabeth Kensington, has everything: haughty British-born façade, successful public broadcasting career in Atlanta, beautiful home, and devoted fiancé. Following her breast cancer diagnosis, Karen returns to her southern hometown of Chattahoochee, Florida, to garner support, seek treatment, and unravel the tangled fabrication she has so carefully woven. Karen embarks on the long and often painful journey to claim the rest of her life. This heart-warming story assures us our family and hometown will always welcome us with loving arms. The novel is the third in DeVane's beloved Chattahoochee series that began with *The Madhatter's Guide to Chocolate*.

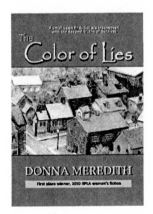

The Color of Lies
By Donna Meredith

Called "the best novel about the complications of contemporary race relations in the South," *The Color of Lies* spins a story of small town webs of connections that transcend color. Forty-year-old widow Molly Culpepper believes her hometown, Alderson, Georgia, is a place of harmony, of white picket fences and harmless gossip passed along at church and the general store—until a fellow teacher chalks a racial slur on the blackboard during Barack Obama's presidential campaign. Molly Culpepper's self-effacing humor shines through as she juggles her roles as a widowed mother, daughter, and dedicated instructor, all while dealing with a dangerous, growing rift in her community. Meredith's novel manuscripts won back-to-back first place awards for unpublished women's fiction from the Florida Writers Association.

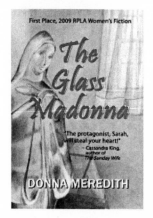

THE GLASS MADONNA
BY DONNA MEREDITH

The Glass Madonna, weaves together stories of three generations of glass workers who emigrate from Germany to West Virginia. Coming of age was supposed to be easy in the '70s, but tradition still bans women from making glass, an art form Sarah Stephens views as part of her family heritage. And regard for virginity is not as dead as Sarah thinks when she gives hers up to a college boyfriend. Uniting the generations is a family heirloom, a glass figurine of the Madonna that shines with unconditional love.

TWO THOUSAND DAFFODILS
BY GAYLE SWEDMARK HUGHES

Gayle Swedmark Hughes tells her remarkable story in this memoir. She was the only woman when she entered her law class at Iowa, she rubbed elbows with governors and Florida Supreme Court justices, and she sat on a bunk with Ted Bundy for a pretrial conference. Despite some difficult moments, Gayle overcame all odds to claim her happiness with her beloved son Lance, and the love of her life, Frank Hughes, who planted two thousand daffodils in her yard when they became engaged.

Wild Women Writers titles are available through amazon.com and barnesandnoble.com in print and electronic versions. Most bookstores can order them.

CPSIA information can be obtained at www.ICGtesting.com
Printed in the USA
LVOW082030030312

271476LV00003B/1/P